BAND OF
INNOCENCE

L E G A C Y

ROBERT AGNELLO

BAND OF INNOCENCE

ISBN 978-09964551-4-5

Published by On the Lamb Productions
Original cover and interior drawings by Louis Manna
Cover design and interior layout by Heidi Miller

BAND OF
INNOCENCE

LEGACY

ROBERT AGNELLO

CHAPTER ONE

Elizabeth

I've stood with this empty feeling inside of me far too many times: always restless and waiting. Honestly, I've done this so many times in my long past that it gets so wearisome sometimes. Now don't get me wrong, I truly love where I am and who I am. This is such a beautiful and quiet neighborhood, nestled here on the outskirts of Chicago. Most of the people are so nice and caring, and as I was saying this really is a very nice, quiet neighborhood.

On summer nights children play in the streets and families are always chatting on their front lawns. Oh, and the smell of edible substances is sometimes overwhelming.

During the winter children can be seen building small dwellings in front of me with the frozen water that falls from the sky and throwing this frozen water at each other. Sometimes I get so worried for these little men and women and how they might hurt themselves with these frozen water balls. I finally found out it was called snow. Such strange names for things, don't you think?

Families make statues out of the frozen water, or snow, putting hats on them and dressing them up to look human. The men always complain about how they have to push it all over and pile it up high but this only makes the children more and more happy. They stand on these hills of snow and come rolling or sliding down it. Why they bother to move it is beyond me. In all my years it's never failed to disappear on its own.

I have learned many words in my long years of living here. When you listen and don't talk you tend to learn more than if you speak and don't listen. I learned that long ago. The things I have learned could fill a book or three. Trees line my street and all the houses are separated from each other by a space where these strange metal containers sitting on round, squishy things transport the families. I have learned that these are cars. Oh my, how these people love their cars. I do like the separation from the other houses though. I have so much room to expand, and expanding is especially good when a new family moves in.

I'm a Georgian Colonial house. Or, at least I was a house. You see when empty and alone, a house is a house, but when occupied a house usually becomes a home. I remember the day I became a home to an extraordinary family — the Lesos. Yes, when the Leso family moved in I was loved again for what I was, but hold on, I'm racing ahead of myself, which is something houses or homes very seldom do. We don't make decisions quickly and never race. We are quite stationary and have time to think about the consequences of our decisions. We also don't think about the future because we revel in the present and are built on the past. The way men and women should be if they want to be happy.

I do have a name but it escapes me right now, which is quite odd because houses never forget anything.

I have been told that I am a very beautiful house in a very beautiful part of a very beautiful city. That's what most humans usually say when they meet me. They also say I have aged wonderfully, thanks, in part, to most of my occupants, or wards as I like to call them.

I think it's the way I was built that has kept me in shape. Although I have to admit that I must rely on people to take care of me. It's such a pity that I've had to rely on people, though. I found that some of them were quite full of themselves and they were less than reliable, with their comings and goings and goings and comings. That's exactly what I started to call them, "comers and goers."

My last family, the ones who moved out recently and left me empty, were full of life in the beginning. Yes from the moment the large one carried the smaller one, the woman, in through the doorway and up my curved staircase I felt a purpose. They really started off, as I said, extremely full of life. Happiness and love could be felt for such a long time until things started to turn. A darkness had started to settle into the daily lives of this once wonderful, loving family. The laughter turned to sorrow and the once pleasant sweet sounds turned into loud voices and shouting. Then everything stopped and again I was alone.

Why do these people always expect me to be perfect when they were so imperfect? A door would warp or a window wouldn't open and right away other strange humans would come in and pull and poke and replace parts of me. So I had quirks, I was just like these humans who built me. In fact houses are just like people, only more reliable, if you ask me, but we do have our imperfections and certainly our idiosyncrasies. We need to be loved and cared for and nurtured.

And of course my floorboards creak, at least they do when I'm occupied. That's the way houses talk. The creaking and cracking of our floorboards are the way we communicate if you only take the time to listen. I once had some people move in who were so set on shutting me up. Can you imagine that? The nerve. More strange men came in and pulled at my rafters and poked at my beams in order to keep me quiet but I would have no part of that. I would not be silenced by a bunch of comers and goers. Well, never mind. What I was trying to say is that these comers and goers move in and fix me up only to leave and give me to another family of comers and goers. Which is why I still think it was the way I was built that has kept me in shape.

As you step into my front door you are met by a large foyer which reveals a sweeping staircase to the second floor. I am oh so proud of this stairway: so regal! All of my doorways have beautifully arched doorways. Lots of time was spent making me and the men who built me were experts in their craft. Brick and wood were finely set so that even after 150 years I stand as strong and sturdy as the day I was built, and as beautiful!

Over the years I was expanded to three stories. They took my top off, imagine that. As you age you do tend to get a little bigger though and the people who love you don't seem to mind. That's a house joke. One family gabled my roof to make more space in the attic. Oh my, I did love the facelift! "More rooms, more life" is what I always would say as I creaked and groaned in appreciation.

I am what most people would also call a welcoming house, one that invites you in before you step through the doorway. There's something irresistible that tugs at you and pulls you in to look around and conveys a comfort to your soul. I am not a house that wants you to leave quickly. I do know those, but I am one that wants you to sit and stay awhile. People seem to especially like sitting around my rather large fireplace in my living room. The living room is lined with built-in shelves and decorated with ornate woodwork, almost like a library. When I was waiting for a new family to occupy me I would often think of all the changes this man creature had set forth on my being. Along the way some-one closed in my porch. That was fine with me, really, because it gave me another room to collect memories and feelings. I also remember when one family used that porch area to see if there were spirits living in me. I loved to play the game too, although no one knew I did; how could they? Why would they? Houses aren't alive. Haha. It was so much fun feeling the excitement of this game and feeling the shock of the soft human creatures in-volved when I ever so slightly moved the pointer without anyone touching it. It took a lot of my energy and I was so much younger back then. I do think back on all the years I've been here. For all my years I have always been most happy when there was a family living in me and loving me.

Houses want families, people who will stay and feed them new memories. Houses live off of life itself. Not the life of the house but the lives of the families that live in them. When a house is happy that's when it talks the most. Just as people get wrinkles as they get older a house gets cracks and splits. These can be fixed by plaster, which is not unlike the makeup that the women folks wear, but the cracks always seem to come back. A lot like wrinkles, I guess.

They say a house is just wood and brick, no feelings and no memories, but they, whoever they are, are so wrong. A house has a soul. There is a saying that goes "if the walls had ears...." Well guess what? They do. A house carries the lives of all who live in it and it retains the memories of those lives.

I have watched families coming and going for 150 years; some have taken care of me and some have abused me.

My creators built me out of love, brick by brick, and lived here for about forty man years. Laughter and giggles, dancing and hugs were always being given or gotten by these two lovers until the strong one became weak and was gone before the weaker one. I had liked the weaker one, the woman, because this one always smelled so sweet.

The little ones always gave me such joy. They were the glowing ones even though they were the hardest on my poor walls and floors; the ones most full of light. My creators also had that light for most of the years they lived inside me. There was constant singing and dancing in my sturdy frame. The woman made me look and smell so beautiful with lovely flowers from the gardens that surrounded my foundation. I was kept so prim and proper and beautiful; the other houses on the street were always so jealous of me.

The woman also had the most wonderful smell and lovely voice. There would be large gatherings of these human folks till the early hours of the morning. Always laughing and filling me with such beautiful sounds of music. That all stopped when the man person left. Then the woman one no longer made anything smell good. The laughter and songs had turned to crying and weeping until one day I looked around and I found myself empty. My creators, my parents, were gone. What a loss.

New families moved in, then they moved out and then others and it was always the same. I was just another house now. My insides were painted and my walls had pictures hung on them but no one treated me as the house I truly was, a house with a soul, a house with a memory, a home.

Now my waiting was over. Another family had purchased me. What would they be like? What would they change? I do have lots of time to think as most houses do and I wondered what kind of people had come to live in me. I was so nervous, as any house would surely be. I have always known that I have an inner strength as if I were built with one family in mind.

Could this be the reason I felt so excited? Was this why I was put here? Was this my purpose?

Well I didn't have to wait that long and it turned out that this family was like no other I had ever experienced. What love and joy and, oh my, the light. What a pure and radiant light. For a while I really couldn't pinpoint where such a beautiful light was coming from because it shone all around me but then, there it was, I spotted the source. I would have thought that such a big light would mean a big human but it was the small one. The small one was the source. She was special. Oh yes you could see and feel it immediately! Love and warmth radiated from this one as a star radiates light in a dark sky. I would have to keep my eye on this one. How could I not? This little one was going to give me such joy and pleasure as she grew, oh and memories!

I almost even forgot my name until the little light one called to me. When I heard her I remembered that my creators used to call me that. How did this child know my name when even I had forgotten it?

Houses remember everything. Hmmm I will have to dwell on this later. Giggle, oh my I made myself laugh. I love that joke. Get it? A dwelling will "dwell" on this. Oh never mind, only another house would get it. The reason houses take their time thinking about things is because we have the time to think things over and over and over before coming to any decision and even then we continue to think about it.

I was so busy thinking I hadn't even noticed that my rooms were being filled with furniture until that bright little package of light was carried up my front steps. The warmth that filled me that day brought all the memories of my past back to me as if a flood gate had opened. As soon as this little creature was set down onto the wooden foyer floor, this little thing warmed my soul. Yes my soul. As the small one touched my floors I let out the loudest floor "CREAKKKKKKKK." It was one of my most welcoming creaks. I felt like shouting and I guess I got carried away. I'll never forget that day.

CHAPTER TWO

The Lesos

"Creeeeeeaaaaaakkkkk," went my floorboards as the man of the family stepped into the foyer of his new home: the home he bought for his family in this nice, quaint section of the Chicago suburbs. The home that was me.

"Don't worry, honey, we can fix these floors."

Oh no! Had I been totally wrong about this family? Were they just another group who wanted to shut me up, try to keep me quiet? I wouldn't stand for that! But as I listened, I learned who these human were. Over my long years I had learned never to assume, so I didn't. I listened and as I listened I never took my attention away from the little one on my floor.

The little one was Emily; and then there was Bill and Sue. Emily, who I later started calling the night star, was the first human, since my creators, to actually listen to what I was saying. It took my breath away.

"Hello, little child," I softly creaked. Who knew I would get a response!

"Hello Elizabeth," she said responding to my creaky welcome. The woman turned to the little one.

"Elizabeth?" the woman one said.

"Emily, who is Elizabeth?" the man said.

I, by the way, didn't know who they were talking about and then I remembered it was me. Oh my, that's who I was. Hahahaha. That laugh came out as a loud creak and everyone looked around. It had been so long since someone called me that name that I didn't realize they were talking about me. I finally remembered my name. Hmm, to be reminded by such an innocent one was strange but comforting. I will like this one.

"The little one is Emily," I thought. What a lovely name. It was the name of my creator. That, in itself, was quite strange but I didn't want to think about that and miss the action going on in my foyer.

"The house is named Elizabeth, silly Daddy," Emily said as she rubbed her hands across the floors.

"I guess Emily named our new house for us, Sue. Elizabeth. I think that's a perfect name, Emily, but why not Wanda, or Rebecca?" The man had a huge smile on his face with his hands on his hips as he tried to be so smart.

"Daddy, her name is Elizabeth. That's what her name has always been. You can't just change someone's name," Emily gave her father a quizzical look as if to say "Duh."

"Ahhhh. Yeah, I guess that would be rude. So how did you know the house's name, honey?" the man said with a smirk.

"Doesn't she look like an Elizabeth? It's quite obvious. You are a little rude Daddy. She welcomed us when we walked in and you didn't even say hello. Didn't you hear her?" The little one stared up at her parents.

"Wait, the house talked to us Em, uh how?" The man started to laugh nervously.

"Dad, I guess you don't speak house do you?" Emily looked up at her father then down at the creaking floor with a look as if to say, are you kidding me?

"You mean the creaking of the floors?"

"Yes Dad, that's how a house talks." Emily shook her head back and forth. It seems like this happens all the time. How can a five-year-old make a grown man feel foolish you say? Emily has been making Bill feel foolish since she could talk.

As Emily sat there on my foyer floor a young woman walked up my front stairs and in through the front door. Thin and tall and quite striking, this woman carried a silver cane. She wasn't depending on it to walk but she carried it as if it were protection from some unknown danger. She carried it with a purpose. She also had the same light that shone from little Emily. She had long black hair with a silver streak that framed her face which made her a quite striking image and I have seen many humans in my day. As she stepped into my foyer she smiled and looked around.

"My Elizabeth, you are quite the beauty, aren't you?" the young woman said and I just had to creak a big thank you.

"You are quite welcome, Elizabeth," this young woman said.

This was Lillian Leso, Bill Leso's older sister and Emily's protector and babysitter.

Oh my, these two speak house. How wonderful! I hadn't felt this much joy since my first brick was placed.

I remember the mom and dad just looked at each other as they shook their heads.

"Two peas in a pod," Bill whispered to Sue, his wife. Emily started to giggle. "You're right, Aunt Lily, she is very pretty and really nice." Emily got up and jumped into her Aunt Lily's arms. Aunt Lily, with her cane tucked under her arm, swung the night star around and gently put her down on my wooden floor.

There is something special about these two. Never have I seen such a glow and warmth coming from these simple man-things.

"Creak."

"Oh you'll get used to Bill, Elizabeth, he really is a good soul," Lily said.

Bill looked at his wife and shrugged his shoulders.

"Well Lily I guess you were right about this house. It does feel very comfortable and Sue hasn't even started painting or hanging pictures yet. Although she does know what kind of furniture we need."

I noticed the woman hit the man in the arm but I knew it was in a loving and gentle way. These people were not prone to violence as others who have lived in me have been. Look at my patched up walls and try to figure out what got thrown and who threw it. I remember each and every injury.

"Lily, I don't know but it feels like I've always been here. This house is so inviting," Sue said as she looked up at my circular staircase and arched entrances. I, for one, love my stairs, which I think are the best part of me.

The man smiled at the woman and a soft glow of love seemed to radiate from him.

"My oh my do they shine so!" I creaked in a whisper.

"Only the good ones, Elizabeth," Lily said.

She heard me, hahaha.

"We were looking for a house that had an eat-in kitchen, a large backyard and a bright sunny living room." Sue said to Lily.

"And we got none of that," Bill chimed in.

"What you have here my dear brother is a house that has a soul to her. For once, Billy boy, just stop and feel your surroundings. Take a breath. Don't listen or talk but feel." Lily has always wanted for Bill to experience the joy of just being.

"I do sort of feel it," Sue said. They all waited. Bill closed his eyes and they all looked at him.

"I, I, hold it, hold it, nah I don't feel it," said Bill.

Everyone started to laugh and a creak of the floor can be heard even though no one had moved.

"I like these ones," I creaked out loud.

Every morning this little creature of love, Emily, wakes up in the room the larger ones fixed up for her and says: "Good morning Elizabeth, how are you today?"

I always answer with a creak or strain: "I am wonderful and I so love watching over you while you sleep, my little night star."

Light just radiates from this little one like a true night star.

As I said, houses can see and feel these things.

I have seen this glow before in some of these man creatures. Never as bright as this one, but all these creatures can glow. Some just don't want to or have forgotten how. Well that's what houses have noticed, if you wanted to know.

I knew this was a special child. One to watch. Eventually I would come to love this new family more than any of the others. These were the ones I had been built for, the ones I had been waiting for all these years. Oh my how the time has flown. I could go on and on and believe me I will but I have to stop for now.

Thank you so much for allowing me to tell you my story, but the real story is just about to begin. Robert, the creator, is going to cut me off very soon. So enjoy the adventure and if you have any questions, just ask me. I'm right down the block.

"Creak (enjoy)!"

CHAPTER THREE

A note from the author

Now you might have thought at this point this story would be all about houses, and believe me Elizabeth can go on forever. It's called house prattle but as the author of this book I need to stop her or she would go on forever about houses and their likes, dislikes and such. In all actuality this could be just about houses, and how interesting houses really are when you get to know them. But this story is about the souls that attach themselves to these supposedly lifeless structures. Most people think of houses as an investment or as protection from the world outside: the cold, the heat.

They say a home is where the heart is but a home is where the souls are, lived and stored in the walls and beams and floors of these beautiful buildings. Don't get me wrong, this particular house does have a part in this story but who can tell how big and where exactly Elizabeth fits? The way life twists and turns neither she nor I, the author, truly know what part she has but she does have a part just like any house when given the chance and attention it truly deserves.

This is the first of a series of books about the Band of Innocence. As you will come to learn, the Band is a group of children that for thousands of years have come to the rescue of this planet when the darkness has threatened all who live here.

Chosen for their innocence, they have accepted the powers that have been granted to them. They carry that innocence on their wrists in the form of a band of light. It's their innocence flowing from their bodies. As these special children grow into adulthood they lose that little bit of pure innocence, they can no longer be part of the band and another group is initiated into this elite force of good. Some of the most successful and famous people in the world, past and present, were in the Band of Innocence. They all have their own stories. You would know them if I mentioned their names. Most became beacons of hope and love but some succumbed to the darkness, the greed and pain of the world.

Jeez, now I'm going on like Elizabeth. Sorry. There are so many stories to tell but this particular story is about the Leso family and how Emily Leso became the leader of this band of children that steer the world into the light and hope of a beautiful future. Let the truth provide and let the innocence guide.

CHAPTER FOUR

The Story

The years have passed for the Leso family since their move into Elizabeth, as the years always do when they encroach upon the life of a family. Seven years have gone by to be precise. Seven years of such joy and love. Elizabeth loves the Lesos more than any house has ever loved its occupants. Watching the little one grow and learn. She is a powerful little human but she needs protection. Elizabeth knows that.

Bill Leso is an older version of the young man that carried his daughter up the stairs of their new house. He has filled out a bit and his hair is going grey but he still has that boyish grin. The stresses at work have kept him busy for the last couple of years: late nights and long weekend business trips. He has had a tough time working for a non-profit group in the present world economy and he has tried to not worry Sue, his wife, with the burden of his daily stress.

Sue Leso is a pretty blonde woman and at thirty-five years old looks to be in her prime. Tall and thin, Sue dresses well but modestly. She wears her hair pulled back into a ponytail and is always well-dressed — never sweats or jogging suits — and is an unbelievable organizer except when it comes to clothes. Her dressing area looks like a bomb exploded!

Tonight is a big night for Bill and he is going to forget about the daily grind and enjoy this weekend's festivities. He stands in his bedroom, looking into the bureau mirror and struggles with his bow tie. The Lesos are dressing for a formal event. They are about to leave for a weekend-long party for Bill's company. This is the promotion event everyone in the company waits for all year. Promotions are given out and announced at a lodge that has been rented where they celebrate the successes of the company. This year the successes were slim but they weren't nonexistent. It's all paid for by Bill's boss to show his appreciation for the hard work they all do.

On the bureau next to him there are pictures of Emily in various stages of life, from when she was a baby to the last one where she is standing with a skateboard which reads "Emily at 11."

There are clothes scattered everywhere around the room.

"God, I love my wife but sometimes I wish she were a little more organized," Bill thinks.

"What, honey, did you say something?" Sue calls from the bathroom.

"Did I say that out loud?" he thinks, then smiles.

"No honey," he answers as he shakes his head. "I really have to stop that.

Sue, you've tried on about a hundred dresses and they're all on the bed. We really need to get going and my jacket is somewhere under these clothes."

"Bill, this is a very important event and I need to look perfect. It's been a long time since we've been out. I can't look too good but need to look good enough to not feel old or fat." Sue Leso starts to giggle. Sue steps out of the changing room.

"Does this dress make me look fat, Bill?" She knows how he avoids answering that question as she laughs to herself.

"This tie is driving me crazy," says Bill, knowing he's avoiding the question. "I hate these things, Sue. This tie is killing me."

"Oh, come on, it's just for one night and besides you didn't answer my question Bill Leso."

"I didn't? No, you're right — I didn't. What was the question? That's it. I'm not wearing this tie. I haven't worn this tie since the party we had in the old house."

Bill knows he shouldn't have brought up the old house; it just stirs up bad memories for Sue. He looks over at his wife and sees her demeanor go from happy to thoughtful. She had nightmares for months following that incident. To this day she still thinks about it.

Sue's face immediately becomes concerned.

"You look so gaunt in that outfit, honey," he says sheepishly.

"Oh so funny Bill Leso, it's too late." She starts to smile.

"Does this tie make me look fat?" Bill asks, trying to get his wife's mind out of the past.

"I hate thinking about that mean old house. Sometimes that night just washes all over me, Bill. That's why I will only let your sister sit for Em. Your sister was right about that house. I feel so much better living here with Elizabeth. I feel so safe here. She really is a special house."

Sue looks around at the room and almost feels a warmth coming from the house. She hears a soft whisper of joy but she knows it can't be; it's just a house. Sue hasn't really let herself go as Emily and Lily have in giving this house a life. She just thinks that this is a really comfortable house as opposed to that dark house where they lived before. She never felt safe there. It seemed so cold and angry at times.

"You know, Sue, we really need to remember what happened," says Bill. "Emily was sleep-walking. It had nothing to do with that house. We have to let Em grow up without that thought lingering around us. What happened then was then...that house was old... that's all. You're so superstitious. My sister really got to you with all her magic mumbo jumbo."

"Lily did not get to me. I just agree with her sometimes. This is going to sound horrible but thank god she is still single. She is always there for us. Your sister is such a great catch, I can't understand why she hasn't married and had kids of her own. She would make such a great mother but then again if she married she wouldn't be here for Emily like she has been."

"She doesn't want anyone. She's happy being alone and I'm a little jealous sometimes."

"Hey, what's that supposed to mean?"

Bill starts to laugh. "Just kidding..."

"I just thank God she's here. It's tough not to think about that night. We almost lost Emily." Sue's mind races back in time to that night in the old house.

Seven years prior, before they found Elizabeth, the Lesos had purchased an old Victorian house on the outskirts of Chicago's northern suburbs. The house had seemed so quaint, so regal. It could have been a splendid house.

On one particular Saturday night, Bill and Susan had a big party. Lily was there to watch Emily who had just turned four years old. Seemed that Lily was always around since Emily was born. Lily did not like that house from the first day she stepped through the front door. She immediately felt a cold, mean feeling crossing her body.

The Lesos had a large plot of land. It was about an acre, which in this area was hard to come by, especially for the price they paid. They had gotten a good deal through Bill's boss. He had a friend in real estate so he pulled some strings. His boss went out of his way to help with this deal because he didn't want Bill to leave the company. Better to keep his best people happy than have them looking somewhere else.

This house was surrounded by plush gardens, large weeping willows and a pond filled with water lilies and Koi fish. The pond was quite large. Man-made, it had a small waterfall and flat blue slate stones so you could sit by the pond and watch the fish. Yes, very quiet and serene. The pond was built to the right of the house along a small gravel walkway. It needed some tender loving care because grass and weeds were coming up from the gravel and there was moss growing along most of the stones used as walls for the pond. Huge water lilies floated on the top of the water and every now and then a fish would surface and then plunge back into the dark waters.

Anyone else would have looked at this as a wonderful piece of property. Isolated but still near the city. Lily looked at it as a cold and foreboding area. She never went near the pond. Too many shadows.

"It's under trees, Lily," Bill would say but Lily knew better. These weren't regular shadows, these were "them."

When Lily got to the house that night she stood outside, at the bottom of the front stairs, and looked at the lights coming through the front windows. Her brow furrowed for a moment as she felt a slight chill. She shook the chill off and then started up the stairs towards the front door, all the while listening to the sounds of the party coming from inside. All the lights were on and the noise she heard could wake the dead but this house was so far removed from the rest of the houses she knew no one could hear the festivities. As she walked up the front stairs, she pulled her wrap tighter feeling the chill again. It had been a warm spring night but still she felt cold.

Lily was dressed in a long blue skirt. She almost seemed to glide up the stairs as the skirt flowed around her body.

As soon as she entered the house her brother spotted her as if he had been waiting for her.

"What's he up to?" she said to herself.

"Hey Lil, thanks for coming. It's been a long time. What, since this morning?" Bill Leso tries to be funny and while his humor often misses its mark it always makes him laugh.

"Bill, I don't like this house. How many times have I said this?" said Lily looking around as she walked through the door. Her long black hair was tied back.

"Every time I see you, Lil. The house is fine; you just need to relax. Emily couldn't wait to see you but she couldn't keep her eyes open. She fell asleep under the couch so I brought her upstairs. She is quiet and safe in her bed, her and Olster." Olster was Emily's stuffed bear. She never went anywhere without Olster.

Bill noticed that odd look on his sister's face.

"Sis loosen up...have a drink. Relax. Forget about the house? What? Did ya feel a cold draft in Emily's room again? There are a million people here. What's going to happen?"

Lily smiled uneasily and walked with her brother into the kitchen, still looking as if something was not right. She smiled and walked through the crowd of people that usually congregated in the kitchen at parties.

"I'll be right back, Billy, I want to check on Emily," Lily said as she walked towards the stairs in the kitchen that led up to the second floor. Thunder could be heard in the distance, reminding everyone that a huge storm would be traveling through the area.

Lily reached Emily's room and peeked in and saw her niece asleep.

"Ah so sweet," she thought.

Emily was sleeping soundly with one arm around her bear. Lily looked all around the room and everything looked in place. All quiet and peaceful. So why was she so nervous tonight? Something just didn't feel right or good. She walked over to the big-girl bed, as Emily called it, and looked down on the sleeping beauty. The glow that came from Emily was blinding sometimes.

"You are the future," Lily thought and pulled the covers up under Emily's chin. "Ah my angel you couldn't wait for me."

Lily turned, breathing a sigh of regret. She bent over the bed and gave her niece a soft kiss on the forehead. She looked around one more time and then went back down the steps, never noticing the dark shadow coming up the front steps. The thunderstorm settled over the house. The wind picked up outside but the people at the party didn't seem to notice.

Lily walked down the stairs and back into the kitchen and was immediately spotted by her brother Bill again.

"Lily, come on in and meet my boss, Phil Calton. Phil, this is my lovely sister Lily."

Phil Calton was a self-made millionaire who dabbled in social and environmental businesses. He had helped many smaller organizations get on their feet and literally turned certain neighborhoods around. His name was on the short list with Warren Buffett and Bill Gates.

"I've heard so much about you, Lily. Bill is always saying how I need to meet his sister and I must say you are more beautiful than I could ever have imagined or he could have described."

"That is so sweet. I also have heard about the wonderful and generous exploits of a certain Mr. Calton."

"Oh stop. It's Phil, please."

"Phil. Really, that is so sweet. You can still call me Lily — oh wait you have." Lily blushed a bit but something started to gnaw at her. She had almost let herself go but a feeling deep in her chest started to build. An anxious feeling of doom.

"Well I'll leave you two alone. You kids get to know each other." Bill turned to Lily, winked and then tended to his other guests leaving Lily alone with his boss.

"So, Bill says you're into the spiritual thing. I love the ethereal. There are so many mysteries to life," Phil said.

Lily stopped listening to Phil. It's not that she wasn't interested and this was so not like her but something was not right. Lily was always present when someone was talking. She always listened to every word the other person said but she couldn't shake the chill.

All of a sudden a huge crack of lightning lit up the sky outside the stained glass windows in the living room and the room lights flickered. One of the party guests screamed, then there was silence. Then everyone started to laugh.

Everyone except for Lily. She looked around for her brother, Bill, but couldn't see him.

"Wow, that was really loud huh?" Phil said but Lily was gone.

Lily left the kitchen and headed toward the foyer. There she noticed a dark shadow in the hall, right by the front door.

"Lily are you ok?" she could hear Phil's voice but it sounded so distant and she ignored his calls. The shadow seemed to be on the wall and the floor, like a large stain. All the lights in the house were on yet this shadow remained, dark and inky. The dark shadow seemed to move, traveling down the wall and onto the floor. Lily started to hurry to the staircase leading up to Emily's room but stopped when she realized the dark shadow on the floor seemed to flow out the front door. There on the staircase she noticed a wet trail leading from up the stairs to the front door and the front door was cracked open.

"Oh no," Lily said as she noticed Olster, Emily's bear. Fear gripped her. Emily never went anywhere without Olster, but there he lay at the bottom of the stairs.

Lily's first reaction was to run upstairs but her instinct told her to run out the front door. She threw the door open and ran onto the porch.

"Emily!" she shouted.

There was another crack of thunder and then a brilliant bolt of lightning that lit up the front porch. There, on the porch and leading down the front stairs was a wet trail. Lily held her cane tight and followed this trail down the stairs and around the side of the house. She headed down the gravel path that led to the Koi pond.

At the edge of the pond Lily noticed one of Emily's socks, lying on top of one of the blue stones that surrounded the pond.

Shadows were dancing all over but they seemed to be darker around the pond. Almost pitch black. Even with the bright crack of lightning the shadow never went away.

"This is not a normal storm," she said.

Lily rushed over to the pond and peered into the waters. The silver cane she held in her hand was glowing and she raised it above her head with two hands for a second and then slammed it into the pond water. The darkness seemed to retreat from the silver cane, as it glowed even brighter. The globe on the top of the cane started to spin, and the water started to bubble as if boiling.

The cane slowly turned in the water as Lily held it and the water started to slowly separate. As the water parted it reveals Emily entangled in water lilies at the bottom of the pond. The water lilies were wrapped around Emily's wrists and ankles. She was being held down by two large Koi fish with slightly human faces. These Koi were about three feet long with arms and legs. Half-human, half-fish. When Lily called out to them they turned to look at her, and bared their pointed, razor-sharp teeth. The Koi hissed at Lily. Emily was unusually quiet and stiff. Lily knew she was in a trance of some sort. If she didn't act quickly her niece would surely die either at the hands of the Koi or by drowning in the pond.

"Let her go. By all that I am and all that I have been, you cannot have her. Let the innocence of this youth protect her."

The Koi turned back to Emily. They were ready to pounce, but a glow started to emanate from Emily. The Koi looked confused. They opened their mouths and snapped at Emily's neck but their teeth couldn't penetrate the light surrounding her. This was her innocence protecting her. Lily struck her cane twice into the water and a ripple of fire ran out from the cane spreading across the water.

"Truth and innocence will cast away the darkness and reveal you for what you really are...fish."

As the fire spread across the water it avoided Emily but engulfed the water lilies and Koi. The Koi let out a loud scream of pain and let go of Emily. The darkness that had enveloped the pond quickly slipped into the night. A low hiss could be heard. With that, Lily reached into the pond and grabbed Emily as the water flowed back. The Koi had turned back into fish. At this point everyone from the party was rushing outside, with Bill and Sue in the lead. Emily was still not moving and her eyes were rolled back in her head.

Lily, holding Emily with one arm, touched the globe of her cane to the child's temple. A small spot of light glowed against Emily's head and Emily started to move.

"Oh my god...how did she get out of her bed without anyone noticing? How did she get out here?" Sue ran and grabbed Emily. Lily handed Emily over to her mother.

Emily was just awaking from her trance when she noticed everyone standing around her.

"Mommy I'm cold. Where's Olster?"

Sue gripped Emily tight. She looked up at Lily and put one arm around her sister-in-law's neck.

"You are an angel, Lillian," Sue said as she looked at Lily.

Bill handed Olster the bear to Emily who grabbed him with both hands and hugged him tight.

'Where have you been, mister? You just can't leave me like that," Emily said to Olster and then hugged him again. Bill and Sue started to laugh, partly because Em was so cute and partly from nerves.

The very next day a realtor came by to put up a For Sale sign in front of the Leso home. A month later the Lesos moved from that house. Lily told her brother that the house was not right. It had chosen sides. Bill told Lily she was nuts even though he had felt the chill leave his body as they drove away. He looked in his rear view mirror and swore he saw shadows engulf the house. Of course he would never tell Lily.

"Oh no, not going to admit to that one," he thought.

Before the big move, Lily had decided she needed help in watching Emily. So Lily gave Emily two Siamese kittens. They looked like normal kittens but these were not ordinary kittens to say the least. These cats had a purpose. To protect.

"Lil, come on, do we really need these fur balls," Bill said turning to Sue.

"Oh my, how cute Lily," Sue cooed.

"Bill, they will be no trouble at all. They will practically take care of themselves," Lily said with a wisp of a smile.

"Hey wait Lil, I saw that Grandma Natu smile. No, come on, I don't want two cats in the house. Sue?"

Bill looked to Sue and could see her holding one of them in her hand.

"Oh Bill look how cute they are," Sue said as the kitten started purring.

The other kitten started rubbing against Bill's pants leg. Bill looked out the window and saw Emily's pre-school bus pulling up.

"I have to get rid of these things before she sees them," Bill thought.

"Oh you know they are really cute. Let me see both of them," Bill said as he reached for the kittens. Both kittens ran behind Lily.

"Bill stop it. They know what you are planning. Let Emily see them. You are such a brat," Lily said with a smile.

Bill looked down as the door opened and both kittens ran towards the door but instead of running out they both jumped up onto Emily.

"How cute, kitties." Emily giggled.

"Emily, your aunt wants you to take care of them," Sue said with a large smile wrapped from ear to ear.

"And your Dad wants his sister to take care of them," Bill chimed into the conversation.

Sue hit Bill in the arm.

Emily was on the floor with both kittens crawling all over her and Bill knew that he had lost this battle. Actually Bill knew the war was over long ago. He was outnumbered and outmaneuvered in every way.

When Lily was alone with the two kittens she bent down and both kittens ran over to her, as if she called them.

The kittens meowed immediately at Lily.

"Oh no, he's OK. Don't let him bully you."

The kittens meowed again.

"You two must watch out for this child my little darlings. I have brought you two here to help me keep an eye on her. You know what the stakes are. This is the blessed one. The one of light. She must never be left alone or we will have lost the war. Do you both understand?"

The kittens started meowing as only Siamese cats can. A language of their own. They cried and seemed agitated until Lily picked them both up and looked around the foyer of this cold house.

"Yes, we won't be here that much longer and I know, I feel it too." Lily knew the cats didn't like the house either.

The cats both looked at each other and then at Lily, meowing their acceptance of this mission.

"Good my two little buttons." Lily put the kittens down and scratched their heads as they started to purr.

These two cats, Scarlett and Rhett as they were named, from that day forward would not leave Emily's side. Ever. When Emily went to school the cats would sneak out the door and follow her. Never seen but always there they would watch like sentries at their post.

That mean house is now a memory but one that won't fade very soon.

CHAPTER FIVE

The Weekend

"Creeeeaaaaakkkkkk."

The creak of the floorboards snap Bill and Sue out of the dark past and back into the present. They both jump.

The creak is the precursor to the ringing of the front door bell. It's Elizabeth telling everyone that someone is at the door.

"Rinnnnnnggggg. Rinnnnnnnnnggggg."

"Jeez, Elizabeth, stop doing that to me. I almost had a heart attack from that creaking," Bill says with a smile, all the while mentally thanking Elizabeth for taking their minds off the past.

A fourteen-year-old Emily can be heard calling out.

"Mom...Dad, Aunt Lily is here."

They pause to look at each other. Bill takes Sue in his arms and holds her. He always knows when she needs a hug. The chill she felt leaves her body.

"Well thank god we have Elizabeth," she says. A large creak can be heard.

"Ahhh yes, Elizabeth. You know I thought I would never say this but I truly love this house and now I'm even thinking of her as a her." Bill starts to laugh.

Another groan can be heard and Bill smiles. "Me too Elizabeth."

Bill thinks, "Now they have me talking to the house," and he shakes his head. Then he looks at the time on the bedside clock.

"Sue help me with this tie...would ya?"

"Oh, Bill, I was just thinking of when Emily was born."

"Honey I love you, you know that and I do love reminiscing but I think I'm cutting off the circulation of blood going to my head," says Bill as he struggles with his tie.

"I thought it was cut off a long time ago?" Sue giggles.

"It's been ten years since we almost lost her. What would we have done?" Sue has tears in her eyes as Bill puts his hands around his neck and jokingly gasps for air. She walks over and helps him out of the tie and reties it for him. She smiles because her husband is such a child sometimes and then kisses him on the cheek and pats his head.

It's funny how in a span of seconds the mind can go from one thought to another and then to another.

Sue starts to think of when Em was born and how Bill handed his newborn daughter to his sister Lily. How she swears Emily smiled and looked into Lily's eyes. The newborn looked as if she were reaching up to touch the amulet around Lily's neck. This amulet was given to Lily by her Grandmother, Grandma Natu as she was called by Lily and Bill, before, or as Lily likes to tell if, after she passed on.

Sue has never heard Lily say that her Natu had died. It was always passing or shifting but then again Lily was into the spiritual thing that sometimes Sue didn't understand and Bill didn't want to. Lily had been much closer to her Grandma than Bill had been.

"I don't know Sue, Natu was a little strange in her ways. I used to catch her talking to the plants and worms. I thought she was a bit wacky but Lily loved her so much," Bill had once told her.

No matter how strange Lily was Sue also knew that when Lily was at their house there was always a feeling of calm. Such a peaceful feeling. Sue always overlooked anything considered weird about her sister-in-law. One strange thing was the cane Lily carried. Lily was a woman in her 30s and in great shape but she was always carrying that cane, which was another gift from Natu. The cane was handed down to Lily after Natu passed. It always seemed strange how Lily would sometimes talk about Natu in the present tense.

"Well, strange or not I wouldn't trust anyone else with my daughter," Sue thinks.

"How do I look, Sue," Bill says, looking quite dapper.

"So handsome. Let's stay home and lock ourselves in our room." Sue smiles and then lets out a little growl.

"Oh wow, sweet or dangerous, uh which could be sweet, well dangerously sweet." Bill starts to laugh.

Bill looks at his wife as she puts a wrap around her shoulders and his heart almost bursts with pride.

"I am so into you, Mrs. Leso," he thinks. "You look glamorous. I am the luckiest man alive."

They leave the disheveled bedroom as Bill looks back and thinks what a mess his wife is and then laughs because he would have it no other way. They walk down the semi-circular staircase and they hear Lily humming the wedding song and Emily is by her side laughing, both are looking up as they walk down the stairs. Bill Leso is constantly tugging at his collar as he walks down the stairs. As they are coming down Bill can see a large bag of dog food in the middle of the foyer.

"Uh, did we get a dog that no one has told me about?" Bill says with a sort of laugh. "Is Les back?"

Bill flashes back to that dog. "What a dog he was," Bill thinks. No one ever knew what happened to him. A wave of sadness overcomes him and then it's gone as he looks down at his daughter.

"No, this is the food Emily wants to bring to the waterfront shelter tomorrow," Lily says and she moves the bag against the wall.

"So, Em, you feeding a pack of wolves?" Bill starts to laugh.

"Makes me think of old Les, what a dog, huh Lil?"

"Oh, Bill, he loved you so," Lily looks sadly at Bill, knowing Les was his best friend growing up. They are interrupted by Emily.

"Dad, there are so many hungry puppies in that shelter and I figured we could afford a bag every now and then. Right, Aunt Lily?"

"Right, Emily."

"But oh my, don't you both look like you're going to an award show? Truly a beautiful couple," says Lily.

"And the Oscar goes to my mom and dad." Emily starts to laugh.

Bill had noticed as he was walking down the stairs how beautiful his sister looked. He really needs to get her together with his boss. His boss still talks about the night he met her and that was ten years ago. Occasionally they would see each other but Lily was so hard to pin down to a schedule. She would show up unexpectedly but not show up when expected. Sue once said that she would be annoyed with Lily for this but Lily always showed up when needed. That in itself was extraordinary.

Lily stood with her long black hair braided in the back. A thin wisp of grey broke the darkness at the front of her hair and it was pulled back to the side of her face. She was a tall woman — about 5'8" — and had the best posture of any person he knew. When she walked in a room every head would turn. Men, women and children gravitated to her, as well as animals of all sorts. Barking dogs would stop barking. Squirrels that would start to run when you walked by would stop and watch Lily float along the sidewalk. Yup, Bill swears his sister floats. She has a way of walking that seems so soft and easy.

Children and animals would seek her out and just circle her everywhere she went. At any party, if you wanted to know where your child was he or she was probably sitting with Lily listening to one of her stories. These were stories of heroes and heroines. Love and teamwork. You always got a sense that when your child sat with her for a little bit, he or she walked away a changed little person. Glowing just a little bit.

There was a natural glow to Lily.

"Those are my Glimmers," Lily would say.

Seeing her inspired peace and tranquility. If you had a crying baby, you would just hand it to Lily. The crying would turn to cooing. Even adults were captivated by her beauty and serenity.

Bill always told Sue that Lily had candy in her pockets and that's why kids followed her even though they both knew she hadn't touched a piece of processed food since she was a child. That lifestyle has touched the Lesos' whole family.

Emily, even as a baby, had only eaten organic food. Seems her body couldn't take any sort of processed foods and Lily had been a staunch proponent of them feeding her just healthy things.

Sue looks down at her little girl. She has grown so much over the years.

"Give me a kiss baby and listen to your aunt." Sue looks around and says "Elizabeth, look after them, OK." Sue really does think this house is special. Bill just rolls his eyes then he hears the loud creak. No one is walking but the house creaks.

"I give up," Bill thinks.

"Oh Mom you know she is looking out for us. Now you and Dad have fun."

Emily looks up at her Dad and notices how uncomfortable he seems.

"Are you alright Dad?"

"I hate this tie, Em. I feel like I'm being choked," he says as he pulls at his collar.

"All right my little Poobah. You and your Aunt have fun. If you want you can sleep in the cave tonight. Lil, thank you for coming up with the cave playhouse in the basement. All she wants to do is sleep down there." Bill stretches. "Not good on the old back."

Bill straightens and puts his hands on his lower back.

Emily pumps her fist in excitement. "Yay we are sleeping in the cave!"

"We will be back tomorrow night. All rules apply, Emily," her Dad gives her a wink.

Lily had designed a cave in the basement out of blankets and cardboard. That's where Emily hung out most of the time. All of the stories Lily told were told in the cave. They had even put up cave drawings of figures they found online and in magazines just to make it seem real and sometimes when Aunt Lily read her stories the drawings did look real. As Lily told her stories the walls would transform into rock and the drawings seemed to come alive, but Emily knew that it was all in her imagination.

"Just watch out for the bats." Bill laughs.

"Thanks, Dad, I'll wear a hat."

Emily jumps into her Dad's arms and hugs him tight. Sue and Bill each give Lily a kiss on the cheek and walk out the door into the night. A car is waiting at the curb and they soon speed away.

"Thank God for your sister," Sue says as she settles into the back seat of the limo and kisses Bill on the cheek.

"Thank god for you, Mrs. Leso. Without you my life would be empty." Bill turns Sue's head towards his and kisses her deeply.

The driver looks at them in the rear view mirror. A dark shadow sweeps across his eyes and a smile crosses his face. A sinister smile. The shadows play on his face and then are gone.

As the front door closes and Bill and Sue leave, the room brightens a bit. Aunt Lily walks into the kitchen to prepare the night's menu. Emily follows Aunt Lily to get the large bag of nuts and fruit leathers. This was what her friends called "Emily food." Emily could only eat naturally grown products, like fruits, nuts and vegetables, and it seemed as if she was rubbing off on all her friends at school. More and more kids were bringing "Emily foods" to school and staying away from the processed stuff they served.

The principal was having a fit because he had a stake in the company that supplied the chicken nuggets and mozzarella sticks. The more kids that brought in good food from home the fewer kids bought food from the lunch menu and the less money he made. Greed is such a bad trait in anyone.

"I think I'm seeing a trend here and we may need to make a change in our lunch menu," the principal had stated recently. "That is going to cut deeply into my profits," he thought.

"No one is eating the fried chicken fingers," he had told the distributor.

Yup, Emily was indeed making her mark.

"OK little girl. Let's go into the dark cave of truth. I have two great stories to tell you tonight — a double bill. The first is about a boy who finally finds a home and the second one is about children your age."

Emily runs and grabs the battery-powered lantern from the shoe rack in the hall closet and Emily and Lily go down into the basement. The basement is completely covered in blankets and cardboard. The walls of the basement have blankets tacked to them so there is no walking room at all unless you go into the cave. There's a small entrance by the stairs that you have to crawl through to enter the cave. At the entrance is a sign that says "Beware." Lily and Emily crawl into the make-believe cave and sit down in the first large chamber. Lily opens a book and starts to read a story about a little boy named Zach and his dog Ibbykabibby.

Lily turns the lantern on and the glow casts shadows on the walls of the cave.

"So Zach was chosen to go to town and get supplies," Lily starts the story.

CHAPTER SIX

Zach and Ibby

The sun was still low in the sky when Zach and his dog Ibby started out from the orphanage to go into town. Every year around fall, one of the children who had come of age was sent through the forest, over the mountain, and through the fresh meadow into town to pick up some supplies. Oh, and the latest gossip. Zach had just turned twelve and was considered a young man. Now it was his turn to assume all of the responsibilities that come with growing up.

Zach stood about so tall and was quite thin. He wore blue overalls and always had on a neatly tucked-in plaid shirt. His hat had a button on the front brim so that the top could be snapped down, which is the way Zach always wore it. Pulled down and close to his eyes, Zach would peek out from under the brim of the hat, because that's the way the men in town wore them. When he wanted to be noticed he would stand up straight and push the hat back on his head. Zach had his jacket slung over his shoulder, since it was fall and the weather could get quite crisp. He was always prepared. When Zach walked, he always walked with a galumph. Up on one leg and then down on the other, in a rhythmic gait.

His dog Ibby was not a small dog, but also not a big dog. He was somewhat of a handsome dog, and also the happiest looking animal you would ever see, with brown spots and big floppy ears. Ibby's tongue always hung out of the side of his mouth. Sometimes his back legs were just a little faster than his front legs, causing Ibby to run sideways. His front legs always seemed to win, and his back legs would go back to their correct position. Ibby was Zach's best friend, and always would be.

Down the narrow winding path these friends started on their first of many journeys. The wooden cart that was used for carrying supplies and firewood and sometimes for fun hayrides was being pulled by Zach.

Zach remarked to himself just how narrow the path actually was. It appeared that the old wooden cart he was pulling would just barely fit. As they walked down the path, Ibby and Zach saw the beauty of nature. The trees were changing into the most wondrous colors. Zach, who had a very good imagination, imagined that he was moving through a forest of fire that was lighting his way to town. Of course there wasn't really a fire; it was the brilliant color of the leaves, bright red, orange and a very soft yellow.

"What a wonderful life we have, Ibby. I can't imagine anything being more wonderful than this right now." Zach spoke to

Ibby often, and whenever he talked to Ibby, Ibby would always turn his head sideways and bark a reply.

Of course as soon as Zach commented on their wonderful life, his thoughts wandered to a foggy memory of a familiar dream. It was his favorite dream, one that he told all the other children back at the orphanage. When the young children were sad and felt there was no one else in the world for them, he would share this dream with them, and it gave all the children hope.

Zach would sit with his arms folded and take a deep breath and have everyone close their eyes. Then he would weave the tale of a friendly old woman who loved all children. Her name, he seemed to remember — or possibly made up — was Nona. She had a small cottage in the woods. It was a friendly place with bright colors on the door. When the front door opened, the smell of freshly baked cookies and bread would fill the air. Her round wooden table had a beautifully colored tablecloth and on top of that sat a vase filled with the most fragrant wildflowers. She had stained glass windows that allowed the sun's rays to beam through, making colors dance throughout the room.

The light made the entire floor look like a rainbow! Nona's fireplace was always neatly stacked with wood. No going cold here on a long winter's night! No siree, not with Nona! Then there was the bed. Ahh, unlike any bed you could imagine. It had a quilt that was filled with such fluffy down! Mmmmm, so warm and soft! When it was time to go to sleep, she would come and cradle you in her arms, only if you were small enough, of course, then she would sing a beautiful song that made you feel safe and warm. Off to sleep you would go. Zach would often find himself humming that song, and all the children would drift off to sleep, with Zach eventually falling asleep as well, with the song still in his head.

Reliving that dream in his mind, Zach let out a sigh as he walked with the cart, wishing that Nona really existed, but he knew it was only a dream.

"Never you mind, Ibby, let's go to town and see what we can

bring back for everyone. Don't tell anyone, but I brought extra money so I could buy you some very yummy dog treats."

Off Zach galumphed, whistling the song he always whistled, the one Nona sang to him in his dreams. Ibby was running and sliding into things as usual, making Zach laugh and forget that it would be hours before they would arrive in town, but arrive they did. Zach looked for a place to rest before picking up the supplies for the orphanage.

Zach liked the orphanage. He always said he had more brothers and sisters than any boy in the world, but he sometimes dreamed of what it would be like to have his own real family.

Once the supplies were neatly stacked in the cart and Ibby had just enjoyed the special doggy snack Zach had purchased, the dynamic pair started back to the orphanage.

Zach and Ibby had only gone a short distance when they heard a voice call out. "Where ya going young fella?"

Zach stopped. First Ibby's front feet stopped, followed by his back feet, causing him to end up sideways on the path. They both looked around and didn't see anyone, so thinking that they imagined it, they continued to walk on.

Zach started whistling again and Ibby ran alongside of him, his back legs trying to keep up with his front legs, all the while panting through the side of his mouth. Again, a voice, very clear and commanding, and sort of scary said, "Don't just walk away, I asked where you were going! Be polite and answer a question when it is asked of you, young man!"

At that point Ibby looked kinda scared, but Zach, who was twelve years old, stood up straight and tall and looked around. He pushed his cap back on his head and waited.

There was no one to be seen. Then out of the corner of his eye, Zach saw something move. He turned, and there on the lowest branch of the biggest tree was a very large black crow. This crow seemed to be staring at him. Looking him up and down. Now Zach had never heard a crow speak, or any other animal for that matter, but since there was no one else around, he figured he would just go over and ask this crow the obvious question.

"Excuse me, Mr. Crow," Zach said in a very grownup gentlemanly voice, "were you talking to us?"

The crow seemed to clear his throat, and to Zach and Ibby's surprise, said, "Of course I was talking to you. You don't see anyone else around that I might be talking to, do you? Are you suggesting I'm a little crazy, off my rocker, not having my faculties in order, and would just be sitting here in this tree talking to the air?"

"But I never heard of a talking crow," said Zach, trying to be as polite as possible.

"We don't bother talking to humans, young man. Reason being, is that they don't talk to us, and the problems I hear about your sorts...well I'd rather not get involved, if you get my meaning."

The crow winked and nodded his beak at Zach in a way that implied perhaps Zach understood perfectly.

"The reason I addressed you in particular is because I'm a great writer and I am working on a story about young men who travel alone on meadow paths with dogs who can't keep their tongues in their mouths and their back legs — well, I guess you'd say, back!

I also kinda figured you to be a little different, since you were talking to your dog. My mother always told me that a human who talks to animals can't be all bad, and as you know, all mommy crows know what they're talking about. So are you going to stare at me all day? Let's start with a simple question. What is your name?"

"My name is Zach and this is my dog Ibby, and we're heading back home after marketing, sir. I don't mean to sound rude, but do crows have names too?"

"Of course they do, and my name is Lou Wisebird. I'm sure you have read some of my books. I'm quite famous in the literary world. It's a pleasure to make your acquaintance, Zach, and you too Ibby. I have been watching you since you started on your way, and if you're going up that way, I just might go with you. But if you're going that other way, since I have nothing planned, I might go with you that way too. Matter of fact, if you're going in ANY of the directions you can go, I just might go along to keep my eye on you, for my book that is."

Zach and Ibby realized that Lou had decided to join them on their journey back to the orphanage.

"It would be a pleasure to have a noted writer accompany us on our short journey," said Zach, and they all began down the path again, with Zach whistling his song, Ibby with his back legs trying to outrace his front legs, while panting, with his tongue hanging out of the side of his mouth, and Lou, caw, caw, cawing to Zach's song. They made a very interesting trio!

After some time, they heard something wooing and hollering in the distance. "Ouch, ooch, eek, ow, owwwww!!!! Oh my, everyone look out, I'm coming through!" Then out of the bushes appeared a raccoon with a swarm of bees all over him.

"Look out, ouch, oh my!" he cried. It was really clear this guy was in trouble!

No sooner did he run out onto the path, he ran across the path and off towards the other side of the path. The three travelers watched as the raccoon leaped high into the air.

SPLASH! INTO THE COLD STREAM HE WENT! SPLASH, SPLASH, SPLASH! "Take that, you bees," the raccoon cried, "take that!" Out of the water came a very wet raccoon. He shook himself off, sending water flying everywhere.

"Oh, I am so sorry if I have gotten any of you wet. I had a minor disagreement with some honeybees. You see, I love honey so much, I overstayed my welcome, and unfortunately, sometimes staying too long can be really painful."

Zach could not believe what was going on. First a talking crow, now a talking raccoon. With his eyes as big as saucers, the raccoon looked at Zach. Zach could not believe his ears, but here he was listening to a raccoon talk, and a very wet raccoon at that. Zach decided the right thing to do was to introduce himself and his friends.

"Ahem, excuse me, Mr. Raccoon," Zach said, clearing his throat. "I couldn't help but notice you. May I introduce my friends? This is my dog Ibby and my new friend Lou Wisebird. My name is Zach."

The raccoon sighed a long sigh and said, "My name is Jaahhn." Zach, being the gentlemen he was, said in a very gentlemanly voice, "I am pleased to make your acquaintance John." But Jaahhn just sighed and said "My name is not John, but Jaahhn." Jaahhn looked Zach up and down and said with a sigh, "So young man, which way are you headed? Because if you're going THIS way I might just go with you, and if you're going THAT way I just might go with you too, because my honey day is over." He then let out a long sigh.

Zach said "Sure, Jaahhn, come along with us, and maybe we can find some honey along the way."

Jaahhn stood still, shaking his head as stray bees flew out of his fur, occasionally taking a quick bite. Jaahhn picked the last bee out of his fur, flicked it and was ready to go.

So off they went with Zach whistling his tune, Ibby with his back legs competing with his front legs, Lou caw caw cawing to Zach's tune, and Jaahhn just sighing and scratching his bee bites. They walked for some time, when Zach noticed it was getting late in the day.

"Say, anyone feeling hungry?" Jaahhn asked. "You know, it's getting kind of late, and since this journey is taking a little longer than I expected, I have built up an appetite."

"I do feel sort of peckish myself," stated Lou. Zach looked at him with his eyes rolling. Lou said, "No pun intended, Zach, but I really am hungry. All of this flying around has made me very hungry indeed." Zach was just having so much fun talking to Lou and to Jaahhn that he had forgotten all about food!

"How about some dinner, Ibby?" said Zach. With that, Ibby almost knocked Zach down. He was wagging his tail and wagging his tongue so fast that he became one big blur of fur!

"OK, let's see what we have to eat." Zach reached into the cart, pulled out some honey for Jaahhn, and some bread for Lou. Out came a bone from the butcher shop for Ibby, and for Zach, a sandwich he had been saving for this moment.

Slurping and chomping was all you could hear. Jaahhn, every once in a while mumbling "thank you," and our friend Lou cawing and singing a song. Zach never knew that crows could sing. He would find out later that one of Lou's distant relatives was a robin, and that is where he got his singing talent from.

"Yes indeed," said Lou between bites, "I knew right from the start that you were a good one to talk to, Zach, and don't think you won't get a mention in my book. Why, I think I will dedicate a whole chapter to my travels with you. Of course, all the other crows won't believe that humans can talk to crows, but who cares?"

"Thank you, Lou," said Zach. Zach was very happy today. His life felt so good with his new friends.

Jaahhn started to yawn, and Ibby started to curl up beside the cart. Even Lou was starting to put his beak behind his wing. Everyone looked as if they were ready for sleep. And sleep they did. Later, when Zach woke, he found they had all been sleeping for hours, and the sun was starting to set. He knew he would never make it back to the orphanage before night set in.

Zach, who was not fond of sleeping outside, looked up and thought he saw smoke in the distance. He walked ahead and saw that the smoke was coming from the top of a chimney. Zach woke Lou and asked if he would fly ahead to see if there was anyone in the home attached to that chimney.

"If not, maybe we will have a much warmer place to sleep for the night," remarked Zach. Well, you don't have to say things twice to a crow, and off he went!

"There doesn't seem to be anyone around, and it looks like the cottage is empty," said Lou, as he flew back from the cottage that stood in the clearing. With that news, the entire group got up and decided to go to the cottage.

As they got closer, Zach noticed the neatly kept garden with its beautiful assortment of flowers. There were flowers of every color, shape and size. Zach could hear Jaahhn sigh, and he knew what he was thinking.... where there are flowers, there are bees, and where there are bees, there's HONEY!!!

Lou flew to the windowsill and started pecking on the window, but no one answered. Zach then tried the door, which opened easily, so they all went inside. There were flowers everywhere. The walls were painted with many colors, and the fire from the fireplace seemed to make everything in the room dance. From the inside, the cottage seemed so much larger. The setting sun cast rainbows across the floors, something that seemed very familiar to Zach.

In the corner of the room was a cupboard. Zach called out one last time to see if anyone was home as he started towards the cupboard. No one answered, so he opened the cupboard door, and to his delight, it was full of jams, bread, fruits, nuts, and even a big jar marked HONEY.

Feeling comfortable in the cottage, they sat down and started eating. Suddenly they heard a noise. Cautiously, they got up and backed towards the front door, when from across the room, another door slowly opened, and a hooded figure stepped out. At that point, no one knows what happened. There was screaming going on everywhere. Zach screamed, then the hooded creature screamed, then Ibby screamed. Leo cawed, and the hooded creature screamed again. Jaahhn was huddled by the front door mumbling something about being SOOO close (to the honey, we think) as Lou tried to regain some control.

In a split second, Lou flew towards the hooded creature and pulled the hood from its head. There out from under that hood was an elderly lady with long, flowing gray hair. She stood very straight and tall, and there was a sharpness to her face that the years hadn't taken away. She was also noticeably upset. When Zach saw it was an old woman with a friendly face under the hood, he and his friends were very relieved.

"My friends and I are so sorry we scared you, but we knocked and called out, and no one answered. We had walked a long way and were very tired," said Zach.

"Well it seems to me that I may have scared you just as much," said the woman, obviously regaining her composure. "I don't get many visitors, and had just gone to the cellar to fetch some cider. You are all very welcome to stay the night, but first, you must tell me how a young boy, a dog, a crow, and a raccoon have come to travel together."

As Zach spoke, he kept getting the feeling that he had met this woman before. Her manner and her face seemed quite familiar. After dinner they all relaxed, except for Jaahhn, who had both his paws buried in the honey jar! They sang songs and told stories until it was quite late, and the last thing Zach remembered was the lady tucking a blanket under his chin.

The sun rose early, and Zach woke from the dream he sometimes had when he was warm and cozy in a nice soft bed. He would dream of a house that was nestled in the woods and a very tall, regal woman, who would grow some of the most beautiful flowers he had ever seen. In the dream, he called her Nona. Also in this dream, he would wake up to her singing the song he always sang. Zach would run into her arms, and she would hug him and tell him how much she loved him. Ibby was always in that dream also, with his tongue hanging out of the side of his mouth, and panting for joy. Times like this made Zach wish he wasn't an orphan, and that there really was a Nona he could run to.

As Zach was getting out of bed, he heard a song. He shook his head and smiled, because he thought he was still dreaming. He was hearing the song he always heard in his dreams. The one he always whistled. "Since I'm still dreaming, I might as well go downstairs and see Nona," thought Zach.

Zach ran downstairs, but something was different about everything. Lou and Jaahhn were sitting at the table along with Ibby and the old woman. She hadn't turned around yet, so Zach started whistling his song. The same song she was now singing.

The old woman dropped the dish she was holding and startled everyone. Then she slowly turned around with large tears in her eyes. Zach somehow felt this was not really a dream anymore, and didn't know what was going on.

"Where did you learn that song, little man?" said the old woman, as she tried to sit down in a chair by the window.

"I've known that song ever since I was a baby. I've always had a dream of a woman named Nona. She taught it to me, but like I said, that was only in my dreams," said Zach. He didn't know how she knew this song either, because he had always thought this was a song he made up.

The old woman slowly approached Zach and started to hug him. "Years ago a baby was taken from me, and I searched a long, long time for him. This was the song I used to sing to him. You see, little man, MY name is Nona, and that baby, I'm sure now, was you. You are my grandchild, dear boy!"

When Zach wiped the tears from his eyes, he noticed that Lou, Jaahhn and Ibby were also feeling the effect of this chance reunion. Zach looked up into Nona's eyes and couldn't help but smile. He was home.

The story has such a happy ending to it and it makes Emily smile.

"I can't wait for the next story," Emily says. Emily knows that as her aunt warms up she always gets better and better. Her stories start to really come alive.

Emily hears a sound and turns her head to face the cave entrance. She can see two large shadows. Normally anyone would be startled or scared but Emily knew exactly what the shadows were. They were her two large Siamese cats sauntering into the makeshift cave. Stretching and yawning, it seems that they were sleeping somewhere and, when they woke up and saw Emily gone, they went to look for her.

"Oh my where has she gone now? I was having such a nice nap by the fire," Rhett had said to Scarlett in his Siamese cat voice.

"I know she's always up and about but you remember what Lily said, always keep your eyes on her," Scarlett says as she lifts a leg to lick her paw.

"Let's get going and find her."

"Creeeeaaakkk," says Elizabeth.

"Ahhhh thank you Elizabeth, she is in the basement, I guess they are in the cave they built. It's snuggle-in-her-lap-time and back to sleep." Rhett lets out a long yawn as the two cats scamper towards the basement steps.

"Scarlett, Rhett what took you so long?" Emily says as she opens her arms to the two cats. The cats brush against Lily who puts out a hand to pet them as they make their way towards their ward. They both brush their heads against Emily and then settle into her lap curling up against each other. They are settled and purring now.

"Mmmmm nighty-night Scarlett," Rhett meows.

"Sweet dreams my dear," Scarlett meows back and they both fall straight to sleep.

"Aunt Lily...Scarlet and Rhett are the best gifts you ever gave me. I love them so much. They always sleep by my side. I still haven't seen that movie yet...but I love their names anyway."

"Oh, Gone with the Wind is a wonderful movie but you have plenty of time to see it. It is really a classic. I picked these two little ones to protect you..." Lily stops her sentence.

"From what?" Emily looks puzzled.

Lily looks at Emily and decides to keep the whole truth tucked away for now.

"From feeling all alone."

"I never feel alone with you around. I also have these kitties, my friends and Elizabeth."

A creak is heard in the floorboards above them. Lily knows Elizabeth heard Emily and the house is happy.

Emily leans over and gives her Aunt a hug. She notices the white band on her wrist that appears, depending on the angle, to glow. She has seen this glow before but always attributes it to a light from somewhere. It's probably a reflection from the lantern Emily thinks. It's such a faint, soft glow that it's almost impossible to make out.

She looks her aunt in the eyes. Lily feels Emily is going to ask her a question. The dreams she has been having are starting to be more and more real. Not a dream so much as a walking fantasy. Practice for what's to come.

"Aunt Lily, why do people have to hurt things that don't hurt them?" "Why honey? What do you mean by that?" That wasn't the question she expected.

"Today at school Mrs. Bankin was talking about how some species of animals are going to be extinct because people are killing them. That means that the animal is gone for a while, right?"

"No, Emily, extinct means gone forever. Never to return. Imagine if all the elephants in Africa were gone forever. That's what extinct means."

"Why would someone want all the elephants to be extinct, Aunt Lily? Are elephants mean?"

"No, Em, but some people are. Greed is a very bad emotion, Emily. It makes you blind to what's right and wrong. It makes you not care about others and think only of yourself. You become less of who you could be by satisfying only your needs and not feeling the pleasure and the joy of what you can bring to others."

Emily's face brightens up.

"Like Santa Claus and Christmas. Cause Santa doesn't ask or take anything for himself. He just leaves us gifts and presents. Except for the cookies."

"Just like Santa. We all need to give from our souls because that's where the love is held. That's where the light shines. Giving of yourself is the most precious gift you can give. Money and power are nothing if you don't have a loving and caring soul. That's why in December they call it the Spirit of Christmas. It's your soul and spirit touching others through giving, from your soul. It also creates the little Glimmers in our lives and in our world."

"Oh I love my Glimmers, Aunt Lily. They make me shine."

Years ago Lily explained to Emily that Glimmers are little beings of light that illuminate around a person who is kind and truthful. Everyone is born with Glimmers surrounding them but if a person lies or is mean their Glimmers turn dark and they become Dimmers. Sad and glum. If you do an unbelievably good thing or tell a spectacular truth you can have Glimmers born around you. The more good you do the brighter you glow. That's why Emily shines; it's her bright Glimmer glow.

Emily continues to listen intently for the next story. She always listens to her aunt. Her voice is so warm and captivating, lower in pitch than most women but soft and kind.

Bill Leso said the reason Lily was always surrounded by children had a lot to do with her voice. As Emily listens she continues to pet her cats who have stopped purring and are fast asleep. They know that they are in the best place in the world and they would give their lives to protect this little one. That's why they are here.

"Tonight, my little cave dweller, I have a special story and one of your favorites," Aunt Lily says with a sly grin. She knows Emily loves this story and tonight it will be the truth and innocence that comes through. Tonight her squire will become a warrior if everything she has seen of her niece is true.

"The Band of Innocence?" Emily is so excited. Every time Aunt Lily has told this story it seems to get more and more real. As if she were part of the story.

"Exactly, but tonight it will be a little different, my dear. We have lots of time and it seems that neither of us is going anywhere this weekend."

Before they had come downstairs Lily noticed the rain starting to fall. This would be a nice storm that would last the weekend, giving her all the time to initiate Emily and see if the fantasy turned to reality. Years of waiting had been leading up to this moment.

"Will this moment fail the goals of all good or will light and love triumph against the dark?" Lily thinks.

Lily knows that Emily is the true light and worries little but there have been major defeats in her life and the world cannot afford another.

With that Aunt Lily starts to read. The story starts a long time ago — before life began here on this beautiful planet. Emily is lying down and starts to stare at the amulet around her Aunt Lily's neck. As she stares she thinks she can see little stars blinking in the stone. She has never seen her Aunt without that amulet. A little purple teardrop of a crystal but now it seems to be coming alive with light. Little specks of light seem to pop up in the amulet as Lily starts the story.

"I want you to relax Em, because tonight a new chapter of the Band of Innocence will be revealed to you. A part of the story you have never heard and in this chapter you have a leading role."

"Me? I don't understand."

"No need to worry honey," Lily says with a giggle. "Lie back and close your eyes, we will be taking quite a long journey tonight."

CHAPTER SEVEN

The Creation

It's the beginning of time. Five figures are sitting in a semi-circle. Mist seems to hover all around them. Together they are studying a small orb that's blue and green. On closer look it is a planet that appears below them. This is a meeting of the Elders, the Gods who will decide how to develop this creation, this planet.

A female God stands and begins to pace. The temperament on her brow seems to change continuously. Surrounded by bursts of lightning and wind, she is Sif, the Goddess of the Elements. She passes by a man sitting upright on a chair made of vines. He is completely engulfed in a forest of green foliage. Small flowers of multiple colors bloom to the right of him as he folds his hands. This is the Plant God, Wiraquocha. He folds his hands as a vine wraps around them. He gives an inquisitive look to the woman directly across from him.

Lying on a marble platform, this woman points to a spot on this newly formed planet. Her hand slowly morphs into the paw of a cheetah, then her arm and the rest of her follow until she has completely transformed into this beautiful cat. She licks her paw and rubs her head with it.

"Purrrr," comes from her throat. A deep, heavy growl.

She then morphs into a falcon. Spreading her wings and shaking her head before she morphs back into her human persona. She is the Animal Goddess, Minona.

To her right is the shape of a man. His body is made of flowing blue water. He is the Water God, Unktahee. He puts his hand to his chin and then quickly points to the round planet as if having come up with an idea, but then retracts his arm. Water from his sudden movement sprinkles to his right and hits the arm of a large figure made of molten rock and fire, causing a small bit of sizzle and smoke. The hiss and sizzle draw a perturbed look from the Fire God, Tu Di Gong. The Water God, Unktahee, stands and turns towards Tu Di Gong, bowing his head. Looking forward in realization, the Fire God does the same.

The Animal Goddess, Plant God and Goddess of the Elements all follow suit. Nodding their heads as if in reverence.

Entering the circle from the mist that surrounds these Elders and floating just above the planet are two beautiful shiny, granite feet. The sparkling black feet stop and stand over the orb. This is Mother Nature herself — an old woman with striking blue eyes and high cheekbones. She is visually striking in every way. Her hair is made of trees, thick and green. Her skin is a gleaming dark granite. Her nails made of gems. She radiates and sparkles. In her hand is a silver cane with an orb as the handle. A closer look reveals that the orb is similar to the one they are looking down on. With a lift of her cane, the planet begins to glow.

"I have called on you, my children, and have gathered you all to construct what will be our greatest achievement. After much practice it is now time to bring this wonderful planet into being, Tu Di Gong," the old woman turns to the large, threatening red and black figure. He smolders and wisps of smoke can be seen coming from his body.

"Yes Mother..." he answers in reverence with his head bowed.

The Fire God's eyes blaze as his hand hovers above the small planet. Flames shoot from his mouth down into the sky of this glowing orb.

As he does this the planet's surface is revealed. Volcanoes can be seen erupting and shooting fire into the sky. The land rumbles as an earthquake rattles the dirt hills.

"Wonderful, your volcanoes will create constant change on this planet by reshaping the land. Let this be the genesis of the Spirit of Fire."

Mother Nature turns to the water figure.

"Unktahee, my love, we need oceans and rivers."

The Fire God interrupts, "Mother. Perhaps I can cover the face of the planet and this time water can be beneath me."

Mother Nature smiles a bit, "No...no my love...we tried that before remember. It didn't work out all that well." All the gods laugh and Tu Di Gong snorts with smoke coming out of his nose.

Unktahee smirks and places his hand over the planet.

The scene on this planet shows the water of a river foaming and churning as it travels across the newly formed land. The oceans begin to cover much of the planet's surface. The giant waves on the shoreline break and then go crashing down into the surf.

Mother Nature looks over at Tu Di Gong and sees him smoldering.

"No need to get hot, my child. As you are vital to the core of this planet, the water in these oceans and rivers are like the blood that runs through the veins of the body. They will keep all things alive. From this powerful source will come the Water Spirits. To make our circle complete, I will need all of you. This is a collective effort, my children. You need to work together to achieve a beautiful world but we still have a little more to add to the recipe."

In the distance over the ocean there is the faint image of the God of the Elements, Sif, standing with her wooden staff held high in the sky. She inhales deeply and spreading her arms, she lets go of a deep breath. Clouds appear in the sky and the Sif's breath becomes the wind that moves the clouds. The first sounds of thunder can be heard as a light rain begins to fall. Lightning lights up the sky.

"Ah my Sif, create the wind, rain and the snow. Bring both your enveloping warmth and your bitter cold. Allow the weather to change like your moods. It will be up to you to balance and nurture all future living things. It is with you the Spirits of the Elements will be created."

The water from the raindrops forms a small puddle on the land. In the reflection of one of the puddles appears the Plant God, Wiraquocha. He reaches into a small, worn pouch around his waist and sprinkles a glowing substance onto the wet earth. The rain slowly stops. A small green sprout shoots up from the ground.

Wiraquocha leans down and touches the leaf of this first sprout and as they watch, plants and trees of all kinds rise from the newly formed ground.

Mother Nature smiles and a rainbow of colors light up the skies. She turns to her children: "Wiraquocha's creations will thrive on this newly formed land. I want these plants to have a language and an intelligence, if you will. From this intelligence will spring the forces of the Plant Spirits. Last but not least we need the animals, the children of this planet."

The Animal Goddess, Minona, begins to lift her hand over the planet but then hesitates. A worried look covers her face and she turns to Mother Nature.

"Mother I have a surprise for you. I know I may have overstepped my bounds by not unveiling this creation sooner."

"My dear what have you done? You know nothing should be hidden from your mother. It's not another platypus, is it? Please, I know you may have extra parts but that was just," Mother Nature giggles, "was just wrong."

All the gods start to laugh.

Minona looks around and smiles knowing that the platypus was just really thrown together as an experiment and even though it looked misplaced, she loved it as she loved all her creations.

The smile from Minona's face quickly faded and she looked down again.

"No, Mother, I know I may have been unfocused with those little babies but I have come up with a new creature. I call it a human. It has more intellect and compassion than any of the other creatures I have created. It has intelligence rather than instinct and has the innocence of all my children. These humans will protect all we have created."

Minona looks down. "I thought we needed a caretaker. This is what has been missing in our worlds. This human has an uncanny ability to love and cherish. I just don't know if the intelligence should have been left out." Minona's shoulders are slumped and her head is still hanging down.

Mother Nature walks over and lifts her child's head. She stares into Minona's dark black eyes. Minona looks up at her mother, seeing the ultimate love that she has for all her children.

"Intellect is all relative, isn't it my child? As caretakers they will need intelligence to make decisions. My child, you have piqued my interest. Show us more."

Minona holds her hands out with her palms facing upwards. A baby forms in her hands. The cries echo across the planet.

All the gods look at Minona's outstretched hands and smile except for Sif.

"Oh my, how beautiful, sister. Really outstanding. Well done," Wiraquocha says.

"I don't trust this," Sif says under her breath.

"Sister you are so suspicious," Unktahee says to Sif.

"No, I just don't think these creatures need to think. Let their instincts guide them. Why make them intelligent? Minona, you make them like the gods we are."

"Sif, you know our time is short here. Who will watch out for our creations when we have gone?" Tu Di Gong says looking worried.

"Let the rain and wind look after our planet," Sif says as a lightning burst springs from her hand into the sky above the spinning globe.

"Now, now, my children. This human was a wonderful idea and you should be praising your sister for her ingenuity," Mother Nature says.

"Are you jealous, Sif?" Minona says.

"I don't get jealous, I get angry" — a brilliant bolt of lightning cuts across the heavens — "but I think this will be trouble. You mark my words." Sif's words echo in thunder.

"Temper, temper my love." Mother Nature puts her arm around Sif.

"The world is set. Let's watch for a little while and see how these humans do. If it doesn't work out I will let you bring on the floods like the last time." Mother Nature knows that their power is weak and they need to rest. She prays that these new humans will appreciate the wisdom and compassion Minona has instilled in them.

A smile comes across Sif's face.

"Oh my yes, Mother that would so please me."

"Good, my dear. I want to praise all my children for the wonderful job you have done for this world. Everything fits perfectly.

Now Minona, populate our creation with your children."

All the gods look down at the earth which is glowing with water and plant life. The land is covered by meadows and forests.

The piercing screech of a bird can be heard. It is an eagle. The eagle is Minona in one of her many animal forms. As she soars over the land and meadows we see through her eyes gazelles on the lush plain along with zebras, lions, and water buffalo. All feeding and running in this paradise.

"Minona, it is your responsibility to create the beings that will populate this beautiful world and from these animals a strong and noble energy shall emanate. This is the Spirit of the Animals. The goal should be to have all things created flow together — living hand in hand. The cycle of life should regenerate itself with plants, animals and elements all coexisting in one harmonious melody."

An early human stands on a hill overlooking the animals down below.

Mother Nature smiles. "We have given our creations the potential for the purest of good."

Early man can be seen admiring the meadows that are teeming with plants and animal life. His face shows a calm, serene smile. The Gods, in their pride, never notice a dark shadow slowly crossing the hilltop. It moves ever closer to man. Noticing a chill which he has never felt before, the man turns to see the darkness getting closer. Man steps back and then runs away down the hill.

The man turns and speaks to the animals in a foreign tongue that the animals seem to understand. Both man and animal turn to see this darkness and start to run from it even as the darkness goes unnoticed by the gods who are resting after the creation of this planet.

Through the eyes of its creators, the earth is a wonderfully peaceful place. As man, animal and plant all mingle together, man speaks in a language that is indecipherable to today's humans. The man then stands and speaks to a tall blackberry bush. The bush lowers its branch in recognition. The bush allows the man to pick its berries which he in turn feeds to a mammoth black bear by hand and pops some in his own mouth. The man then rests his head against the large beast's chest and quickly falls asleep.

The Elders gather around Mother Nature as they peer down on the small planet.

"Mother, it is everything we dreamed. The harmony between all living things is...is beautiful," Wiraquocha the Plant God says.

Minona looks at Mother. "And what should we call this wonder?"

Tu Di Gong, the Fire God, lifts his big head and smiles. "Brimstone, perhaps?"

Mother Nature stands silently looking at this newly formed world. She then looks around at her children.

"This planet will be called Earth. It will be up to the life spirits you have placed within your creations to protect this land... from now until the end of time." As she says this she smiles. Light pours from her mouth and eyes and this world called Earth starts to slowly spin.

The gods rest and let their creations prosper, never noticing the darkness that hides in the shadows of this world.

In this lush world everything lives in harmony. Thousands of years pass as man multiplies over the globe always leaving enough for others and never taking more than his fair share. The plants give nutrition and medicine. When a man child is born the plants and animals all celebrate. It's an easy life and as all things pass so do these men, plants and animals but they are always replaced by others. As they are replaced, the new order follows the law of the old order. Until......

CHAPTER EIGHT

The Lost Path

Man and all the other inhabitants live on the beaches and in the hills and caves and there is always enough heat and food and water for all.

The mountain folk are a wonderfully gentle people. Living on berries and nuts, they like all mankind have sworn never to kill or take more than their fair share. One particular tribe lives in the mountains that are now called the Alps. This is one of the larger clans of early man living in a giant cave which, this morning, is taking in much of the early light.

The cave has a huge back hall where music is played every night. All the people eat together as any family would. Dinner is a large gathering with hundreds of tribes. Men, women and children all lining up for food, with people laughing and dancing.

On this particular night a chill has settled in the air. Some of the people feel it but most just go about their business. As everyone drifts off to sleep a large man with a dark black beard sits smiling. This is the leader of this particular clan. His smile reflects his joy at the lives he is responsible for. He sits very still watching the group as they lie asleep. He seems to be staring at a young man curled up next to what looks to be his wife. This young man is his ward. He has watched over this lad since he was just a small boy. The young man and woman lie next to the remnants of a dying fire and beside them is a basket of fresh fruit.

The large man does not notice the dark shadow that slowly seeps into the cave along the wall behind him. The shadow snuffs out the light on his face and the broad smile becomes a dark menacing grin. His dark black beard develops a silver streak. He violently stands and grunts as he crosses over to the young couple and grabs the woman out of a dead sleep. He then grabs the fruit. As the young man stands to question the bearded man's action in disbelief the large man picks up a log from the fire and swings the club at the young man, knocking him to the floor. The older man holds the log over his head in a sign of dominance. Suddenly a second man charges the older one until a brutal fight breaks out. The shadow swallows the clan as the fighting continues.

All over the world arguments and fights break out.

"Mother, come see what is happening," cries Sif the Element

Goddess. The Elders, now all looking a great deal older, peer down in dismay at the actions that have transpired in the cave. Mother Nature shakes her head. Mother Nature, looking tired and worried, rests on a large marble slate. She places her cane down and massages her brow. The Elders gather around her.

She sighs, "Oh dear."

Unktahee the Water God speaks first. "The guardian spirits have let man multiply too quickly. This is not good."

Minona turns to the spinning globe. "The humans had agreed to never take more than their fair share. Now look, man is losing his ability to communicate with plants. The same appears to be happening with the animals. What is this darkness? I am not sure what is happening. Mother can you see where this is going? Can we take one glimpse?"

They all stare at the cane Mother Nature is holding. Peering into the globe on the handle may give them some indication where this is heading.

"No," Mother Nature says sternly.

The Fire God Tu Di Gong steps forward, "But Mother, Minona is right. We must see the direction man is heading. Then maybe we can decide to end this and start again as we have done before."

Mother Nature slowly gets to her feet. She sadly and slowly turns her back.

"I must dwell on this my children."

Her image begins to fade in the clouds as only her voice can now be heard.

"You all know how I feel about such things. Looking into the future is not permitted. We have grown old, my children, and now we must allow Earth to take its natural course."

Mother Nature fades away, leaving all the other Elders looking at each other in disbelief. Then they turn their eyes back down toward the Earth. The Earth begins to spin faster and then faster. As this happens we see in the globe the images of different violent confrontations around the world. We see arguments and fights.

We see greed and lies.

There is a beautiful scene of a mother bear and her cub by a lakeside.

"Maybe things aren't that bad," say Minona the Animal Goddess. "Look at my bears. So peaceful and calm."

The sun is beating down as the bears drink from the lake and the sun light shimmers from the golden rays. A peaceful calm encompasses the lake. The sunlight suddenly begins to be replaced by a dark shadow. The bears look up and run back into the forest as the shadow gets bigger and the serene lake side is replaced by the noise of screams and shouts. Man has entered a new stage. This is war. Men fighting other men. Fire raging out of control.

The Elders, ever older, watch the battle by the lake unfold.

Sif is stunned, "Do you see what is going on with our creation? This darkness has turned man. I knew he should never have been trusted and never created." She looks at Minona.

"Mother approved it. I also came up with bear, buffalo, birds and fish. It was Mother who let me have an animal that had free will, someone who could create great and beautiful things. I feel so bad. This was not what I planned," a tear can be seen in the corner of her eye.

"I have a surprise, is what you said," Sif states in a mocking tone.

Minona begins to cry.

"There, there sister. How could you have known? Man looked so perfect and innocent." Unktahee puts his arm around Minona.

Wiraquocha looks over at the seat Mother Nature had been sitting in. "Mother has left her walking stick. Let us look into the globe and see where this all leads."

The silver cane with the spinning globe on top is leaning against mother's chair. The cane sparkles as the globe rotates. The Earth, with all its clouds, land and seas can be seen so clearly as the globe spins.

"You heard Mother...the future is off limits," says Minona. The look in her eyes says she is too scared to see where this is heading.

Her eyes are wet and red with tears.

"Then why would she have left her cane? We need to find out where this is leading," Sif answers. "Let's see how your creations, dear sister, affect ours."

"Sif, stop it. Don't you see how bad Minona feels?" Tu Di Gong stands close to Minona in support.

"I warned you all." Thunder can be heard as Sif's voice rises in anger. Lightning flashes around her.

"Free will, caretakers. I knew they would be trouble. Weak and easily corruptible is how I saw them but no one would listen to me."

"Enough." Wiraquocha walks into the center.

"What is done is done. Our sister had the best of intentions. Let us see now where this is headed."

Sif grabs the cane as the Elders gather around. The globe at the top of the cane, that has been slowly spinning, now produces an image. It is of a serene Japanese river bank, just beyond a rice field where the wind is blowing the grain back and forth. The Elders seemed relieved at the beauty the future holds. The Animal God smiles as a group of sika deer walk into the image. A few red-crowned cranes land at the water's edge. This is Japan in the future.

"See, all is well. Look at the serenity, the beauty," Unktahee says.

The sun ripples off the top of the rice field as the sika deer graze in the foreground by the river bank. A giant red-crowned crane dips its large head into the water in search of a meal. A dark shadow falls across the riverbank but this shadow seems different. The sika deer run for cover back into the rice fields. One of the giant red-crowned cranes spreads its wings and in a sign of fear the top of its head turns bright red. The shadow continues to make the river bank darker as a whistling sound is heard.

The Elders watch through the cane as a large explosion destroys the entire riverbank. We see the reflection of the future in each one of their horrified eyes as a mushroom cloud ascends into the sky. The faint images of the aftermath can be seen in their pupils. Minona lets out a scream. The sphere at the top of the cane goes dark.

Minona is trying to hold back her emotions but she cannot. She again starts to cry. Feeling the pain of all her babies is too much for her.

"What have I done?" Minona cries.

"I know what Mother said but we cannot let this happen. Entire species destroyed." Sif starts to point to each of the gods.

"They will destroy your plant life, poison my sky, pollute your water and erode the land your fire has created. This is enough we must stop this monster we call man," Sif's voice resounds across the heavens as a huge clap of thunder.

Tu Di Gong's voice resonates across the heavens so loudly that all on the planet look up. "Sif is correct. At our age, we must act now before we are too weak to make a difference, while man is still small in numbers. This can be done in no time. Quickly."

Sif the God of the Elements steps forward, a cyclone forming in her hand.

"Allow me then. Mother had said I could. I will wipe the Earth's slate clean so we may start again without man and his shadows and greed."

Wiraquocha looks worried. "No. We should all have a part in this. When Mother comes to ask what happened...we will take responsibility together."

Sif has other ideas "Let me take care of it. A giant tsunami or two and we can start over one last time."

As the gods bicker about who should end the world Mother Nature appears from the mist.

"My children." Mother Nature stands looking at the Gods. They are all startled and turn toward her. Like children caught taking cookies from a cookie jar. She steps out of the darkness looking older than she did before. Cracks can be seen in her once smooth black granite face. She walks hesitantly.

"You will do no such thing. You have sealed the fate of this planet by looking into the future."

"But, Mother, we see now where man is heading. We were unaware how bad this was going to be." Sif speaks as lightning blasts around her.

"No, Mother this has to stop." cries Unktahee. "My oceans and seas are being sickened and left filthy."

"I will not let them continue to pollute my air and fill my sky with dirt and death." Sif is the most temperamental of all the Gods. She is holding a bolt of lightning in one hand. Mother Nature looks at her and knows she, of all her children, has always been the hardest to restrain or predict just as the weather has always been and always will be. She steps forward and takes her cane from Sif.

"Ahh my children, I know how you feel but you have seen things to come and now they will be. You have sealed the future of this planet. We must take responsibility for what we have done and for what we have seen. Thoughts become realities and your actions have helped form a future for this planet."

Wiraquocha puts his hand on his chin. "So must I now just sit by and watch as they destroy all my children. The plants and trees I created and cared for and loved. The innocent plants and animals are now subject to these cruel whims of man. This wasn't the original way, Mother. How did the path of compassion become overgrown with greed and hate?"

"My child," Mother Nature puts a hand on the Plant God's shoulder. "We could not suspect that a darkness would be created in our garden. It's a blight that we did not foresee. We will certainly not just stand by and watch the pure be corrupted and do nothing. No. We will intervene." Her worried look warms a bit.

The Elders turn as Mother Nature slowly makes her way back toward her chair. She uses her cane to support her walk.

"But not by destroying them. Destruction is not our way, we are creators."

"I don't mean to interrupt Mother" — but Sif always does — "We are older and the Guardian Spirits within us are growing weak as the time passes. We gave the humans a chance, we must start over." She raises her arms and thunder and lightning shoot across the sky. All the people on the planet are looking at the sky because they have never seen such light or heard such loud thunder before. Men and women scurry and run for protection into their caves or under their huts.

Mother Nature smiles and sits as she is too old to stand for long.

"Ah, Sif, my love," Mother has a tender spot for this child, always so headstrong.

"Again what are we if we destroy what we have created? How do you fault the humans if your plan is the same — to destroy? It's this darkness that corrupts."

Minona spins with frustration in her voice. "Then how? The humans have lost the innocence which was bestowed upon them. They refused a gift of wonder and joy. A blessing that they have been granted turned into a curse. I say we stop it now."

Mother Nature's grin becomes a full smile.

"Have they all fallen victim to this darkness? Is all of man guilty of the sins of his brothers? Is the innocence truly gone?"

The gods stand and all wonder why Mother is smiling. They look at each other and then Sif, the God of the Elements, has the look of realization. She turns quickly towards Mother Nature.

"Mother, the children."

Mother knows for all her faults and instabilities Sif is the most intuitive of all her children. Tu Di Gong broadens a huge smile of rock and brimstone. "Brilliant Mother, the children."

Mother Nature sheds a tear of hope from her left eye. As it falls to her hand it becomes a stunning purple teardrop amulet. The deep color swirls in the silver casing. She carries the amulet and sets it down right above the planet Earth. It floats above the spinning globe.

"Yes, the children. They will be our last hope. They will be... our Band of Innocence. My children, circle this amulet with me."

The Elders stand in a circle holding hands, bowing their heads.

"We will search for the most pure of heart. They will be chosen to combat the darker energies that are motivating the people of the Earth."

Mother Nature takes a deep breath as she begins to shake slightly. She closes her eyes. The gods who had looked so worn and tired regain their grandeur from younger days. They seem strong and powerful again as they all lend their powers to each other. Even Mother Nature's black granite face seems to mend with the cracks smoothing out into their former beautiful black granite perfection. They are all pulling strength from each other and they know that when they stand together there is nothing to stop them.

"I need all of you now. This creation will take the last bit of power we have. Follow my thoughts." Recessed in her black face she opens her eyes and the purest white light shoots out across the skies.

The Group of Elders, gripping hands, begin to convulse. A flash of brilliant white light and a loud thunderous explosion knocks their bodies to the ground. Again they have reverted to the worn and tired-looking gods. As they slowly get to their feet they see hovering above them a sword of bright light. It's slowly spinning and glistening; next to it a brilliant silver suit of armor. It shines like a star in the dark night. As the elders resume their places in the circle they stare in awe at the vision of the sword and armor.

"We...we did it," says Tu Di Gong looking a little confused, "Uh but mother what exactly did we do?"

"This is the Sword of Truth. The leader of our Band of Innocence will use it to vanquish the darkness. The Armor of Innocence will be used to protect their souls and bring them the knowledge of the ages."

Mother Nature raises her silver cane skyward. The sword and armor spin downward disappearing into the amulet.

"We will hide the sword and armor in this amulet. We will

also hide our remaining powers. For this shadow will try to possess them all. At the right time the amulet will reveal its secrets to the most untainted, the most innocent and it will release a new age of wonder to this ever-darkening world." The Plant God reaches down and picks up the amulet and studies it with wonder. Unktahee, the Water God, turns to Mother Nature.

"So...who will lead this Band of Innocence?"

The Plant God hands the amulet to Mother Nature and she secures it around her neck. As the gods stand around her they are all slowly absorbed into the amulet.

As the Earth continues to spin through the ages of mankind, we see a terrible series of wars: Alexander the Great, the Ancient Roman Empire, the Mongolians, the Crusades, the French Revolution, the Revolutionary War, and the Civil War in rapid succession. In each of these battles we see a glow of light and a small band of children but the darkness continues to grow across the spinning globe and a faint menacing laughter can be heard.

As Mother Nature stands alone above the Earth she watches all that has been going on upon her once beautiful planet.

"The power of my children is safely within this amulet, with the sword and the armor. We have suffered some defeats but I feel a bright future for my children. My children and I have yet the strength to try one last time and we will."

CHAPTER NINE

Haran Kazan

The year is now 1971, and so many things are going on in the world. The Vietnam War is still raging, but the atmosphere has changed and people are just tired of it. John Lennon's "Imagine" is one of the top songs of the year along with Rod Stewart's "Maggie May" and the miniskirt is still the rage. Michael and Jennifer are the two most popular names for kids.

Chicago is still getting over the riots from previous years and its sports teams aren't doing so well. The Cubs have never won a World Series but are actually starting to look good.

On the outskirts of the city a large white building stands with a large parking lot surrounding it. The building is very modern. It's raining and the flashing lights of an ambulance can be seen rushing in through the gates of the emergency room parking area. This is St. Mary's Hospital. St. Mary's is known as one of the best hospitals in Chicago. The 2nd Floor east wing is quiet tonight. This wing is where all the rich and famous come for treatment. It's where they hide after their plastic surgery or for more serious ailments. This is where they get the special attention that the rich expect.

A raven-haired nurse walks in straightening herself as if she is just starting her shift. A middle-aged administrator with bad highlights and glasses seems frantic as she is going through paperwork on the desk. She keeps looking down the corridor where a large man is standing. He is about 6'8" and weighs 300 lbs. His large foreboding body stands in silhouette looking out a window. He is bald, with a black goatee. His face is stern and cold. Shadows seem to play all across him.

To his rear, there is a less substantial man with thinning hair who is calmly berating a petite, blond nurse. They are standing in front of room 14D. The entrance to this room is staffed by two large bodyguards on both sides of the door. Hospital personnel are continuously entering and exiting.

Two nurses stand together and the one with raven hair is looking very flustered. Her name tag says Nancy. She looks at the other nurse and in a low voice says. "This is nuts, Dierdra...they called me back on four hours rest after 12 straight in the E.R. This better be good. Who is that hassling Sally? I mean what is going on around here?" Nurse Dierdra Hall doesn't look up but quietly answers Nancy's question.

"Nancy...Heellloo?...Haran Kazan is going on. That's what's going on."

Nurse Nancy Wilkins continues to study Kazan, then looks at Dierdra as if still not getting who this is. Dierdra stops and looks at Nancy in disbelief.

"You've never heard of Kazan? He is one of the wealthiest or is the wealthiest man on the planet...Talonthorn group? If there is someone who doesn't want the Vietnam War to end, it's that man over there."

Nancy looks puzzled. "What do they make?"

Dierdra looks at Nancy "More like what don't they make! Mostly defense contracting...weapons and such. But Kazan would have his company knit socks for entire countries if he could make a buck off it. They will contract with anybody...democracies, communist governments, rogue dictators...Ah there it is!"

Dierdra straightens her glasses and grabs the paperwork. She turns to approach one of the men surrounding Mr. Kazan. Dierdra had seen this gentleman before in front of the press. She would have rather had her kidney removed than approach this man. Tall, with glasses, he seems to be British given the accent and his voice is quite loud for being in a hospital.

Dierdra turns back to Nancy. "His money knows no ideology. It only knows pain and suffering. Now look busy because you don't want to get involved in any of this."

Dierdra scurries down the hall. In her hands she has the paperwork that was asked for, or more like demanded, by this British gentleman. Nancy watches out of the corner of her eye as Dierdra gets further down the hall.

As Dierdra gets closer with the papers the man's right arm extends out without even looking for the papers but expecting them to be there. Never looking at Dierdra he takes the papers from her hand. He scans the paperwork briefly and then throws it over his shoulder. The papers go everywhere. Dierdra bends down to pick them up. Nancy races to help.

The man is Graham Wellington, Haran Kazan's right-hand man. In his late 20's he stands about 6'1" and has a very thin body.

Wearing round glasses with short blond hair Graham has a cold calculating stare. No compassion can be seen and none will ever be given by this man. Money is the god he praises.

Born in England, he was a brilliant student but was always being bullied by his peers for his studious looks and ways. He swore he would get his revenge on everyone including his Mum and Dad who always wanted an athletic boy. He once overheard them say that they wished they didn't have such a girlie boy but a boy like the neighbors had. Ricky Prentiss. Ricky was the middle school star soccer player. The girls loved little Ricky. Graham is the one that smirked when Ricky's parents looked in his room one day and he wasn't there. He was never heard from or seen again.

"Oh poor Rick," was all Graham had said when he heard the news. They never found any clues to Ricky's disappearance.

The summer after Ricky disappeared, the Wellingtons all went on vacation to Italy. Graham was the only one to return home. He attended school as scheduled and continued about his life. The school found out months later when they tried to contact his parents because Graham had won the prestigious math and science award in his school. The police did an intensive search but never found them. When asked, Graham said they left and never came back. That's all. Nothing more.

He ended up living with an aunt until he was eighteen and then moved out.

From eighteen to the present his history is very sketchy. Always being very close to crooked dealings in money, drugs and weapons but not close enough to ever be prosecuted.

The hospital staff is constantly running back and forth as Graham turns to no one in particular. "This was not our agreement," he says in a very thick British accent.

"See...right here...the hospital agreed to provide the staff from the East Wing," Dierdra says sheepishly not wanting to really look at this man. She is pointing to one of the papers she has just picked up from the floor.

Graham has no problem interrupting her as if she weren't even talking, "No...You were not to provide the staff of the East Wing but you were to provide...the Wing! Where is this Mr. Roberts? I need to speak to someone in authority, not some nurse."

Just then, a heavy set man in his late fifties wearing a fine blue suit exits the elevator with a forty-something doctor with thick black hair and bushy eyebrows. The chubby man extends his hand to Wellington. His overcoat is wet from the rain that started earlier in the day. Graham ignores the handshake.

Dierdra gets back to her feet with the rest of the papers being held close to her chest.

The heavy set man is Dennis Roberts and he is in charge of the hospital. He has worked his whole life to get to where he is and this is not where he wants to be right now. He is a doctor; has been his whole life and a really good one. He has the mind and heart for this job but he didn't sign up for this part. He's oblivious to the politics of health care. He just wants to make people well. To help the needy and those in pain. That's all.

"Hello, I'm Dennis Roberts...Chief Executive Officer and this is Dr. Hanagan, the specialist you requested. I understand there is a problem, Mr. Kazan?"

The mistake Mr. Roberts makes is he addresses Kazan and not Graham, which infuriates them both.

"Ah, Mr. Roberts, I think you need to first address me. Graham Wellington. I'm the person who contacted you and made all the arrangements. It would be to your benefit to deal with me because once you have to deal with Mr. Kazan then you may wish you had stayed out in the rain. The problem we have here is that Mr. Kazan had requested the wing of this hospital, not more useless staff running about like headless poultry."

Roberts can't hold back and blurts out, "That's crazy. I would never have agreed to such a request. We are the leading pediatrics hospital in a major metropolitan area. I can't accommodate...."

Graham pays no attention to what Mr. Roberts is barking

about and he doesn't care. He turns to look into Mr. Robert's eyes. He has dealt with these kinds of useless men. Men who feel that everyone is born equal with equal rights to health and well-being. What a load of garbage that was.

"I spoke specifically to Mr. Kazan's concern for germs, distractions and unwanted publicity...Do you know the annual contributions Mr. Kazan makes to this institution?"

Just then a large hand comes down on Graham Wellington's shoulder. The hand covers all of Graham's shoulder. Graham is not small in stature but he looks like a child next to this enormous man. Graham's face turns slightly sour as he knows he has failed Haran Kazan but he looks at Roberts with a "You really should have dealt with me" look. The huge man steps forward as Graham's shoulders slump and he steps aside. Haran Kazan's large menacing brow is shadowed with a dark black stain. These shadows seem to dance all around. The lights in the hall are bright but the shadows are all around.

Kazan's voice is low and thick. A cross between Darth Vader and Batman. "Mr. Roberts, perhaps Graham hasn't articulated to you just how much I would value that my requests be met."

Dennis Roberts thinks for a moment. "I can negotiate with this man. He doesn't sound that threatening." Dennis is totally wrong. "Mr. Kazan, I have too many children that I would have to..."

Kazan steps forward and closes the gap between himself and Roberts. Getting ready for the kill, as he would say.

"You know, yesterday I was speaking to Eli Blanderbaum... and Nicholas Scarboza...and Catherine Sharp... and..."

The doctor who has been standing there wringing his hands turns to Dierdra.

"Who are these people?"

"Members of the Board of Trustees," Dierdra says quietly.

Kazan continues, "This is a fine institution...you do enjoy running it?"

The dark shadow spills from Kazan's face and begins to cover Dennis.

Dennis Roberts thinks that Mr. Kazan is a reasonable man and will see how this could hurt his patients. Dennis Roberts has made a huge mistake today by assuming Mr. Kazan has anything but his own interests in mind.

A slight smile crosses Kazan's face and Roberts seems to relax until Kazan goes in for the kill.

"You have two boys in high school? Correct? I am sure they have grand aspirations for future education... and the cost these days. I donate to any major university worth its salt. Mr. Roberts...I have a long reach. So...one parent to another, you can understand why I want the best for my newborn son. Do we understand each other?"

Dennis Roberts starts to realize there is no negotiating with this man.

"Dierdra...Nancy...start clearing the East Wing."

The doctor who has been standing there looking completely out of place in this group of men shakes his head, which gets Mr. Kazan's attention. His name is William Hanagan and he will soon realize it was better to just comply with these demands and remain in anonymity. Kazan breaks into a slight smile.

Nurse Nancy and Nurse Sally look at Dennis as if he were crazy.

"Doctor, is something wrong with my request?" Kazan says in a slightly louder voice.

"This is unethical...those children are at risk," the doctor says thinking he has the well-being of his patients in mind.

Dennis interrupts quickly. "Doctor don't make this any worse."

Nurse Sally turns to Dennis with a stern look. "And what are we supposed to do with all the children on this floor?"

Dennis starts to get angry because he knows that the longer

this goes on the better chance he could be on the unemployment line tomorrow. Kazan will just go above his head and that would not look good to the board. "Double them up...use any room if you have to. I don't know ... tell them...tell them we are checking for a gas leak or something...well go!"

The nurses pause in disgust. Then begin to move. Dennis, feeling guilty, lowers his head and walks away. The doctor stares in disbelief at Kazan. Kazan stares him dead in the eye.

"So Doctor Hanagan...I have chosen you to deliver my heir. They say you are the best pediatric doctor in the country?" Dr. Hanagan says nothing. The two large bodyguards stand on opposite sides of Dr. Hanagan.

"You had better be." Kazan pats the doctor on the cheek as if to say "Good boy."

Nurses and orderlies frantically begin to move patients out of their rooms toward the elevator. There is yelling and chaos as Kazan's demands are being met. Haran Kazan's wife is now wheeled into a room at the end of the E wing. She appears to be in pain. Her complexion is white and pasty. The doors slam shut behind her.

CHAPTER TEN

The births

With all the chaos that is attributed to a gas leak doctors and nurses are called from all over the hospital to help get the patients in the E wing to other parts of the building.

Down in the emergency room another patient is about to be admitted.

A young man runs up to the reception desk.

Doug Leso is a doughy type of man. Not in great shape and a little wide around the hips. His hair is matted back with sweat all over his face. He looks like he has just stepped out of a shower. His shirt is half out of his trousers with a couple of the buttons not exactly buttoned right. He scrambles up to the desk, almost oblivious to the chaos that is going on in the hospital. Patients are being moved across the E.R. to different wings. Nurse Nancy is trying to help the receptionist with all the charts that are being moved around along with their respective patients.

Doug runs up, frantic. "Someone, help! I need a wife, my doctor is about to baby a deliver!"

Nurse Nancy and the receptionist look at each other, then look at Doug Leso.

"I am sorry sir, we know what you mean, but right now we are dealing with extraordinary circumstances. We are both short-staffed and out of room. It would be in your wife's and the baby's best interest to go downtown to Memorial."

"Downtown? No...no...no...she'll never make it. Look at her!" Doug points to an old woman standing next to him.

"I am not an O.B.G.Y.N. and don't want to be offensive but I'm thinking there isn't going to be a baby here anytime soon," the nurse says to Doug.

Nurse Nancy looks up at the old woman and finds herself staring into the most brilliant blue eyes she has ever seen. The old woman is leaning on a silver cane. Her hair drapes her face as a wisp of a smile accents her mouth; the nurse and receptionist fall into a trance.

"I'm sorry my son is a little confused. This is his first child. His wife is actually still in the car but the poor boy is beside himself," says the old woman. "I'm his mother, Lillian Leso."

Lillian Leso is a stately woman with a strong, straight stature. At five foot ten she is tall and quite thin. She has long grey black hair which looks like silk. Her eyes are crystal blue and they sparkle when she speaks, and when she speaks, you can't help but listen to her. Everyone calls her by her nickname, Natu. It started long before her son Doug was born. No one knows where she got that name.

Doug puts his hands to his temples as if trying to remember an important fact.

"Geez...She was...Oh my God did I leave her in the car?"

Doug Leso goes running out of the hospital. As he goes out a very pregnant woman passes him on the way in.

Natu watches her son pass her daughter-in-law through the revolving doors and turns to the nurse "Oh nurse...this is my daughter-in-law, Milly."

"Once again we believe we might have a gas leak so I would suggest you try and make it to ....."

Natu holds up her hand and the nurse stops, "Surely there must be somewhere for her to deliver. She really needs to get off her feet. Her water broke about an hour ago and she's in a lot of pain."

Milly Leso's face is locked in pain. She is slightly doubled over holding her belly. "Nurse, I don't know but this doesn't feel right. There was lots of blood when my water broke and...ah!"

Milly doubles over as the pain spikes. Natu leans to help her as the receptionist rushes from behind the desk. Nancy calls Nurse Sally from in front of the elevator.

"Sally, I know what we were told but this woman and child are in trouble."

"I just don't know where she can deliver. Every room is double, triple occupancy right now. All the operating rooms have patients in them on gurneys and no one is getting any help because the whole staff is moving people from the E wing. Our patients are being put in utility closets for God's sake. Hey wait, we still have the chapel I guess...I will have to pull a doctor to deliver the child."

With no wheelchair in sight Sally runs around the desk and grabs the roll-around chair from behind the desk for Milly to sit in.

"Don't worry sweetie...what was the name?"

All Milly can do is moan even louder.

Natu looks around listening and then seems to realize the urgency of the situation and answers for Milly. "This is Mildred Leso...Milly. I beg you please help her and my grandchild. Time is very short and I need to be vigilant. There is no time for formalities. This can all be done later, she isn't going anywhere. Please."

They look into Natu's crystal-blue eyes. They are shaken by her voice and stare and they shake their heads yes in reassurance. As they wheel Milly away in the office chair, Natu stands alone. She begins to sense something.

Not hearing any of the chaos surrounding her, Natu looks skyward and then feels something from the corner of her eye. She notices a dark shadow that quickly slinks down the walls and slips under an elevator door disappearing in a second. "Was that my imagination or are they here already?" she thinks.

Just then there is more commotion at the entrance of the hospital as Doug charges his way back into the hospital. He looks more disheveled and sweaty than he did when he left if that's possible and he approaches the security guard at the door. Doug grabs him by the arm as the guard tries to pull away.

"Come with me...call the police. Someone delivered my pregnant wife. I mean someone took my wife...who's pregnant. They took her and left the car! Don't look at me like I'm crazy...they do this stuff ya know. ...remember Charlie Manson! Some crazy hippies could've kidnapped her for the baby! Maybe she's delirious and wandered off and she's going to end up having my son on the street."

Natu walks over to calm her boy. When he sees her he leaves the guard who is still looking at him as if he were nuts.

"Doug, Doug, Milly's okay; she's in good hands. Why don't you check her in so I can go and see how she's doing and then just meet me in the chapel?"

Doug looks bewildered and mumbles under his breath, "Chapel?"

Doug goes over to the desk sweat pouring all over his face with huge sweat stains under his arms.

Doug gets to the desk where Nurse Nancy is standing and looks at her with wide unresponsive eyes, "I'm having a baby, I mean my wife, well we're having. . . ."

Nurse Nancy has seen this before. Probably his first child, "It's okay, I get it. Please just fill this out. Of all the days for your wife to have a baby. This kid is gonna be something."

As Doug fills out the forms, Natu heads to the elevators. She presses the button and the doors open. The elevator is painted hospital green with one of the fluorescent bulbs flickering. A cool breeze gives Natu a chill. People are in the elevator as the doors start to close then open and then close again. The doors start acting erratically and the people in the elevator start grumbling and pushing the alarm.

Natu whispers lightly, "So that's how you want to play it," not looking at anything in particular but taking in everything.

She turns, smiles and stamps her cane. The elevator doors open and the people come out. She decides to take the stairs.

"You can't stop me from taking the stairs now can you," she whispers under her breath. As she goes down the stairs she notices a cold breeze following her.

"So you are here. You want her out of the way? You fear her purity and strength. Oh does the light of life scare you, my old friend?"

Natu hears a laugh from a faint, distant voice. Natu stamps her cane twice and smiles and the laugh is gone. She sees the sign for the chapel pointing down the hall and she can feel Milly's cries. She heads for the double doors that go down to the chapel.

Back on the 2nd floor of the East Wing Doctor Hanagan emerges through his own set of double doors. He is sweating and looking very worried.

"Mr. Kazan your wife is in serious condition. The baby is being stressed and there is a chance that if we get the baby out in time your wife won't make it. She's lost a lot of blood."

Kazan stands up and walks over to the doctor. "Just tell me, what are you trying to say?"

"We may have to abort the child to save your wife because...." He is interrupted by a lack of oxygen as Kazan's massive hands grasp his throat. The doctor can't speak as Haran Kazan tightens his grip. The two bodyguards block the view so no one can see. The hall starts to get darker as a shadow falls across the floor and the air suddenly has a chill about it.

Kazan is now in a quiet rage. He will get what he wants, if not by negotiating then by force. Force is always, happily, plan B.

"This is what I call an end to negotiations. Now you listen good and listen hard to what I am about to tell you. I came here with the intention of leaving with my son. And I will leave with my son...no matter the risk to the mother."

Wisps of cool smoke come from his mouth as the temperature of the room goes cold. With his other hand Kazan grips the doctor's hand and squeezes so hard you hear a crack. Doctor Hanagan's eyes begin to water from the pain.

"I can't imagine you being able to keep your status as a world-class physician without the use of either hand...Do we understand each other?"

The doctor tries to nod yes.

"The baby is what matters. He is my name...my legacy. Everything else is just a vehicle."

The doctor again tries to nod.

"They say that the eyes are the windows to your soul. Do you know how many 'windows' I watched close when I was fighting in Korea? Do you know how many animals I've had the opportunity of helping cross over? You are just one more window. Remember, Hanagan...first the child...then the mother."

Kazan lets the doctor go and the doctor collapses against the wall and grabs his hand, flexing his fingers to see if they still work. Dr. Hanagan tries to catch his breath. The two bodyguards pick the doctor up and dust him off as Hanagan feels his hand come back to life. Hanagan tries to contain his fear and avoids looking into Haran Kazan's eyes. Kazan straightens his suit coat as he composes himself, running his hands across the sides of his head as if he had hair to push back. He does this when his rage subsides, to compose himself.

He looks at the doctor, knowing that he has made his point.

"Deliver me my son."

Kazan looks at the clock. It's 10:30 AM.

At the same time in the chapel Natu looks down from the clock on the wall. She looks over to where a thrown-together triage center has been put up near the altar. There are work lights on stands casting shadows on the walls. Through the curtain, she can see the doctor and nurses fretting over Milly. Doug Leso comes through the chapel doors and runs up behind Natu.

"Hey Mom, is she okay?"

"I don't know, Doug. They finally pulled a doctor to care for her. Now that you are here I need to return to the hall."

Doug's brow reacts peculiarly to Natu's need to leave but he quickly runs up to the curtains and moves to his wife's side. Natu steps into the hall. A shadow emerges from down the corridor. It spreads covering the floor. Soon it seems to be all around but it won't go near Natu. Natu closes her eyes and slightly raises her cane. It begins to glow softly. The shadow slowly starts to recede.

"You are all around like buzzards circling but there is no carcass here, my friend," Natu whispers. The shadow is gone.

She cracks the chapel door and peeks in. There she sees a doctor speaking to Doug. The doctor puts his hand on Doug's shoulder. The doctor returns to tending to Milly as Doug rubs his brow.

Natu closes the door. Seconds later a worried Doug emerges.

"The doctor says that the heartbeat is very shallow. They might need to induce labor but Milly has lost so much blood that they don't want to chance it. They're doing more tests and he told me to pray." Doug is sweating more than usual.

Natu takes Doug by the hand and they go back into the chapel. They sit in the last pew and watch as the doctor, with a nurse, works feverishly behind the curtain. Natu clutches the teardrop amulet around her neck. She is staring at the wall and falls into a trance. Doug looks around the chapel.

The work lights that the building people have set up cast an ethereal glow in this room. Shadows play off the statues of the saints. As Doug looks at these he notices shadows moving across their faces and the serene smiles start to look like wicked grins. He starts to notice the eyes of these statues moving back and forth in menacing movements.

Doug loses his breath for a moment and then sighs. He closes his eyes and when he opens them the statues are back to normal with the serene smiles. He turns to his mother but her eyes are closed and she is breathing heavily. He knows exactly what's happening.

"You're gone again. Every time something happens you grip that amulet and disappear...off into your own world. I remember that time...what was I, six?"

Doug starts mumbling to himself.

He remembers the time when as a boy his dog ran away.

"I remember when Petey ran away, you vanished on me then too. I even tried to shake you. When you finally came around I asked if you were okay. All you did was smile. Petey came running up the steps wagging his tail. He was dirty as hell, but I always thought that was pretty far out. Now your grandchild is on the way and...Mom, I might need another miracle like Petey."

Doug starts to notice it's getting a little chilly and that there's a shadow creeping from under the door and across the floor of the chapel. It almost looks like someone spilled ink from outside the door and it was seeping into the chapel. The shadow seems to surround them. He stands to see why the walls and the ceiling are lit but the floor is dark as night. The shadow appears to move away from Doug's feet as he moves.

"That's odd," Doug thinks. This shadow looks like it's alive. So black and it seems to move. As Doug studies this shadow, the doctor interrupts him.

The doctor seems nervous and clears his throat to get Doug's attention, "Mr. Leso we're still running some tests so this may take some time. I know you're worried and I want to keep you well informed but I have to be frank...it doesn't look great. Let's hope for the best."

Doug turns to sit down and looks at his mom. She's now looking up at him and that wisp of a smile comes across her face. He looks back at the floor and the shadow is gone.

"It's going to be okay, my beautiful boy." She has always called him that when she knows he needs reassurance. This brings Doug back to his earliest days as a child and he does feel a little more at ease. "Both Milly and the baby are going to be fine."

"How do you know that, Mom, you heard the doctor?"

With that the doctor quickly reemerges.

The doctor doesn't hesitate to interrupt them "Mr. Leso, we do have a serious problem. The baby is under stress and if we induce labor now the baby could survive. But your wife....it doesn't look promising. She's lost a lot of blood. If we wait the child's health will be put in jeopardy. I can't make this decision for you but one has to be made quickly."

Doug collapses back into the pew. His shoulders are slumped. He feels the pressure of a decision only an adult can make.

Doug starts to choke up. "Oh geez. Mom, what do I do? I should have gotten here sooner I knew...."

His mom interrupts him. "Doug, stop. Don't go back there. Stay here in the present. Listen to me. State your intention. The decision you make will be the right one. The future is for you to create right now. Don't look or think about the past. What do you want, Doug? How do you want the path of your life to run?"

"I can't live without Mills. She's my life."

"Baby boy, you don't have to live without Milly. Look at your future, here in the present and state your intention. What do you see?"

The chapel begins to get a little chilly and dark. Even the staff feels this as one of the nurses pulls her sweater tight around her body. As Doug listens to his mom he starts to focus and the chapel around him starts to blur. The image of his wife lying at the foot of the altar fades. His mom taught him at a young age how to visualize what he wanted his life to be and so far it has worked. He has the woman he foresaw when he was a young man in college. He has the life he had seen as he was growing up. All has worked out for Doug until now. As his mother speaks Doug falls into a trance.

He hears her voice deep within his soul and he whispers, "I see, I see..." "Doug, if you want your wife and child to survive look at them in your future as if it were your present. Just like anything else you have ever wanted. Don't forget all I have taught you."

Natu's silver cane starts glowing ever so softly. She holds the amulet around her neck and as she looks the chapel lights start to dim.

"This must end quickly. They are getting too close but it really is all Doug now," she whispers.

Doug Leso closes his eyes.

He sees himself standing outside the house he has always wanted. The house and life he has always been grateful for even though he didn't have it yet. These are the teachings of his mother. Doug sees himself standing outside this house. Black clouds are rolling by and he can hardly see it's so dark. As he speaks, stating his intention, light starts poking through the blackness. It breaks through as if the darkness was no longer able to hold the light back. Thin blades of light shoot out and illuminate the ground. By the end of his visualization the sun is shining. There on the front porch of the house is Milly.

It all seems so real. Doug is still sitting in the pew, but his eyes are still closed tight and he is off into his future. Natu is watching her son with a sense of pride. Gone is the face of a man in pain and worry; Doug's facial expression is one of amazement.

Doug starts to speak out loud. He doesn't hear himself but he can feel his words deep within. "I see them. Milly is giving birth. A little head is coming out and a body and the doctor holds the baby up...it's a...it's a girl. Oh my God! It's a girl! Mom, I see Milly and my baby coming home — us taking her to school — me giving her a horseback ride around the living room...."

A huge smile crosses his mom's face.

"I have taught this boy well," she thinks.

"That's it, my boy. That's your future...no matter what you decide in this present moment."

The chill in the air goes away and the room brightens as Doug opens his eyes. Even the nurses notice the difference. One of the nurses unbuttons her sweater. The chill is gone.

Doug turns and stares into his mother's eyes. The doctor approaches once again.

"Mr. Leso, what do you want to do? We have no time."

Doug continues to stare into his mother's eyes. Without turning his head to address the doctor, he takes a deep breath.

"Induce labor, Doctor, we're having a baby."

The doctor notices that while Doug Leso looked at his mom a wisp of a smile came over both their faces. The same, exact smile. Doug looks at his watch and it's 10:41 am.

At the same time on the 2nd floor Haran Kazan looks up impatiently from his watch. He turns back toward the window. Graham Wellington is down by the administrator's desk either constantly chirping at the help or talking on his cell phone. Even though Kazan's son is being born his businesses need constant attention. There's always money to be made. The bodyguards are standing as statues on opposite sides of the door. Doctor Hanagan emerges; the red marks from Kazan's hands are still around his neck. He appears defeated and very nervous. The bickering between Wellington and the administrators has stopped. The hall quiets from any activity that had been going on. Hanagan clears his throat. If there was ever a time he wished he had taken that civil service job like his mom had wanted him to it would be now.

"Uh...Mr. Kazan?"

The doctor avoids looking up into Mr. Kazan's eyes.

Kazan stares at the doctor and can smell the fear in him. He has felt that in so many of these weak pathetic animals. "Is the baby alright?"

Doctor Hanagan hems and haws a bit then nervously says, "Your wife, I'm sad to say...."

Kazan cuts him off immediately. "I asked about the baby, my son!"

"The baby is fine, Mr. Kazan. He's healthy and alive but I regret to tell you your wife...."

The doctor flinches in fear thinking Kazan was going to exact revenge for what has happened to his wife. Instead Kazan merely brushes him out of the way and enters the operating room. Kazan's eyes scan the entire room. There are motionless feet on a body which has been covered on the table. Kazan continues to look about the large room without regard for his wife. The room is not a pretty sight. It looks as if a war had taken place. There is blood on the floor and medical items askew throughout the room.

Finally his eyes rest on the corner of the room by the window. There a nurse is holding a bundled infant. He rushes over to where the nurse has the baby. He takes the baby from her hands and looks into the baby's eyes. The sunlight is streaming in from the windows.

He tries to contain himself. Haran Kazan has never given way to excitement and has never let his emotions grab hold except for now. His voice starts softly and controlled but then for the first time he loses control.

"My God...My God. Jason. I have waited so long for you. You will be what I am...and more. You will have the life my father could never give me. You will grow to be powerful, intelligent and above all else...a man. You are a Kazan! Haran Kazan has his legacy."

As he turns with the baby he notices his wife's lifeless body.

"Ah Nicole, we have a son, and you have made me so happy. We have also avoided a nasty divorce and for that I thank you. Hahahahaha." The laugh echoes throughout the East Wing halls. People down the hall of the hospital all feel a chill in the air.

The sunlight that had been illuminating the windows of Nicole

Kazan's room is now muted by the shadows that follow Kazan. The once sunny room is now engulfed in an inky, black shadow and an eerie laughter can be heard coming from somewhere.

Meanwhile down in the basement Doug and Natu are standing in the hallway outside the chapel. Doug is staring at the poor sick children who are being moved into the chapel space because of the gas leak everyone keeps talking about.

Natu is off somewhere on her mental field trip, as Doug would call it, holding tight to her amulet. Doug is pacing but does not look worried. Now he has a quiet confidence and calm to him. The doctor finally emerges from the operating room.

"Doctor, may I see my wife and daughter now?"

The doctor thinks that this question is so puzzling given the fact that last time they talked, just a couple of minutes ago, the lives of his wife and child were held in the balance.

"I'm sorry, Mr. Leso, but don't you want to know how it went?"

Grandma Natu stands close to the doctor, "We know how it went, Doctor. You did a fantastic job. When can we see the child?"

"How do they know that they both survived?" the doctor thinks.

"I must tell you that what transpired was simply...remarkable. I don't know how it happened. One moment everything looked so grim. Her heart rate started to plummet and we tried everything. We really thought we would lose both your wife and the baby. Then, without doing anything, it all turned around without explanation. The bleeding stopped, both the baby's and your wife's heart rate increased and we now have a healthy baby girl... oh and mother. There are times when there is no scientific explanation. This was one of them. I hate to run but we are short-staffed. We will continue to monitor her."

Doug shakes the doctor's hand and the doctor sees the tears in his eyes. The doctor turns to hug Grandma Natu but he looks in her eyes and thinks twice about it. They just smile.

"Thank you, Doctor. Fine work under such tough circumstances," Natu says with a wisp of a smile.

The doctor begins to walk down the corridor away from the chapel but he pauses. He turns and walks back towards Natu, who is going into the chapel, as if he remembers something. He hesitates for a moment, as if he has decided to forget the whole thing, but instead he calls her.

"Excuse me ma'am. You know when the baby finally came, I held her up. I swear she smiled at me. I've never seen a newborn smile like that."

A wisp of a smile comes across Natu's face, "Maybe she was just happy to see you, Doctor."

The doctor stood for a moment mesmerized by Natu's crystal blue eyes and her smile, then he smiled, turned and continued on his way. He would never forget that day or that woman or that smile. From that day forward whenever he was feeling down or having a bad day all he had to do was remember that smile. That smile would brighten his soul and that brightness would stay with him for the rest of his life. As the weeks go by this doctor decides to quit the hospital and join Doctors without Borders and until the day he dies, when things go wrong or he feels down, that smile comes back to light his way. It brings him solace in his times of need. That day he became a different man, all because of a supposed gas leak.

Doug and Natu go back into the chapel. They rush to the curtained area and pull back the curtain. There is Milly and the baby. The baby's eyes are wide open and when Natu enters the room the baby starts to coo. Doug goes over and kisses his wife and Natu moves closer to the baby. Milly looks tired from the ordeal but manages a smile.

"Honey, I was so worried but Mom was right."

"Your Mom's always right, Doug," she says with a breathy tired voice.

Natu comes around the side of the gurney and touches Milly's head. "It was Doug that saw this, Milly. He's the one that helped it along."

Doug is quiet; he has spotted the baby. His baby. His little girl, the one he saw in his vision. The exact same one. Both Natu and Milly are staring at Doug as they see the tears come down his cheeks. Both women start to tear up.

"Oh my I can't believe it. She's so beautiful." Doug can hardly speak.

Natu looks over at the little baby. "Doug she looks like Milly. Doesn't she?"

"Oh no, Lillian I think she looks like you. A little Natu."

"Hahahahaha I don't think so dear. She has your beauty and your eyes."

Doug bends over the little bed and can be heard whispering, "Alice, Alice, Alice. Isn't that beautiful, dear? Alice Drew Leso. It's like a song. I can't wait to tell everyone. I even ordered the cigars with little Alice's name on them. I could have gotten 'It's a girl' but instead I had Alice put on them." Doug holds up the box of cigars.

"Doug honey, don't be angry but I had a thought as the baby was being born. I know you really like the name Alice Drew but I saw another name in my head. Just hear me out. I want to name the baby Lillian."

"Lillian? That's my mother's name."

They both look at Natu and she smiles a smile that lights up the room. Doug, who is now holding the baby, passes her back to Milly.

"Lillian, I owe so much to you. You are so much a part of this family that I would like to bless this baby with your name."

"But what about the cigars? Geez, Milly, I love the name Alice. Now don't get me wrong — I love the name Lillian because of course it's my mother's name — well you know that don't you? No offense Mom, but crap on a cracker, Milly."

"Doug, watch your mouth, I love your Mom," Milly looks at Natu and smiles.

Milly passes the baby over to Natu. The baby reaches up and takes hold of the amulet; a major feat for a newborn. A sparkle of light quickly appears and disappears inside the amulet. No one sees it but Natu and the baby, Lily.

A wisp of a smile comes across the baby's face, the same smile that often appears on Natu's face.

Jason and Lily grow as the years pass. They share the exact same birthdate, to the minute. But through the years they lead completely different lives. Jason grows with the shadows while Lillian grows with the light.

CHAPTER ELEVEN

Growing in light and dark

Haran Kazan finally had his legacy in his son, Jason. Everyone else was incidental, including his now-deceased spouse. He no longer had use for her or any memory of her. She was buried as a pauper in an unmarked grave and any memory of her was erased before Jason was brought home from the hospital. All pictures of Nicole Kazan were thrown out and burned along with her clothes and other personal effects Kazan had allowed her to acquire.

The whole mansion was scrubbed clean of any memory of Nicole Kazan, as if she never existed.

Jason's nursery, for which no expense was spared, had been prepared months earlier. The room is bigger than most three bedroom homes. It has contemporary style and is completely sterile. Dark colors swirl across the walls and floors, interlaced with black inky shadows. The room also has shelves full of toys that are neatly displayed. The toys, upon closer examination, are all war toys: tanks, guns, missiles and hundreds of weapons of destruction.

A woman who is dressed in a dowdy black dress organizes the large bassinet that is holding this infant. Her hair is grey and her face is sallow, drawn and wrinkled; there is no emotion on her face, just black shadows that dance around her eyes.

There is a black teddy bear to the right of the infant. A camera lens can be seen in the belly of the bear. Haran is always watching his son and will always be watching him. Haran Kazan fears no man, let alone an infant, but children have a tendency to turn on their parents as Haran did so many years ago. The look in his father's eyes was priceless when they led him away that dark night. His mother who pleaded with Haran to tell the authorities the truth looked so pitiful. He hated that pitiful look. Throughout his life he has seen that look on a number of occasions. The nanny who tends to Jason is stoic to the point where she will not even blink in her guarding of this infant. Haran found this woman during a trip he took to Russia. She was a deaf mute. She was someone who relied fully on Haran, someone the shadows had picked. As she straightens the room a large dark shadow moves across the room and rests on the baby's face. The baby smiles not a sweet baby smile but an adult smile of joy. The joy one gets when he wins a game or overcomes an adversary. It's a menacing grin.

A mobile hangs over the infant with planes, warriors and missiles: a mobile of destruction that is perfect for, well, this infant.

Through the nursery's huge double doors, in the background, is Haran Kazan's massive office which lies right across the long hall. Haran has the phone in one hand rested over his shoulder and a cigar in the other. Haran Kazan can be seen berating a pleading man. He has a large bottle of Scotch with him and only one glass. He takes a sip. The man is evidently distraught but Haran just sips his drink and smokes his cigar. There is an insidious grin on Haran's face.

The office gives him a straight view of his son. He laughs as he sees his son throws things onto the floor from the crib.

"Hahaha. Even at this young age he knows what he wants and doesn't want."

As time passed Jason became the spitting image of his father, in looks and temperament. Jason was a mean and nasty child. Unhappy only when he wasn't causing pain and grief in another's life, Jason not only picked on his peers but adults too. In the beginning he would just torture small animals and the kids he went to school with. Other children, the smaller ones, would avoid him like the plague but even this passed as he grew. Jason would take advantage of the weak to the point where he didn't even notice them. As if they were ants, he would just step over them rather than be bothered to crush them under his foot. There was no need to bother with these people who were so far beneath him. He had other plans in his life and he could not be bothered with that waste of energy. He treated everyone the same, with disrespect — even his father. Haran loved seeing his prodigy grow into a powerful young man who didn't have the normal weaknesses of these poor, pitiful, small people.

There was a slight period where Haran had to steer Jason back in the right direction. Imagine a Kazan scared of the dark.

"This can't be," Haran said to himself but after a couple of episodes Haran stepped in and slightly altered his son's fears. It was necessary.

"Just a slight detour," Haran told himself. No one ever knew what happened behind the massive doors of Kazan Manor and no one will.

From the time he could socialize Jason would command attention and if it didn't come easily he would take it by any means: hitting, throwing, or breaking.

Jason knew at a young age that he could do whatever he wanted and his father would take care of everything. From paying off teachers and parents to bribing officials Haran always made sure his son was never in trouble. Well, never caught in trouble because whenever there was trouble Jason wasn't far away.

From burning buildings to terrorizing animals and children, Jason was the first on the list, but somehow whoever looked at that list always skipped to number two.

Across town time also passed for Lily. But Lily's time passed with hope, love, compassion and light: pure, innocent white light. Lily grew in a modest, normal home. Her bassinet was pink with a lace canopy. Her room was full of dolls and Lily was a smiling infant. A smile that was contagious. A smile of joy at nothing in particular but as she grew she said that her smile was caused by the light. Even at night Lily always said there was enough light to keep her smiling.

Doug and Milly Leso would often stand in Lily's nursery and feel the peace and joy that would emanate from their child. When Lily was brought home her mother placed her in an older, second-hand bassinet, one that had been handed down from Grandma Natu. Milly had hand-painted it making sure that it would be ready for Lily when she arrived home. She had painted unicorns, rainbows and stars.

"Doug, do you remember how Lily would kick inside my stomach when I was painting that crib for her? It was like she was jumping for joy."

Every time she finished a painting on the crib a couple of dance moves would happen in her belly.

It got to the point for the Lesos where Doug would put his hand on Milly's belly right before she finished a star or animal and could feel Lily dance and kick.

They would often stand over Lily and admire her as the moonlight rested on her face. Lily remembers lying in her crib and staring up at her mobile toy. To this day she remembers the little stuffed objects that hung over her crib. There was a sun, a waterfall, a flower, a rainbow, and Noah's ark with small animal heads sticking out of the ark. Her parents said she would lay there and coo. Lily also remembers the faces of six figures looking down at her but never knew who they were. Whenever she felt scared these faces would reassure her and comfort her. Her parents could not believe what a good baby she was. Never crying and always enjoying her time alone.

"Hey Mills, have you noticed that Lily talks in her sleep sometimes?"

"Yes I have. I asked her yesterday morning if she was awake last night."

"Is it normal for a three-year-old to do that?"

"She said she was talking to her water friend."

"Oh, that's reassuring. The other day she called out something and when I asked her she said that she saw the dirt man." Doug holds his head.

"Oh, honey, all kids have imaginations like that." Milly starts to laugh at Doug.

"I wonder how she is going to feel about sharing us." Milly leans closer to her husband.

Doug is so involved in thinking who the hell the dirt man can be, he doesn't realize what Milly is saying.

"Uh Doug did you hear what I said?"

"Yeah something about staring at something with us."

"No Dougie, sharing us."

"I don't understand."

"I'm pregnant again."

"WHAT! Oh My God!" Doug jumps up and races around the table to hug his wife. Yay, oh god! When, how, oh jeez."

"I think when we were on vacation last month and on the how, I think you remember that night." Milly starts to giggle.

"Oh this is so great. I can't believe it. We need to tell Mom."

"She knows. She told me."

"Huh?" Doug said, confused.

"She told me to go to the doctor and that there was a surprise coming in eight months."

"I hate when she does that."

"She says it's a boy."

"YAYAYAYYAYAYAY whoo hoo. We are complete. One boy for you and one girl for me. Oh reverse that, or not." Doug starts to laugh and hugs his wife. The glow from them lights up the room.

Lily is going to have a brother but as she grows she also will contend with the darkness, which is the Kazans.

As Jason and Lily are getting acquainted with their new world, there are those that are going to steer their futures. One towards the light and one towards the dark. Two young souls born at the same time in a world that needs all the light it can get. One soul fighting to keep that light and the other fighting to extinguish it.

Haran Kazan is one of those that will manipulate the lives of everyone, in darkness. Jason has gotten too big for his nanny to handle him.

One day the nanny is gone and Haran Kazan has a new mission for Graham Wellington, his most trusted man. Graham seems to be stating his case to his boss.

"As second-in-command your new job is the boy...end of discussion!" Kazan loved military jargon although he was never in the military. That was for the poor. He was too busy making money and taking orders from someone else was never his strong point. If orders were to be given they would come from him.

He has always called Graham Wellington his second-in-command as if there were a war going on. Well there is a war going on, he would tell his men. The war is between Kazan and everyone else.

Graham gets up and walks to the double doors of the nursery right across the hall from Mr. Kazan's office. He steps into the nursery and with disgust shuts the doors.

"A babysitter," he says to himself. "I thought I was going to be a negotiator or a point person not a diaper boy." He puts his head against the doors.

"Oh well, Graham old boy. Buck up and don't dawdle," he says to himself. He accepts his role and turns towards the boy, Jason.

As time goes by these children grow and the world gets darker. They have run into each other in those five years and the light always seems to balance out the dark. It frustrates Jason but Lily doesn't dwell on it; Jason does.

Natu has her granddaughter Lily, now age five, on her lap as they sit on an old country porch swing. She is reading her the book The Giving Tree. A baby's cry can be heard in the house.

"No!" is all they hear. It's Lily's new brother Bill using his favorite word. Well, his only word.

Lily lays her head back on Natu and admires the beautiful amulet around Natu's neck. Lights seem to play in the amulet. Not on it. It's not a reflection but light deep inside the amulet which seem to mesmerize Lily as she reaches up to hold it. As Lily grows older the thought of holding that amulet always stays with her. From the time she could talk she remembers always calling it the magic thingy.

At the same moment Natu and Lily are on the porch swinging on that old wooden swing, explosions are going on across town in the forty thousand-square-foot house owned by Haran Kazan. The fuse to a small explosive charge is lit by Graham Wellington. The fuse runs under some dirt and the charge has been placed in between a group of toy soldiers. Graham quickly scrambles away. An animated Jason Kazan is now five years old and is wearing an army helmet and camouflage shirt.

Jason is quite excited. His favorite game is war. Well, destruction is his favorite thing, and war gets him as close as possible. He crouches behind the couch and yells "Fire!"

With that the army men explode. Jason smiles as a dark shadow moves across the play room that looks like the toy store itself exploded in the room. Toys fill the room but mostly war toys. Tanks and guns are all over.

"This wears on me, but I do get some joy at blowing things up, Hahahaha" Graham Wellington thinks as he hands the fireworks to a servant at the door and quickly exits.

CHAPTER TWELVE

Lily and Jason

Years continue to go by as Lily and Jason establish themselves in a world fraught with destruction and chaos.

On a sunny day in a quiet suburban neighborhood a moving truck pulls up to the curb in front of a modest row home with a For Sale sign in the front yard. The sign is marked Sold.

The house is a two-story, blue-shingled Colonial that looks identical to the houses on either side. It has a small porch on the front with white shutters that flank all the windows. One of the shutters is hanging crooked.

A chipper Doug Leso jumps out of the moving truck. Right behind the truck a Volkswagen station wagon follows. Out of the vehicle steps Milly and Doug's mother, Grandma Natu, admiring their new house.

"Hurry up, you two," Doug yells out. "Home sweet home."

Natu and Milly both turn towards the station wagon and out of the back seat springs an eight-year-old Lily followed by her four-year-old brother, Bill.

As they head toward the house from the car Bill wets his finger in his mouth and sticks it in Lily's ear. Lily swats it away as if he were a mosquito. As she does this, she notices a stray dog limping up the street. She runs up to it as an anxious Doug yells, "Honey, no, be careful, you don't know....." and gives up because Lily never really listens to him anyway. The dog is holding its paw up and there is blood on its fur.

Lily immediately begins to care for the dog's bloodied paw.

The dog has hair coming out from all over. Not especially thick but kind of straggly. His face is covered in hair. The hair is grey, black and brown. He actually looks like a couple of dogs mixed into one. Not a dog you would say is very handsome but more peculiar.

"Come on, honey. Please be careful. That dog may have rabies or some other disease and I want us to all go inside together. You can see your new room," Doug says trying to coax his daughter away from the stray dog.

Doug motions to the front door of the new house but Lily won't leave the stray dog's side. Doug realizes his daughter is never going to leave a wounded anything and reluctantly joins his daughter in caring for the animal. "Dad, can we keep Les?"

"Who is Les?" says Doug.

"Dad, this is Les," Lily says pointing at the dog.

"Oh Lily, we just moved in and I don't know. It's nice you named him but we aren't ready for a dog. Mills?"

Doug always deferred to his wife when he knew he was about to cave in to his kids. Milly was putting a vase down on the porch of the new house as she turned to Doug, "What, honey?"

Milly walks towards them as Doug gets up to meet her.

"Oh my, where did this dog come from?"

"I don't know, hon, but talk to your daughter, please. Lily wants to keep this dog. I don't know, Mills. Please talk her out of it."

"It's Les, Mom, and he's not an 'it,'" Lily says looking up at both of them with her big brown, "oh please" eyes.

Milly is totally distracted, but starts walking over to Lily.

"It's less than what, Lily?" Milly asks.

Doug looks at Milly, "No, the dog's name is Les." Milly looks so confused.

"He told me," Lily says as she pets Les's head.

"Oh, honey, I don't know. He looks like a stray and we have so much unpacking to do," Milly says.

Doug turns to Milly and whispers, "I see a little bit of terrier in him but the rest is pure Martian." Milly elbows Doug in the arm and Les the dog whimpers.

"Dad, Les heard that, now apologize. He is very sensitive about his looks."

"Well not all of us are," says Milly, patting Doug's belly.

"Oh come on, Lily, he heard me, really?"

"Dad, he not only heard you but he understood you were making fun of the way he looks."

Doug looks down at Les as the dog bends his head down, looking totally despondent.

"I can't believe this. Ok, ok, Les I'm sorry for making such disparaging remarks about your appearance." Les looks up as if he's smiling and gives a little yip.

"See Les, it's ok. He's not like you said he was."

"What?" Doug says, looking offended.

As all this was going on Natu and Bill walk over. Bill seems a little fidgety.

"Oh Doug, can we go inside? Bill needs to use the facilities."

"Geez, Bill how many times can you go in one morning?" Bill is looking totally out of sorts. Doug wonders how a kid of six can drink four quarts of Juicy Juice in two hours.

"It was all the Juicy Juice he drank in the car," Milly says as she goes over to Bill.

"I know Mills but the kid is a sieve. As soon as it enters his mouth it comes right out."

Natu notices the dog. "Oh Les, what happened to your foot?"

Doug looks at his mother and is stunned yet again.

Les looks up at Natu and seems to bow his head and whimper.

"Oh my, thank you. You too," Natu says to Les. "I didn't know you were coming today."

"Uh were you expecting him, Mom?" Doug is trying to take this all in.

"Oh honey, as much as I expect rain on a sunny day."

Doug looks at his mom and then up at the sky. He looks around and everyone is looking at him except for Billy who has his legs crossed.

"Okay, well then that was sure fun and as always I totally give up. Let's bring Les inside and tend to his foot. Why not? We have a new home, I have a new job and now we have a new, well an old, new dog."

As Doug says the word old Les cocks his head and looks up at Doug. He limps over and licks Doug's hand.

"Yeah, yeah," Doug says and pats Les's head.

Over the years Les became a fierce protector of the family, especially of the younger one, Bill, and it seemed like Les knew what the future held. Bill was very important to the life of this planet as we shall see although it would seem this story is about Lily. How Les got his name is easy. He was born with it, as Lily said to her dad, "We call him Les because that's what his name is." Doug knows when his daughter says these things it's best not to argue or question. Just go along with whatever happens because when it comes down to it it's always so much easier.

Les saved Bill's life on a number of occasions. One in particular was when he pulled the boy from the path of a runaway truck. If Les weren't around Bill would have surely been mowed down and Doug and Milly would have been living a vapid and empty life with no purpose or meaning.

That is what sometimes happens when a child is killed. Their grief would have overcome the whole family. They would have mourned their only son and neglected the gift that was Lily. There would have been no joy in the years following Little Bill's funeral. People would have felt so bad that they would stop coming over to visit because they wouldn't want to see the couple so despondent. Milly would just sit in the living room holding a picture of Billy, probably the one where he is holding his baseball bat.

You never really get over the loss of a child, especially a child with the potential Bill had. Actually, the world itself would never get over the loss of him and his legacy. Every holiday would be the same, year in and year out. Lily would overhear all the conversations of how if Bill were still here, about his laugh, about his prowess. Lily would grow to hate her dead brother, never realizing her true potential. The world would have been a much darker place for it but all that was saved by a Martian-looking dog named Les. His quick reflexes and relentless vigilance were what we all count on in our companions. Les's fondness for Bill also helped. Les truly liked Bill and always watched him out of pleasure not just necessity. A pleasure reserved for an owner and his pet. Or a father and his son. A proud pleasure.

Les kind of thought of Bill as his son and as any father watching his offspring, Les was there to pull Bill from the street just as the truck came rolling down the hill.

"How can he hurt himself?" Les would say. This helped Les in his protection. Always thinking ahead of a given situation.

Oh yes the darkness was out to get both children but Bill was the one that its sights were on for now.

The driver swore he had the hand brake on and the police did find the brake on but this didn't stop the truck from rolling down towards Bill.

Bill was coming off of the school bus on a beautiful fall day. When the bus pulled away Billy looked both ways as he was taught and started walking across the empty street as he did every day. On this day though, his green toy soldier suddenly slipped from his backpack. Bill didn't notice until he got to the other side of the street. He looked back and then realized his toy had fallen onto the street.

Billy didn't think of anything at that point and just turned and was about to step into the street when powerful jaws grabbed his backpack and stopped him mid-step. As Billy was pulled back a truck came roaring by and crushed his Power Ranger toy exactly where Billy would have been standing.

No one but Les had noticed the black inky shadows that rested on the truck and on the street that sunny September morning as Les waited for Billy. These shadows swirled around on a perfectly sunny day and then there was the low evil laughter that only Les had heard. Oh yes, it may have sounded like wind but Les knew it was them. He had been warned by Natu to be on guard. That shadow had no business there but to create pain and death which Les would have no part of, then and until the time he moved on. Les had hurt his foot for a reason that day the Lesos moved into their house. On that day he took over the protection of the Lesos in preparation for Grandma Natu's eventual passing.

That was what he was there for, to protect.

"I'm leaving soon, my friend," Natu had told him. "It is your job to watch over this family now. I know you to be a strong and vigilant protector. Be so. They are always looking for a way to get to the youngsters and the youngsters will always look for a way to get in trouble."

Les bowed as if accepting his mission from his queen. Les had the sole purpose of watching and protecting.

As Lily and Billy grew into the light an eight-year-old Jason Kazan was growing more towards the darkness.

"Look at this, my how pretty. Say goodbye, stupid plants. Mrs. Carson says plants can talk and hear. I don't hear you screaming." Jason laughed as he stamped on a row of tulips.

The lovely flowers do scream but Jason is not the right person to hear them.

Life finds him riding his motorized bike through an exquisite, botanical garden. He is tearing up some beautiful Birds of Paradise and Ecuadorian Roses much to the displeasure of the head gardener and his men. This garden is cared for all day long, seven days a week and the crew is the same gardeners who work at Chicago's Botanical Gardens. They stand and stare as Jason does a jump onto a large brick patio. He sends dirt flying onto Graham Wellington's suit pants as Graham sits comfortably reading the paper. Graham peeks out from his paper, wipes the dirt from his pants for a second then returns to it as if nothing happened. Jason grins as a shadow covers his face.

"Hey Wellington, can we shoot those birds again today?"

"Uh, master Jason, the birds have been avoiding this side of town since you started killing them."

"So get more. I want to watch them fall to the ground. Come on. Don't let me have to take this up the ladder. Hahahahaha." Jason rolls over with a despicable, guttural laughter.

Across town is a modest house with another garden, somewhat smaller but much more lush than even that of the professional gardeners. In this garden plants of every kind can be seen. Yes a smaller garden but still a garden with some amazing plants.

A ten-year-old Lily runs up to her Grandma Natu who is working in this garden. Lily is dressed in a Girl Scout's uniform and she hands Natu a Humanitarian award.

"Another award. Hahaha my Lily you are a wonder."

Natu, who now looks much more fragile than before, smiles with pride and hugs young Lily. Les comes trotting into the garden with a rawhide bone crushing one of the violets.

"Oops," says Les in a whimper.

The two turn as if they had heard something, not Les's whimper but a short and gentle scream. Well they not so much heard it but felt the poor flower being stepped on.

"Oh my Grandma. The poor thing." Lily gets up and runs over to the plant.

"It's ok, Les you didn't mean it," Natu pats Les on the head.

"Whew," Les thinks.

Natu follows Lily over to the fallen flower. Lily looks up at her grandma as Natu smiles and nods her head yes. Lily smiles and holds the poor flower as a light can be seen radiating from her hands. She helps it upright and amazingly it stands tall on its own. Lily listens for a minute as if she hears something and then says "You're quite welcome," and turns back to her grandma.

"Ah Lily, the gift of love is oh so powerful, isn't it?"

Meanwhile a ten-year-old Jason Kazan along with two of his buddies, approach a nerdy looking heavy-set kid with thick glasses. This is the Wilson Academy for Gifted Children. The people in the neighborhood call it the Wilson Academy for Privileged Children because only the children of the rich and powerful come here. More problems are caused here by these children than in any part of town. They are above everyone else and above the law most of the time. Protected and nurtured, most will grow up greedy and mean.

The children are all eating in the cafeteria and are all dressed in the uniforms of this fabled private school. The meal is a duck confit and dessert is a thick chocolate mousse. The nerdy kid immediately becomes intimidated, looking down so he won't be noticed, as the group approaches him.

"Hey Jasper, you really are packing it away. I think we need to save you from yourself." Jason turns to his friends and they all laugh.

The cafeteria monitor turns away because he knows who this boy, Jason, is. He is the son of the man responsible for the whole new study wing. No matter what happens Jason is untouchable.

Jason pushes the spoon of chocolate mousse up into Jasper's nose and squirts ketchup into his pocket. Jason then snatches the duck off his plate, takes a bite and puts it back. Laughing, the group moves on. As they walk away all the children separate so as not to be caught in Jason's crosshairs. The last person to interfere was forced to leave the school because their father ended up in a scandal and lost everything. People know one thing at the Wilson Academy: you don't mess with a Kazan.

CHAPTER THIRTEEN

Life without Natu

1982 is a year that Lily and her family will never forget. It's the year that Grandma Natu left them. Natu quietly slipped into a deep sleep one night and didn't wake up. The doctor didn't call it a heart attack but said her heart just stopped.

It had been six months since Grandma Natu had died. It was now the summer of 1982 and the neighborhood was alive. Sprinklers on the front lawns, paperboys delivering papers and a milk truck delivering milk. In the background you can hear "Eye of the Tiger" playing on someone's stereo.

The Leso's house and the one next to it have RVs parked in the driveways. The house next to the Leso's belongs to the Parkers. These two families are preparing for their annual camping vacation. Milly Leso and another woman are running back and forth between their houses and the RVs.

The air has a slight crispness to it. It's one of those mornings that when you take that deep breath you feel revitalized, knowing it's going to be a beautiful day.

Milly stops what's she doing and starts talking to the other woman over the four-foot white frame fence that separates the property lines of these two houses. The fence was put there by Doug to stop Les from bothering the Parkers who swore he was never a bother, except for the occasionally wet and slimy newspaper that would sometimes have to be pulled out of his mouth. Les considered the paper his and it didn't matter on what property it landed. Doug actually had done a good job on the fence which was unusual for him given his tendency to get disinterested in such projects.

Doug would always say, "Good fences make good neighbors."

Milly thinks Doug did such a good job because Mr. Parker made some remark that Doug didn't know which end of the hammer to use. Doug would actually be good at these projects if he would focus, but he didn't. The tree in the back had a treehouse which was more like a tree ledge. He managed three cross beams and that was it. Bill would sit there with his friends and balance on the beams but no one ever called it a tree house. Bill would always say "I'm going in the back on the tree beam." It used to upset Doug for a bit but he realized that that's exactly what it was. So Doug would take visitors in the back and say that his house was the only one with a tree beam.

"Yup, three of them," he would tell folks.

Milly is talking to Mary Parker, Lily's best friend's mother.

"Every time we go away he gets lost on some errand. This time it's batteries. Last time, it was rope. Jeez, I think he just makes these things up. And I'm left packing the camper," Mary looks quite upset.

"That's okay. You'll get a lot more done without him. Doug went in to deal with the kids. Every Saturday it's the same thing. Yelling and screaming. I told Doug let's just get Lily a small TV for her room. But Doug doesn't want anything that could take her away from her school work. I feel so bad. She really misses her Grandma Natu. It's been just over six months and I still can see the look in her eyes. She holds onto that silver cane like she's waiting for Natu to show up for it. So sad. She lived a long life it's just...I miss her too. She was always someone I could talk to and she understood Lily so well. They were like sisters rather than granddaughter and grandmother. They had a certain bond I can't describe."

Mary Parker hates to see her best friend so upset and puts a reassuring hand on Milly's shoulder. "It's such a shame. She was so healthy, then all of a sudden...I think this trip will be good for Lily. Mia has been talking about it all week. Hopefully it will be a pleasant distraction for Lily."

"I hope so. I don't know what else to do. Summer is almost over and I don't want her going into the school year with this weight on her shoulders. She's only eleven. It's too young to have a loss like this." Milly wipes a tear as Mary reaches into her apron and pulls out a tissue.

"It's so senseless. One day she is gardening and the next moment she's gone." Milly blows her nose and reaches across the fence and hugs Mary.

"Thank god we had you guys. You helped us get through this and we will never forget it."

Inside the Leso house trouble is brewing. No matter how innocent and pure you are all common sense leaves when a younger brother is introduced into the picture. Patience is a virtue but little brothers are a nuisance. Young Lily and Bill Leso are arguing in the living room of their home like they usually do on a Saturday morning. Lily is watching Faeire Tale Theatre when Bill walks over and switches on Bugs Bunny. Lily gets up and tries to switch it back but just as soon as Lily sits down Bill quickly gets up and switches it back. Les is sitting between them watching them like he's at a tennis match. His head goes from Lily to Bill and back again.

"Billy I was watching that..."

"We always watch your shows Lily why can't I watch mine. Old stupid Faerie Tale Theatre ...I want to watch Bugs and the roadrunner, your show is stupid!"

Lily has had it and turns her head and screams "Mom...Bill is calling me stupid again."

Lily gets up and turns the channel back to her show. Bill gets up and stands in front of the TV blocking the set. Bill begins skipping back and forth singing the Bugs Bunny theme substituting some of the words with the word "Stupid".

"Stu..Stu...Stu-pid. Stu...St...St ...Stu-pid."

Lily looks at her brother with resignation. "Fine. Put on whatever you want. I give up."

Under her breath she whispers, "So annoying."

Les lies down with his head on his paw and just looks up. "Jeez this has tired me out."

Lily, shoulders slumped, walks into the living room. In front of a window is a small round table with many pictures on it. Some are in single frames but some are in fold-out sterling silver frames. Lily picks up an antique frame with a picture of her and Natu in it. Her eyes begin to well up. Her mother notices this as she walks in from the front door with a couple bags of groceries in her hand. She notices Lily holding the picture with her shoulders slumped and knows Lily is crying. She puts the groceries down and slowly enters the room.

"Oh baby, I just want you to know that I just spoke to your

brother and I am going to make him apologize...especially for playing that cassette tape of you and your girlfriends talking about Darren last night at dinner..."

Billy had recorded Lily and her friends, during a sleepover, talking about boys and of course found a not-so-perfect time to play it to everyone.

"Mom, it's not Billy..."

Milly knew what was wrong but was hoping to break Lily out of her grief, "I know baby it's not Billy. Look sweetheart I know how much you loved Grandma Natu...There is no easy way. It is just going to take some time."

Lily holds the framed picture close to her chest and looks up at her mother with tears running down her cheeks.

"I know this is our family's big camping trip. I don't want to hurt the Parkers' feelings... I'm just not in the mood this year. I love Mia...she's my best friend and everything but I can't get into the camping spirit. Dad and Mister Parker really get into it, but it's not that they don't see enough of each other working together. Everything I do...I see, hear or smell reminds me of Grandma Natu. I still hear her stories about the spirits of the earth...and the spirits of the oceans and the animals. Sometimes I feel like she's not really gone...but she is, Mom...She is gone." Lily starts to cry again, rubbing her nose with the arm of her sleeve.

"You know full well what your grandma would want you to do. She would want you to think of happy things. How about your father speaking to your class during career week? Come on, that was sort of fun, well maybe it was fun, might be a bad example because I would think having your dad in class might be awkward."

Lily smiles a little but nods her head yes.

"It was awkward, for him," Lily smiles again as her mother kisses her on the head and picks up the food packages. Milly turns one last time before going into the kitchen to continue her packing for the trip and sees Lily kiss the picture and put it back on the table. Lily closes her eyes and thinks back about her dad in her class.

It's May 17th and it's "bring your dad to school day." The kids of St. Peter's middle school decided that if they were going to have to go to work with their parents, which they hated to do, that they would make a day where they could totally humiliate their parents. So today Lily's dad is the next victim. Usually the kids would ask totally wrong questions and sort of confuse the parent who had shown up but today was different. They were getting snacks.

Doug Leso is standing in the front of the classroom. On the desk is a wide variety of Nature's Resource products. Lily is staring at her father with admiration.

"Finally, here is one of the products that I developed and it just turns out to be my daughter, Lily's, favorite. Actually, she also had a hand in developing it. I'll never forget her first words when I baked the first one. She said to me, after spitting it out, "Dad, how did you ever make edible cardboard that's crunchy?""

All the children laughed and Lily got slightly embarrassed but she knew that in time her dad would embarrass himself.

"These were made to taste like the famous vanilla cookie Vienna Points. We call them Newport Vanillas. They are made of all natural ingredients, so they're good for you. Now I'm not saying you should eat a whole package, but maybe eat half," which is followed by his nervous laugh. Doug is trying to be funny but the old teacher standing in the back does not seem amused.

The teacher seemed to not like Doug from the moment he walked in. Doug had felt that. He knew that. It wasn't anything she said but it was the way she looked at him. No smile, no nod of approval and no handshake. She stared at Doug and pointed to where he should set up. She seemed annoyed with everything he did or asked for. Doug could have been right in his assumption given the circumstances but it turned out that morning Mrs. Spencer got word that her son had been injured in a car accident and when she got out of bed she tripped and her back went out again. The pain was so severe she had to take the muscle relaxers that she had never wanted to take but they did numb the pain. Both in her back and her heart.

Mrs. Spencer's son was just on his way to turning his life around. Years of drug and alcohol abuse had taken its toll on the whole family but she stood by him all those sleepless nights. Now he had a good job and he was off the drugs and stopped drinking. So life turns around and rewards him with a traffic injury. Another reason for him to go on painkillers. Oh my God, how will we handle this she thinks as Mr. Leso comes into the classroom? Between the worry and the painkillers she has so little energy that she just points to where he is setting up. Maybe she should have called in sick today. Doug didn't know this so he assumed she was just a mean teacher.

"I mean a couple of cookies. I was kidding when I said half a package," Doug says feeling completely awkward. Lily always notices when her dad gets nervous, because he starts to sweat from his upper lip and she could see the sweat start to form. Lily starts to laugh a little and her dad looks over at her with a pleading look. "Help me."

She raises her hand and her dad jumps at the chance to have someone else talk. He had told Lily that if I look at you raise your hand because I'm in trouble. He called her his ringer.

"My dad is right. These are my favorites but my little brother loves the Chocochunks. They also are made from all natural ingredients. Sorry to interrupt, Dad."

"No, no that's fine, Lily, thanks. So as I was saying the Newport Vanilla's taste just like Vienna Points but are all natural which means they are good for you. Yup they are good for you and they taste like they aren't." Doug was very proud of that tagline. He wrote it so why shouldn't he be, except for the fact it wasn't a good tagline. But it did kind of make the point.

"I'd love to try the Chocochunks, Mr. Leso," Andy Rivers says. He's the first to raise his hand. Andy loves food but Lily has been helping him try to stay off of the bad stuff. The processed foods and fast foods so many kids eat.

"Mom, I invited Andy over to study," she would tell her mother and of course they would offer him dinner and Lily would make him stay over.

"Here, Andy, have you ever eaten roasted peppers and kale?"

Andy started to get healthier and became more athletic. He even joined the softball team. That was Lily's influence. She would trick all her friends into eating well or doing some sort of community service and it was her attitude that did it. Her attitude and her light. She could brighten up any room she walked into.

A kid in front of Lily licks his lips as Lily's dad starts to hand out cookies. Lily's smile fades as she thinks about the word Vienna. Her grandma always talked about how the best part of her life on this planet was the time she spent in Vienna.

Lily remembers sitting with her grandma in the lush gardens surrounding her home. She remembers her grandma opening a book to a picture of a beautiful statue.

"This is the statue of Athena. I had the privilege of viewing this in person many times when I visited Vienna. That's where I met your grandpa." This is the only time she ever saw her grandma's light fade, when she talked of her husband, which was very rare.

Everyone remembers a first childhood memory. Whether it was a doctor's visit, a new dog, or just a distant memory of lying in your crib. The thing that stands out in Lily's mind is the light that blinded her coming from her grandma. She remembers, as a baby, the first time she opened her eyes and saw Natu standing above her, she could hardly make out her warm, wise and beautiful face. The light so blinded her.

After Natu had passed Lily would always sit and daydream of the stories her grandma would tell her. She remembers always looking up at her grandma and into her crystal blue eyes. The way her long silver and black hair would frame her soft, smooth, olive-colored skin. Her grandma's amulet always seemed to glow and sparkle. If there were things that Lily would remember about her Grandma Natu they were the amulet, her silver cane, her eyes and voice. Sometimes she would stare so hard at that amulet she wouldn't hear anything her grandma would say. She wouldn't hear the words but she heard the voice. Soothing like ocean waves as they hit upon the shoreline. The world would seem to disappear and Lily would feel as if she had stepped out of her body. All the sounds and smells of this world except for Natu's soothing voice would be replaced by totally new ones. Everything else that had to do with this world would disappear and would be replaced by the sights and sounds of Grandma's story. The story would actually come to life.

Lily would walk the streets of Vienna with her grandma and smell the fresh flowers and grass. Sounds of waterfalls and birds whistling. There would be people laughing and voices singing.

"Oh my, the bird's songs are so beautiful," Lily would say as she soaked in the sounds and sights of Vienna.

"Are you in my amulet again child?" Grandma would say and it would snap Lily out of her dream. Natu knew it was her doing. "Prepare the child," she was often heard saying to both Doug and Milly, although neither knew what that meant. Lily would snap out of her dream but retain all she'd heard, smelled and saw.

"It was a dream, wasn't it?" she would always ask. Natu would stroke her hair and say, "Everything is a dream, my child and you can dream anything."

The trips she would take through Grandma's stories were astounding. Climbing mountaintops, helping small children and animals that had been abused or forgotten. Lily, in her dreams, met so many people of different cultures and did so many things to help this planet. She remembers stories of rain forests.

Standing in a forest covered with butterflies, walking with a cheetah, standing at the end of a rainbow and so much more. Lily would always wake up with her head in Natu's lap. How her clothes got so wet and dirty was always a mystery. They would look at each other and just start to laugh. What adventures they would go on, distant parts of the world while never leaving the gardens that surround their home, or that's what Lily thought.

"You can go anywhere you want, Lily. Just think it. That's why a book is like a time machine. Using your imagination as the vehicle to take you to places you would or could never go. The mind and soul of a purity is so powerful."

"Am I a purity, Grandma?" Lily would often ask.

"Yes, my dear, I do believe so."

In these adventures Lily would always be walking next to Natu and listening to her explain life and love and happiness.

"As you want to be treated Lily, so must you treat every living thing. Every living thing including this planet you live on. She is alive and she needs as much love and care as any person or animal needs. She is yours to live for and on and with. Love her, for she is the mother to us all. You can't change nature but you can love, protect and nurture it."

Lily learned so much from Grandma Natu's stories and went so many places.

All the good memories would then be replaced by the thoughts of that terrible morning when she got the news.

On that morning when Lily was in her bed, under the covers nice and snuggly, her mother quietly came in and sat down at the edge of her bed. Doug, her father, had bloodshot eyes as he walked past Lily's bed over to the windows. It had started raining just as Natu passed over that morning. It seemed that the world was mourning the loss of his mother. Heavier rain had not been seen in this part of the country for hundreds of years. Lily opened her eyes and felt the loss. She knew Natu was gone.

Natu had come to her in a dream. Kissing her forehead and telling her she hasn't left her forever but there is just some business that needs her attention.

"This body isn't who I am, as you will see. Love all and love always. I will return to you my child."

That morning her Mom was holding Grandma Natu's cane. Lily's eyes opened and saw her mother with tears in her eyes as she looked over at her Dad who had just covered his face with his hands and was shaking his head slowly.

"Lily, sweetheart, we have some sad news to tell you about Grandma Natu."

Deep inside her daydreaming about all these past events Lily is abruptly shaken by a loud trumpet blast that rattles the quiet library. She is taken away from that moment of the past and brought abruptly into the present.

"Why must the present be so loud?" she thinks as she holds her ears.

Lily jumps as she is startled and almost falls from her chair. She is jolted back to reality by her brother Bill, playing his toy bugle in her face.

Blahhhhhh. Blahhhhhh. Blahhhhhhhh.

Lily screams, grabs the trumpet and throws the trumpet against the wall. It's purely a reaction, she doesn't mean to break or hurt anything, she is just startled. The trumpet hits the wall and you can hear the cracking of plastic.

Billy looks at Lily then at the wall and screams, "Lily, I think you broke it. That was my favorite bugle. I was going to join the cavalry with that and kill Injuns."

Lily just stares at her brother, not in anger but in solemn bewilderment. She didn't want to upset him but he really did startle her.

"Love everything, love everything," Lily keeps repeating under her breath. "Even Billy," as a smile comes over her face.

Doug Leso struggles down the steps with three bulky sleeping bags as the two start to argue. This is more than an argument. This is a World Wrestling Federation brawl. "Are you ready to rumble" is all Doug can think about right now. Just what we need as we prepare to be stuck in an RV for a couple of weeks. Ahhh I love getting away with the family. He smiles, realizing how cynical he can be. Even with the sibling brawls he does love, and even better, likes his family.

Bill is first to speak as always, "Dad, Lily broke my trumpet. My favorite

trumpet. How am I going to call the cavalry?"

"Are you serious? You almost blew out my eardrums." Lily turns to her dad. "Dad, Bill almost blew out my eardrums."

Doug walks into the library after putting the sleeping bags by the door. "Okay that's it. Both you guys go upstairs and get ready we're leaving in about, I would say, five minutes and I don't want to hear that someone" — Doug looks at Bill — "has to go to the you know where, to do you know what. Understood?"

Bill looks down and nods. He remembers the last trip when they were going to Aunt Carol's and as soon as they turned the corner he had to go to the bathroom. Some children or animals fall asleep in the car as soon as a family trip starts. Bill always has to go to the bathroom.

"I would like to hear how much you two love each other....or maybe even a little Q*U*I*E*T on a Saturday morning...but I will settle for a simple 'yes Dad' if you two will just please get ready."

Both kids simultaneously say "Yes Dad," but not before they let out two huge sighs. Then they jump up and run upstairs to get ready.

CHAPTER FOURTEEN

The Trip

The Leso/Parker wagon train, as the two fathers had started calling it right from the first trip, leaves on time again. The men have always been so proud of their ETD, estimated time of departure, but never talk about their ETA, estimated time of arrival, because they never make it to their destination when scheduled. The blame can be attributed to Bill having to go to the bathroom or a lack of good directions. Paper maps is all they had back then. No GPS. Whichever it was no one was blamed and both families had more fun than most. When it started there were four to five families but slowly as the families moved away it became just the Lesos and Parkers.

The Lesos and Parkers finally make it to their campsite in the mountains. A six to seven hour trip that usually took four; but who's counting? This is the seventh trip these two families have taken together. Lily can remember her earliest memories of going on vacations with the Parkers but the only difference was that Grandma was with them.

Lily and Bill look out the window of the RV with Les in Bill's lap as usual. Lily is holding Grandma Natu's cane. As she gazes out the window she imagines herself on a horse riding on the shoulder of the highway. Keeping up with the RV, jumping the railings and going up and down the hills. As she stares the images change and she sees herself gliding on two white discs and racing the RV. Lily sees herself dressed in silver holding a light beam in her hands. She floats alongside of the RV flying around trees and bushes and signs.

The movement of the RV slowly lulls Lily to sleep. The round globe at the top of the cane starts to glow slightly without anyone noticing it.

Dreams of flying and children with superpowers swirl in Lily's head. Plants growing in deserts, rain and wind being summoned from the palm of a hand, rock turning into a red, steaming liquid and through all this Grandma Natu's face would keep appearing. Lily is startled as the RV comes to a stop and when she rubs her eyes she sees that the wagon train has reached its destination.

The dreams seemed so real but now they fade from her thoughts and memory except for the face of her grandma. A tear forms in the corner of her eye and she wipes it away. Her heart gets heavy for a moment and then she takes a deep breath and gets out of the camper.

The night air is crisp. "Natu used to love it here," her dad says to her. She said it added years to her life, a place to feed the body and soul.

"To be comfortable alone with oneself is to be at peace with the world, Doug," she used to say. Doug puts his arm around Lily as they both look around at their campsite. At the same time they both look up and say "Wow."

Lily looks up at her dad and notices a tear coming down from his eye. He brushes it away and looks at Lily. "I do miss my mom, Lil. I guess I always will."

There are so many stars that the sky looks like a blanket of snow. All around are the sounds of the night animals and wind. Cicadas can be heard all around as a chorus of nature welcomes them back to the campsite they have come to year after year. Doug and Mr. Parker hurry to get a fire going because the first fire means hot dogs and marshmallows. Bill is dancing and singing his hot dog song. Lily and Mia talk about school and boys. While Mia talks about boys, Lily just daydreams about animals and plants and her grandma but she is feeling a sense of relief. She is not weighed down by the feeling of emptiness she has carried for the last couple of months. She actually feels relieved for the first time since grandma passed.

"Hmmmm why do I feel so good?" she wonders.

Lily is unaware that it's the night air. Also she is more like her grandma than she could ever imagine, feeding off the energy that nature provides.

Hot doggie night, as Bill called it, is always so much fun. Her dad and Mr. Parker take out their guitars and play all their favorite songs. Her dad is really into the Beatles so they all sing "Hard Day's Night." Mr. Parker does his Van Morrison songs. Lily didn't know who that was until Mr. Parker told her all about him. Then Bill does his Hot Dog song and everyone just laughs uncontrollably.

"Hot dog doggie, is the doggie ok, hot dog doggie, it's a wonderful day to eat hot dog doggie hot dog doggie."

"Why again am I protecting this kid," Les says to himself and then starts to howl to Bill's song. "If you can't beat 'em, join 'em," Les thinks and then starts jumping up and down.

Bill is such a wacky little boy. He can't dance but he tries to, he can't sing but he tries to. He has no fear of sounding or looking bad. Bill will try anything no matter how many times he fails and usually he won't give up until he succeeds. Unfortunately he will never be a dancer or singer but it doesn't stop him. He also loves when he can make people laugh. Lily does love him so much even when he's a pest.

"I wish more people were like Billy," she says to Mia.

"Uh, he is a freak, Lil. Hahahaha."

"I know," and they both laugh.

Milly comes up behind Doug and puts her arms around him.

Doug looks up at her, "Check it out," he nods towards Lily, "I haven't seen her laugh like that in months. I knew this would be good for her."

"Oh my. Look at her laughing with Mia. I'm so glad Lily has a friend like her. Someone to make her laugh like that."

"Are you kidding? Thank God we have him," as Doug points to Bill trying to do a cartwheel. Doug and Milly start to belly laugh.

"I wish I wasn't so worried about what people thought of me like him," Doug says about Billy. "The kid has no ego, or way too much ego. I'm not really sure."

As the night wears on the fire starts to die down and Lily cannot eat another thing. Bill is feeling sick because he ate so many marshmallows.

"Mom, I don't feel so good," he says.

Milly looks at Billy, "Well we can count on two things, your Hot Doggie dance and your vomiting marshmallows. A perfect ending to a perfect beginning." Milly leads Billy behind one of the tents.

Since Lily was born she has had no desire to eat sweets. She has eaten some but never liked the way they tasted or made her feel. She has always gravitated to fruits and vegetables. Her mom and dad thought it weird for quite a while having a child that only eats what's good for her.

"What the heck, kids eat garbage and it's supposed to be a constant battle to keep snacks to a minimum," Doug used to say to Milly. "We have a child that watches what she eats. What are we to do? Just watch?"

"Doug, you have Billy to watch."

"Oh right," Doug looks relieved.

Doug and Milly never, ever had to watch her because Lily watched herself. It seemed that Lily would treat her body as the temple it truly is. As for Bill he treated his body like a warehouse. Bill was the typical kid, always getting hurt and stealing cookies from his dad's office.

Once Milly was cleaning and found dozens of empty Chocochunk boxes under Bill's bed. When Doug got home that night they both, after laughing a lot, approached Bill and asked him about the boxes.

"I love them and got to have them," is what he said. Again they laughed. Bill did promise to ask first before he took anything from Doug's office and kept to his promise. Doug and Milly knew two things above all about their kids. When they promised something they kept to it, and they never lied. The Lesos were truly blessed with two extraordinary children but then again Doug's mother was an extraordinary woman and Doug didn't even know how extraordinary she was.

As the night gets longer the adults and children are finally settled into their tents and are entering their REM cycles but Lily is the only one who can't fall asleep. She opens her eyes. She leans herself upright in her sleeping bag. She holds her head still as if listening.

"Strange, what are those voices I keep hearing? As if someone or something is trying to call me. I just can't make out what they're saying and there are so many of them. Les, is that you out there?"

Lily sits up and looks around. Lily whispers loud enough for her Mom or Dad to respond but not loud enough for whoever was out there to hear: "Mom?...Dad?....I think...I think I hear something. The voice sounds... it sounds like...it can't be...."

"Where is that dog when I need him? He's always around but now he's nowhere to be found. Wow, what a nice rhyme."

The fire in the center of the campsite is still glowing with enough light that Lily can see the RVs in the glow of the flames.

Shadows seem to be dancing on the sides of the campers but not just any random, shapeless shadows. Forms of animals and people seem to come to life in a weird sort of dance along the sides of the white paneled RVs. The shadows take shape and then disappear. Some are flat against the campers and some seem to come away from the side and dance around the flames. A bear, a wolf, trees with leaves moving on roots. All these shadows dance by her and then drift into the night.

Lily calls out again to her mom and dad in a desperate whisper. She gets no response so Lily instinctively reaches out for Natu's cane. She holds the cane close to her. The cane seems to be providing some sort of security and warmth to Lily. She holds it like a child holds a blanket for comfort. The voices seem to come from everywhere and get louder and louder. She can't believe that no one has woken up. She covers her ears and at that instant all goes silent. She removes her hands and all she hears are the sounds of the night.

"What was that? It seemed so loud," Lily wonders. She strains her neck to listen but the voices are gone. Well whatever she heard is gone because now she can't really be sure it was voices. Lily yawns deeply and lies back down on her sleeping bag. She snuggles with the silver cane under her chin trying to get warm from the chilly mountain air. As Lily closes her eyes and falls asleep, the cane slightly illuminates.

The night is uneventful and the fire eventually goes out. As the morning sun comes up there is only one creature awake. That creature is a little brother who is intent on being the thorn in his sister's side. Les is lying still after sleeping right by Billy's side.

"Should I stop him?" Les thinks and then just settles down on the ground to watch. "I was told to protect him, there was nothing said about modifying his actions."

As Lily sleeps, a small hand lays a tiny Garter snake across her face. The hand belongs to a mischievously smiling Bill. Lily jumps up with a shriek as she is startled. Bill laughs so hard he falls over.

Lily checks on the poor snake who went flying, then turns her attention to Bill. The commotion wakes the rest of the Lesos and the Parkers.

Bill runs out of the tent and starts dancing around. "Wake up, little Lily! We are going to the caves this morning. The caves, the caves, we are going to the caves."

"Bill Leso, do you have to be such a pest? I didn't get any sleep last night. Why are you up this early? And for your info I am not going to these stupid caves. Okay."

In the same breath with a matter-of-fact attitude Bill yells, "Dad, Lily's yelling at me. When are we going cave exploring? Can we go now?"

Doug and Milly are sleeping in the RV and hear the commotion. Milly immediately looks at the clock. It's 6:30 am. She then puts a pillow over her head and turns over on her stomach. Through the pillow Doug can hear a muffled, "They're your kids, Doug, you need to take care of them." Doug can't see her smiling.

"Oh I love that, whenever war breaks out I become the United Nations peace keeping force. Wasn't it you at the hospital with me when they were born? I could swear it was you. I don't forget a face or a backside that cute." Doug slaps Milly's butt.

"Doug, stop. That hurt," she half giggles.

Doug gets up and puts on his sweat pants and shirt. He wears sweat pants a lot, not because he works out but he does sweat. Ever since he was a kid whenever he got nervous he would sweat. Really sweat. When he asked Milly to marry him he literally had to be wiped down. He looks in the mirror and again thinks of what a blessed life he lives. He has a beautiful wife, two wonderful but spirited kids and a full head of hair. Mike Parker has got the little dish on his head already. He'll be bald in five years Doug thinks. He tousles his hair feeling good about his looks and steps into the hot sun of the morning.

The campsite looked the same as it had for centuries. Maybe a little more worn with families coming every year but the big trees still stood where they had for as long as Doug could remember. Doug started coming here when he was just a baby. Grandma Natu felt it necessary for him to feel a part of nature — to experience the wild. Back then there was nothing around here. This used to be two hundred thousand acres of pristine woods. Home to bears and wolves. Raccoon and beavers. Even the drive up made you feel you were in a remote part of the wilderness. Doug remembered being in the car for hours and not seeing any sign of life except for the deer on the side of the small road. He would tell his mom every time he saw an animal standing at the edge of the trees, yelling out their names. Sometimes groundhogs, sometimes deer and once they even saw a bear with her cubs.

Now all that stood of this massive forest was twenty thousand acres of state forest. The state felt it necessary to sell off some of the land to developers and lumber companies. Urban renewal is what they called it. Urban renewal means rebuilding cities — mainly putting money into poor neighborhoods. Urban sprawl is more like it. Natu called it Urbomination. The killing started when the building and gentrification of nature's playground began. As houses and families started to move in the people felt threatened by the animals that called this place home. Bears and wolves were being killed because they came too close to houses. The same bears and wolves that had lived there for thousands of years were being caught and killed because they did what was natural to them. They hunted. Doug would see his mom crying each time they came up here. He never saw the dead and dying animals but his mom always said she felt each innocent soul being hurt by the greedy and cruel side of man. She always seemed to take responsibility for the actions of these people.

"I am so sorry," he would hear her whisper in the car as they passed the cut down trees and buildings going up.

Back in those days the animals would come up to the camp site with no fear of being hurt. Grandma Natu had a special gift with the animals.

"Mom, how do you do it? They just come up to you."

His mom would just smile that wisp of a smile.

"They like me," she would say.

Animals from all over would come to the campsite and flock to his mother. Birds would fly onto her arms when she extended them.

Doug remembers seeing his mother standing with bears and wolves behind the campsite when she thought everyone was asleep. Like a queen holding counsel but things have changed. The animals were slowly driven away as progress stole their lands and homes.

The ride was also not what it had been. No longer calm and peaceful. It was quicker but had lost all its thrill. Gone were the twisting and turning roads that wound through a beautiful, remote country setting. No longer were there trees and hills for as far as the eye could see. Now strip malls and car dealerships lined the road. The two-lane highway had been replaced by a six-lane superhighway, congested in most places with honking horns and car exhaust. The dirt road that used to go to the campsite was now paved and well maintained. As you drove up you could see all the cardboard cookie cutout houses lining the perfectly manicured cul-de-sacs. Each house had the big bay window, two-car garage and brick or stone facades. Swing sets could be seen in the backyard with each house looking identical to the next. Built for money and not for love, these houses were cold and lonely. There was no feeling of love but there was a feeling of life. Yes, life without love or compassion. A shame.

And all the trees were gone. That's what Doug noticed the most. Instead of putting the houses in between the trees someone decided it would be better or easier to just cut them all down. The people who made money knew what the deal had truly been.

There was a deal set up between the developers and lumber companies. It was quite profitable for both of them. The developer cut down the trees and sold them to the lumber company for a small profit while the lumber company supplied the lumber to build the houses for a small profit. The developer received wood that was cheap, making more money on their houses and the lumber company procured a bounty of good wood for a song. That song is playing for a lot of people today. The song is Greed.

Doug is brought back to reality by a screaming little girl who is threatening to de-bowel a certain little boy.

"OK, what the heck is going on with you two? Your Mom and I were sleeping as were the rest of the animals in this forest."

Doug turns to Bill and tries to look parent-like.

"What is your problem little man. When you wake up early and no one else is up count to one thousand before you move a muscle. This will give me at least another half hour of sleep." Doug starts to grin.

"Dad, he put a sweet little snake on my face. Isn't he going to get punished?"

"Lily is right. You should be punished, Bill. Tell your sister you're sorry. It is way too early to be yelling and fighting."

Bill looks down and says, "Sorry."

Lily shakes her head because she knows Billy isn't really sorry but she'll take whatever she can get at this point.

"Now, let's wait until the Parkers get up before we start to make any more noise."

Doug hears a sound from the Parker's RV and turns to see lights coming on in the windows.

"Oh well, it's too late for that. Bill, looks like you've taken care of that as well."

Mr. Parker, still half asleep, peeks his head out of his RV to see what the noise is all about. His wife is looking out one of the windows and so is Mia.

"OK change of plans, forget going back to bed. First breakfast, then washing up and then Hemlock Caverns."

"I might as well start the coffee and when Mike gets out we can start setting up a nice little campsite style breakfast. I really think these caves are going to be great. They have been around for thousands of years," Doug says with excitement. Always one for adventure, Doug realizes it's where his son gets his enthusiasm from.

Milly Leso stumbles from the camper in time to hear Doug. "Sort of like the pack of Nutter Butters I found in your backpack, Billy, from last year's trip."

"Have you planned out our military strike for today, Colonel Doug," Milly starts to giggle.

"God I love her giggles," Doug thinks. It always reminds him of when they were dating and she would giggle at everything he did or said. He used to call her the giggling girlie. It made him fall so deeply in love with her, besides her being the prettiest woman he had ever seen.

Ignoring Milly's sarcastic comments, Doug pulls out a brochure from Hemlock Caverns. This excites him to no end. Doug has always been an information hound. He would read the credit card application brochures from cover to cover.

"You just don't know what you can miss if you don't read the information they supply, that's why they supply it," he would always say. As he opens the brochure you can see handwritten notes scribbled in crayon. It's Doug's handwriting but Billy's crayons. Brown, Billy's least favorite color. Doug saves them so as not to waste the crayons Billy doesn't use. Doug is also a little cheap.

The notes list the game plan for the day. Every place they go Doug has a game plan. That's why Milly always calls him the colonel; it's because of his vacation tactics. Everything is drawn out and planned the night before. She even once bought him a military helmet so he could wear it as he planned his family's next mission. He always told her it was all in the ground assault.

When they went to Disneyland he stayed up all night figuring the best route to take to avoid long lines. Now Milly would think her husband was a little compulsive, which he was, but his plans always seemed to work. They would always get to an event or ride at the right time to avoid long lines or avoid not being able to get in at all. A master planner he was, but also a master pain in the neck.

"Hurry, let's go. We have ten minutes to get to Thunder Mountain otherwise the line will be too long." Doug barked orders out like they were on military patrol.

"Let's go, let's go. Move it."

The kids would fall right into line.

"Yes sir," they would say.

Behind Doug the Parkers are yawning and stretching as they stumble out of the RV.

Mia runs over to Lily and they start talking like young girls talk, in excited whispers. Soon giggles abound as the two walk over to Lily's tent. Lily preferred sleeping in a tent because that's what she and Grandma Natu used to do when they would come out on this yearly camping outing. Actually Natu used to sleep right outside the front flap of the tent, lying right on the dirt. Lily didn't like being outside like that because the dark sometimes scared her. Natu used to say that sometimes she needed to feel the earth beneath her. It gave her strength and balance. Even when they took a walk Natu would stop sometimes and put her palm on the ground. Not on the concrete or pavement — it always had to be dirt or grass.

"I need to see how my child is feeling," she would say and then smile. She always said that you can't count on anything but the earth under your feet. Towards the end Natu would look sad and tired after seeing how her child felt. Lily always thought "her child doesn't feel well."

After a great family breakfast Doug Leso calls out, "You ready, kids? This might be scary." Lily is lost in thoughts of her grandma as her brother Bill walks up to her.

"Lily looks a little scared. She's scared that's why she doesn't want to go," Billy says with a smirk.

Doug looks at Lily and notices something is bothering her. She appears preoccupied. A frown has settled on her face. He continues to clean up the breakfast dishes but keeps an eye on his daughter.

Lily walks over to the far side of the campsite and Milly sees her sitting there with her brother standing just inches away from her. She prods Doug to go over and see if she is ok. A small poke of an elbow into the side was all it took. After being married for so long you get to know what different pokes mean.

Doug turns and sees her sitting on a log holding Natu's cane and staring at the smoke from the fire.

Doug slowly walks over to her.

"Are you scared of the caves Lily because they have ghost and spiders?" Billy says to tease his sister but Lily doesn't react in the slightest.

"Hey, Billy boy. Do me a favor? Can you run into the RV and get me some more of that wonderful coffee your mom is heating up?"

Bill points to the cup of coffee Doug is holding in his hand.

"All right then go grab me the Coffee Mate."

"Aww come on, Dad, why don't you just tell me to get lost?"

Doug is about to split a gut from his boy but his daughter needs him so he holds onto any laughter and just says, "Get lost."

Billy smiles and says "K" and walks off to do what boys normally do when left to their own devices: either cause some sort of trouble, get dirty or hurt themselves.

Doug watches as his son leaves, knowing all the things that might happen to Bill as he tries to keep himself occupied but then sees Les get up and follow him.

"I swear that dog is human. Weird how he watches out for Billy. I guess someone has to," he thinks then turns his attention to Lily.

His daughter has that look on her face. The look of a girl who is lost, lonely and grieving. His thoughts of Billy fade so quickly when he looks at Lily. His soul hurts. His mother was so much more than a grandma to Lily. She was a figurehead, a teacher, and foremost a friend. A friend that never let Lily down. Natu talked to her as a child would talk to another child. He swears that the innocence Lily possesses, which is an incredible gift, was equal to the childlike innocence his mother possessed. His mother was a unique woman. Children and animals especially gravitated to her. People always felt like they had known her for a long time. With her piercing eyes and that captivating smile Natu could charm the chrome off a car fender.

"Look Lil. I know you are hurting. But if you live in the past you'll miss the present. And we both know your Grandma Natu wouldn't want that. My mom was all about living for the moment. Remember she would say, 'You can't do anything about the past and the future is uncertain. The present is all you have.' Your grandma loved caves. She would stand in them and take deep breaths. Remember she used to say she is breathing the breath of her child. Come on. You'll feel closer to Natu if you come with us and I promise you'll have fun."

Lily looks at her dad with an incredible sadness in her eyes. Doug puts his arm around her. He grabs the shiny silver cane that Lily had laid next to her and then hands it to her. Doug turns away for a moment so Lily can't see the tear that is forming in the corner of his eye. He is also still hurting from the loss of a woman he was born to but always felt he never really knew. There were secrets about her and his father that were never spoken about but that didn't stop him from loving her more than life itself. He will forever feel an emptiness, but he has to be strong for his daughter and his family.

"Besides if you don't go, I am going to leave Billy back here so you can watch him."

This makes Lily crack a smile. She would rather lick the fur off Les.

"Well, you drive a hard bargain Dad. Let's explore some caves."

Bill pops his head out of the RV evidently listening to the whole conversation.

"Yay, when are we going?"

CHAPTER FIFTEEN

Hemlock Caves

The two families are the first ones to arrive at Hemlock Caves. The caves are brilliant. The walls and ceilings tell the story of vast changes to the earth. As the tour guide talks about the caves, Lily is admiring the vast beauty of her surroundings. Suddenly she looks behind her. She has the feeling that she hears something or she is being watched. Out of the corner of her eye she sees a slithering shadow. When Lily turns it quickly disappears.

The guide hands out small lanterns to every member of his tour. He then proceeds to take the group deeper into the caves. Mia looks amazed. Bill is hanging close to his dad.

The guide speaks of the history of the caves.

"If these caves could talk...the stories we would hear. In the late 1800s a group of explorers were trapped when one of these cave walls collapsed. They were never heard from again. The Indians in this region always thought the caves were home to the shadows. Evil forces intent on destroying their lands. They sealed them up. Massive walls of rock were put in place. These caves were only uncovered around 40 years ago but as I said scientists think that they were actually lived in millions of years ago. They have found traces of a fire pit and skeletons."

Mia moves closer to Lily. "Is he just trying to scare us? Because if he is trying it's really working."

"Hey Lily what's that behind you?" Billy starts to giggle when Lily turns around.

She turns back just in time to give Billy her meanest look but she actually did see something move so she looks again and whatever it was is gone.

As the guide keeps talking Lily starts daydreaming. The group of people led by the guide keeps walking as Lily stops. Once again Lily sees something disappear behind a rock formation. She walks back slowly to investigate. She is using Natu's cane as a walking stick. She can hear the tour guide voice becoming faint in the distance. She now feels something wicked behind her. Lily feels a cold breeze on her neck. She hears a low, dark laughter. She quickly spins around to see if it was behind her but there was nothing. When she turns back, still walking, she walks right into the cave wall. The guide's voice is gone. So is her group, so is her family and so is the path.

"Ouch. Where'd the path go?"

She quickly tries to find her way back. Her hands start moving along the walls and searching for a door or an opening or the path would be great. Lily starts getting nervous.

"What happened, am I dreaming?"

Lily begins to call out sounding a bit concerned, "Dad?... Mom?...Mia?"

She thinks, "I would even be happy at this point to see Bill. I must be really desperate."

Lily turns around to go back from where she just came from but now there is a wall there too. She is completely perplexed.

"This was not here a minute ago and rock walls don't just appear out of thin air so I must have fallen and hit my head. Logic wins out all the time as Dad says," she whispers to herself. She holds the lantern high in front of her and sees a path to her left.

She didn't see this before and it seems to be the only way to go, down this rocky path. The cave is lit just enough, with the lantern glowing, for her to see the walls and floor around her but too dark to see anything that's up ahead. As she walks she looks behind her and the path she had just come from is pitch black. The path before her is also pitch black.

"This just keeps getting better. Thank God this is just a dream."

As she walks a little farther she notices the walls are covered with etchings. Like cave drawings, the same ones that Mr. Fulman talked about in history class.

"They look so real," Lily says to herself.

On the wall are figures of men on horses holding swords up high above their heads, birds flying and animals running. The etched figures seem to come to life. There's a series of drawings showing trees growing, blooming with leaves and then turning into people. She sees rivers flowing as fish jump out of the water, turn into people and then dive back into the flowing waters. A sword appears on one of the walls and it shoots a bright light, lighting up the cave and for a moment blinding Lily. She stops and rubs her eyes.

The drawings, which had started on the walls, now seem to race around her, in front of her and behind her. She reaches out to touch them but her hand goes through them as if they were just smoke or ghosts. Lily is so taken by what she sees she begins to lose any of the fears she may have had. Battles are played out in the air in front of her. She sees children running and leaping into the air only to turn into birds.

"This is the best dream I have ever had," she whispers and then the images fade back into the walls. Lily touches the drawings on the walls. They are cool to her touch.

Up ahead she thinks she can make out a slight glow. She can hear a murmuring coming from down the path.

"Are those voices?" she asks herself. "Whew, there they are. I thought for sure I was lost. I must have just got turned around. Mom, Dad I'm coming, wait up."

Lily hears the slight murmur of voices getting louder and continues in the direction of the light and sound feeling relieved that she has found the group.

Lily walks down the path. The light seems to be coming from an opening in the rock wall up ahead of her on the right.

"Hmmmm, I'm not sure about any of this. I don't think this is the group but maybe it's another one and then they will call my mom and dad," she thought. That seemed to make perfect sense as most things do when you really want them to.

Lily slowly gets to the entrance and peeks around into the opening, her right hand on the cold, stone wall. As she peers into this chamber her breath is taken away by the magnificence of this cave. What she sees is like a scene from a movie. Beams of light seem to radiate from the center of the room, spinning and hitting the walls, lighting them up.

Lily steps into a chamber which is huge. The walls are stone and marble and go up high to a vaulted ceiling that she can barely see. She does see rock formations hanging down from the ceiling.

"Are those stalagmites or stalactites?" she wonders. She wasn't too keen on her science classes. At the end of each formation is a figure, reaching down.

As her eyes dart around the stone cavern she sees, carved into the walls, statues, hundreds of them. As she stares a brilliant burst of light strikes her in the face. Her hands immediately cover her eyes and she rubs them. She tries to focus but all she sees is a huge ball of white. She stumbles further into the chamber as she lets go of her hold on the stone wall.

As her eyes adjust she looks around at the walls, trying to avoid the bursts of light coming from the center of this chamber. She notices that the statues are children. Some of them have the body of animals with children's faces and some look like children with tree limbs as arms. There are some that are dressed in armor holding swords. These statues line the walls as if on display at a museum. She has seen exhibits like this in New York City when her family went to visit. She remembers the Museum of Natural History and all the statues and stuffed animals in display cages. Well that's what she had called them.

Light beams are circling around the walls, occasionally hitting the statues.

Even though the statues are the same color as the rock walls, every time a light hits them they seem to become more animated and have color and depth to them. They seem to be alive for that brief second. She also swears that they move into different poses as the light passes them.

"This is so strange," she thinks.

She stares at one statue holding a sword above her head. As the light touches her the child seems to come to life and changes from a standing position into a crouched position with the sword at her side. The instant the light touched her she looked like a normal child with long brown hair and dark skin. She actually looked like her friend Mia. Then the little girl became part of the wall again. Her little-girl features turning to stone.

She laughed a little to herself, "Mia carrying a sword." Mia had the biggest Barbie collection Lily has ever seen and was now getting into those American Dolls.

"She didn't even know which side of the bat to use when we played whiffle ball," she thinks.

All past expressions and catch phrases start to fill her head. About a month ago she read Alice in Wonderland because her grandma would always talk about that book. The phrase "curiouser and curiouser" kept popping into her mind because that's what this was, curiouser and curiouser.

"Lily down the rabbit hole," she thinks.

"Maybe I'm in another dimension, a dimension of light and sound, hey wait that's from that show my dad watches." Her thoughts have gone media mad. She giggles a little. "Okay I've definitely hit my head so I might as well just enjoy this wonderful dream."

As she cautiously moves further into the chamber she sees that the room is being bathed in light of every color. Swirling and reflecting off the walls. Lily then remembers the line from The Wizard of Oz, "we're not in Kansas anymore Toto" and steps back a little, trying to find the safety of the stone walls. Her thoughts go to the Wicked Witch and she immediately gets a little frightened.

"I need to come up with my own phrase," she thinks. Lily goes farther back up the path she had come from but her curiosity gets the better of her and she peeks around the corner taking in all the sights. She is hidden by the rock wall.

She looks up the path and it is pitch black.

"Hmmm, no going back," she thinks and looks back into the chamber.

Her eyes start to adjust to the lights swirling around and she sees in the center of the chamber that the source of light is coming from the center of the cavern. There in the middle is a white pedestal with a teardrop amulet floating above it, in mid-air.

"Wow, that looks exactly like the one Natu used to wear," she thinks noticing it looks a little bigger and it is much more brilliant in color than Natu's.

Lily always held that amulet when she was being rocked in Natu's arms as a baby. When she would lie in Natu's lap Lily would always reach up and hold it.

Natu's amulet was a muted purple color. This amulet is filling the hall with every color imaginable. The light coming out of this gem is incredible.

Getting her courage up again, Lily slowly steps away from the wall and enters the chamber. Her eyes are fixed on the glowing amulet. She doesn't see anything but the spinning light, as if hypnotized. The light that splashes out of the amulet covers Lily and totally transfixed, she approaches the center of the chamber towards the amulet.

Lily doesn't notice the five hooded figures that step out of the shadows and surround her.

These five figures are wearing different colored cloaks, all with hoods hiding their faces. Lily's eyes dart around for a second but she is drawn to the amulet. She notices that the white pedestal that the amulet hovers over has figures carved into it. Five, to be exact, and the top of the pedestal is in the shape of a woman with arms extended upward as if she is trying to grab the amulet.

Lily is in a trance but she is now aware that she is being surrounded by the five faceless figures. The dripping of water can be heard in the distance causing an echo in the cave. For a moment she smells flowers, sweet and soothing, like the ones in her garden.

"I'm dreaming, I'm dreaming. Keep telling yourself that, Lily."

She can hear these figures speaking but she can't seem to move a muscle and can only stare into the amulet.

Lily can hear these figures talking to each other. Their language is so strange but Lily understands everything that is being said around her.

"What if she's not the one?" the red-robed figure says. Wisps of smoke can be seen escaping from beneath this one's robe, as a red glow can be seen in the darkness of his hood.

"She has to be, there is no one else. We cannot wait because time is very short and if we do not hurry our creation will succumb to this darkness," says another one of the figures. This one is dressed in a brown robe. She has the voice of a woman and at the bottom of her robe can be seen hooves; horse's hooves instead of legs and feet.

"Curiouser and curiouser," Lily thinks and then smirks as her attention is pulled back into the light of the amulet. Lily is seeing the beginning, the end and possibly the future of this world. Stories of long ago are being shown to her as if on a video screen. All of it coming at her like a blur but she is still aware of all that is going on around her.

A tall figure in a green robe is the next to speak. "Mother, she is the one. She has the innocence we have hoped for, I can sense this." This figure stands taller than the others and out of the arms of his robe where you would expect hands are leaves and small branches.

Lily can hardly breathe. She is transfixed by the amulet but still understands the conversation between these figures and knows that they are talking about her. She can sense that these figures have surrounded her but is still captivated by the lights that are being thrown at the ceiling and walls by the amulet.

One of the figures is dressed in white and her robe is constantly blowing as if it were surrounded by a breeze even though there is no movement of air in this huge cavern. She also carries a large wooden staff.

She is the next to speak. "But is her heart strong enough? Can we jeopardize all we have created through nepotism? Are we sure we want this, this girl could be our last hope." She turns to a dark spot in the cave, "Mother, please, are you sure?"

A voice can be heard from the darkness. A figure emerges in front of the amulet. A woman's shape takes form but she is silhouetted by the blinding light. This woman commands the group's attention by just being. This is the one figure that the rest have been addressing as Mother. She is a tall figure with a thick, dark-green head of hair that looks like a forest. Her face is chiseled black granite stone with piercing blue eyes. Her robe is multicolored and she floats as she moves.

"Nepotism, is that what you think my dear, dear Sif? Hahahaha." Her laughter fills the hall but something about that laugh seemed so familiar to Lily. "Ahhh my temperamental child. You are all my children, just as this young one is my child. In fact all the children who came before her and the ones that will come after are my children. Is it because she is a child of my blood? Let's remember so are you my dear. And you," she points to the others. "Her heart is strong enough. I know her. She is the one." Her voice rises as to make this the final word.

The red-robed being lifts his arms and says in a gravelly voice, "It does not matter what we think Mother. In the end it's the armor that will decide."

"That is right, Tu Di Gong," Mother says to the red-robed giant as a smile crosses her face.

"Where have I seen that smile?" Lily says to herself.

The only figure who has not said anything steps forward. He is dressed in a blue robe and moves fluidly and effortlessly.

"We will have our answer soon. She hears us and will soon understand what is expected of her."

"Ah yes, Unktahee, you are always so easy to sway," says Sif under her white robe, with a slightly sarcastic tone in her voice.

"No, my dear sister, I just know that what will be, will be. Why fight something when you can just let it go and let it happen. You are so easy to excite and sometimes very temperamental. My waters run freely, going around obstacles rather than trying to push through them like your storms. Gently and easy. Our answer will be unfolding in moments. You need to be more like Minona, she has the patience of the great animals that she has created."

"Purrrrr," says Minona. The hooves sticking out from beneath her brown robe are a contradiction to the purring that escapes her throat as she touches Unktahee, but the purr and low guttural sounds match her hands which have changed into the paws of a very large cat.

The mother raises her hands above her head and the amulet continues to spin. It spins slowly at first as it had since Lily walked into the chamber but starts to speed up.

"Tu Di Gong, Unktahee, Minona, Sif and Wiraquocha, we have gathered here again to bless our next child into the band. My children, we are here to give our souls and powers to the next generation of saviors. What is, is, and all that has happened cannot be changed. We bless this child of the future, of the present and we pray that she is accepted today by the armor of innocence. Love, trust and compassion will rule the day and our new band will lead the way into a new age of light. Let the truth provide and let the innocence guide." With that a clap of thunder echoes through the cavern. Sif smiles a little because she knows that it's her thunder that punctuates the great hall. She looks around very satisfied.

The light from the amulet is blinding now and it's spinning so fast Lily can't even see it.

Lily breaks out of her trance and starts to back away. Moving the way she came in. She bumps into the green robed figure and as she goes to push away from him a vine shoots out of the cuff where a hand should be and wraps around her wrist. She quickly pulls away to run. The vine lets her go.

"Mom! Dad! Help!"

She runs back up the path but the way she came is now blocked by a stone

wall. Her hands run along the stone walls but there's no way out. Lily is now scared.

"Lily...come here my dear."

Lily slowly turns. "Who, who are you? How do you know my name? Where are my Mom and Dad?"

"You know who I am. The reason I know your name is because it also happens to be my name," the mother says.

The silhouetted woman steps out from in front of the light toward Lily. The mother is holding the silver cane that Natu gave Lily and her looks have changed. No longer are her features of stone and forest. The mother steps out of the shadows and reveals her identity. It is Lily's grandmother, Natu. Only her face looks different. She looks tired and ashen. Older. Her eyes are sunken and there is little expression on her face. Lily gasps in wonder.

"Grandma Natu? It...it can't be you."

"It is me, my dear. Now come. There's a place here for you by my side. Time is so short."

Indeed there is a spot for her. She walks slowly over to her Grandma's side. Lily gives Natu a warm hug and then takes her place in the circle. Six tall figures and Lily. In the middle of the circle Lily can see the amulet still spinning with every color of the spectrum coming from it. Now this all makes sense to Lily, well more sense than what she walked into, okay maybe it made no sense but at least she knows it was her grandma's amulet spinning around.

"Lily my child. These are the Gods of the world. My children. They are the creators and caretakers. But they have become weak with age and the constant assault of the darkness on our creations. Truth and innocence strengthens them. All the stories I told you have been to prepare you for this moment. Let me introduce them."

With each introduction the hooded figures reveal themselves. They pull their hoods off and their cloaks drop to the ground.

"This is the God of all that grows. His name is Wiraquocha. He is the God within all the plants and trees you see."

The God of Plants is a seven-foot-tall Inca king with plants entwined over his body. A golden staff and jaguar crown.

"Here is Minona, she is the Goddess of the Animals. She is the caretaker of all the creatures that walk the earth."

The Animal Goddess is a black warrior princess. She has the greenest cat-like eyes and the darkest ebony skin Lily has ever seen. She is holding a spear and shield.

"This is the unpredictable Goddess of the Elements, Sif. She controls all the wind, rain, lightning and thunder."

The Element Goddess pulls back her hood. She is a Norse Valkyrie with helmet and battle staff. Her hair is yellow and is parted into pigtails. Her stare is cold and Lily can see ice forming in and around her eyes. Lily feels the piercing cold stare go right through which sends a shiver down her spine. Lily's grandma notices and puts her arm around Lily but doesn't say a word. Sif has always been the most uncontrollable of all her children but she accepted her for who she was. Deep down Sif had a good heart and loved the creation they had named Earth.

"This is the God of Water. Unktahee, come my child," Grandma beckons to the God of Water. "He has control of the seas and the oceans and all that live there."

The God of Water is a figure shaped like a human but has bubbling seas and oceans as a body and face. He has a broad smile, which is warm and comforting.

"Where would my world be without Tu Di Gong, the God of Fire and Earth? He can be hard and unmoving and yet mold his way around any obstacle."

The Fire God has a less human shape than the rest. His body and head are made of fire and stone. His body has molten lava traveling through it. Smoke can be seen lifting from his body and the smell of sulphur permeates the air.

"And you, Grandma. You're just my Grandma Natu, right?" Lily looks up at Natu.

That wisp of a smile comes over Natu's face, the smile that has been part of her life for so long: the same smile that Lily had when she was born and will always have. Her dad has it and it is unique to this family, as a beauty mark is to some families or the chance for twins. A smile that is both warm and inviting. It mesmerizes the people who are blessed to receive it and those people never forget that smile or the person that offered that smile.

"Well my dear," Natu giggles, "I am your Grandma Natu but some have called me by a different name."

With that Grandma Natu takes off her robe and her face changes. Gone are the old features only to be replaced by an ebony face with small trees as hair. Her eyes are the blue of the skies. Here stands the Mother herself. She is beautiful beyond words. Her body has all the elements of the Earth wrapped around her. Water, skies, animals, plants all cover her body. She is not just the spirit of nature, she is nature herself. The best that was ever created. As Lily looks at her grandma up and down another transformation happens. Natu sees that her granddaughter is overwhelmed so she changes back into the form that Lily is more accustomed to, that of grandma Natu.

"Oh my child," Grandma Natu shakes her head, "I am Mother Nature, my dear, and my time here is short. I and my children have stayed here too long and we are weak and tired. When we first created this wonderful planet we wanted it to flourish. A darkness existed but was unseen at the creation and now it is increasing in our world. Every age has seen more and more of it. The children who have come before you have fought valiantly and hard. You and your band will also be called on to stand tall against that which corrupts. I know you can't grasp all that I need to tell you but my dear you are cast into a very difficult role. I feel you to be the most innocent child on this planet. One who has been born to the role of leader.

"Since you stepped into this hall you have been accepting all the information you will need to be the great leader we hope you to be. The one to save my creation, your world. You will be the light in the darkness, the sword, the truth."

"Me? Okay so I walked into the wall... hit my head right. In a minute I'll wake up and this will be a dream. Where is the nurse?" Lily closes her eyes, knowing when she opens them all this will be gone. She then opens them and nothing has changed.

"Oh my. My dear, dear Lily. Remember all the stories I read to you about the Band of Innocence. All those stories I read to you were true. They were meant to lead you to this exact point; to prepare you to take your place amongst the children in this hall of creation. Look around, Lily, there is the spot for you."

Lily looks to where Natu points to a place on the cavern wall and there seems to be a space that's too large for one figure. She realizes that the spot is meant for more than one child.

"That space is bigger than just me, Grandma."

"It's for you and your band."

"Okay hold on. So the stories about the Band of Innocence were real? I always thought it was a fairy tale not a real story."

"Yes my love, I know it's hard to accept but it was all real. Those were real stories about real children. About the Band of Innocence. We are hoping that you will be their next leader. These are extraordinary children with fantastic powers bestowed upon them by these spirits, these creators." Natu points to her children who stand around the amulet. "I believe you to be the most innocent of all innocents, so stand my child and do not move because this is the moment we have been waiting for, the moment that will prove me correct in the assumption of your brilliant light."

"But Grandma, who are all these children on the walls? They seem to come to life when the light hits them. Are they real kids?"

"These are the children who have come before you. They are the innocents who have battled against the darkness throughout the ages. You can see their names my darling. See there is Martin, Teresa, John, Robert, Abraham, Rosa and all the other children who through their innocence and faith battled the darkness even when they became adults." As Natu points to the statues they seem to come to life and nod at Lily.

"Some of them you know and some you might not. You also have a very important part in this story, my dear. When you have faith and beliefs that no one can change, you yourself can change the world as these children did. Nothing stopped them from their beliefs and a large part came from the innocence they held onto from their childhood. But now we must get back to you." Natu laughs, loving the inquiring mind of her granddaughter.

"Now you must stand still and trust all that is going to happen. Do not move."

The amulet has been spinning, muted beams of light have been flashing against the walls but when Natu lifts her arms a burst of white light comes from the amulet and a large thunder clap. Lily covers her eyes. The light fills the chamber and shines a warmth on her skin that penetrates her soul. The warmth that man had felt before he walked a path that was different than the original way; a safe and loving warmth.

The spinning of the amulet starts to slow and then stops. It hovers, bobbing a little in midair, above the pedestal. The outstretched arms that came up from the pedestal slowly move and take hold of the amulet. Lily didn't even notice the arms moving, she is so overwhelmed.

"When did that happen, is everything in this cave alive?" Lily thinks.

She looks at the pedestal and it looks different than the one she had seen when she walked in. It now had movement to it. All the carvings on the side of the pedestal have become very animated, slowly moving as if the figures etched into the pedestal were alive.

The hands holding the amulet turn the face of it up toward the ceiling. A bright white light shoots up revealing the true height of the ceiling. Lily now sees more faces and carvings. It seems like thousands now.

A silver liquid starts to drip out of the amulet, running off the sides of it and dripping down onto the pedestal. Lily thinks it looks like the time Billy unscrewed the top of the maple syrup and when she went to pour it all the syrup came rushing out and overflowed over her plate and off the table. Thick and oozing. The silver liquid, like the maple syrup, drips down the sides of the pedestal and puddles on the floor.

It starts moving towards Lily. Lily starts to back up as the liquid gets closer but feels a gentle hand on her back. She looks up into the eyes of her grandma. The wisp of a smile returns to Natu's face and it eases Lily immediately. The liquid is now touching Lily's feet. It looks like it would be cold but Lily isn't chilled. It slowly starts to travel up her leg covering her like a second skin. It covers her jeans and then shirt. Lily holds her breath not knowing if it will cover her face. It reaches her neck and stops. Lily looks down and she is covered neck to toe in a silver armor.

"Now do you see? The armor knows," Natu comments to the other elders.

"She is strong of heart and innocent of soul. She is the chosen one. We have our warrior of light. Lily the armor has chosen you. Step forward my child and reach into the amulet's light."

The light is so bright that Lily has to squint and still she can't see what is in the beam of white light. For a second she thinks she will burn her hand but as Lily reaches into the light she feels a hardness, an object that her hand instinctively grabs hold of and as she grabs it she feels a slight vibration. Her hand slowly comes out of the amulet and she sees in her hand a sword of the most beautiful and brilliant white light. The handle which should have been hard to hold, because it was so big and her hand was so small, molds to her hand and the weight is perfect for her. Heavy enough for substance but not heavy enough to tire her arm. It's an extension of her arm actually and she feels like it's been there forever.

The handle has the same carvings as the pedestal. All the figures are intertwined.

Natu turns and smiles down at Lily.

"This is the sword of truth. It will help you on your journey, but, Lily, I must warn you, never, never use it in anger. Anger will take away your power, it is the darkness dimming your light. You will lose your innocence and the darkness will have won a major battle."

"But how will I know how to use these gifts?" Lily asks as she takes the sword in her other hand.

"The amulet will guide you, my darling. The amulet will be in your care now. I am handing it over to you, my child. I am too old and weak to carry on the fight. It's time to give this battle up to a new generation. One of hope, compassion and youth."

Lily looks down and there around her neck is the amulet. The muted purple glow radiates across the cavern walls. The statues of the children on the walls have moved and they are now all bowing to her. Hundreds of heads looking down all around her and then in an instant they are statues again.

"We must leave you now, my child. The past is inside you. You have all the memories of the ages. The armor and the sword are all you need. The amulet is your connection to us."

Lily looks around at the creators and one by one they start to fade and as they fade their bodies start to circle over the pedestal in a spiral shape, like a tornado. As she stands there the creators are pulled into the amulet. All are gone now except for Natu, Mother Nature.

Natu looks at the children on the wall and smiles. The children on the walls smile back and bow. She then turns around to Lily.

"I must go now, child."

Her appearance changes to Grandma Natu for an instant and then back to

Mother Nature. Piercing blue eyes and dark black granite skin reflect the light of the amulet.

"Grandma Natu. Please don't leave me. I have missed you so much."

"I will always be with you in the amulet. Never let it go. You will meet your band mates soon and will carry on the fight to protect and save this world and the ones who suffer from greed and hate. May the truth provide and the innocence guide."

With that phrase echoing in the air, Grandma Natu starts to fade, she reaches out one last time and touches Lily's face. A gentle touch that skims Lily's cheek and then her body becomes absorbed into the amulet. There's a burst of light as every color of the spectrum fills the whole chamber. Light can be seen hitting every part of the chamber along with whispers that seem to be coming from everywhere, growing louder and brighter and brighter and louder. Lily, with eyes wide open, tries to adjust to the burst of color but she has to close her eyes. The sound begins to get too loud as Lily covers her ears while keeping her eyes closed tight.

Lily stands with her eyes closed and her hands over her ears. She starts to sway a little bit. She feels as if she is losing her balance.

As she starts to fall she feels hands grabbing her. She slowly opens her eyes. A silhouetted figure can be seen but she can't make out who it is.

"Grandma?"

Slowly she starts to focus and sees the face of her dad. She feels her dad's arms around her, holding her up and can hear the guide asking if everything is alright. Her dad helps her over to a large boulder and sits her down. He turns and picks up Grandma Natu's cane that Lily had dropped.

"Lily, are you okay? Lily, honey, are you alright? You almost fell over and you look white as a ghost. Did the guide scare you with his stories?"

"No, Dad, I think I'm okay. Dad, was I here all this time? I mean, was I with you guys, here?" She tries to get up and starts to look around.

"Here being relative, yeah you were standing right by me, holding my hand. Or I think it was you." Doug smiles, thinking okay maybe this isn't the time for jokes although his mind quickly goes into a science-fiction movie where aliens take over the bodies of family members. But that thought quickly passes as he tries to concentrate on his daughter.

Doug pauses as he sees his daughter is looking distraught. Lily is still a little unsteady on her feet and leans into her dad for support.

Everyone is watching and the guide asks again if everything is alright. This is the guide's first day and he wants no trouble.

Doug waves off the guide and gives him the thumbs up sign, as if to say everything is alright and the guide continues his speech which is winding down the tour. Billy is right up front listening as if he is hypnotized. He is the only one to not turn around.

Doug sees him and thinks to himself how he loves boys. They are so easy. A snack, a ghost story and sports and a boy will thrive. You may not hear from them until they're in their twenties. Girls on the other hand take so much work. He laughs to himself because he knows he loves both of his children more than life itself. He just wishes girls were easier to understand. Duh, welcome to the world of every man on the planet. It's funny how so many thoughts can run through someone's head at any given moment but Doug's mind goes right back to his daughter's well-being.

Doug kneels down and looks at his daughter and realizes that she looks dazed, like Billy looked when he got his first concussion, with many more to follow.

"Lily, you don't look so good."

Milly is standing with Billy and Doug calls out to her.

"Hey Milly, come here. Lily looks a little sick."

Flashes of the past rush through Lily's head. She sees the caves but not in the present, she can feel the age in them. She can feel the people who were trapped in them and the animals who lived in there. She feels as if she knows what the ground is thinking and feels. Lily is absorbing the vibrations from beneath her. She can feel what the trees around her are feeling; the breeze is carrying voices. She is being overwhelmed. So many feelings of past and present. So much joy and pain coming from all around her.

Lily closes her eyes tight. She shakes her head to stop all these thoughts and feelings. Reaching out to her dad she grabs the silver cane. As she touches the cane all these sounds and images stop. She grabs the cane with two hands, holding it tight.

"What happened, Dad?" Lily says still feeling woozy.

"It's okay, honey, why don't you sit down again and I'll get your mom to get you some water."

Lily's Mom rushes over.

"Lily, honey, you look white as a ghost." As Milly kneels next to her husband, she puts her hand on Lily's forehead to check for a fever as all mothers do as soon as they think their child is sick. Milly moves her hand down and holds Lily's cheek. Cupping them gently as she lifts Lily's head she looks down at what is hanging around her neck.

"Where did you get this?"

Milly immediately takes hold of the amulet and looks up at Doug. Doug shrugs his shoulders. He has learned long ago never to ask questions, just go with it. It's so much easier.

Milly looks back and forth between Doug and Lily. "Wasn't this Natu's?"

She holds the amulet around Lily's neck. A light flickers ever so faintly. Doug and Milly exchange quizzical glances as they hover over their daughter.

"Lily, honey, where on earth did you get this?" Milly looks at Doug who just assumes the "I have no idea" look. They both look at Lily.

"Grandma Natu gave it to me." She looks up and smiles that wisp of smile.

CHAPTER SIXTEEN

Kazan

The building that houses Talonthorn Enterprises should be a towering structure, with ornate marble columns and a huge glass facade. It should have all Italian tiles in the lobby and a staff of hundreds to cater to the rich and powerful that frequent Kazan and his meetings. Talonthorn Enterprises makes so much money each year its offices could cover a whole block and for that matter it could own a small country but instead Kazan's company is in a nondescript old building in the financial district of Chicago.

If you were to take the elevator to the 5th floor and turn right you would walk down a corridor with worn dark red carpet and dim lighting. The walls call out for someone to come and freshen up the paint. If you continued down the hall to the fifth door on your right it would look just like the second, third and fourth doors on your right. Room 525. Just another office door, to another office in another office building. The carpet to this particular room is more worn than the carpeting that runs down the hall and the door has scratches on it. All the doors have faded green paint but if you looked closely you would notice there are no locks on this door or any of the other doors. Matter of fact, there are no door knobs.

One of the lights in the ceiling flickers at the end of the hall exhibiting all the signs of a failing ballast in a fluorescent lighting fixture. This hall seems too ordinary and forgotten. If you stepped through the door of Room 525 you might expect to see stacks of paper piled up on a desk with accountants on the phone or maybe an insurance company with a receptionist who smells of stale tobacco and doesn't look up at you but asks who you are here to see.

That's where you would be wrong. If you were allowed to step through that door you would walk onto tile that was brought in from Africa and cost as much as a small two-bedroom house. Each tile. Two bodyguards would politely ask you to remove your coat and then would wand you for anything that could be of use to someone who had the intent to harm the occupants, and there are plenty of them. One target would be the owner himself, Haran Kazan. The master of deceit and torture, murder and hate. This is why he employs an army of men to protect him, his son, his minions and his endeavors.

The office's foyer stands forty feet high and sixty feet long. It seems like one of those cartoons where the little duck character steps into a tent and the inside is as big as a palace. The ceiling looks as if it was painted by Michelangelo himself. Thoughts of the Sistine chapel would enter your mind.

The walls are made of wood from endangered and expensive

rain forest trees which are broken up by the placement of heads of animals that have met the fate of all who fall into the crosshairs of Haran Kazan. As you walk down the hall of this tribute to pain and death you smell the fear in the air. The fear these animals felt and the fear everyone has of Haran. The carpet runner is soft as a cat's fur. Actually it's made of woven tiger fur. It must have taken the lives of hundreds of tigers to make the soles of expensive Italian shoes feel comfortable.

Typical Kazan. The ultimate humiliation.

At the end of the hall are two large wooden doors. The doors are made of tigerwood and stand at least twenty feet tall. They are arched and at the top is a huge wooden bust of Aries, the god of war, with two swords crossing under his face. This is Kazan's conference room. His War Room, as he calls it, because everything is a war to him.

Two large men stand on either side making sure no one gets in who isn't expected and no one gets out until Mr. Kazan says they can leave. It has happened on occasion that certain people never got out, they just sort of disappeared. Poof, gone. This hasn't happened too often though because most of those people don't even make it in through the hall door. They disappear long before standing in the hall and wondering what the receptionist looks like on the other side of the door.

In the conference room a long, finely crafted wood table runs the length of the room. The table itself has to be fifty feet long. The legs are carved into figures holding the table up. All of the faces appear to be in pain, as if the table is too heavy for them to hold. Kazan likes pain. He loves to breathe in fear and hate just like you or I would breathe in the smell of fresh-cut grass.

The high ceilings and picturesque view are offset by Haran Kazan's menacing frame at the front of the room. Dark shadows dance around the walls, which should during this time of the day be bright and sunlit. Most of the shadows seem to settle near and around Kazan. They are dark, inky, foreboding blots.

Kazan looks much older than he was the day his son was born, but he is still an intimidating presence. There are ten older men all wearing blue suits, sitting spaced perfectly on each side of the sizable table. Kazan is standing by a PowerPoint screen at the front of the room. The graphic in the presentation shows Talonthorn Corporation, Kazan's main revenue source. The graphic reads "Profit Outlook" and it seems that profits have been dipping for several consecutive months. Kazan's frame paces through the little light and growing darkness that's shadowing the screen. The members of the board do not look very happy. Actually they look just plain scared.

"These graphs tell it like it really is, gentlemen, and the numbers are like no numbers that I have ever experienced since I designed this company. It was constructed to be recession proof. If there is war we build weapons, if there is peace we plow the conquered land. We drill, we construct. So which of you fine gentlemen would love to stand up and explain to me how this is possible?"

The men around the table sink lower into their seats as if they won't be noticed. They all look as if they would rather be anywhere than here.

"So anyone? What is going on?" His voice has a booming sound in this conference room. He had it designed for just this quality.

"This is the sweet spot, Mr. Kazan. If you stand right here your voice will boom across the room," his architect had told him. His architect was right. If Kazan stood at the front of the room, in that certain spot, no matter where he was and no matter how quietly he spoke you could hear him. Something to do with acoustics.

The room is dead silent. No one makes eye contact with Kazan which in itself he despises.

"Cowards," he thinks. Useless pieces of flesh and bone.

Kazan switches the screen. The graphs change to a video news article about drilling being halted in the Arctic. In the photo a giant tanker is frozen as hundreds of thousands of seals surround the tanker.

The screens switch back and forth showing different angles of this big ship. These shots seem to be coming from satellites or reconnaissance planes. They are grainy but with some enhancements, which Kazan has taken the time and money to do, clear images can be made out.

The scene changes now to a large oil tanker sailing through sparsely icy water at breakneck speed. Behind it can be seen a trail of oil. The ship seems to be leaking its cargo but is not stopping to do anything about it.

"Gentlemen, the Apostle — which we all know had a little leakage problem" — he laughs a little, "was on its normal oil run and here is what happened and what we pieced together."

Into the camera shot you can see a small young hand reaching down, where some oil sludge washes up on the shore next to a dead herring. It seems like the hand of a young girl. The camera pulls out and the young girl is shining in the sunlight. The young girl stands in a suit of armor and points to the ship, the Apostle, with a sword of bright white light. A young Asian girl can be seen standing next to the armor clad girl and instantly transforms herself into a sea lion. She leaps into the water and resurfaces only to make a loud call into the night. A call that radiates across the ocean. Shortly after her war cry, which really can be nothing else, thousands of sea lions can be seen swimming towards her and they all head towards the ship. They surround the liner, forcing it to stop.

Kazan starts to narrate the events happening on the screen.

"Now, gentlemen, I quote from our own internal resources. August 13th. In a strange and unexplainable scene hundreds of thousands of sea lions surround a large Talonthorn oil tanker forcing it to stop. The weather then turns unseasonably cold, freezing the Apostle in place."

In another video piece, caught from a security camera on the tanker itself, a pale thin boy can be seen blowing air out of his lungs and the water actually freezes around the big ship.

As the group watches they see another young boy's body changing and dissolving into a liquid form. He shapes himself into the crack of the cargo hull that has been leaking oil from the big tanker. The pale boy hovers by the crack in the hull and blowing cold breath freezes the liquid to prevent any further oil leaks as the sea lions howl. A bright light comes from the shore. It's the little girl in the armor holding her sword in the air.

"The crew would have to be rescued and the ship would remain locked in this frozen water until the oil could be transferred without incident. We are now being sued by every conservation group known to man. The government is now investigating but we all know how that goes. I pretty much own every politician, so the Feds are not our concern. It's these do-gooders that will cast a public light on our operations. Gentlemen I have prided myself on keeping Talonthorn out of the public eye. The people of this country didn't even know we existed, until now." His voice explodes. "HOW IS THIS POSSIBLE?"

No one answers. Instead, the men all seem perplexed and scared. As Kazan studies their faces and looks for an explanation he thinks, "Fear, that's all I see. Weak and pitiful fear in their eyes, as in the eyes of the animals I have killed. It makes me sick to be surrounded by this weakness. At least the animals had the good sense to run from me. Ahhh, but I did love looking into their eyes right before they left this world. The questions and pain in those weak windows."

"So no one. Hahahaha. Ok I have some more information to share today with you fine men."

A collective groan can be heard from the men around the table as if the news they were hearing wasn't bad enough.

"Oh yes, my fine colleagues, we haven't finished."

Kazan clicks to a new article.

The headline reads "Talonthorn makes no progress in building defense plant in Brazil."

The text at the bottom of the picture gives the date. June 5th.

The picture shows bulldozers covered in thick vines with a

half-built compound that looks abandoned. Trees are growing out of the windows and vines cover the front of the building.

The video again is cut together and goes from some black and white to color video. The camera shows a thick rain forest. Trees as far as the eye can see then over one of the hills we see emptiness. The camera pans from left to right showing a fleet of bulldozers which are clearing a roadway through dense rainforest that stretches for miles.

The lower third title reads "May 21st."

Swaths of thousand-year-old trees lie splintered and broken. Dead animals can be seen on the sides of the destruction being created by these powerful machines. Gunshots can be heard among the bulldozer's engine roar.

"We set up lots of robotic cameras at the banks of the Amazon River to scan the perimeters to watch the progress of our operations, as always, but it seems the best footage came from our crew chief. With millions of dollars in cameras and recording devices what we have is home video from a local's camera," Kazan says, looking agitated.

The camera is capturing the progress of the front loading machines. These machines are ripping trees and plants from the ground where they have thrived for thousands of years. In one frame, though blurry, three small figures can be seen walking up from the water's edge. They are heading towards the workers and the big machines. The video, which has been enhanced, starts to bring these figures into focus. The figures are children. Three young girls. The video zooms in and these are not native children.

Every once in a while the camera hits a reflection of bright light coming from the trio. Seems one of the girls is wearing some reflective clothing. This is strange in itself but some still photos have been edited into this piece. What they show is incredible. The stills, snapshots taken from some of the workers' cameras, clearly show two of the children getting to the shore on a crocodile. The pictures are in succession.

The large croc hits the shore and the two children climb off its back. The next picture shows three children and no croc.

"So with all our technology and cameras set up all of this has been captured on one man's camera and a couple of Polaroid cameras which we had to confiscate. Again, how is this possible? You gentlemen have a great deal to think about and I suggest you continue thinking because I will want answers at the end of our little presentation."

The crew chief was filming the progress his crew was making to possibly impress Mr. Kazan. Little did he know that what was going on in the background is what really impressed his boss and that because he didn't get the job done he was fired and sent back to Guatemala with nothing to show for it, not even his camera.

In the video you can see the trio of little girls take cover in the forest as the construction crews continue to wreak havoc over this pristine forest. Off to the side another child can be seen approaching the trio. It's a young boy who can be seen entering the camera frame and walking up to the girls. They all peek around the trees watching the construction crews destroy a forest that took Wiraquocha a thousand years to nurture and grow.

The voice of a professional in-house correspondent can be heard as the video screen projects different images. Some of the footage is of men yelling and some of workers throwing their hard hats down and running. Men are brushing their heads violently, trying to get things out of their hair.

The screams are of fear and the only word that anyone can make out is diablo, Devil. Dark blurs fly into and out of frame. It's hard to make out the flying black figures attacking these men but it's quite clear that the men are in full panic.

"The much anticipated Talonthorn military industrial complex was delayed yet again as local workers refuse to participate no matter the salary. They were driven by fear from what they were calling the presence of the devil but that has changed to 'children of the gods.' Reports of small children, bats and magic have caused massive delays. None of the workers were injured and one worker was even rescued by one of these children when he almost fell into the foundation of the now defunct building. As you see on the video, albeit very grainy, a young boy can be seen helping to pull out a confused worker and even dusting him off. The child says something to the worker who then kneels as the boy touches his head. This worker stands up slowly, turns and walks slowly up the same path the other men are running up. The workers who encountered these children claimed that they had seen and felt a light; a peace."

The video ends with a young girl motioning toward the camera and the video goes black.

"That camera was purportedly destroyed by a stream of water produced from the finger of that young girl" Kazan explains. "Most of this next footage was captured on cell phones we confiscated from the workers," Kazan says as he paces.

He has seen this footage over and over to try and find out who did all these special effects and how.

"Magic children. Children of the gods. Whose gods are they talking about? Not mine. Ridiculous," he says to himself.

Kazan hits his remote and another piece of video starts to roll.

"I hope you are all enjoying this. It has cost me close to a billion dollars in losses for this wonderful production."

The footage is blurry but finally comes into focus. A small boy walks out of the forest and as he walks he seems to transform into a tall female Viking warrior. A helmet is on her head and she has long blonde pigtails. In her hand is a long wooden staff. She raises the staff and holds it up to the sky. A large clap of thunder can be heard from her staff and a streak of lightning breaks the sky. This once sunny day starts to cloud over. A perfectly clear sunny Amazon day is now dark as night. A small Asian girl stands in front of the camera and as if by magic transforms herself into a vampire bat. A loud high-pitched shriek can be heard coming from her as she takes flight. Seconds after her ear-splitting scream thousands of black bats descend down upon the workers. The workers go scrambling back up the path they have just cleared. The foreman is trying to stop them. As he turns he runs directly into a little girl with armor. He stares at her brilliance in the darkness. The girl holds a sword of the purest white light over the foreman's head. Light envelops him.

Her voice can be heard over all the yelling: "You must move this facility to a place better suited for your planet."

Mesmerized, the man nods his head in agreement, as if a light bulb has gone off in his head, and in a calm manner picks up his bag and walks off as if hypnotized. Once the area is cleared the Viking queen who called upon the clouds turns back into a little boy and the dark clouds roll away while sunlight returns to fill the sky. The vampire bats fly off, presumably returning to the cave where they sleep. The band of children gathers once again on the trail. There are six of them.

A little black girl, who stands with the rest of the children, starts to change. She gets bigger and taller. In her place now stands a bronze god and he is dressed in an Inca-style outfit with a large jaguar head piece. He raises his arms and as he does they change into vines and branches. In a split second the man is gone and in his place a dense rain forest starts to grow. In minutes the new growth that this plant man fabricated quickly populates the torn-up area with new plant life. A large tree that appeared in the middle of this growth starts to shrink and change shape. It turns back into a little girl.

In the background you can see some of the workers hiding behind trees making the sign of the cross and kneeling on the ground in prayer.

Kazan stands in front of the screen and put his hands on the long table leaning towards his board members.

"What has been documented as fact is that there was a vast number of vampire bats seen in the middle of the day and that the cleared rain forest was quickly able to regenerate itself. Oh and we are losing billions of dollars. Billions. Gentlemen, ponder this thought while I take a smoke."

Kazan, always in control, does not like losing his temper. He needs to think and unwind. He goes over to a humidor on the table and takes out a cigar, putting it under his nose to take a long sniff.

"Ahhhh one of the luxuries of life," he thinks to himself.

"Every problem has a solution," he whispers under his breath, "the strong find that solution and never care who gets hurt or how dirty they have to get." His father used to say that to him before hitting him. He loved his father for his strength and hated his mother for her weakness.

He sits himself down in a large chair and cuts off the end of the cigar, grabbing a lighter that has been implanted in an extinct owl. He pops the head off the owl and flicks the lighter. It comes to life and he takes long and large puffs.

The image of the Brazilian article is still with him.

"Children of the gods. I will stop this insanity," he thinks.

He puts his feet on the table and crosses his thick legs and looks at these weak losers sitting there with blank stares on their faces.

"What is going on? Someone is out to get me and no one has ever done that before. Hahahaha, I have an enemy. Well I have many people who hate me but no one is strong enough or stupid enough to contend with my power. I will crush these people or gods like fleas. I will find out what and who's behind this."

Kazan is getting angrier with each word.

"Oh well, sometimes the smoke doesn't help," he thinks out loud and flicks the cigar across the room as some of the men surrounding the table duck.

"Vampire bats in midday?...Ice storms in August?...Young girls with swords? Can someone please tell me what is going on here?"

A man, Harold Palmer, slouched two seats to the right forms a sarcastic grin.

"Ya know...It's not nice to fool with Mother Nature." Harold thinks it would break up the room a little bit. The room is dead silent. More silent than it was before and some of the men sitting near Mr. Hill start to move their chairs. Blood stains don't come out of these expensive suits very easily. Many of the men look down or look away. Harold realizes he shouldn't have opened his big mouth.

"Ah...Mr. Kazan...what I meant was..."

Kazan interrupts Harold, "No, no, Harold a sense of humor is a good thing to have in a downturn. As a matter of fact they could use some cheering up in the Arctic, with things going so poorly. I am sure you will be able to provide them with the comic relief they so richly need. Dress warm, Harold."

Kazan rings for his bodyguards and points over to Harold.

"Please escort Mr. Hill to my private plane. Tell my captain to fuel up for a non-stop flight to the Arctic. Bon voyage, Harold. Keep them laughing."

Harold gives a pained nod "yes" to his boss as he is led out of the room. No one turns their head or looks at Harold as he is walking out.

"Mother Nature...No, you see Mother Nature is when you get the occasional September hurricane...not this, after this, after this, and after this," Kazan says as he cycles through newspaper articles of freak mishaps that have cost him money. He starts ripping at them and when he's done he sits back down and grabs another cigar.

"Now gentlemen, anyone? Any other explanations? I pay you to make me money. You have not done your job. Hmmmmm. What to do, what to do? I know. YOU'RE FIRED! All of you get out."

The room clears instantly and everyone in the room feels completely lucky at having gotten away with just a firing. They all bless themselves that they aren't Harold. Shipped out on the next flight to the Arctic, oh and he is lucky. Some people just disappear, never heard from again. Then there's the occasional blood splatter. Kazan pays really well if you survive working for him. As everyone leaves, Kazan slams his hand down on the table so hard that the wood splinters.

He walks around the table and out of the door into a sitting room. Crossing the hall he moves toward another nondescript set of doors. These doors again open up into a huge cavernous room. There are pictures on the wall of all the Kazans. This is Haran Kazan's office. It was also Haran's father's and his father's father's and so on. His family's company was a small widget company that had been in business for a hundred years until Kazan took it over. Kazan learned quickly that there's more money in death than in the public good. The darkness helped him realize this and Kazan flourished along with his company.

The walls are a rich mahogany, from floor to ceiling. The floor is marble with a bearskin rug in the center of the office. There's a large desk towards a big bay window at the end of the room. The ceiling is a cathedral type with a large chandelier hanging down from the center. The chandelier has to be 40 feet in diameter with 5 tiers of crystals hanging down, each piece from Tiffany's. On one side of the room the wall opens up to a bay of computers and at three computer pods three men sit. They are all typing feverishly.

He walks towards the man in the middle and leans over him. All three are very nervous after hearing the encounter in the boardroom.

"This, gentlemen, is costing me a fortune and may cost you your jobs or more! Has anyone found out who this girl is?"

One of the computers has a picture of the little girl with the sword on its screen. It looks like the picture from one of the articles and is quite grainy when magnified.

"We are rendering the picture, Mr. Kazan, and hope that it will get a bit clearer, then we will run her through our database."

Mr. Kazan stands tall and looks at the three young men.

"I never hope. Hope means you are relying on something not seen or felt. I don't believe in anything if I can't grab hold of it, crush it with my hands or shoot it." Kazan smiles because he knows these men are now really frightened. He has come to the conclusion that people work better when they fear for their lives.

As Kazan looks at the computers the door behind him swings open and in walks Graham Wellington, Kazan's son's nanny. Graham has round glasses and was once the second-in-command in Kazan's secret service. Now he's a nanny. Granted he makes ten times what he made before but he's still a well-paid babysitter — extremely well-paid.

Kazan seems annoyed. "Graham, what are you doing here?"

"Mr. Kazan, you must have a look at this."

"Again Wellington, why are you not with my boy? He is your sole purpose."

No one ever raises their voice to Haran Kazan but if there was ever a time Graham knew it was now.

"Sir, I insist you look, just look."

Kazan reluctantly takes the binder and opens it. There sits a picture of a small girl.

"Wellington, I've seen this and we have all this information on these computers which these fine men are extracting." The three men never look up.

"Mr. Kazan, turn the page. Please."

Kazan turns the page and looks up to Graham with a big dark grin.

"This is who you have been looking for; all of them. You might be shocked to know that they are all children. I think they are all between twelve and fourteen years of age. There are six of them, or that's how many I counted."

Graham leans over his boss and leafs through the pages to show him the kids. The dark shadow returns and creeps across Haran's face. Like ink it remains as a big smile across Haran Kazan. His smile is more frightening than his yelling. The black stain runs off of Kazan then rests on Lily Leso's picture. As the shadows play around Kazan, Graham feels cold.

He points to the first page and the figure on it.

"The leader is Lily. She is the glowing kid with the sword and the reason she glows is that she has some sort of metal suit that fits her like a glove of sorts. From what I could find out through my connections and in my spare time while I was waiting at Jason's target practice I came up with the rest of these kid's names and what they do."

"Next is the Asian girl who I was able to find out has a gift with animals. She's the one who looked like the crocodile. Callie Yung."

Graham goes through each kid by turning each page for Kazan. If there is anything Graham Wellington can do it's put on a great presentation. Each sheet has a picture of the child with name, age and powers.

Nora Smith is the African girl with a penchant for plants.

Carlos Rodriguez plays with the wind and rain.

Gregor Rathustern seems to have an affinity for dirt and rocks.

"And Edward Carl is always wet." Graham looks at Kazan to see if he's laughing but he isn't. "It seems he can control water. You saw him on the Apostle video."

"Did you do all this behind my back, Wellington, while you were supposed to be watching my son?" A threatening tone is present in Kazan's voice to the extent that Graham moves away a bit.

"Ah sir, I did this all on my own time and between the things Jason needed to do. I never shirk my responsibilities, sir, I promise."

Kazan then said something he very rarely says to anyone.

"Good job, Graham, my boy." A smile creeps across Kazan's face and shadows dance all around Kazan as if there were a tribal dance going on. It makes Graham feel sort of sick and sort of cold.

Graham has always felt a chill whenever he's in his boss's presence. It wasn't a draft or anything like that but it was a bone chill which could be felt deep in his soul, if he believed he had a soul, which he didn't. He did, however, always see the dark shadows play around Mr. Kazan. Especially when he was busy working on some situation. The worse the game would turn out for his opponents the darker the shadows. Graham looks around and sees that the shadows are having a field day in this room today. He smirks thinking it's like a shadow convention. Dark and thick is how he would describe them.

But what really sticks in Graham's mind is the phrase, "my boy." Yes he's done it. Now the promotion and for god's sake, please get me away from the little psycho's presence. Jason is not an easy child, which is a huge understatement and actually he may not even be a child. He may be the Devil incarnate. Graham's mind is running away with itself.

Kazan turns his attention to the three men sitting at the computers. None of them have turned around for fear of being noticed but now they are.

"All right, I guess that'll be it for the day, gentlemen. Everyone but Wellington here is dismissed."

The three men, without question, grab their jackets and leave, quietly and quickly. They march out without even looking around, just straight ahead and out the door.

Graham Wellington moves around the desk and now sits in front of Kazan in one of the large, soft chairs. The desk is nothing short of huge, just like everything Kazan has. It's made of marble and wood. Large legs that look to be made out of elephant tusks end with ball and claw feet. On the desk are pictures of his son Jason, from when he was just a baby to various stages of his life. The last one is Jason holding a shotgun standing beside a tiger. One foot is on the animal. It reads, Jason at 14, first kill. A large smile is on the boy's face.

Kazan continues to study the paper work as he chews on his cigar.

"Graham, Graham, Graham, my boy you have done extremely well. Now tell me again how do we reverse this curse? Supposing this is a curse we are under which I still don't buy. Children, Graham? Kids my son's age? Beating me? Now that we know who they are let's just end it."

"That might not do it sir. It's not really a curse — well it's your curse — but what I really mean is we need to look at their history.

It seems these kids do have authentic powers which I can't seem to figure out. There also seems to be some lineage to this going back as far as time itself. The folklore goes something to the effect that these children are here to protect the weak and frail but the powers they have will be lost as they mature into adults. A natural fading, if you will. Then another group will take their place. In none of my snooping have I seen any adults who can do this and it's always a different group of kids."

"So if we eradicate them then another bunch of brats takes their place?"

Graham looks at Kazan. "Exactly, sir. I think we need to beat them or have them beat themselves."

As Graham speaks Kazan is closely studying the book. The shadows on the walls seem to congregate around Kazan and some settle across his face as he closes the book.

"Graham, we are losing billions every day. I can't wait that long. A natural fading, please. I am already hemorrhaging money. I can't wait for a bunch of kids to grow up. We need to make them grow out of these powers quickly."

Kazan can feel his rage building and Graham sees this as well. As his boss starts to get angrier Graham thinks the shadows are getting darker and thicker.

"I'll let it go a little bit longer," Graham thinks. "Maybe if I play this out I can get a promotion and be paid what I'm truly worth but I can't let it go too long. That in itself would be really dangerous for me."

"There has to be something we can do now and I'm not even sure I believe this crap. Everything has an explanation and you want me to believe in a myth, folklore?"

"Sir, it's all documented. All through the ages. I'm not sure how or when it started but these kids seem to be real. Always changing but the basic premise is the same. To stop people like us." Yes, "us." Include myself in this and I'll solidify an alliance.

Kazan sits back and crosses his large arms. "There's more,"

he thinks. "I'm not going to play this game anymore. It's time we ended this dance."

"Graham what are you not telling me?"

Graham gets a little worried as a dark shadow crosses his boss's face where a smile starts to emerge. The smile says, "I've got you now, Wellington and in this chess match you're in checkmate, remember that."

"So spill it and we'll talk about you getting your promotion and raise. What else is there?"

"I've spent lots of time on this sir and it's not for personal gain." They both know this is a lie. "The only other way is if they use their power in anger. It was documented that a band of these kids had lost their powers this way. Not many, mind you, because it seems that the kids chosen have an innocence so pure that they cannot be corrupted."

"Everyone has a price, Wellington, and everyone is corruptible." Kazan smiles again, reliving all his great moments in corruptibility.

"Well sir, here you might be wrong. The only instances where they failed were when one of the kids acted in anger. Seems that there has never been a member corrupted but anger has ended, I think, one or two of these bands from achieving their goals. There seemed to be a lapse of these children of light for fifty years, after World War Two. It took a while before they surfaced again. There also was a period during the Middle Ages that the good was gone. Hundreds of years it seems. Then during the Crusades. You see, Mr. Kazan, using their powers in anger will void them of their innocence, their purity. I do realize that the whole thing seems farfetched but I do have a lot of documentation on this."

Kazan stands and walks over and stops by a fireplace in his office. You would think that the light from the fire would cast away the shadows that played around him but not these shadows. No, the light has no effect on this darkness. Over the fireplace sits a painting of his son Jason. The same picture with the tiger, only painted by an artist. Kazan rubs his chin.

"This Lily Leso is evidently the leader of this group sir, so maybe if we could . . .," but Graham is quickly interrupted.

"I have a plan. We'll set her up and make this Lily Leso angry. Make her lose her cool as the kids say and so along with that will go her so-called innocence. If this is true, which I still have my doubts, we will take away her innocence and her power. You see Graham, I don't believe in hocus pocus. I do, however, believe in the great power of the mind. And the way I am losing money, I will stick the pin in this voodoo doll myself. Here is what I want to do."

Kazan lays out a plan and Graham listens intently.

"And if this doesn't work?"

"Well, unfortunately, you know what we have to do if it doesn't work. These kids or whatever they are can no longer be allowed to disrupt my plans. Business is business. If this doesn't work then I have men who will make these kids just disappear."

"Then there will just be others to replace them. I think our first plan will work. Mr. Kazan. This may or may not be the time but I was hoping this would earn me that promotion you mentioned."

Haran Kazan walks over to Graham Wellington and places his hand on his shoulder. His huge hands wrap around Graham's shoulders and the long thick fingers come down across his chest. They both look at the painting of the adolescent Jason.

"Wellington, you do realize there is no promotion from where you're at. You have the highest position in the whole company. You get everything you want, sometimes before you want it. I have trusted you with my most prized possession, my legacy, my Jason. That is where you will stay and you will stay for as long as Jason and I need you."

Graham looks down in disappointment but he does know there will be monetary compensation that will follow if all goes as planned.

"Now no one is to know what we are about to embark on. I want this to be hush hush son." Graham has a moment of joy at

Kazan calling him son and then he just feels a little uneasy, almost dirty as shadows play across his face. He feels suffocated but then that feeling quickly ends only to be replaced by joy as a big smile crosses his face. A seemingly forced smile. Forced by shadows.

CHAPTER SEVENTEEN

The Trap

Outside the city of Detroit there is a landfill that had been closed by the federal government. It seems that non-regulation had helped make this site one of the top five landfills to make the Superfund list of the most toxic dumps in the United States. The dump is surrounded by high fences and razor wire. It looks like a prison, not to keep anything in but to keep everything and every-one out.

Now the non-regulations have made some people very rich but in turn it also made some others very sick. There was an unusual spike in cancer cases in this small neighborhood around the dump and when it was found that pharmaceutical companies had been dumping toxic waste into this landfill for years, everyone distanced themselves.

No one counted on the toxins leaching into the water system and people starting to get sick and die. Then, and only then, did the feds step in. When children start to get diseases like leukemia and die officials get uneasy no matter how profitable doing nothing is. No one wants a dirty money trail to be traced back to them. The government officials who let this happen and made out financially were the most vocal against this travesty.

"How could this happen? We'll get to the bottom of this." Typical.

The private sector that caused this mess was then forced to stop all dumping. The federal folks decided that after such a large number of cancer cases and the snooping of reporters it would be better to just close the dump and make like nothing ever happened. But as we said when children die it's not so easy to walk away.

Funny, but even with an impending civil suit and a ninety percent rise in cancer cases some politicians were still arguing about the rightness of closing the site. How the company would be impacted. The locals actually took the ill and dying to Washington and camped outside a couple of official offices waiting for a representative of the government to meet them. Instead a stern-faced secretary came out and was very nice. She told everyone that their Congressman had their best intentions at heart and that he would push for an investigation and compensation. Money is always good to give people who are dying because that's when you need it most.

The people had been heard. Yes, heard and some of them paid off but the rest started to file a class action suit. It turns out that their representative was also part of a foursome that played in Florida every winter with the CEO of the company that was dumping the toxins into the landfill. The folks even named this certain politician in their lawsuit. That's around the time the fences and razor wire were put up and no more trucks could be heard or seen. Then a big sign showed up saying "Closed. Environmental Hazard. Keep Out."

Their representative also took all the credit for shutting down this dangerous landfill to protect his constituents. In typical political fashion he condemned the company who did the dumping. But behind closed doors he sat and counted his money and thanked God for the great health care that was provided to him and his family, thanks to the kindness of the people he was killing. While he spoke at the press conference announcing, "I will not tolerate this atrocity to be leveled at my people," a dark shadow played across his face. His smile was a bright black in the middle of a sunlit day.

This was some sort of victory for the lower-middle-class neighborhood that took the brunt of watching their neighbors and themselves get sick and die. The sick and dying received ten thousand dollars each — just enough to cover the cost of a really nice funeral.

You would think that a person would have a little more integrity than to put toxic waste in a dump located a couple of blocks from an elementary school and a church. Golf isn't that good a reason to kill people. Or is it? There hasn't been any activity at this site since the closing two years ago but that all changes tonight.

The night is dark and peaceful as three large trucks pull up to the gates of this closed-down landfill. The lettering on the side of the trucks reads toxic and hazardous materials. A night guard, who is supposed to tell people the dump is closed, can be seen talking to the driver in the first truck.

"Talonthorn Corporation," the truck driver says.

The security guard sounds angry as he looks around expecting something to happen.

"You cats weren't supposed to show up until 1:00 am. Man, you know how hot you guys are for dumping this stuff. We're supposed to be closed and you come here advertising toxic waste.

How about I just call the feds and turn myself in. Don't your bosses know anything about being a little discreet?"

The truck driver hands the gate attendant an envelope which contains a wad of money. The gate attendant has six kids and this envelope has ten years of his salary in it. As soon as he realizes how much money he has just received he opens the gate.

"Shut up and go count your money," the driver says.

Behind the trucks a junkyard dog can be seen picking through garbage and without anyone's concern, follows the truck through the gate and into the dump. The guard sees the dog but he's too busy counting his money for the third time and who really cares about another dump dog anyway. Usually he would take out his gun and shoot it but he is too busy thinking of the things he can do with his newfound fortune. The dog disappears behind a gate and reshapes into Callie Yung, the little Asian girl, the shape changer.

A vine along the fence starts to move and then transforms into a small African girl; it's Nora. The truck pulls back up to a deep hole. Two men jump from the cab and run to the back of the truck. They are looking around because their prime objective is not to be caught. These men are dressed in yellow HazMat suits and start to unload large chemical drums from the trucks.

"These things seem awfully light. What's in these things?" one of the men asks.

A tall man who looks like he is in charge says in an English accent, "That's not your concern, is it. Shut up and just unload these barrels." It's Graham Wellington.

As they start to unload the barrels no one takes notice of a point of light coming toward them.

This spot of light can be seen hovering just above the tree lines. From this angle is could be a star or a reflection of a street light but it is neither of those. If one of these men had taken notice they would be able to make out a small figure. It was Lily in her armor gliding on pads of light.

The moon casts a pale shadow and it is difficult to see but Lily knows that Nora is reshaping herself back into a net of vines and is creeping over the open hole. The plan is to catch the drums before they fall into the open pit and hold them so as not to make contact with the ground.

The children are all connected with a telepathic link. Knowing and hearing what each is doing and saying. They are always talking to each other without ever saying a word. This is the work of the armor that Lily wears. It keeps the children in tune with their leader and with each other. They were there to stop these men from unloading any of this toxic sludge.

The wind starts to pick up, blowing dust everywhere making it difficult for the men to see.

"Where the heck did this wind come from?" one of the men says as he wipes dust from his eyes.

Carlos, the element child, has commanded the wind to blow hard to slow these men down while Nora covers the hole in vines. Water starts to bubble up from the ground making it muddy so the men are having a difficult time walking thanks to Edward Carl, who controls water. Edward has also made the ground under the wheels of the trucks wet so the tires start to sink a little.

"Where the heck did all this water come from? Is this toxic or something?"

"Keep unloading. I don't care if you are standing on plutonium, your family will have enough money to live a comfortable life once you are gone. Keep going," the man in charge yells but Graham knows what is going on and the plan is working perfectly.

An owl can be heard in a tree overlooking this place. Keeping a look out is Callie, in the shape of an owl making sure there are no other men around that could interfere with their mission. Right outside the front gate in the middle of the entrance a bump starts to form cracking the asphalt in the road. It gets higher and higher blocking the front gate.

This small hill wasn't there when the trucks rolled in because they would have never gotten inside the dump and now they can't get out. If you looked at the dirt mound closely it seems to move ever so slowly, growing bigger.

Gregor, who has the power of the earth, is using his power now to make sure the entrance is blocked. The guard doesn't even notice the large dirt pile that blocks the entrance because he left as soon as he got paid. He hated this job and with the money he got tonight he is going to make a change in his life. Unfortunately he will spend it in a couple of weeks and now not only will he be out of a job but he will be arrested for leaving his post at a federal Superfund clean-up site. Greed is a nasty thing.

Lily floats over the fence and settles behind one of the trucks as she watches all this action taking place.

"Good, As soon as the drums are being held by Nora the police will be notified and these men will be trapped," she thinks; the other children nod in agreement.

The armor which is usually glowing like the sun has dimmed so as not to be noticed. Nora has spread her vines across the large hole but in the dark it was very difficult to see her. As the men get ready to push the drums over the edge of the hole Lily notices out of the corner of her eye a man talking to the tall man and pointing into the hole.

"Go get the torch and we can cut our way through this," Graham says to the man.

The man runs off and comes back with a blowtorch. In the dark the torch blazes against the ground. The man kneels down and starts to burn the vines that cover the hole. Lily cries out to Nora mentally. Lily gets no response.

Lily screams as the glow of the torch touches the vine. The vines catch fire and start to burn.

White light pads appear beneath her feet and she rises into the air. She flies towards the man with the torch her hair flying behind her.

"No! Nora! No!"

Lily's screams are all for naught because the man sets more of the vines ablaze.

All the men turn toward her as the one man continues to burn Nora.

"Oh my Nora," Lily screams looking around for her band members but with the dark shadows dancing around she can't see anything but black. Lily's face becomes enraged. A large shadow dark and inky falls across it. The once pleasant smile and little girl look changes into a mean, angry look. She lifts the Sword of Truth which is glowing with colorful power, gone is the pure white light. Her hair is swirling as she flies towards the man with the blow torch. As she gets closer she raises her sword high above her head and swings it towards the man.

"NO!" A scream is heard from the children standing there but it's too late. The man collapses sheared in two by the power of the sword. All the other men see this and stand watching. Her armor which is always a bright pure white light is now dark and black as if a light switch had been turned off on a once glowing bulb.

She settles back onto the ground and strikes an offensive pose with the sword out in front of her. She keeps it in front of her and circles around looking for more men "Come on, come on you cowards," she screams but the men just stand there looking at her.

Shadows play all around Lily and a dark, deep laughter can be heard in the distance. All Lily can think of is retribution. Her sword swinging around ready to cut down anyone around her until a soft hand touches her shoulder. She turns as if to attack but it's Nora and she's alive.

"You're...you're alive...but how?"

Suddenly giant work lights illuminate the dump site. A large projector screen can be seen on one side of the dump. Lily looks down to see the man with the blowtorch is actually a mechanical figure. He is shorted out now but his legs are still moving. Lily, stunned, drops the sword to the ground. Its light extinguished, it is now just a handle. The once bright light that shaped the sword blade is gone.

Slowly the other children appear and walk over to stand with

Lily. All of them are confused as they look at the projector screen. The men who have run into the dark all come back and stand around the children. They all take their headgear off and laugh.

Gregor, who was at the entrance of the dump, walks over and shakes the toxic drum. He knocks on it and it produces an empty sound.

"It is empty, Lily," he says in Russian but the children don't understand him any longer. They can tell by the sound that it's empty but it seems all communication between them is gone.

Lily looks stunned. "We've been tricked. Oh no what have I done? I couldn't see anything but that darkness."

Lily looks down and the once bright armor is dark and now fading along with the sword. Slowly the Sword of Truth and the Armor of Innocence disappear in a vortex back into the amulet around Lily's neck. Light is pulled from the other children and is also absorbed into the amulet. The children all fall to the ground. They look dazed and confused but they know what has happened. Anger has won the day. The darkness is joyous in its victory. Around the world there are more robberies and murders. More people than ever before are stealing from other people and hurting animals. Rain starts to come down. Earth's mother is crying.

Suddenly Haran Kazan appears via satellite on the large screen. He is holding the burnt vines that Lily thought were her friend. Looking around, Lily and the others realize there are cameras mounted throughout the landfill.

"Ahhhh, Lily. My poor girl. Technology is something, isn't it? You are starting to realize now that you have made a most grievous error and are powerless, you are no longer pure — are you? Haha. You have caused me quite a headache with these little games. Well, now the games are over. Once again I win. Isn't it past your bedtime children? Go home, kids, while I still let you. If I ever hear from you again it won't be just you I take down it will be your whole lineage. Nighty night, and sleep tight."

The lights shut off and the men get into the trucks and they pull away leaving the now powerless Band of Innocence.

"He is right. He wins," a little boy says in Spanish.

The children start to fade away being taken back to their homes leaving only Lily to stand alone. Lily grabs the amulet. A tear forms in her eyes. She has failed. The amulet glows then the glow goes out. All is dark. Yes it has won. The darkness has beaten this band. Her teardrop falls and hits the ground. A slight sparkle can be seen. Almost unnoticeable but a sparkle just the same. All these events fade and Lily finds herself in her bedroom.

She wakes up as if she was in a bad dream. Lily can't get last night's events out of her mind.

"How long has it been? I can't seem to remember," she thinks to herself. "Oh my god I failed my planet, my friends and grandma."

She climbs out of bed and the sun is high in the sky. She starts to shake with her head down and slowly slumps onto the floor.

As she sits there, in her room, she sees a newspaper on her floor. As she turns the pages of the newspaper she comes across a page about oil drilling in the Arctic. Her mouth opens wide and she turns on the TV. All she sees is war, greed and suffering.

"I can't believe I let everyone down. I failed Grandma Natu and my brothers and sisters and the whole world. Am I the only leader to have failed? Oh my God, what have I done? Now there is no one to protect the weak and innocent."

Lily holds the amulet around her neck. She is crying now. Tears stream down her face. She begins to remove the amulet but she doesn't notice that it begins to glow.

"I can't wear this any longer. I was not the one that they wanted or needed. I wish I was never part of this band."

As she struggles with the clasp the amulet starts to glow brighter and Lily looks down at it. As she takes hold of it light starts to pour out through her fingers. It turns her once dimly lit room bright in all the colors of the rainbow and in this light a figure appears. It's Grandma Natu in her Mother Nature state: dark ebony granite skin, hair as thick as a forest and eyes as blue as the waters of the Mediterranean.

"Lily. Child what are you doing? Stop. Do not take off the amulet."

"Grandma....I've failed. I acted in anger. Someone else needs to wear this amulet. Someone other than me."

"No, my child. Listen to me. This was all foreseen before you were even accepted."

"What do you mean, foreseen? You knew I was going to fail?"

"You didn't fail. You did what you had to. Sometimes from failure great success is won. Sometimes when the battle is lost it's to win the war, my dear."

"I let you down. I let my friends down. I let the world down."

"You let no one down. It was meant to be. You must prepare for the Pure One's arrival. The dark forces are looking away now. They think they have won and the light is gone forever. They are busy corrupting and destroying, the things they do best but we now have a chance."

"I'm not sure I understand Grandma,"

"Your brother Bill will grow and have a child. She will be the pure one. The savior.

She will be the most innocent of the innocent. You will be her protector and guide because you are special, my child, and will always retain a little bit of that pure innocence that you have deep inside you."

"That is your mission. That is your calling. You needed to go through this to make you who you will become. Your innocence will always be with you because that's who you are and you will always be a part of the Band. Innocence leads to greatness. Look around you at the world's leaders. The great ones were part of the Band. The children on the walls of the cave. Remember? Martin, John, Theresa, Susan, Alexander. All these children were strong and famous. They were leaders because of their innocence. They never forgot their dreams. Their beliefs. Their faith in themselves and others. That's you."

"So my losing was actually my winning. Okay, I hit my head again. I don't understand."

"You were close to your time with the Band Lily. You had grown. When people grow they lose a certain part of that pure innocence. People can hold onto some of it but most choose not to. You my dear will never lose that part of you. We needed to have the darkness think that we had lost. Remember that when you failed it was merely a prelude to a future success. Enjoy the failure as if you had won. You are right where you should be."

"When will she come, Grandma?"

"Soon, my dear. Rejoice you have done your part and your part is not done. I will always be with you."

Outside the hall of Lily's room Milly Leso is standing and hears her daughter talking to someone. She can see light flickering under the door.

"Lily dear. Are you okay?" Milly asks as she puts her ear to the door.

She knocks on the door but Lily doesn't answer.

"Honey. Are you okay?"

Lily doesn't hear her mother and is sitting in the middle of the room with light all around talking to Grandma Natu as Milly opens the door. As soon as the door opens all the light gets absorbed into the amulet and the room is back to normal.

"Are you alright honey? I heard you talking to someone."

"Yes, Mom, I was talking to Grandma."

"Uh Lil, you know, I think, uh never mind," Milly stammers.

Milly looks around the room and then at her daughter who is sitting cross legged on the floor and with a raised eyebrow, Milly slowly closes the door and steps back into the hall. She pauses and shakes her head then walks away. Lily smiles and holds the amulet.

"I can wait and then we will come for you, Mr. Kazan," Lily whispers to herself.

CHAPTER EIGHTEEN

The Future

It seems like only yesterday that Lily sat in her room speaking to Grandma Natu about her failure and now here she sits with her niece. The pure one. The one to lead the new Band. So many years have passed since the Band was active in its role as protector and guardian of this planet and a lot has been lost. Species of plants and animals have disappeared, the air has become more polluted and the seas have been battered and bruised with oil and garbage spewed into them. Most of this destruction was led by one man, Haran Kazan.

"If only I could have stopped him when I had the chance," Lily thought but that time is over. The past is all a memory which you learn from, and to have a secure future you must act in the present moment. All the teachings of Grandma Natu have not been lost on Lily. Grandma knew Lily would make the perfect teacher.

Lily looks over at Emily and her two cats. She knows that Em is absorbing this story like a sponge retains the water you pour into it. If you pour the water slowly very little is lost. Lily has been feeding Emily information about the Band of Innocence since she was merely a toddler. Slowly, lesson by lesson, Emily heard all the stories and tales of adventure and valor of the prior bands.

Emily, without even realizing these stories were true, heard the tales of Martin Luther King and his band, Gandhi and his band and all the other great leaders and their conflicts and successes. These great people who carried their innocence and beliefs with them like a banner, and gathered millions of followers to carry out their dreams of peace and compassion.

Now it's Emily's turn. Here the cave is so nice and warm as Lily looks at her niece.

"I wish we could just sit here forever. She is so precious and pure. What if she is also corrupted?" Lily's brow furrows at the thought but she quickly pushes these thoughts aside.

Emily looks up at her aunt and pauses with a quizzical look on her face.

"That last story was about you, Aunt Lily, wasn't it?" Emily sits up.

"Yes Em, I was your age. All the stories I have told you have led us to this story, my story," Lily says to Emily.

"Now, I have prepared the way for you. I will look after you and I swear nothing will ever happen to you and you will not fail in your mission," Lily thinks.

Lily continues to read.

Color starts to flicker from the amulet around her aunt's neck. At first it looked like a reflection but then Emily noticed it was actually coming from the amulet itself. At times Emily felt that she was sleeping but all the while her aunt's voice could be heard telling the story.

"Such a soothing voice," Emily thinks.

As Lily continues the story the light from the amulet starts to get brighter and brighter. The colors start to get richer and richer.

All the colors of the spectrum begin to fill the make-believe cave as Emily continues to listen to her aunt's story. Aunt Lily doesn't seem bothered by the light. She just keeps on reading. Emily notices that the story matches exactly what is going on in the cave at this moment.

As Lily reads the story of how the walls of the make-believe cave become real, Emily realizes that the walls of this make-believe cave start to look like a real cave. The blanket walls are gone, replaced by stone. Emily gets up, as Rhett and Scarlett meow, and she touches the walls. She is amazed that they feel like stone.

"This is incredible," Emily thinks.

Aunt Lily continues reading about the young girl not believing that the cave walls have turned to stone.

"Wait, now you're reading about me." Emily says to herself.

"Aunt Lily. Aunt Lily can you hear me," but her aunt just keeps reading.

"I think I'm still sleeping," Emily says to herself in a soft whisper.

In the background Emily hears dripping water that is echoed in these cave walls. All of a sudden the back of the cave, which was just a piece of cardboard minutes ago, is gone. As matter of fact the whole back of the cave has opened up. There is a path that leads down. Both Rhett and Scarlett start down the path and turn towards Emily.

"Meow," they say as if they are calling for her to follow.

Emily turns back towards Aunt Lily but she is gone too and Emily feels the need to follow her cats down the path.

All the while she can hear her aunt telling the story. Lily's voice never stops reading, as Emily listens to exactly what's going on.

"As the young girl realizes that a path has opened up, her two cats lead her down this rock path."

Scarlett and Rhett never leave Emily's sight, turning every few steps to make sure their ward was following them. Emily is realizing that these cats know exactly where they are going.

"Rhett, Scarlett where are you taking me? This is kind of crazy."

"Meow," says Rhett. In some way it's a reassuring meow if that's at all possible.

As she goes down the dark path she starts to see cave drawings on the walls as Lily had seen years before. They seem to come to life and dance around her. She stops in amazement and reaches her hand out to touch them. Her hand goes right through them but they never stop their dance. There are figures on horses with swords and animals running. Trees and plants are growing right before her eyes. Waterfalls and birds flying over mountains and forests all so vivid and all so real.

"This is the oddest dream I have ever had," Emily thinks.

She keeps going down the dark path touching the walls so as not to fall. Light can be seen coming from an opening somewhere down the path.

"Okay, I've fallen asleep and now I'm the one in the Alice in thingy land story," she says to herself, "but instead of following a rabbit I'm following two crazy cats." Both her cats turn and meow at her.

"I'm sorry you aren't anything like a rabbit," Emily giggles.

"You understand everything I say, don't you?"

The cats meow again, saying "yes we do and we are not crazy."

Emily proceeds down the path toward the light. As she comes to an opening she peeks around the corner and now sees where the light is coming from and she lets out a gasp. Just like the stories she was told and like the story she is being told.

The light is coming from the center of a huge chamber. She

looks up and can't even see the top of this cave. As the light spins it reflects off the walls and Emily can see statues all around the cave. There must be hundreds. Each time the light hits these statues they seem to move into different positions. As the light reflects off the walls she sees all the figures on the walls are now kneeling with their heads bent down.

The light is so bright at points that she has to cover her eyes. She slowly walks into the chamber and sees exactly where the light is coming from. Her cats are now behind her nudging her legs forward.

"Meow, meow."

"Hey no pushing, I'm going, I'm going," Emily says to them.

In the center of the chamber, hovering above a white marble pedestal is Aunt Lily's amulet. The gold chain is suspended upwards and the amulet is hanging and spinning slowly like a mobile. Emily is standing in the middle of this huge chamber that is filled with light. She can still hear Aunt Lily's voice reading about exactly what was going on.

"The little girl was mesmerized by the light coming from the amulet. Like all the children that have come before her and the ones that will follow the young one stares while her body is bathed in the warm light that is radiating from this amulet."

Like years before, the amulet starts to drip a silver liquid as it once did for Lily. The silver stream of liquid flows slowly towards Emily, running across the floor until it touches her feet.

Emily moves backwards but is stopped by Scarlett.

"Hey," Emily says loudly and it echoes through the cave. The silver liquid continues to lick at her feet.

The liquid feels cool as it travels up her legs until she is covered by the armor.

Emily spins around looking down at the bright, shining armor. It doesn't feel heavy at all. It feels like her skin, soft and pliable.

A loud meow breaks the silence and echoes through the chamber as Rhett and Scarlett, not wanting to be left out, leap onto Emily and drape their bodies over her shoulders. They are immediately absorbed by the armor. The light from the amulet changes from a pure white light to a spectrum of different colors as in celebration of this event. A coronation, if you will, of the new one. The pure one.

Flashes of the past seem to hit Emily as her body flinches. She sees the creators, the beginning of time and Mother Nature herself.

A murmur of voices, children's voices, can be slightly heard in the background. Emily can hear laughter and talking but she can't understand what any of them are saying. It sounds like recess at her school. The voices seem to be echoing off the walls.

White light starts to radiate from the armor that covers Emily. It seems to extend from her body, lighting up the cave.

"Jeez," Emily says as two oval light pads slowly form under her feet. They are like the circles in the game twister. They are bigger than her feet and she feels so light, as if they are pushing her up from the ground.

"This is insane. Scarlett, Rhett, are you two okay?" Emily says as her head goes from left to right to look at the two silver cats draped over her shoulders. Both cats are moving and meowing that everything is okay with them.

Emily's attention is pulled back to the amulet with all its colors, spinning above the pedestal.

A white shape starts to materialize out of the amulet and Emily hears Aunt Lily's voice continuing with the story: "The young one reaches into the light of the amulet and grabs the sword of truth."

Emily hesitates for a moment, then reaches into the light of the amulet, feeling a hard object. As she pulls the object out of the light she realizes it is the hilt of a sword with a blade of white light.

Emily doesn't seem to notice that she is hovering slightly off the ground. All the light from the amulet is reflecting off the armor. Finally Emily returns, feet to the ground, barely knowing she was hovering above the stone floor of the cave. Emily stands clad in silver from her feet to her neck. Her brown hair cascades around the two silver cats draped over her shoulders. A sheath is attached to her back which is also all silver. The sword of truth glows a bright white as she holds it in front of her looking like a true warrior.

All this is going on as the voice of Lily can be heard through the cave. Her voice echoes off the walls but the other voices in the cave start to get louder and louder.

"The armor accepted the little girl and then the sword of truth presented itself to her. She reached out and grabbed it as the voices of the ages could be heard calling."

The voices are so loud now that Emily can barely hear her aunt. The light starts to glow even brighter as the voices get louder. It all starts to get too much, so that Emily starts to look around wondering if and when it will stop, and then abruptly all the sound stops and the cave goes black for an instant.

The darkness is interrupted by a slight glow of the amulet and the sword. Out of the darkness, Aunt Lily walks towards her niece and then stands before Emily. She looks different. Younger and the silver streak in her hair shines with a bright light.

"It seems we all were correct in assuming it was you, Emily. We actually had no doubt at all. It was foretold that you would be the leader as I was before you but sometimes things take a slight detour. You look the true warrior, but you won't make the same mistake I made; I won't let you. Your light is so bright, the brightest. You have the gift and you will stay pure. Your innocence is so great that you will lead not only this band but this new age of goodness and purity. You are now the leader of the Band of Innocence. All the stories I have read to you have been preparing you for this."

Aunt Lily gets down on one knee and bows her head. The armor starts to glow as it illuminates the walls and all of the statues assume the same position as Aunt Lily.

"I feel like I'm asleep and this cave is all part of a wonderful dream Aunt Lily. I always thought the Band of Innocence was just a story. You do have such a great imagination."

Aunt Lily looks up at her niece.

"Imagination has nothing to do with this, my love. Yes, the Band of Innocence is a story but it's not based in fiction. It is as real as this world you live in. Tonight you will meet the rest of your band. The children you will lead, but before they appear I need to tell you one important truth. Never use the sword in anger. This and this alone will cut short your stay in the Band of Innocence. At this critical time a loss will be devastating to us. I was warned of this but I wasn't strong enough to control my emotions. You have to be. We are losing this planet and the Great Mother is weakening. She and her children, with their last bit of power, will wipe the Earth clean of all living things so they can start again if you do not save us. They have done that before. We are mankind's last hope."

"What do you mean, Aunt Lily?"

"The Mother has wiped out all that have lived here before. She and her children have brought floods and earthquakes to try and cleanse this world. Each time they destroyed everything to start over and keep this a pure planet. But each time the darkness has crept in and corrupted the world. The creators may erase all they created and just be done with this planet this time. We must not let that happen."

"The children you will meet tonight have heard the stories I have read to you in their own dreams. All of these children think they are asleep but tonight they will wake to a new beginning. You are the most innocent being in the world and these other children are also the world's most innocent. Tonight they will realize who and what they are, and what they are going to become."

Lily turns around and on one side of the cave are six pods. These tall cylindrical portals line the wall and they glimmer and glow different colors. One is green, one is blue, one is brown, one is white, one is red and one just sparkles with bits of light. Each cylinder is made of rock but has a glass front, like a window that you can look into. Light skips across each pod as they reflect the glow of the sword and the armor.

"How could I have missed those?" Emily thinks.

The portals start to glow even brighter and images start to appear in them. In each cylinder a child can be seen materializing.

The first pod, the green one, holds a heavyset boy with a basketball under his arm. He's dark skinned and wearing shorts and a Chicago Bulls jersey.

The next, a yellow pod, has a black girl with very feline features. Her long hair is braided and she's wearing a black track suit. She is tall and athletic looking.

Next to her is a small blond girl, in the white pod, with skin as white as snow. Her features are quite elfin. Her hair and eyebrows are almost as white as her skin. She is dressed in blue jeans with ripped knees and an "I Love NY" t-shirt.

Next to her is a girl with pigtails. Her hair is black and her skin is dark against the blue glow of this pod. She is dressed in American Indian attire. Her skirt is fringed along with her shirt. She has a headband and a large bird sits on her shoulder. The bird is snow white and it too is looking around incessantly.

In the next pod is an Asian boy. The pod he stands in glows a bright red. He has long black hair and he's dressed in all black. He, out of all the children stands with his head held high and chest puffed out. He does not look the least bit confused. He looks ready.

The last cylinder has a small black boy. He is by far the smallest of all the children and he also looks the most nervous. He looks to be the youngest and there are speckles of light that flicker across the glass part of his pod make it look like the sky, full of stars.

Lily steps towards the portals as the glass doors start to slide open and the children, looking confused, except for the one boy, step out of them. A smile comes across Aunt Lily's face.

"This will be the first band that has a guide. I hope I am up to the task."

These are her wards and she will protect them like they were her own children. As a mother lion protects her young.

"Welcome my children, welcome to the Band of Innocence. You have been chosen as the most innocent and heart-strong in the world. You are needed today to fight the ever-spreading darkness. We all have met but never in person. Your dreams were more real than even you could have ever imagined."

The boy with the basketball looks at Lily, then at his basketball and in Spanish he says, "It looks like we aren't in Peru anymore, Toto."

The other children don't understand him so Lily repeats in English and somehow even the children who don't understand English understand her.

There is some giggling but the children are still looking around in awe of their surroundings. The amulet that has been spinning ever so slowly starts to speed up and light seems to jump out of it. Beams of light that are very narrow spin around the chamber. Every once in a while a beam will hit a child and be absorbed into that child. Different colored light hits the different children.

The Asian boy jumps as the light pierces his body. The little girl with the pigtails opens her arms, accepting the light and giggling.

"Do not be frightened, children; the creators are accepting you as their hosts. You will have powers and memories of the ages. You will be the new heroes of your generation. Good is the new way, you are the new light and you have all been born with both."

Emily is witnessing the host process. Images of the creators can be seen in the light that is being ingested into these children. The elders or creators are accepting their hosts. The children start to turn into the elders who have inhabited their bodies.

The boy with the basketball turns into a large man with plants and vines wrapped around him. He looks like an Inca king, gold staff and Jaguar crown.

The black girl with the braids turns into a fierce warrior princess with spear and shield.

The blond girl turns into a Norse Viking princess. She is holding a battle staff and is wearing a helmet of silver.

The Indian girl with the white bird on her shoulder turns into a human form made of water and foam.

The Asian boy turns into a large figure made of stone that glows from molten rock that runs continuously across his body. Wisps of smoke can be seen coming from his body.

The small black boy remains unchanged. He seems so tiny next to the alter egos of the other children. These creators or gods of this world look at each other and smile. The plant god flexes his arms as if he had not used them in quite some time. The Viking warrior holds her staff above her head.

As the creators relish their freedom from the amulet Emily turns to her Aunt Lily.

"Aunt Lily, who is the little boy? He has no one to stand with?"

"That is Jimmy. He will be the soul of this group. No one stands with him but he stands with many. Yours is the only Band that has one with his powers. His power comes from his innocence just as your strength comes from yours."

"Now, children, I think it best to introduce ourselves. You all know who I am. You have seen me walk in and out of your dreams. Santiago, you start. You and Toto." Lily laughs. So do some of the gods.

The first elder starts to talk as he changes back into a kid. He is speaking in an ancient language but all the kids understand him.

"I am Santiago Cordon from Peru. I have within me the power of all that grows: the power of Wiraquocha. I hold in my hands the seeds of life. I feel what the plants feel and see what the trees see." Under his feet beautiful thick grass starts to grow.

The warrior princess with shield and spear steps forward and bows her head. She is dressed in a long dress made of fur and beads. Her form changes into that of the young girl with the tight braids.

"I am Paka from Kenya. I have the soul of Minona the animal elder inside of me. I can become any animal and talk to all animals. I have created them and will die protecting them as they are my children."

The Norse Viking is the next to speak. Again, like the others, she bows her head in reverence and begins to take the shape of a small girl.

"I am Edda from Norway. I have control of all the elements: rain, wind and thunder. I can bring down snow and call for lightning."

The creature made of water is next to step forward. Although shaped like a human the water and foam keep swirling all through him. Pools of water are left where he stands. As he speaks his body turns into that of a small girl with black pigtails.

"I am Fala and I am a Choctaw Indian. I am being taught to be a shaman. I possess all of the knowledge and magic of my ancestors — The Great Spirits. My people were one with the spirits, as I am. As you can see, sitting on my shoulder is crow. Crow has one eye in the spirit world and one eye in the real world. He is the bird of my ancestors. I also have the water spirit, Unktahee, within me. I can control all the seas and oceans."

As the last large figure steps forward the ground seems to shake. This large stone man speaks with a gravelly voice. As with all the children this elder spirit takes the shape of the child who is hosting him. An Asian boy is revealed.

"I am Victor. I'm from Tibet. I have the Earth Spirit in me, Tu Di Gong. I can be as unmovable as stone yet as liquid as molten lava. I have the knowledge of the centuries that the Earth and rock have gained."

All eyes are on the little black boy who doesn't look up. He seems lost in this group of children. The children start to hear him talk even though he doesn't say a word. He is talking with his hands.

"I am Jimmy Curtis. I come from Los Angeles, California, and I am hearing impaired. I am also an empath. That means I can feel emotions all around. I can start an emotion in someone as long as there's just a spark or seed of that emotion already in their soul. I have no one inside me but many inside of me."

Emily looks up at Lily. "I can hear everything he is saying and I understand the other children as well. How's that possible?"

Jimmy smiles so Emily realizes he understands her. "How can she hear me?"

"The armor, Emily that you are wearing has given everyone here the ability to talk to one another and understand each other without you even having to speak to them. You will always be connected even when apart."

At that moment the lives of these children are revealed through the armor. Each child sees themselves and the others from their births up to this day.

CHAPTER NINETEEN

Emily Leso

Each child almost lost their lives at the hand of the darkness. Emily Leso had a near-death experience at the hands of evil koi fish. When her Aunt Lily was asked what her life's mission was, she responded with, "I guess I was put here to watch over Emily."

As Emily grew her innocence and truth grew along with her. She always had a smile for everyone and was always ready to share either her toys or supper with her friends, and everyone else — I mean everyone was her friend.

During her first year in kindergarten a child entered the class in the middle of the year. This child was Terry Kingston. Terry was born with a spinal disorder and was confined to a wheelchair. When the teacher introduced her to the class all the kids were quietly staring and some were whispering.

"Class please quiet down. This is Terry Kingston and she is a new student here. Is there someone who would like to mentor her and show her the ropes?"

Immediately Emily jumped up and asked the teacher if she could be Terry's partner for the day.

"What happened to your legs, Terry?" asked Emily. Terry was shocked. No one ever asked her what was wrong; they just stared. Terry looked into Emily's eyes and was filled with the compassion this child had for her. It was like a pure white light sprang from her body. Terry found herself smiling ear to ear, something she hadn't done in a long time.

"I was born this way, Emily. I wasn't as lucky as you."

"You were very lucky Terry. You were born and now you're my friend."

From that day on Terry and Emily were inseparable.

Terry's mother found out what had happened at school and went straight to the Leso's house shortly after to find out who this child Emily was, because Terry could not stop talking about her.

Sue Leso was in the kitchen when a loud knock on the front door resonated through the front hall. Now that could have startled Sue but just before the knock a loud creak could be heard coming from the front of the house.

"Better than any alarm system," Sue thinks.

"Thanks Elizabeth, I'll get the door," Sue says, smiling. Another creak signifies Elizabeth saying, "You're welcome." Sue walks to the door shaking her head and smiling.

"I love this house," she thinks. Sue opens the door expecting the delivery of groceries but instead, standing there, is a stern-looking woman with her arms crossed.

"Mrs. Leso, I'm Carla Kingston. Is your daughter Emily?'

"Why, yes. Is something wrong?"

"Now I'm not sure how to say this but I want to be totally honest with you, Mrs. Leso."

Carla Kingston is a tall, heavyset woman. Her brown hair is pulled back tight into a ponytail. Dressed in a grey pin-striped suit she is definitely looking down on Sue. She is wearing thin metal framed sunglasses.

Sue immediately thinks "Uh-oh."

"Why don't you come in, Mrs. Kingston."

"Thank you."

As Carla Kingston walks into the foyer of the house she feels a warmth that she has seldom felt, a welcoming feeling.

"What a safe place to be," she thinks.

"Creak," goes the foyer floor.

Sue can't help but smile. "Even Elizabeth is on her best behavior," she thinks.

"Now what seems to be the problem, Mrs. Kingston? Oh and call me Sue, please."

Sue was expecting a response to that, as in "And you can call me whatever." Sue got nothing.

"This may not be good," Sue thinks.

"Well Mrs. Leso, my Terry has been confined to a wheelchair and when my daughter was introduced in front of the class today your daughter was asking a lot of questions about what happened to Terry and why she's in a wheelchair." Mrs. Kingston steps back with her arms folded, a very defensive position some might say.

Sue felt so bad. "I'm sorry, Mrs. Kingston, but Emily is very open and truthful, possibly to a fault. I hope she didn't hurt your daughter's feelings."

Carla's stern face softens and she smiles. Her arms find their way to her sides which opens her up to Sue and her warmth and compassion.

"Call me Carla, and on the contrary my daughter and I find this immensely refreshing. Your daughter Emily has included Terry in all the activities that took place in school today. It's as if Emily doesn't see that Terry is different. She just wouldn't take no for an answer."

"She doesn't see a difference, Mrs. Kingston, I mean, Carla. Emily says she only sees the light in people. The brighter the light the better she sees and you and I know that Terry isn't as different as some may think."

"Mrs. Leso, can I be frank with you? Terry has always thought of herself as a regular girl confined in a wheelchair but most folks don't get past the wheelchair. She has never truly felt accepted until she met Emily. Now all that is wonderful and I want to thank you and your daughter but there is just one thing that I really need you to tell your daughter for me. Your daughter taught something to Terry which is driving me crazy."

Susan thinks, "Oh no what could this be now?"

"Terry now answers to everything, with 'That's the way I roll, Mom.'" Carla holds her head and shakes it.

Susan didn't know what to say until Mrs. Kingston started to smile. The two women start laughing.

Emily's light gets brighter every time she shares her light with others. The more she gives the stronger her light becomes. Giving her compassion to Terry only made Emily stronger.

Another thing that keeps Emily pure is the foods she eats. Only pure, organic foods can enter her body. Aunt Lily has vowed to keep the poisons from entering Emily, the processed foods that will zap her strength. The purer the foods the more Emily shines and the stronger her light becomes.

CHAPTER TWENTY

Edda Stahl

Edda Stahl was born in Hamar, Norway on January 15th. Her family had for generations performed as the premier aerial artists throughout Europe. The Flying Stahls were so famous that Kings and Queens would attend every one of their performances. People would line up for days to get front-row seats to their shows. These events were always sold out for weeks and months ahead of schedule. They, in fact, were royalty. Edda's great-grandfather was knighted by Christian VIII, the King of Denmark, in the mid-1800s.

On the day Edda was born it seemed that the whole world darkened. Clouds covered the sky, huge black storm clouds congregated and one of the worst snowstorms to hit Hamar in centuries happened on that particular day. The world was dark and foreboding.

Vor, Edda's father, thought, "These are the darkest clouds I have ever seen. Could this be a bad omen?" He quickly pushed that thought out of his mind. Today was to be a joyous day. His daughter entered this world no matter if the world celebrated or not. He felt in his heart this was a blessing but his eyes and mind were more than a bit concerned.

Vor and his wife, Kirsten, had thought they would never have a child, that is, until Edda was conceived. The doctors had told them to adopt because they would never be able to have a baby on their own and just when they had given up Kirsten became pregnant.

Kirsten's mother had told them that they needed to relax and the gods would bless them with a child.

"Kirsten my dear, forget about babies and babies will find you," she said with a smile. "Worry begets nothing but more worry," was another saying of her mother's.

Kirsten was almost nine months pregnant when the day finally came. She woke up her sleeping husband. On that morning it seemed all odds were against them getting to the hospital. Dark and ominous shadows seemed to shroud the Stahls that morning. Kirsten had woken with pains in her belly and knew it was time to go. Vor looked outside but said nothing. No need to worry Kirsten with such details. He would find a way to get her to the hospital.

They opened the door to at least three feet of snow and a biting wind. A dark shadow seemed to descend on the pair as they stepped out. Black and inky is all Vor remembers it being.

As Vor placed Kirsten into the car she looked deep into Vor's eyes and he knew the baby was coming soon.

Without her saying a word, Vor said, "It will be fine, Mama." Just hearing those words from her husband calmed her heart.

He smiled and closed the door of the car. That dark shadow

followed him around the car as if it were trying to consume him. He slowly backed his car out of the drive and the blizzard seemed to get worse.

"How can this be?" he thought. "How can this storm get any worse?" But it did.

He couldn't see anything behind him and drove on instinct, having backed out of that driveway a thousand times before. He thought he heard a low, mean laughter as the darkness increased but attributed it to the howl of the wind.

As he pulled back into the street he looked at his wife. Never has he loved anything or anyone as much as he loved Kirsten.

"How will we get through this, Vor? I cannot see anything in front of us. It is so dark," Kirsten said.

The dark shadow had the little car in its grip and the snow came down so hard that the wipers could not keep up with the snow.

"We will make it, Mama. Now close your eyes and breathe."

As Vor took a deep breath he looked out of the front window and his eyes grew wide. It was a miracle.

The snow started to clear and there in the sky Vor thought he could see the face of a woman. At first Vor's thoughts quickly went to a game he played when he was a boy. Lying in a meadow and looking up at the sky. All the clouds would take shapes of horses and people. That's what this seemed like. The snow and clouds seemed to be forming a face, but this was different. When he played his cloud game the clouds would take shape and then break up but now the snow and clouds were forming a more visible face. The face started looking less like the clouds and more like a human face. A woman with striking blue eyes and long blonde hair. Her skin had a silver blue tint to it.

The face was just sitting there in the clouds. He could not take his eyes off of this apparition. He watched as she drew in a huge breath and blew a wind that separated the blizzard's snow so Vor could clearly see the road. Vor thought this had to be a hallucination but the snows parted and Vor had always been the kind of man that would jump at any opportunity. He wasn't going to wait for this apparition to disappear.

Before he stepped on the gas Vor looked up one last time. He swore that the woman in the clouds winked at him. The low laughter he had heard turned into a hiss and the dark shadow was gone. The snow kept falling all around them but not in front of them. It seemed that the snow was avoiding the car.

"How odd is this, I think I may have lost my mind," Vor thought and stepped on the gas. He drove quickly while the storm parted in front of him. They were actually making better time than if it had been a clear morning. There was no one on the road except the storm and the Stahls. As he neared the hospital he came around a tight turn.

The same dark shadow that covered the ground when they first got into the car was back. He could see it blanketing the road up ahead. This darkness hid the fact that ice had formed across the road exactly where the turn was tighter than most.

"I hear that laughter again," Vor thought but did not say anything.

He never saw the ice because of the dark, inky shadow and even if he had slowed down he would have had a hard time staying on the road.

"Oh Vor, the baby is coming," Kirsten was moaning.

"Hold on, Mama. Hold on."

Vor felt the car skidding around the turn.

"Oh no we aren't going to make it," he thought as the car started to slide off the side of the road. In moments the car would crash into the snow bank.

"This can't happen. We are going off the side of the road," Vor thought in that split second.

At the exact moment Vor thought all was lost a huge gust of wind swept across the little car, pushing it back onto the road.

Again the shadow ahead was gone and a hiss could be heard as if gas was escaping.

"Hahahaha. Oh my. The gods are truly with us tonight," Vor said out loud and without thinking gave the car more gas.

When they arrived at the hospital the nurses ran out to the car and were amazed that anyone could have made it in this storm. They quickly took Kirsten into the hospital and when Vor looked back at his car it was consumed by the storm. He looked up at the sky but saw only darkness and snow.

"How did you get here, Mr. Stahl?" a doctor asked him.

"A lot of luck and imagination," Vor said with a smile as he dabbed the sweat his forehead. Vor realized at that moment that the impossible became possible by some miracle.

"This baby wants to be born very badly, or some other force wants this baby born. Whatever the case, I'm finally going to be a father," Vor said to a nurse.

The hospital was working on generator power and the staff was short of nurses but since the storm was so bad there were no patients coming in so all the attention was on Vor and Kirsten.

It took only an hour and the Flying Stahls had a new addition to the family.

In the birthing room the doctor was telling Kirsten to relax and breathe. A nurse, who didn't look familiar to the doctor, stood by Kirsten whispering to her. Whatever this nurse was saying was calming Kirsten down. The doctor did notice the nurse's crystal blue eyes. At one point he was mesmerized by her.

"Doctor, the patient," the nurse quietly scolded him.

"Yes, I'm sorry, I just don't remember you, nurse."

"Is this the time for introductions or do you have a child to deliver?" the nurse said. Her cheeks raised above the mask so it was evident that she had a huge smile.

The doctor looked down at Kirsten. "Right, yes."

The doctor worked feverishly and in a matter of moments a small blue baby emerged.

As the doctor held the baby he looked at this miracle baby's face.

"Oh my god. This baby just smiled at me," the doctor said.

"Maybe she is happy to see you Doctor," the nurse said. The doctor looked at the baby and then back up and the nurse was gone. He looked around the room and he couldn't see her. Matter of fact he never saw her again.

The doctor's attention was quickly drawn to the blue child. He started to get worried, thinking that no oxygen was getting to the baby but the baby was cooing and moving her hands and legs. He took the child's temperature and it was normal.

The baby was handed to Kirsten. "Oh my little miracle. My little Edda."

Kirsten was crying when Vor came into the room.

"Why are you crying, my love?"

"Oh Vor, these are tears of joy. She is so beautiful."

"She is, but isn't she a bit blue?" Vor said, turning to the doctor.

"Mr. Stahl, Edda is completely healthy in every way. We will do more tests but I think the blue color is coming from the emergency lights reflecting on the baby's skin." The doctor had no idea, but this explanation sounded perfectly rational.

The doctor would always remember that night. A couple arriving in a storm that stopped the whole town, a nurse with amazing blue eyes that disappeared and a blue baby that smiled at him. What else could possibly happen? A drink was in order and that's what he did. Edda was moved into the pediatric ward where her skin color changed closer to a normal tone.

The generators were working overtime and the staff prayed that the storm would break before the generators did. A patient down the hall needed some attention so the pediatric nurse left Edda cooing and giggling in her little newborn bed. As soon as the nurse shut the door a darkness crept into the room. Low laughter could be heard coming from some distant place. All of a sudden the heat stopped in the pediatric ward. Edda was the only baby born that night so she was all alone. The temperature quickly plunged. In the twenty minutes it took for the nurse to come back the temperature went below 20 degrees. The nurse screamed as she ran into the room.

"Doctor, doctor come quick."

Vor heard this also and two other nurses quickly ran towards pediatrics.

As the doctor checked the baby Vor's breath was quite visible due to the drop in temperature.

There in her little bed Edda was making little happy noises although when the doctor took her temperature she registered 55 degrees. The doctor kept taking her temperature because most people would be dead but this baby seemed to thrive in the frigid weather. The nurses and doctor agreed that there was a rational explanation, something scientific, but Vor knew that the gods had given him a special child.

As Edda grew Vor and Kirsten realized that the cold or heat never bothered Edda. She could stand in waist-high snow with no shoes on and not even be bothered, let alone get a chill. She did retain that slightly bluish color, though. Her hair also was so blonde at times it seemed close to white. Someone said she looked almost elfish except for the fact that her ears weren't pointed. She was actually quite beautiful.

There were days when Kirsten would have to tell her to go inside and get dressed for the weather.

"Edda, please put on your boots."

"Why, Mama I don't need them."

"Yes but we don't want others knowing that. It might make them feel bad that they need to be bundled and you don't."

Edda didn't want anyone feeling bad, that's why she became a prankster. She could always get people to laugh but would never play a joke at someone else's expense. During the winter she would make the most wonderful snow statues. The snow would almost melt in her hands and mold to her wildly imaginative thoughts.

Edda, as all the children who grew up to be in the Band, was very allergic to processed foods. The doctor at birth told her parents to only give her organic foods since she looked so frail but Edda was anything but frail. Her looks were quite deceiving. She was the toughest kid in her school and not by strength but by tenacity. If Edda Stahl wanted to do something everyone knew she would be able to do it. When she ate the purest of foods it seemed her light would grow, her inner strength would increase and the joy she would spread could be felt by everyone.

Edda took to the trapeze like a bird takes to flight and her family knew she was blessed. She did have one near-death experience as all the children did when the darkness knows you are its enemy. When Edda was three her uncle strapped her to his back and took her high up to the top platform of the performance arena.

"Let's see if she has the Stahl courage, Vor," Edda's uncle, Karl, said to her father before his ascent. One hundred and fifty feet into the air Edda's uncle climbed, and all the while Edda was giggling and clapping her little hands.

Without anyone being aware of it, a dark shadow crept into the tent. It followed Edda's uncle up the rope. It seemed to almost be chasing Edda's uncle to the top platform. A low, ominous laughter could be heard in the distance. Vor heard this and a chill crept up his spine.

"Where have I heard that before?" Vor said to himself but he continued to watch his daughter go higher and higher with his brother.

The platform was so high it actually went through the top of the tent. As they settled on the top, overlooking all the countryside, Karl unstrapped Edda and held her high above his head. Edda could see all around for miles and she screamed in excitement. A small crowd had gathered to watch the baptism of another Stahl but the darkness had another idea of how to baptize this child.

The black shadow had settled on the platform, wrapping itself around Karl's ankles. Karl felt a chill around his feet and looked down and at that moment something happened that has never happened to a Stahl. He lost his footing and started to fall off the platform. Karl reached out to grab a rope but with that he let go of Edda. Edda's uncle grabbed the rope with one hand and tried to grab Edda but she slipped through his hand.

"EDDA!" Vor screamed from below as everyone held their breath watching this small child plummet to the earth. In the instant it takes to lose the grip of a loved one, out of nowhere, a circular cloud formed up from the ground, a cyclone of sorts. In a mere millisecond the funnel cloud cushioned Edda's fall and gently dropped her into a pile of hay that was off to the side of the arena.

"Oh my god, my child. I can't explain what happened. Karl did you see that?" Vor turned to his brother who rushed down and was white as a ghost.

The dark shadow that had almost taken over the whole arena quickly slipped out into the countryside and disappeared. Beaten again.

Edda never had another near-death incident. She flourished and grew. Well she didn't really grow that much but what she didn't have in height or weight she made up in her aerial performances and on the balance beam. Edda almost seemed to float. Her father said Edda always rode a favorable wind.

The snow and hail always seemed to beckon to her and the wind always made her smile. Yes, she was blessed and she blessed everyone she met.

CHAPTER TWENTY-ONE

Santiago Cordone

Born outside of Umasbamba, Peru on November 23rd, Santiago Louis Philip Cordone Aldez was one of three children. He was the youngest son born to Diego Louis Cordone and Maria Sofia Aldez. When Santiago was born the doctor remarked that the baby smiled at him. "I have never seen a baby smile like that before."

A nurse who had been coaching Maria through this birth looked up at the doctor. Her eyes were a piercing crystal blue. "Maybe he's just happy to see you," she said, and then she turned and walked out of the room. The doctor asked the other nurse who that was and the nurse looked around and asked "Who?"

When Santiago was taken home his relatives and friends came to the house and everyone seemed to say what a special child he was. He had such a calming effect on everyone around him. He seemed to bring peace everywhere he went and people would always smile. Wherever he went things always seemed lighter and brighter. Dogs would stop barking and people would become silent and stare when he was around. The strangest thing was that the flowers people sent for his birth, cut flowers, never died as long as they were in his presence.

When his mom would go into his room she swore that all the flowers and plants looked healthier than they had the day before. The flowers would lean towards the baby even after Maria would arrange them nice and straight in their vases.

Santiago's mom would sometimes take some of the arrangements and put them in other rooms because she loved the scent of these beautiful flowers but when she did, the flowers would start to die. Santiago's father had taken notice of this and started taking the baby around to trees and crops that had the blight. Every time Santiago sat next to a plant that was dying that plant would become healthy. Diego never told anyone about this because he was frightened that someone would think he was crazy.

"We must never tell anyone about this, Maria. This must be our secret. Santiago is a blessing sent to us and we must protect him," Diego said to his wife.

Maria looked down at the floor and said, "But dear husband what do we do? Every time he is around flowers and plants they seem to lean towards him. They want to be closer to him."

Diego cleared his throat and held Maria and said, "We will keep him safe my darling. Here on the farm he is safe from everyone. His brother and sister love him and they will help us protect him. We have been blessed."

"He will have to attend school, my dear husband. What will we do then?"

Diego kissed Maria on the head and said, "We will worry about that when the time comes. For now he is safe."

Well that's what they were hoping but things sometimes turn out differently. When Santiago was a toddler he had two near-death experiences. On both occasions the family remembers a darkness creeping over the land.

The first was on Santiago's third birthday as the family went on their traditional walk through the Amazon jungle. Diego, who was a descendant of the Inca, wanted to take Santiago to the ruins at Machu Picchu where they would bless him into the family. Diego took each of his children to this sacred place when they turned three years of age but he knew that Santiago was different. Diego knew that Santiago himself was sacred. Since Santiago was born the crops had never been more healthy and bountiful.

As they walked through the trails, the branches of the trees and plants seemed to beckon towards the family. Diego brought his machete to cut away any undergrowth but was a little shocked to see there was none. It was like all the plants and trees cleared a path for this family and led them on.

"Papa, I have never seen such a clear trail before." Santiago's older brother Luis had remarked.

Diego and Maria were in awe of this. The last time they walked this trail it took many hours of cutting away underbrush and branches from trees. As they walked the trail unveiled itself to them. There was no thinking about where to go because the plants opened up before them and closed up behind them.

After walking for a while the family started to get hungry so they sat in a clearing that so happened to appear to them and ate some of the food they brought. Santiago's mother put him down on the ground to tend to her other children and Diego. Santiago immediately started to crawl away. In no time he had disappeared into the jungle and when the family looked around he was gone. They noticed a darkness that had crept across the jungle floor and when they turned to look at it, it too was gone. The darkness followed Santiago.

"Oh my God! Where is our little boy?" screamed Maria. "Santiago, Santiago!" Maria's voice was trembling.

"Santiago, Santiago," yelled Pena, Santiago's older sister

"Oh no!" thought Diego. Luis and Diego ran from side to side looking under each bush and behind each tree.

Santiago could hear the calls from his family but felt so at home in the jungle he just continued to crawl. As he crawled all the plants stretched their branches and leaves out to touch him.

Santiago laughed because the leaves were tickling him.

A Camu Camu bush offered its fruit to him. Camu Camu fruit has forty times more vitamin C than any other plant in the world and Santiago quickly started to eat it. The calls of his family grew more and more faint until he could hear them no more.

"He will never survive out there and night is coming. Diego, what shall we do?" Maria said. It was starting to get dark and Diego needed to protect his family so he decided they would camp right there and look for Santiago in the morning. He had a strange and calm feeling in his heart that Santiago would be alright but his mind had other thoughts that weren't so pleasant.

As Santiago sat in a small clearing he started to get tired as any three-year-old would. He lay down on the jungle floor and a group of acacia trees surrounded him. They laid their branches on him to keep him warm and Santiago fell asleep.

The Cordon family could not sleep. Maria was up sobbing and thinking she would never see her baby again. Diego remained positive until he heard the roar of a jaguar. Then he started to worry that his son was alone and fair game to any animal in the Amazon. He started to pray.

"Hahahahahaha." A low laughter could be heard across the jungle floor.

"Did you hear that, Maria?"

"What, Diego?"

"That laughter. It must be my imagination," Diego said but knew it wasn't his imagination; it was something evil.

A dark shadow crept through the jungle until it found the sleeping child and covered Santiago as he lay asleep.

The jaguar that Diego had heard had gotten the scent of Santiago and was making its way towards him. Santiago never really knew of the danger. As the jaguar got closer and was ready to pounce on the sleeping Santiago, the trees scooped Santiago up and proceeded to pass him from branch to branch. The dark shadow tried to reach out to grab the child but the trees were too quick and the darkness receded back into the jungle with a hissing sound.

When morning came Maria sat up because she had finally fallen asleep and there in her lap was Santiago sleeping soundly. The trees had placed him back into his mother's arms. Diego still talks about that night and refers to Santiago as the "prince of the jungle."

Since the day he was born Santiago had only eaten foods that were grown naturally. He seemed the healthiest when the food came from the Amazon jungle but he ate any organic food as long as it was grown naturally without any additives.

As Santiago grew his family noticed that when he ate, which he loved to do, the plants and trees around him would all seem healthier. The first and only time he ate processed food was at a birthday party for a cousin. A strange darkness had fallen over the party when all of sudden Santiago got violently ill. Santiago fainted and his breathing became shallow. The darkness followed the family as they rushed him back to the farm and put him in his room. His mother noticed that when they placed him in his bed the flowers around him started to wilt. They immediately called the doctor. The doctor rushed to the farm but could not find anything wrong with the child.

"It seems like food poisoning but all the children ate the same thing," the doctor said. Santiago lay white and still.

"All we can do is pray," said the doctor and they all left the room.

The darkness crept up the walls and was about to cover the whole room when silently through the window a Camu Camu plant extended a branch and dropped its fruit in Santiago's mouth. Instantly the color in his face came back and he started to fidget. There was a loud hiss and the darkness was gone.

"Whaaaa," Santiago cried out.

Diego heard his son and ran into the baby's room just in time to see the branch of a tree go back out the window. Ten minutes ago Santiago was near death and his skin was ashen but now he was crying for food and looked fine.

"Prince of the Jungle," is what Diego was thinking.

Diego could not believe what he had seen but there on Santiago's cheek was sticky red juice. Diego put his finger to the cheek of Santiago and scooped up the red liquid. He tasted it and knew it was from the Camu Camu berry.

The doctor, who also happened to be the village priest, ran in and proclaimed it a miracle. He said the hand of God came and touched this little child. With that he made the sign of the cross and ran out to tell the people about the miracle that had blessed the Cordone family. The Cordone family never gave processed foods to their children again.

When Santiago was five years old he fell in love with basketball. His father took him into Lima, the city's center, and there he saw his first basketball game. His dad wanted Santiago to play soccer like his brother Luis but Santiago had basketball fever. From that day on all he talked about was basketball and would watch every game he could. His hero was Michael Jordan. His dad even had to put up a hoop so he could practice and Santiago always carried around a basketball.

It was always funny to Diego to see this small boy carrying around a full-sized basketball and trying to shoot it into the hoop. The hoop was so high and every time Diego asked his son if he should lower it Santiago told him no.

"Father, Michael would never shoot with a shorter hoop."

Santiago would spend hours practicing. The neighbors and relatives would come by just to sit and talk and watch Santiago try to make a basket. Rain or shine Santiago was out there trying his hardest. His father and mother always were impressed at his commitment to everything he did. He would try and try but could never reach the basket. Every day he would stand under the basketball hoop and throw the ball as high as he could and then one day he got it in. Everyone in the village cheered as this little child seemed to accomplish the impossible.

Santiago grew up strong. He had such an innocence about him that everyone loved to be close to his glow. He treated everyone with respect and honesty and never judged another person by what he heard or what they had done. He was the biggest boy in his 4th grade class in height and weight, but was also the most athletic and he always fueled his body with organic foods.

Santiago is one of the seven children that make up the Band of Innocence. He was chosen for his innocence, as most of the children before him were chosen. The pure food is just an added bonus, a fuel to keep him focused and clean.

His parents always would watch in wonder at the glow around Santiago after he finished his meals. His food seemed to add to the pure light that generated from his soul.

CHAPTER TWENTY-TWO

Paka Kalu

Paka Kalu was born on a sunny bright day in Kenya, Africa. She was born on February 12th to be exact. Her father was out in the bush that day doing what he normally did, looking for poachers. Katow Kalu had been a game warden all his adult life. His love of animals started when he was very young. What better job for a lover of animals than to become their protector.

As I said, the day his fifth daughter Paka was born Katow was out following a trail of poachers. Someone had been trying to kill elephants for their tusks to sell on the black market. The tusks are ground down into powder to be used as an elixir, possibly for strength; who knows, but these people would kill the elephant and remove their tusks, leaving their bodies to rot.

Katow had seen baby elephants standing by their dead parents for days. It broke his heart and he wanted to track down every last one of these poachers and bring them to justice.

As he moved towards the area where some men had been seen he felt something cold held close to his head.

"Stand very still," the voice said. "Hand over your rifle and kneel down on the ground."

"I am a game warden and whatever you're doing here is illegal," Katow said with no fear. He got down on his knees as he handed his rifle to the man behind him.

"We know who you are and that's why we are going to kill you. We can't have you interfering anymore. I am so sorry, my dear fellow, but you came upon us just as we were going to kill a white tiger that a couple of moments ago was over there but has run off, thanks to you." The voice was that of an English gentleman. "My ward will stop at nothing to get this animal. You know he is quite a collector and if you had only waited ten minutes then two lives would not have been lost today."

"You won't get away with this. You will be tracked down," Katow said.

"By whom — one of your daughters, perhaps?" The English man laughed.

Katow froze at the mention of his daughters.

"How do you know of my family?" Katow now was scared. Not for himself but for his children and wife.

"We know all about you. You have been a thorn in our side for a long time. Now just stare straight ahead until my boss gets here. I'm sure he will want to do the honors of blowing your head to Kingdom Come."

As Katow was kneeling on the ground he noticed a small monkey off in the brush. Katow stared at the monkey because the monkey was staring at him. "Why is the monkey staring at me?" he thought.

"That monkey is now motioning to me."

The monkey had his finger to its lips as if to say to Katow be quiet. Then it winked at him.

"I've gone mad or I'm already dead," Katow whispered.

"What did you say? I can't wait for my boss, old sport. I'm sorry, but your death will guarantee your family's safety. Ta ta." As the Englishman started to pull the trigger a little field mouse ran out of the grass and up the pants leg of the would-be executioner.

"Blimey, what the heck?" the man shouted. He started to slap at his pants but the mouse ran up and down his legs as the man did a sort of weird dance. The mouse started to give him little bites.

"Ouch," the man shouted.

Katow was still kneeling but the yelling of this man brought the attention of the others in his party.

"Wellington, are you alright?" a voice screamed.

Katow looked over and the little monkey was waving to Katow to come quickly. Without thinking he got up and ran into the brush where the monkey was standing.

"Stay low my friend, you are safe. We need to get you home. Your daughter is being born," the monkey said to him. It was a female voice and all Katow could say to himself was "Minona." Minona is the Goddess of the animals.

All the men from the group ran towards the screaming and found the Englishman dancing and slapping his trousers. The field mouse scurried out of the man's pant leg and ran off as a mean-looking man with a rifle walked through the circle of men.

"Wellington, do you know you just lost us our prize today. My father won't be happy."

"Sir, I was attacked and it wasn't me that lost the tiger. I had the goody-two-shoes game warden and something ran up my leg. Look at the bites." This man Wellington pulled up his pants and there were little spots of blood all over.

"Where is the cop anyway?" All the men looked around.

"He got away. I'm not sure where he went. I was too busy being bitten."

"Let's get out of here. I will get this prize but evidently not today. Dammit, Wellington," the leader storms off as the men follow him.

Wellington looked around and yelled into the air: "We will be back warden and you best stay out of our way."

From where he was Katow noticed that even in the bright sunlight dark, inky shadows danced all around these men.

"There is no time to waste. Your wife needs you. Go."

Katow had forgotten about the little monkey who saved him. When he turned he was no longer looking at a monkey. There standing next to him was a woman holding a spear and shield. She had long braided hair and the facial features of a black leopard and large green eyes that sparkled in the sun.

"Minona," Katow whispered.

"Growwwwwwlll," the woman smiled. Her face changed into the face of a black leopard. Her lips pulled back and she showed her cat like fangs. In the next instant her body changed into a small hummingbird that floated in the air but as this little creature flew off Katow heard her whisper "Hurry home they need you."

Katow stuck his head up from the brush and looked around. All the men were gone.

"I may have heat stroke," he thought. He ran to his truck and got on the radio.

"Chacha, come in. Chacha, come in." The radio crackled and then a voice could be heard. It was Chacha, ex-undercover soldier and the man in charge of security on this reserve. There are things that Chacha has seen and done that sometimes makes Katow shiver. That being said there is no one Katow would trust with the safety of his family more than Chacha. Chacha would give his life for the Kalus.

There had been a rebellion against the past regime in Kenya and Chacha had some involvement in that rebellion. Katow was on his nightly tour when he found Chacha and three of his men. Chacha was the only one alive. The others had been butchered. Katow thinks that he must have scared off whoever did this horrible thing before they were able to get to Chacha.

Katow took Chacha back to his house and the Kalus nursed him back to health. From that day on Chacha has never left the Kalus. A strong protector and a very close friend.

"Hey old man, how are you?" Chacha responds on the radio.

Katow cuts him off. "There is no time to play. Take two or three men and get to my house. There may be trouble and Sinci is about to deliver the baby. Have them bring weapons and be on guard."

"What is the matter Katow? Is everything...."

Katow interrupts him. "Just go, please, and I will meet you there. Do not let anyone near the house, Chacha."

Katow steps on the gas and a large billow of dust comes up from the back wheels of the truck. As the truck leaves a small monkey can be seen waving and holding his hand over his face as he starts to cough from the dust.

Katow races home and as he gets there he sees a group of villagers standing outside the house. They are all talking and whispering as they stare at the house.

"Oh God, I am too late."

As he jumps from the Jeep he sees the armed men and recognizes them as Chacha's security force.

He quickly pushes his way through the group of villagers and into the small house.

He runs into the bedroom and sees Chacha standing by Sinci.

"Is everything okay?" he says as he looks around.

"My husband, I am sorry," says Sinci.

Sinci and Katow met when they were in grammar school and Katow fell in love with her instantly. He would go home to his mother and father and tell them how he would marry Sinci someday.

She is the love of his life.

"You my love are the light in my life," he would tell her.

"Why are you sorry my love? Are you alright? Is the baby alright?" "We couldn't wait for you. The baby needed to come," Sinci says.

"Pushy little thing, you best watch this one," says Chacha with a laugh.

"So the baby is okay?" Katow is looking for the baby and then sees the doctor in the other room. He rushes over.

"Doctor, is the baby okay?"

As the doctor turns Katow realizes this isn't the normal doctor from the village.

"The baby is fine, Katow. A beautiful baby girl."

"Who are you? I have never seen you before doctor. Where did you come from? Where is Doctor Carter?"

The doctor is a woman with the bluest eyes he has ever seen and she holds out a small bundle. A small smile is on the doctor's face that seems to mesmerize him. He doesn't move.

"Katow, your baby girl," the doctor says as she again offers the small pink bundle to him.

Katow, shaking his head, looks down and as he holds the package of pink fabric the doctor unfolds the corners and there lies his newly-born daughter.

As soon as Katow looks at the baby's face, the baby smiles. A little wisp of a smile. A smile very similar to the doctor's.

"My daughter just smiled at me," Katow says quietly.

The doctor had turned to leave and as she was passing him he heard her say, "Maybe she is happy to see you."

"Uh, thank you Doctor." Katow turns but she is gone.

"Chacha," he calls out, "where did the doctor go."

"What doctor?" Chacha says. Katow would never see that doctor again.

Katow looks around confused but, at that point, forgets everything except the knowledge that this is his daughter. This is Paka.

As Paka grew her father would watch her.

Every once and awhile he would look at Paka and her eyes would seem to look very cat-like. Then she would blink and they would be normal again. Was it his imagination? He couldn't really tell.

He did know that she had a special talent with animals. He thought he was tied to the animal spirit but he saw that Paka could actually be the animal spirit. She grew up with very few human friends. There were a couple of children she would play with but she was always seen with animals, dogs, chickens, horses. All would follow her around. As if they were guarding her from something.

The Kalus would sometimes take in injured animals from the reserve and Paka would never leave the animal's side.

"Oh don't worry, my daddy will help you," she would tell the animal.

The sight of a four-year-old petting a female lion who had gotten into a trap was a marvel to behold. At first they would keep her away because of the danger but they kept finding her in the cage with all sorts of creatures and never once did any one of them ever attempt to hurt her. Paka always knew what was bothering the animal.

"His tummy doesn't feel good, Mommy. He thinks it's something he ate," she would say and she would be right.

Katow was paid to notice things and he would point out to Sinci what he saw.

"Look at the way the animals are always looking around as they follow our Paka. They seem to be watching out for something. I have never seen anything like this."

When Paka was three years old her family was having a picnic out on the reserve. It was to celebrate her sister Awino's tenth birthday. There were about twenty-five people present.

"To my beautiful, or one of my beautiful daughters, Awino, please come here I have a present for you." Awino was getting her great grandmother's ring. A ritual that started long before even Katow was born.

"Soon you will be a woman, my first child." Sinci stood up to hug her daughter.

The family started to applaud never noticing the black shadow that was creeping around the camp site. A dark, inky spot. Paka was sitting alone playing with a sparrow that was hopping around. The shadow settled around Paka and the bird started to chirp and hop away. Paka started after the bird and walked into the surrounding brush.

The shadow seemed to be everywhere now. As Paka stumbled along she entered a clearing. There in the clearing was a pack of hyenas.

They all turned at the approaching child. Paka saw them and of course had no fear. Why should she? They are her friends, as all animals are but here something was different. There in the middle of the group of animals was one black hyena. The shadows played all around and over this animal. The other hyenas started to back away but this one bared its teeth. Foam and drool dripped from its mouth.

At the party Paka's sister Barika, who was just seven years old called out to her little sister.

"Paka, Paka. Where could that child have gone?" she said feeling very motherly.

"Barika, where is, Paka?" Katow shouted across the table of food and desserts.

"She was right here, Katow," said Sinci, looking a little worried.

All the guests started to stand and look around.

"Growl, grrrrrrrrrr, rowlllllllll....."

A large skirmish could be heard in the brush.

"Oh no, something has got my Paka," Sinci screamed.

The men grabbed their rifles and ran off in the direction of the ferocious noises coming from the brush. As they approached the area the animal sounds stopped dead.

"Let's fan out. Something has taken my child and I will not let her go."

The men with the rifles fanned out and one of the men saw hyenas running away.

"Katow over here — hyenas!" his friend Chacha screamed.

"Oh my, no please my lord watch over my Paka," he thought as he ran towards Chacha. You could hear the clicking of guns getting ready to shoot.

As they approached a clearing they all stopped. There at the edge of the clearing was Paka in the jaws of a large brown and grey hyena. The hyena was holding her by her pants so Paka was just hanging there.

"Hello father. I'm going for a ride," Paka said as she swung in the jaws of the hyena.

Chacha raised his rifle to shoot and slowly Katow pushed the barrel down.

"Wait Chacha. Everyone put your guns down."

"But Katow, that hyena is going to run off with Paka and have her for an afternoon snack," Chacha said.

"If she were, she would have already done so. Plus you may hit Paka."

The hyena stood staring at the group of men and slowly walked forward with Paka in its powerful jaws.

The crowd backed up except for Katow and Sinci. The hyena slowly walked over to Sinci and laid Paka down at her feet.

"Good doggie," Paka said and petted the animal's head. The hyena licked Paka's face and slowly turned and walked off into the brush.

"I can't believe my eyes, Katow," one of the guests said.

"Katow, what just happened?" Sinci clutched her daughter.

Katow looked around at the guests who were standing in disbelief. He leaned over to his wife and whispered, "Minona."

No one ever talked about that day, as if it had never happened, but it did and everyone knew it did. Everyone also knew that

Paka was a special child. She would tell her father when an animal wasn't feeling well and she was always there to comfort any animal if it was hurt or dying. She would cry uncontrollably at the death of any animal.

When she was five her dad found a litter of three puppies. He realized too late that they were Rhodesian Ridgebacks. The family had already fallen in love with them. They grew to be little ponies — well, that's what Paka used to call them. She would ride on their backs and they were never far from her. They would follow her to school and wait for her to come out and follow her back home. They slept at the foot of her bed every night.

Paka learned patience, compassion and honesty through those dogs and her mom and dad will always remember how they were always around. One night they were watching Paka playing in the yard with her dogs and they all heard a hyena call.

Sinci turned to Katow and kissed him on the cheek and whispered, "Minona," as they both smiled.

CHAPTER TWENTY-THREE

Fala Deerhorn

In Carthage Mississippi, on April 17th Fala Deerhorn was born to Leo and Starr Deerhorn. Leo was the tribe leader to the Choctaw Indians in Carthage, a poor community with its fair share of problems.

On the day Fala was born it was raining quite heavily and the skies were dark with black, threatening clouds. Never had Leo seen a storm so vicious. He also noticed a black, inky shadow forming along the ground outside the house. It was raining so heavily that there were reports of flooding and several of the rivers overflowed. This was a monster of a storm.

This storm came out of nowhere. Leo, who was not only the tribe's leader but a holistic doctor, was out seeing a patient on the other side of the reservation when he received a call from a neighbor that his wife, Starr, was in labor and needed him.

There was no need for them to call a doctor since he had delivered most of the children on this reservation but as he opened the door to leave and get in his car he saw that the weather conditions were extremely dangerous. He went back into the house to call for an ambulance, since he thought he wouldn't make it but as he picked up the phone a shadow fell upon it and the dial tone faded.

"I have to get to Starr," were his first thoughts so he put on his hat and ran for his car. "Okay please start, please start." Leo took the sound of the engine firing up as a sign of luck. He slowly proceeded out of the drive, barely able to see.

"I have never seen rain like this, or darkness this pitch black."

Dark, inky black shadows seemed to dance all around the car as it slowly made its way down the road.

"I will never get there with this storm," Leo said out loud.

Then as if by some miracle the rain opened like a curtain around him.

"This cannot be possible. The path before me is open and clear."

Leo stopped the car momentarily. Then he remembered a saying: "A gift not used is no gift at all." He then accelerated his car through the parting rain.

"No rain is hitting my car and I can see the road so clearly now," and as he drove he knew that this miracle had something to do with the birth of this child. He had been having dreams in the last month of her birth. He knew it was a girl because of the dreams and also knew she would be special; how special he had no idea.

The storm was truly incredible. It seemed like a mean rain, trying to stop him in any way it could but the powers that kept the rain away were relentless. Leo drove as if it were his one sole purpose in life. He had a baby to deliver.

He had just a mile to go but that mile included the small bridge that went over a gully.

"With all this water the bridge must surely be washed out," he thought. "What is my choice? I can't go back. Starr needs me. The great spirits will not fail me."

As he got closer to the bridge he could see the bridge was truly washed out. Not only was the bridge gone but so was the road.

"How will I cross this?" The water, which usually was a small stream, was now a raging river. He could see trees and debris being pushed along. Then he had to rub his eyes. On the far side of the riverbank he thought he saw the figure of a man, a rather large man. He couldn't make him out completely but the man seemed to be waving him on.

"Are you crazy?" Leo thought. "There is no road. How will I make it?"

A whisper came to him.

"Trust me." This whisper had all the sounds of rushing water.

Leo looked around his car. "Who was that?"

Again the words whispered, "Trust me."

Leo knew he was crazy for trying, but then again there was no water hitting his car. So maybe crazy was the way to go. He opened the door of the car and stepped out. No rain touched him. It was like a big umbrella covered him. The rain could be seen trying to hit him, almost violently, but an invisible shield protected him.

"This is not just a storm," he thought. "I need to be with my wife so I have no choice."

Leo turned around one last time and saw that the road behind him had been washed out so there really was no choice and with that he took a leap of faith. Well, he will say it was a step into madness but what he would later realize was that it was a leap into the abyss.

He settled back into the car and put his foot on the gas and his car slowly moved forward towards the raging river. With no indication of a road and the river flowing in front of him he clenched the wheel and pushed harder on the gas. As soon as he reached the embankment the waters from the river divided and ran around the car, never touching it. He concentrated on keeping his car going and did not look out the passenger window for, if he had, he would have seen a wall of water coming at him and then splitting.

The river waters were indeed going around his car and then what he saw took his breath away. There in the water-well, not so much in the water but actually part of the water — was the man he had seen earlier on the river bank. His long hair was made of waves of water and he was nodding his head and smiling. Leo whispered, "Unktahee," and the large figure nodded again.

Leo heard the whisper, "Hurry." It sounded like the sound of water rushing by but the word was distinct.

Leo looked at the road ahead of him and he was now on the other side of the river. He looked back and the figure melted into the river and was gone. Realizing he should be getting to his wife's side he quickly gunned the engine and headed home.

As he got to his house the rain started beating down on his car. His sister came running to the door.

"Leo, how did you get here? All the roads are washed out; even the ambulances cannot make it through. The midwife showed up just before the storm started."

"Unktahee," is all he said and rushed to his wife's side. An hour after his arrival, came a new arrival.

Leo had rushed into the bedroom hearing his wife, Starr, screaming in pain. There he found Starr in bed and the midwife in the room with her. He had never seen this woman before but thought she looked familiar. She had the most amazing blue eyes.

He was going to ask where in the village she lived but with Starr being in so much pain he just concentrated on delivering his daughter.

"Questions can always be asked," he thought.

It was a difficult delivery but with the help of the midwife, Fala came out perfectly.

When Fala was born Leo looked at her and he swore the baby smiled at him.

"Starr, the baby just smiled at me," Leo said.

The midwife, turning toward the couple as she was leaving the room said, "Maybe she is just happy to see you," and with that remark went through the door. Leo and Starr looked up at her as she walked out. They never saw her again.

The window of the bedroom became bright with sunlight and the storm in all its ferocity stopped.

"Was that a hiss I heard, Starr?" Leo said.

"I had been hearing very strange things in the last couple of hours, like someone was laughing as my pain increased. Also, Leo, the storm kept getting worse as the pain got worse. Then the midwife showed up and the laughter was gone."

Fala grew to be quite an unusual child. She never cried. Never.

Now there are babies who are quite happy but Fala was always happy. Another unusual thing was that Fala never walked. As soon as she got her balance she ran. She would run to school, run in school, run home and run up to her room or down to the kitchen.

"I like to get places quickly because it gives me more time to be there," was what she would tell her father. Fala had started to speak at eight months old and to run at nine months and she has never slowed down.

"Child, you are going to wear out your feet," her grandma would tell her. Her grandma Sooze was the tribe's medicine woman or shaman. She lived in an authentic Indian tipi that was on one hundred acres of land that was given to her great-grandfather.

Inside the tipi hung dried-out herbs and flowers. There were bowls filled with all sorts of things that she used to make her elixirs and potions. In the old days people thought her a crazy old feeble woman but as present-day people started to turn to natural remedies Grandma Sooze was in high demand.

"See the world is changing and people are now running to receive my tonics. The natural way is always the best way," she would say to Fala.

"They are running because they think I'm chasing them Grandma," Fala would say giggling.

"People are looking away from the modern medicine and coming back to the mother that is nature. I know that this makes the Great Mother very happy."

"How do you know that Grandma?"

"Oh I know her personally and she told me," Sooze would say laughing.

Fala would sit for hours and watch her grandma stir and boil and mix. Sometimes Grandma Sooze would let her taste it and ask what the ingredients were. Fala was getting so good at it that the natural thing to do was to start her education in being a shaman.

"You are only four years old, Fala, and you will be the youngest shaman ever. The youngest and the fastest with all that running around," her grandma would say.

The darkness of the world quickly became aware that a brilliant light had been born and since it could not stop her birth it tried to end her life early. Stop her from realizing her potential and extinguish the light at its source.

The darkness knows the ones it needs to extinguish as opposed to the ones that will just burn out slowly by themselves. Most people give up their beliefs and dreams as they grow. These are the ones the darkness overlooks. It ignores them because they don't pose a threat. They are the half-empty souls. Dim lights. Fala was neither empty nor dim. She was full of life and oh so full of light.

The darkness was intent on stopping her before she could grow stronger and brighter.

On a clear afternoon when Starr was coming home from the

city with Fala in the back seat, the darkness made its move. As they approached the same road that was washed out five years prior a shadow moved quickly towards the car. Starr looked away for a second but that was all it took. When she looked back up a black inky shadow had covered her windshield.

"Oh my God," Starr screamed as the car veered to the side of the road heading toward the water.

All she thought of was Fala but she couldn't undo her seatbelt and the car hit the water with a huge thud. Starr's head hit the dashboard and she was knocked out. She would never wake up again. As the car sank in the river the interior started to fill with water.

When Starr didn't return home Leo started to get worried.

"This is not like your mother. She would not be late without calling," Leo said to his sons. "Get in the car, we need to find them." Leo sometimes had visions and he knew Starr and his daughter were in trouble. As he ran to the car he had a vision that was more vivid than any he had ever experienced. He felt that all the breath had been taken from him. He stopped for a moment feeling as though he was suffocating. This feeling passed quickly and he stumbled to his car.

As he drove, searching each side of the road, he saw a figure standing at the end of a dirt street. It seemed to be that of a woman. She radiated a soft white glow. The figure beckoned him to stop. Her hand was raised. As he stopped the car he jumped out and noticed it in fact was a woman in a white flowing dress.

He stared at her in shock. It was Starr.

"Take care of my little girl, Leo. I love you so."

"What, what are you saying, Starr?" he screamed as the woman faded.

At that point Leo knew Starr was no longer alive and had gone to meet the Great Spirit. She was no longer walking this earth but what about Fala? His grief was quickly replaced by his fear.

Leo scoured the roads but could not find the car, Starr or his daughter.

Leo called the local police.

"Hello, this is Leo Deerhorn. My wife is missing. She was supposed to be home hours ago and she is with my daughter. What do you mean? I have to wait for how many days? My family needs help now. Ah the white man's laws. Thank you."

That night Leo drifted in and out of sleep. As he laid his head down Starr came to him in a dream.

"Leo, I'm so sorry I cannot be with you to raise our daughter. She is very special and has a very important mission in her little life. Please find her and protect her. I will always look over you and my family. My love is waiting until we meet again Leo. Use our people. They will track her down. Do not wait. She is only protected for so long."

Leo woke up with a start. Sweat pouring from his head. The sun was peeking up over the horizon.

"How long did I sleep?" he wondered.

He would resume the search but this time using his tribe. They would track her down and find his girl. Leo called his tribe together and after telling them what had happened he had one hundred and fifty people helping him find his family. They scoured the town where Starr and Fala had been shopping, handing out pictures, then Leo was approached by the Indian trackers.

It took the Indian trackers only two hours to find the tracks of the car. The tire tracks led off of the embankment right next to a small bridge. This was the same place Leo had seen Unktahee five years prior. The police divers were called and they looked for and found the car under the water of the river.

"I'm sorry, Leo. There are two bodies in the car. We think your wife is in the front and your daughter is strapped in the back. We have to tow the car out and you can make a positive identification."

Leo fell to his knees.

"Oh, my poor girls."

He could not stop the tears from flowing. Leo was sobbing from grief when the car was pulled out of the river. The police opened the driver's door and there lying against the wheel of the car was his wife. Her skin was blue and he knew she was safely in the hands of their forefathers. As they opened the back door he waited, preparing himself to see his daughter's lifeless body but rather than a dead Fala there in the child seat, she was very alive.

"Daddy, Mommy is sleeping and I haven't been able to wake her up. I've been calling her but she says she is resting with the great ones. What does that mean Daddy?"

"Oh my god. Great spirits, Fala, you are alive."

Everyone on the shore was astounded. How could this child live under water for nearly two days?

Leo will always remember his mother, Grandma Sooze, walking up next to him and whispering "Unktahee, her protector."

Leo was devastated and joyous at the same time. He had lost his wife but his daughter was alive and then he remembered the ride from the hospital to the house when Fala was born.

"It was Unktahee. My heart is broken but is alive, but why, why not save both of them?" Leo didn't know that one life had to be given to save the other.

His tears were of grief and joy. When Fala was released from the hospital Leo was ready to take her home. They had buried his wife two days before and he had just enough time to straighten things out in order to be a single parent. Two things were about to happen that day to change the direction of his life.

When he got to the house the door was wide open.

"That's weird, I know I locked that door," Leo had said to himself but that wasn't the oddest of things. As he looked at his house his gaze went to the roof and there sitting and staring at him was a large white bird. He had trouble making out what kind of bird it was against the bright light of the sun. He put his hand to his brow to block the sun and to his amazement he realized what was on his roof.

"Oh my spirits, it's a crow, a white crow."

Leo remembered the stories he was told as a child of how the crows changed from a pure white bird to a black one.

"I always thought that it was just a story," Leo whispered.

As he brought Fala out of the car his mother came out of the house and stood on the porch.

"Welcome home, my son."

Leo shook his head because his mother lived on the other side of town and very rarely ventured out, which though he loved her dearly was fine with him. He looked from the roof back to his mother; that's when he saw it. There in the back of the house was his mother's teepee.

"Oh no," he thought to himself.

"You are going to need help with this one, my son. I've moved all my necessary things into the spare room. I will be her guardian and teach her the ways of our ancestors and it seems that our ancestors have chosen her to walk a greater path than we could ever imagine."

Sooze looked past Leo and Leo turned to see the crow on top of the car.

"CAWWWWW." Leo shook his head because the crow screamed right into his face.

"Hahahaha," Grandma Sooze started to laugh.

"Mother, you do not have to stay with us, we are fine."

"Nonsense son. I have to watch over you, the boys and this special package but I think I have help with this one," she said with a smirk.

They both turned towards the crow.

"Cawwwwwwww," it screamed.

Now Fala had two older brothers, Karl and Levon. The boys had been devastated at the loss of their mother but they loved their sister so much and they became the most doting brothers you could find.

One day Leo came home and Levon ran to the front of the house.

"Father, father you need to see this. Please, quickly."

Leo didn't like surprises. He liked the ordinary, the simple and the predictable.

As Leo and Levon came around the house there was Fala running after Karl.

"She just got up and started running Father. She started running and she won't stop."

As soon as Fala saw her father she ran to him. Then back to Karl then to Levon, then back to her father where she jumped into his arms and fell asleep. From that day on whenever you saw Fala she was running. She barely ever walked anywhere and was always the first one at any function along with the large white crow.

As Fala grew it was such a sight to see this little child running at full speed being followed by a large white crow. The crow never left her side. Fala named it Fvla, which in Indian means crow — not very original but neither forgettable.

With her interest in herbs and tonics Fala became Grandma Sooze's apprentice. At age nine she entered the New York Marathon and actually finished: the youngest person to finish the marathon. Her father and brothers and grandma watched as she crossed the finish line. And so did her mother.

As she crossed it a rainbow appeared in the sky. Fala looked up, "Thank you, Mother."

CHAPTER TWENTY-FOUR

Victor Xio

In the town of Lhasa, high in the mountains of Tibet, Victor Xio was born. It was May 15th and there was a threat of rain. The clouds looked dark and mean on that day. His older brother Kanno had come running for their father.

"Father, father," he called as his voice echoed through the Potola Palace where his father was the curator. For years his father, Heng, had taken care of this wonderful building so that tourists could see the beautiful architecture that Tibet had to offer.

"Kanno, what is it? You are out of breath. Stop and tell me what is going on."

"Mother is in pain. She says it's time. You need to come home." Kanno started to pull his father's hand.

Yenna was not due for two more weeks, he thought.

"Kanno, is this another one of your games?" Heng asked his son.

Kanno had been a problem since the day he was born and now at the age of 15 he had gotten into serious trouble, hanging out with the bad element, as Heng used to say. It was difficult for him and his wife to keep Kanno under control.

"Father, I'm telling the truth. Mother is in so much pain. She said to get you. I told you I changed. I want to be a good son."

Heng had seen a change in Kanno ever since it was confirmed that Yenna was going to have a baby. Kanno had touched her stomach and a soft glow came over him.

"I saw it with my own eyes Heng. The light came from my belly and travelled up Kanno's arm and radiated in his heart," his wife had said.

Heng tried to believe Yenna but he had some doubt.

He looked deep into Kanno's eyes and knew Kanno was telling the truth.

He turned to the security guard with Kanno pulling on his arm.

"I must leave, my wife is having my baby. Can you close up?"

"Heng, good luck my friend," the security guard yelled as Heng and Kanno ran from the building. Heng jumped on his bicycle, put Kanno on the handle bars and started off to their home.

As they were going through a small mountain pass Kanno could see black shadows dancing on the mountain sides.

"Father, look," he pointed but his father was too busy concentrating on getting home and didn't see the danger up ahead where the shadows congregated.

On the mountain's side, high above them, a slight rumble could be heard. The mountainside was looking to bury Heng and his son. As Heng rode he felt the ground start to shake and saw the side of the mountain start to dislodge with small pebbles falling onto the road at first and then larger rocks. Heng knew that if this continued the side of the mountain would block his path. He needed to hurry.

"I have to peddle faster to beat this avalanche," he thought, so he started to peddle even faster but as he did larger boulders started rolling down toward them and he couldn't outrace the rock and stone that started to fall onto the road.

At that very instant the most unbelievable thing happened. "What is that?" Heng screamed. Kanno covered his eyes.

As Heng peddled the ground in front of them started to rise up and what seemed to be a huge rock head rose from the middle of the road. They could see the glowing eyes inset deep into the rock.

Heng tried to stop but couldn't and as they were about to hit this huge stone face the mouth of the rock monster opened and swallowed Heng, Kanno, and the bike.

All the while Heng continued to peddle. As Heng's legs pushed the pedals of his bicycle a tunnel formed in front of him and they just kept moving forward.

"Father, what is happening?"

"I do not know, Kanno, but we must get home to your mother. I know she needs us." Sweat was pouring from Heng's face and his shirt was drenched but he never slowed down.

Heng continued to pedal as the dirt and rock walls opened up in front of him and then closed up behind him. Kanno sat wide eyed because it was pitch black. He had no idea if he was moving or standing still.

"Look, Father, a light, I see a light." Heng and Kanno landed back on the road, still on the bicycle. Kanno looked behind them.

The hole in the ground closed up and he saw all the rock and boulders blocking the road. They had ridden under it.

"How did we get past that?" He turned and looked at his father who had sweat streaming down his face but Heng never stopped pedaling.

As soon as they got home, Heng knew that no matter what was happening he was here with his wife. The sun once again sat high in the sky and the wind had a crisp smell to it. He ran into his home and in the bedroom his wife was moaning. There was an old midwife with her but he knew there was no pain medication because they weren't expecting the baby so soon. Heng ran straight to Yenna's side.

"Heng, thank Buddha you are here. Oh my, this hurts so much. My water has broken, I think. Look, see the blood. Should we go to the doctor?" she said but Heng and Kanno knew they had no way of getting there. The avalanche had closed off all routes to the town.

Heng ran into the kitchen and soaked a towel to put on her head and then called the doctor. He tried several times but there was no dial tone. The avalanche must have knocked down the telephone lines.

Heng remembered the doctor had said to make her as comfortable as possible and to call him as soon as her contractions were five minutes apart.

"Do you know how far apart the pains are my love?" Heng said to Yenna.

"I think every two or three minutes. Ohhhhhh here is another." Yenna clenched her teeth. Heng held her hand as Yenna squeezed it.

The doctor also said that she shouldn't be in that much pain. At this point Heng knew he wouldn't be able to get in touch with the doctor.

"Is the doctor coming Heng? I need him here."

"Yes dear, he will be here soon," but Heng knew that no doctor would be coming. What would he do if in fact the baby was stressed?

Heng knelt by his wife, holding her hand. Kanno stood at the door, seeing the look of worry on his father's face. "Father, can we speak?"

"I'll be right back, my love." Heng got up and went into the other room with Kanno.

"Father, is everything alright? You seem so worried. How will the doctor come with the road being blocked?"

"He won't, Kanno. We are alone — you, the midwife and me. We need to do all we can for your mother and pray to Buddha that all is well with your sibling."

The midwife was one of the old women from the village and she really was just there for prayer and to help sterilize towels. She didn't get her hands dirty with birth details.

"What was that?" Heng said turning towards the window. A low rumble could be heard but it sounded like a laugh. A low evil laughter.

"Ahhhhhh," a scream came from his wife.

Heng rushed to her side and there she was about to have her child but something was wrong.

"Heng, the baby is kicking too low in my belly, ahhhhhhh." He had heard of this before. A breached birth, meaning the baby was upside down. Those births never turned out okay unless a doctor or nurse was present. The baby needed to be turned around.

All of a sudden there was a knock on the door.

"Kanno, go see who that could be." I hope it's the doctor Heng thought. That would be a miracle or did I use my only miracle already?

As Kanno opened the door he was blinded with light. He put his hand in front of his eyes.

"How did the sun sink so low in the sky to be blinding me like this?"

As his eyes adjusted to the light there at the front door stood a tall woman with the most brilliant blue eyes he had ever seen.

How unusual to see someone with such blue eyes in Tibet.

"Can I help you Ma'am?"

"No, my child, it's I who can help you. Your mother is going to lose her baby so please let me in and I can save the little soul." This tall woman stood in the sunlight although all around the front of the house dark inky shadows could be seen. None coming near her but all dancing around outside.

"Please come in," Kanno said as he looked around outside. She was also speaking in their perfect dialect. As if she had been born in Tibet.

"Where did she come from?" he asked himself, not seeing any car or bike.

At that moment Heng came into the front of the house.

"I'm sorry, can I help you?"

"I was sent here to help deliver your son. I need some hot water so I can cleanse my hands for the job I will need to do. Your son is in danger and we need to save him. Otherwise they will win."

"I'm sorry but who sent you and who is winning? Did Doctor Kai send you?"

"I came on my own accord. Is it not enough that I have come to help? Do you not need my help?"

As she spoke Heng could see her eyes blazing blue and he was hypnotized by her voice. He could almost swear that her skin was changing, getting darker by the minute, but then she smiled and it went back to normal.

"Heng, let's save your son so he can grow and someday save us."

Heng and Kanno nodded without knowing why and led this mysterious woman into the bedroom.

This strange woman turned to Heng and Kenno and said, "You can leave now. I will call you when you can come in."

Like stunned cattle they walked out leaving this stranger to help deliver the baby.

Heng looked out the window; it had grown darker. Shadows seemed to be playing all over the house. A low laughter could be heard.

"The wind is playing tricks on our ears Kanno," he said but he was worried just the same.

Time crept by and Heng could feel a rumble below the ground. He looked outside and it looked like night but it was late morning.

"I have never seen this before, Kanno. Buddha has stolen the sun."

"Father, I feel the earth moving below our feet. Is it another earthquake?"

Heng jumped up as the little house started to shake and headed for the bedroom. He took two steps and was thrown to the floor by a vicious shake of the house. The whole house felt like was going to come down around them and then in an instant all was calm. Like someone had flicked a light switch. At that moment he thought he heard a baby cry.

As he lay on the floor dust settled down from the roof. Dishes lay all over the floor and Kanno was in a fetal position under the table. Heng looked up at the window and saw the sun light start to stream in. Bright sun, as if the heavens were opening their doors.

Kanno crawled to the front door and opened it. "Father, come and look."

As Heng got to the front door he saw with a shocked look that nothing outside had changed. There was no sign of damage or any destruction. People were walking and bicycles were rolling through the little village. No one seemed bothered by the quake except for the Xios.

Heng then heard the baby cry again and he realized "Oh my Yenna," and ran to the bedroom just as the old woman with the blue eyes was coming through the door. She stopped and handed him a bundle wrapped in a blanket and in that blanket was Victor Xio.

"Congratulations, Heng, you are the proud father of a baby boy."

Heng smiled and looked down at the baby and the baby smiled up at him.

"I have never seen a baby smile like this before."

"Maybe he is so glad to see you, Heng." With that the woman walked out the front door, never to be seen again.

It was a miracle, thought Heng and when Yenna was well enough to hear the whole story about the ride home she just looked into her husband's eyes and said "Tu Di Gong."

"What, my lovely Yenna?" Heng said looking confused.

"'The spirit of Tu Di Gong was with you my love."

"But who was that woman?" Heng said gently.

"Maybe it was him. He can take so many forms, my love."

As Victor grew physically strong and brave of heart it seemed everyone around him became a better person. When Victor was around there was no mischief. He brought out the best in everyone and he never used his physical strength to win a battle or beat someone. He did it with words and emotion but he was immovable at certain times.

When Victor was a toddler he would make sculptures out of practically nothing but rock and dirt. He seemed to be able to mold dirt and rock into beautiful statues of Buddha and animals. The front of the house was full of figures of all sizes. People in the village would come and walk through the statues like it was an outdoor museum and every couple of days there would be another one.

As the Xios were eating one morning a pounding came on t he door.

"Yenna, who could that be? Kanno, see who it is, my son, and then hurry back for your breakfast."

As Kanno got up to get the door it was suddenly pushed in and Chinese soldiers pushed their way into the little house.

"You," the captain pointed to Heng, "I want you and your family outside. Now."

Heng looked at Yenna and nodded.

"What are we to do?" he said to himself as Heng picked up Victor and handed him to Yenna. Kanno was already outside where there stood a half dozen soldiers with grim faces and rifles aimed at the family.

Heng and Kanno also noticed black shadows that danced about the ground and played on the faces of the soldiers.

"Why have you not abided by the law, farmer? These statues are not to be publicly displayed. This is treason. Did you not know that?"

"No I did not. We are so sorry. We will take them down," said Heng to the captain. Heng put Victor down on the ground and turned to get Kanno when he was hit in the back with the butt of a rifle.

"No, the crime has been committed. You will need to be a symbol of what happens to farmers who break the law."

"Leave us alone, please, we will take them down and you can have anything you want just please don't hurt us," Yenna pleaded with the captain.

The captain turned and slapped Yenna and she fell to the ground. Kanno ran towards the captain and that was when the guns all rose and fixed on him. Kanno stopped in his tracks. All the while Victor was sitting on the ground making a rock formation. The rocks started to mold to Victor's touch and in a matter of minutes he had a figure of a rock man.

"That looks like the creature that swallowed us," thought Kanno.

"Captain, look at what the baby has done." A soldier was standing over Victor.

"Well what we have here? A genius baby? After we are finished with you" — he pointed to Heng — "we will need to take this baby to the chancellor." Shadows as dark as ink were all over this captain's face and more were flocking around the soldiers.

"No please, I beg you, leave him alone. He's just a baby," Heng called to the captain. Heng tried to get up to stop the soldiers but as he did all the guns swung around and aimed at him.

Heng paused as he felt a small tremor under his feet. The soldiers also felt this and for a second time their attention was taken away from the Xio family.

Heng took this moment and lurched forward to save his child.

"Stop there," the captain screamed and pointed his gun at Heng. But before the first shot could be fired the low rumbling became louder and the ground started to jitter and ripple.

Like a freight train coming closer, the rumble and shaking built rapidly. The ground started to shake more violently and as it did all the statues that Victor had built started to crumble.

Everyone was having a hard time standing on their feet. The earth started to pulse up and down like a trampoline.

The bouncing of the ground separated the soldiers from the Xio family as all the soldiers started to bounce towards each other. As soon as the soldiers were in a pile, having fallen together, the ground started to rise behind them.

"Heng, what is that?" Yenna screamed. The ground itself took shape like Victor's crumbled statues.

"That is the same rock head we encountered on our bike ride home when you were about to give birth to Victor."

Everyone stared up as the ground rose twenty feet above them. A face slowly formed out of the dirt and rock as a huge gaping hole appeared right below the eyes of this rock monster's face. The eyes in this dirt mound were deep-set and blazing a smoldering red as it stared down at the soldiers.

One soldier fired his weapon but the bullet was just absorbed into the dirt.

"That is what happened to us, Father," Kanno yelled. The same rock mouth that had saved Heng and Kanno opened wide and swallowed the soldiers whole. There was total silence. The big rock head slowly slipped back into the ground.

All was quiet as the Xios stared, but Victor broke the silence.

"Yum yum," said Victor who was still sitting next to his latest statue. The only statue that didn't fall was the one of the rock man.

"Yum yum," Victor said again.

"Where have they gone, Father?" Kanno said as he slowly got up and looked at where the large hole was.

"I don't know, Kanno, but we all saw that, right?"

Kanno could only nod his head yes.

"Quick, get Victor, he is not safe," Yenna said moving quickly to snatch the baby. As she bent down to grab Victor she looked closely at the stone statue he had just made.

"Heng, come quick look."

Heng went over quickly and Kanno followed. They all stared at the rock man.

"Tu Di Gong," Yenna whispered and then they all looked at Victor.

"Yum yum," Victor said and then he smiled that smile he first displayed in his swaddling clothes. The little stone statue's eyes glowed a glint of red and then went out.

A thousand miles away from the Xio's house the ground opened up and six dusty soldiers were literally spit out of the ground. One by one.

The captain looked around and dusted himself off.

"Where are we?"

"I don't know Captain, but I think we are not in Tibet anymore."

"I know that, you idiot. This is never to be spoken about again. I will not have our great leaders perform mental tests on me after I tell them what happened."

These six men never said another word about the incident except every now and then they will remember the day that the ground ate them and then spit them back out as if they weren't worthy of even being buried. They all became giving and caring men when they were reunited with their families. It only takes one incident like that to change your life forever and meeting Victor was that incident.

CHAPTER TWENTY-FIVE

James Curtis

Martha Williams had a troubled youth growing up in Madison, Wisconsin. It wasn't Martha but the system that failed. A system that is supposed to help children sometimes fails to help some, but there will be no finger pointing in this story. Martha just seemed to fall through the cracks. So at 13 years old she started hanging out with the wrong crowd.

The girls she hung out with all wanted to have babies. Even though they were only twelve and thirteen years old they had it in their minds that being a mother was a cool thing to do. These were lonely girls who thought that having a baby was giving birth to unconditional love. Someone who would love them no matter what. None of them thought of the work that goes into having a baby.

There was some drug use and drinking but this wasn't a daily occurrence. Mostly recreational but Martha did turn her back on her school and church group. So when she became pregnant it was no big deal. All of her friends were having babies so she was really just the norm. Yes, normal except for the fact that she was carrying a special package, a special baby in every way.

Martha, as opposed to most of her friends, knew who the father was. He was a rough boy from down the block. Reggie Curtis. Committed to a gang, he spent most of his time in their clubhouse, a rundown storefront on the outskirts of town. No matter — he wanted nothing to do with her or the baby anyway.

"I told you, Martha, running around with that crowd will bring nothing but trouble. Now what are you going to do? You have already quit school and now we have to raise this baby or do you expect me to take care of it?" her father said to her.

"Daddy, I will raise my son with your help or without." It was weird but she knew she was pregnant before she took the test. She remembers waking up in the storefront where the gang hung out and feeling a sense of joy and pride that she never felt before.

"What am I doing here?" she had said to herself. A realization came upon her that her life was important and had a greater purpose. A respect for herself seemed to overwhelm her.

"I need to get better, be better, because I am better," she had told her friends.

Martha stopped all her extracurricular activities. The urge to smoke or partake in any substance abuse left her body when she felt her little package of joy inside her.

"Martha, you are glowing," her friend Cynthy had said to her.

"Oh Cynthy, all pregnant women glow," Martha laughed.

"No, hon, you are really glowing," and it wasn't just Martha feeling good about herself although that had a lot to do with it. It also wasn't the normal, pregnant woman glow, it seemed that everyone noticed a light or hue that emanated from her body. All of her friends, the ones who still hung out with her, felt a certain joy and peace. Each one of them became clean in their own way. They became compassionate, truthful and respectful of everyone and especially themselves. Proud to be who they were.

"Martha, I don't know what it is but you have become such a pleasure to be with," her friends would say.

Her father Frank, who Martha thought drank way too much and probably did, even had an epiphany of his own. One night as Martha was watching TV he touched her belly when she was beginning to show. With that one touch his whole world changed.

He felt a warmth travel up his arm and into his chest, a peaceful feeling in his soul.

That night he had dreams of flying. He hadn't had those dreams since he was a child. He also dreamed of his wife who he realized he had missed so much.

Five years ago his lovely Nico died in a robbery attempt at the corner store. She had gone to get him and Martha food for dinner. That was Frank's job but he was running late from work so Nico decided to go. She knew the neighborhood was dangerous at night but didn't think anything could happen with a simple walk down the block.

Two men rushed in and the cashier fought back. A gun went off and Nico's life ended.

That was the night Frank started his drinking. He just gave up on everything including his daughter but this morning the world looked different. Brighter.

In his dream, he saw his dear Nico and she spoke to him.

"Frank, my love. It isn't your fault I passed on the way I did. You could not have known or protected me any more than you had."

"Oh my, Nico, but I could have been there for you, to stop those bastards from hurting you."

"Frank, you know you couldn't be with me every moment of every day. Let me go and let your guilt float away. I loved you and will always love you. You now have another one to look after. I'm at peace."

Frank woke up a new man. Looking ten years younger, he bounced into the kitchen of his little two-bedroom apartment. He stood up straight without the weight of guilt pressing down on his body.

"I don't know why, Martha, but this morning I woke up and realized that I need to change my life. I need to clean this place up because it is not suitable for a child," he said with a grin.

"I need to take responsibility for myself and for you Martha and I know I can't do it if I'm drinking and playing all the time. Martha, I don't know what happened last night or what you have cooking in your oven but I feel twenty years younger."

Her father became a totally different man. In two weeks he had a job as a cook down the street. He even started looking younger and happier than he ever had.

"This baby is special," Martha thought. She felt it. The warmth, the glow. "How could this be? This child isn't even born."

The night Jimmy Curtis was born was a quiet, peaceful night. No drama in the neighborhood, no car alarms, no dogs barking. People living there will always remember that night as the breath. That's what they called it. It was the night that this neighborhood took a deep, satisfying breath. Jimmy was two months premature. Martha was worried when she started to get contractions.

Yes, the night Jimmy decided to come into this world Martha felt ill and knew that her baby was close to being born.

"Martha, we've got to get to the hospital so I called Rosa next door. She said we can borrow her car."

"But, Daddy, it's too early for my baby to come out. He isn't due for another two months."

Martha felt another contraction and doubled over.

"Oh my god, Daddy he's coming. I don't think there's time. I feel cold, Daddy. Like something is wrong with the baby." Martha stumbled back into the bedroom holding her stomach.

Shadows danced around the room and a low laughter could be heard coming from outside.

Frank looked around and noticed how dark and black the shadows were when just five minutes ago the light was streaming through the window. He picked up his cell phone but the battery was dead.

"Wait, this is weird." He looked at his phone and it was plugged into the charger and the charger was plugged into the wall.

"How can this not work? I need to call 911." He grabbed the phone on the wall and it didn't have a dial tone as a low laughter seemed to come from all over. Frank got the chills as the laughter mixed with Martha's moans.

"Everything was going so well. Oh lord please, please don't let us lose this baby."

At that moment a loud rap came from the door. Frank jumped about a mile.

"Baby, I'll be right back," Frank called into the bedroom.

Frank opened the door and his breath was literally sucked out of him. The most striking woman he had ever seen stood in the hall. He also noticed that the hall was lit up with sunlight while his apartment was dark with shadows.

This woman had the darkest skin and most brilliant blue eyes he had ever seen. She was carrying a silver cane with a globe on the top. The globe seemed to glow. She didn't even ask to or wait to be invited in but walked with authority into the room. The room was dimly lit and the dark red rug made the room look even gloomier, but when this woman walked in the light returned into the room.

"Can you take my coat please, Frank?"

"How do you know my name, and who are you?"

"Frank, your daughter needs our help so let's help her first; for this birth will in turn help us all."

"Are you from the social worker's office? Did Rosa send you?" Frank asked.

"Shhhhh." She put her finger on his lips. "You stay out here and I'll go in there." She handed Frank her cane and turned to go into the bedroom.

Frank was hypnotized by this woman's eyes and the wisp of a smile that enchanted him and before he knew it he was alone in the foyer of his apartment while the bedroom door closed.

"What just happened?" Frank murmured, finding himself alone.

Frank sat in his big overstuffed chair facing the TV. Shadows seemed to play on the floors and all around the room but no shadow moved towards the bedroom. There was the usual amount of noise outside. Car alarms, people yelling and calling out and dogs barking. Frank was wondering why he didn't want a drink. This would have been the perfect time for a cold beer or shot of whiskey.

"I feel I need to experience my life. The good and the bad. Too long have I hidden in a bottle. I'm so worried, yet I love this feeling," he thought. Frank was feeling worry for the first time since he stopped abusing himself and it was all after he touched Martha.

"Something's wrong," Frank said to himself. Something had changed.

He looked around and the shadows were gone and also all the noise too.

He jumped up to look out the window. Usually at this time of the day the air was filled with the sound of car alarms. There had been shouting and music outside but he heard none of that now. Then he heard a baby cry. No, he didn't just hear the baby but felt the baby cry. A huge wave of emotion filled his soul and tears came to his eyes.

"Oh my Lord. What a feeling I just felt in my heart. A warmth, a joy. I haven't felt this feeling of peace since my dear Nico was here."

It seemed to not only affect Frank but the whole neighborhood. Not a sound could be heard outside and beyond. If there was a way of calculating this it would have been noticed that the whole world felt joy in that second. It might have only been noticed by a few but those who did notice it would hold onto that joy forever. Frank was one of the lucky ones.

Realizing the baby's cry he rushed to the door. As he reached the door it swung open and he was presented with his grandchild.

"Frank, here is your grandson."

"Oh Lord, look at this. My God, thank the Lord. Oh my, did you see that, I think he just smiled at me. Is that possible? He smiled at me."

"I think he is happy to see you, Frank," the woman with the blue eyes said as she picked up her coat and cane and headed for the front door. She opened the door, stopped and turned to Frank.

"You are so cute, little baby boy," Frank was cooing.

"This is a special child, Frank. He can't hear you but he can hear everyone. Protect him."

With those words the woman walked out the front door, never to be seen again, but Frank swore he heard her whisper, "They are complete," and then she was gone.

Frank didn't know what she meant but knew that she brought the sunlight back into their life that day. He had run to the window to look out but there was no sign of her.

"How did she get out of the building? There's no other way out."

Frank slowly walked into the bedroom and Martha was there, smiling.

"Martha, are you okay?" Frank slowly put the baby on Martha's chest.

Frank heard another knock on the door.

"That woman is back. I need to thank her."

Frank opened the door, "Thank you so......" but it wasn't the woman. It was an EMS crew.

"Sir, someone phoned in a medical emergency."

"Oh really? My daughter just had a baby."

The EMS workers hurried into the bedroom and Martha and

the baby were placed on a gurney and rushed to the hospital.

In the hospital the doctors and nurses all crowded around the baby. He seemed to be the center of attention.

A doctor walked into the room and looked at Martha's chart.

"You are doing fine, Martha, but your son is very premature. We have put him in an incubator for safety reasons but we don't see any real issues. The only thing I noticed is that he doesn't respond to sound but he responds to people, which is weird. We will have to check him out in a couple of weeks."

"Can I see him Doctor?"

"Are you feeling up to walking, Martha?" Frank asked, hovering over his daughter. He had a new life now. He was the protector.

"Yes, Daddy." Martha smiled. She had a new baby, a new father and a new life.

They walked to the isolation ward and the nurses there helped them put on gowns.

"Oh, Daddy, he's so small. Look at him and so quiet. I have a name for him. I want to call him James. James Curtis will be his name."

Martha's hand slipped into Frank's and if you were watching these two you would see the glow coming from them. Like a soft white light.

"When I get the chance to pick him up I may not want to put that baby down. He may never learn how to walk," Martha said as they both started to laugh.

They did find out that Jimmy was deaf. He was born without cochlea. The darkness had stolen his hearing but the light had blessed him with something else.

It was weird because he didn't hear sounds but always knew when someone was around him. It was like he could feel them and in his own way understand what they wanted. It was like he felt them rather than heard them.

The doctor met with Martha and Frank on the day James was released from the hospital. "Your baby is hearing impaired Martha. His ear canals are underdeveloped but there are things we can do medically when he gets a little older. I'm sorry. The curious thing is that he does respond when someone approaches him or talks to him but we think it must be just a coincidence."

The doctor was absolutely right that if you approached him he turned toward you as if he had heard you. There was no explanation for this. He seemed to hear but he was incapable of hearing.

"The boy can hear," Frank would swear. "He hears better than most people."

"Actually, Daddy, I think he listens better than everyone," Martha would say. "He listens with his soul, Daddy."

As he grew it seemed that Jimmy was always glowing. When his hands would touch his mother or grandfather they would feel pure joy.

"Hold my hand, Jimmy, I need a fix," Frank would say.

That day he came home from the hospital the neighborhood was abuzz about the glowing baby. Some said a miracle child was born and people needed to see him but the new baby was quickly forgotten.

People quickly forgot and went about their lives except for the ones that Jimmy touched directly. If you were touched by Jimmy you had the chance to be changed forever. Why a chance? Because your future is really in your hands and Jimmy is powerful but he can only do so much. You need to want to change; yes that's the key.

One day Reggie Curtis, Jimmy's natural father, came by. Jimmy was only one month old. He had come for some cash because he knew Frank was working.

"Martha you don't even know it's my kid. You can't prove it. So don't go talking crap around the neighborhood." Reggie was irate and pacing. Martha was worried for her safety.

"Reggie baby, he is yours. Why don't you hold him?"

"I'm not holding any baby. What are you, crazy, Martha?"

Jimmy was lying in his baby seat on the kitchen table. His little head was going back and forth as if he actually was listening to the conversation.

"The money you want is on the table, Reggie. Take it and leave us alone." Martha started to tear up and Jimmy, even at one month old, felt his mother's pain.

"Tell Frank I may need more next week."

When Reggie grabbed the money off the table a small hand reached out from the baby seat and touched Reggie's arm. Right on his wrist where his gang tattoo was inked.

Reggie felt a warmth travel up his arm.

"Hey, what is this?" Reggie said.

Now you would think that Reggie, who is six-foot three and two hundred and thirty pounds, could easily pull away from the grasp of a one-month-old baby. But whether he couldn't or didn't want to is still up for debate.

Martha watched in amazement at the change in Reggie.

The anger and pain that surrounded this boy seemed to melt away revealing a caring compassionate young man.

Reggie felt it too. The warmth that was traveling up his arm stopped in his chest, in his heart. Jimmy's hand held him tight. A little hand holding lightly onto the arm of a grown man.

Jimmy's hand clutched Reggie's wrist and Reggie did not move away. Martha was watching and knew Reggie didn't want to move.

There was that spark of compassion and love that Jimmy seemed to be able to touch in people and once Jimmy found it, it was hard for that person to stop the avalanche of feelings that came to the surface. A hardened person could become jello if Jimmy found that spark and ignited the flames in their soul but the person also had to want to accept this gift. Most people want the change even if they don't know it. Reggie wanted his life to change and change it did.

"Martha I'm so sorry," Reggie said, tears filling his eyes. "Damn I don't know what's come over me," he said as Jimmy let go of his soul grip.

Reggie would never be the same. Reggie deep down wanted to change. There was a spark of kindness and goodness in him. He accepted the gift Jimmy gave him without even knowing it. He accepted the change and let it grow until it overwhelmed him.

Even though they never got married Reggie became a father to Jimmy. Not just a father but a friend, a mentor and a role model.

Reggie decided to go back to school and he became a licensed electrician making good money and supporting Jimmy even after Martha decided to go to Los Angeles, intent on getting a job and living in warm weather.

"I won't let him down again." Reggie had told Martha.

"Ya can't trust him, baby," Frank had said, "he is a yard dog and won't be holding to you once he is out of sight."

"You're wrong, Daddy, I see it in his eyes. Reggie has accepted Jimmy in more ways than we will ever know."

Martha was right. When they moved Reggie started sending money every two weeks, and to this day he has never missed either Jimmy's, Frank's or Martha's birthday.

Frank was getting older and the winters in Wisconsin were getting too hard on him so when Jimmy was five they moved to Los Angeles. Frank also converted to Judaism. He had become an avid reader and decided that was the religion for him. Martha followed suit so for all intents and purposes Jimmy also became Jewish.

Jimmy had a tough time in his new neighborhood. He was always smaller than everyone else and he was of a different religion and he was hearing impaired. All that made for long odds against a little boy in a new neighborhood but his powers of reading emotions always helped him. He couldn't hear people, but he could feel them and sometimes that was so much better.

CHAPTER TWENTY-SIX

Playtime

As the stories of each member of the Band end the amulet, which is now spinning slowly again, comes to a stop but still hovers over the pedestal. Lily picks up the back of her hair and the amulet moves towards her. As though it has a mind of its own, it attaches itself around Lily's neck.

Lily puts a hand to the amulet as if reassuring herself that it is there.

"Now that we all know where we came from, let's find out where we are. It is time for you to really get to know each other and yourselves. Your powers are yours for now. You will feel like you have had them all your lives. Your memories are the memories of the elders and they will guide you."

Emily is still a bit overwhelmed by all that has happened.

"Aunt Lily, I am really proud to be picked but I am just a fourteen-year-old girl. I really don't understand why I was chosen above everyone else."

Aunt Lily walks over and brushes her niece's chin.

"Oh sweetheart, you are the chosen one. Your innocence chose you long ago. You're the one the world has been waiting for and even though you are the brightest star on the planet you too will lose some of that light some day and open the way for another leader. Don't worry — everything will become clear and you will understand your role in this planet's life pattern. Not many children are chosen to be in the Band but you, my love, were and are the leader of the Band of Innocence."

Lily turns to the rest of the Band of Innocence.

"I want you all to remember one important thing: you are powerful alone but unstoppable together. Play, my children, because soon your real adventures will begin."

Aunt Lily takes a step back and disappears into the darkness. Her voice can still be heard.

"My young ones, this will be your fortress. It is the Chamber of the Elders. Adventures await you so have fun now and learn and listen to the powers you have."

Edda had already started by making a handful of snow balls. She took one of the snowballs and threw it at Santiago. Out of nowhere a vine came out of the ground and blocked it. All the kids laughed. Santiago looked stunned.

"Did I do that?"

Paka Kalu's body started to change. Paka called out, "Look, I'm a lion. Now I'm a snake. Now I'm. . . ." She disappeared except for a squeaky voice that flew around. "A fly."

A snowball almost squashed Paka as it zipped past her.

"Hey, that was close," she squeaked.

Paka then changed into a panther and leaped towards the stone stairs in the chamber. As she did this, Edda lifted her hands and covered the stairs with snow and ice. Paka changed into a penguin and slid down the frozen staircase on her belly. She laughed all the way down the ice slide.

"Anyone want some Inca berries?"

Here in the chamber Santiago had grown a huge Inca berry bush.

"No, Santiago, I'm fine," Victor said as he raised his arms. With that a huge mound of earth covered the bush and Santiago.

Everyone got quiet. All of the children turned to watch. The mound of earth started to shake and rumble. It started to crack at the top. Out popped one small sunflower. The mound cracked and fell apart as Santiago stepped out. His face was covered with the remnants of Inca berries.

"Anyone have a napkin? Wet Wipe?"

All the children laughed as Santiago handed Victor the sunflower.

"For you, my dirty friend."

"Funny. Don't have a napkin but how about a face full of mud, plant boy."

Victor laughed as he formed a mud ball in his hand. A huge vine picked Santiago up and he went racing around the cavern.

"Come and get me, rock head."

Meanwhile Emily was uneasily testing her newfound powers. She was clumsily trying to figure out her light pads. As she hovered off the ground, they shot off with her at breakneck speed. She closed her eyes and concentrated as she approached a smooth steep wall. Miraculously the pads transformed into a skateboard.

"Now this I can handle," she thought. "Just like my skateboard at home."

Emily, now smiling, takes the turn up the wall. She begins to dart all throughout the chamber, her light pads leaving trails like a shooting star. With a quick change in thought she is changing the pads into all sorts of shapes, from roller skates to a surfboard and everything in between.

As she flies around the cave she sees Jimmy standing and smiling at the goings on around him. Emily heads towards Jimmy. All she has to do is think of slowing down and she does.

The board is an extension of her, well it actually is her. Her innocence is like her arm or leg; almost no thought goes into using either.

Emily hovers right by Jimmy on her light pads. The light pads expand into a long board and she holds her hand out to him.

"Hey Jimmy, need a lift?" Jimmy looks up smiling. He grabs Emily's hand and jumps on the back of the board. With Jimmy behind her Emily picks up speed and swoops around the cavern.

"This is so cool," Emily hears Jimmy say in her head.

Emily and Jimmy speed around the cavern barely hitting the walls. Jimmy is holding onto Emily tight around her waist.

"Your armor is so soft. I would have thought it would be hard and cold," Jimmy says in Emily's head. Her armor does feel soft even though it looks like metal. After a couple of breathless turns with closed eyes her long board floats to the ground.

Edda walks over to Emily with a sparkle in her eyes. Emily recognizes this look. Her friend Tom at school looks like this when he's about to tell a joke or play a joke on someone.

"What could she be up to?"

"Hey, Emily, those little cats on your armor are so very cute. Can I touch them?"

Edda's hand goes to touch them when all of a sudden the heads of the cats grow out of the armor. Both cats growl, extending their large silver teeth, protecting Emily from Edda. In an instant Edda jumps back and the moisture in the air around her freezes, forming an ice shield protecting Edda from these cats.

"Okay. Nice kitty. Rowwwwwwwe," Edda says, just a little nervous.

"Scarlett...Rhett that's not nice. This is Edda. She is a friend."

The cats hear their consort's voice and immediately start to purr. They leap from the armor as their bodies grow in size. No more are they the small Siamese cats that sat in Emily's lap. Now they are two silver cats the size of lions. They start to purr and rub against the ice that shields Edda and it starts to melt. Edda starts to giggle but is still a little afraid as she raises her arms.

"Edda, don't be afraid. They won't hurt you."

"Uh they have the biggest teeth I have ever seen."

"Oh jeez they are bigger than my dog's teeth," Paka says as she transforms into a full grown Rhodesian Ridgeback."

"Hissssss, Growl," Scarlett and Rhett look at Paka, the silver hair on their backs spike up into the air.

"Oops not the best choice," and she quickly turns into a mouse. The two cats are ready to pounce.

"Oh God maybe not this either," as she turns back into Paka. Rhett goes and rubs against Paka now.

"Paka you need to work on your powers," Fala says laughing.

"Actually it's my choices I need to work on, hahaha."

Edda's hands come down and she starts to rub Scarlett between the ears. The children all start to mingle around to watch the cats. They all start to pet their heads. Scarlett and Rhett are in their glory. Rhett lies down and exposes his belly and Santiago starts to rub it.

Paka changes her body into the shape of a female lion and stands almost as big as the two silver cats. Scarlett comes over to Paka and gives her a big wet lick. Paka turns back into her girl form and wipes her face.

"Ewwwwww," she starts to laugh.

Santiago stands to the side and looks around. "Hey, anyone else hungry? I'm starved. I have more Inca berries."

Santiago sits on a rock and another Inca berry bush pops out of the ground as he waves his hand.

"I don't know if anyone is interested but in my country we make cheese from yak's milk and I have some. Anybody interested? It lasts forever." Victor holds out the cheese he brought.

He pulls a bag from a backpack that is sitting on the floor next to a case of some sort.

"I wish I had some pumpkin seeds and almond butter. My aunt makes these things called super balls. My Mom used to feed them to me when I was a baby because I almost died from the food they were buying at the store. Turned out all I could eat was organic food," Emily says.

"That's what happened to me. They didn't know what to do. They finally fed me fresh fish and vegetables and I was fine," Edda says.

All the children yell out how they too can only eat pure food. And each one of them pulls out nuts and snacks of only the purest of foods. As each starts sharing, Fala reaches into a bag that hung from her waist and hands a seed to the crow that stands on her shoulder.

"Hey Victor, what is that little case you have?" Jimmy says.

"It's a guitar my father made me. He made this for my last birthday. I don't go anywhere without it."

"Can you play it?" Paka asks.

"No, I carry it around to impress people."

"I'm impressed," says Edda with a laugh.

The kids all start to laugh as Victor takes out the small guitar.

Paka jumps up and says, "Oh can you play something I know? Do you know any Katy Perry?"

"Ewwww, how about Justin Bieber?" Fala asks.

"Ahhh no. How about some Led Zeppelin?" says Victor and starts to play "Stairway to Heaven."

He looks around and realizes these kids don't know who the heck Led Zeppelin is, let alone "Stairway to Heaven."

"Okay how about a song I wrote last week. The more I think

about it, this just may be perfect for our team here. We're gonna need a theme song."

"All superheroes have theme songs," Santiago says as he stands with his hands on his hips. Very much a superhero pose, except for the basketball under his arm.

Fala comes over and sits in front of Victor. "Oh please play it Victor."

"He is really cute," Fala thinks.

"Santiago, can you give me a drum beat. Bum... Bum, Bum Bum...Bum, Bum." Santiago pounds out a rock and roll drum beat on his basketball.

Victor holds his handmade guitar and starts to sing, the cave adds a natural echo to Victor's voice.

"Did you ever wonder?

Have you truly seen?

Look at your sisters and brothers and the weight they've been carrying.

If you open your hearts to some caring,

You can help them carry the load. Love is all about sharing.

We've come so far but we have so much further to go.

We are all the same no matter who you are or where you've been.

Life is just a game and we all can win. If we stick together."

Edda and Fala are swaying side to side in time to the music.

"Together arm in arm we can right all that is wrong.

Together we march together we sing together the weak are suddenly strong."

As Victor sings the ground under him starts to rumble and push up forming a stage. He is standing now on a small mesa platform.

Sparkles start to emanate from Emily's armor. Pinpoints of light shoot out of the armor and hit the rock walls, lighting up the statues. Emily becomes a human disco ball as the cave transforms into a rock arena.

It seems the statues themselves are all moving to the music. As the cavern is filled with light, Victor's song echoes, while Fala is enthralled. Her mouth is wide open and she can't take her eyes off Victor. Edda turns to Paka and points at Fala.

"Victor has his first fan."

"Together arm in arm we will stand for what is pure,

Brothers and Sisters hearts beating as one we're not alone anymore

We're not alone anymore."

As Victor winds down the dirt-and-rock stage levels out and he's back standing with the children. The kids all start to applaud. The white crow flies down and rests on Victor's shoulder for a brief instant as if saying good job. Victor turns and looks shocked and the crow flies off back to Fala's shoulder.

"Hey Fala, isn't that a crow? Shouldn't it be black? Why is your crow white?" Paka asks enthusiastically as she turns into a black crow momentarily. "Cawwww," says Paka.

Fala turns to the group.

"Did you not know that long ago all black crows used to be white? Would you like to hear the story?"

All the children nod their heads yes.

"The story goes like this. The crows were friends with the buffalo. Every time my people would try to sneak up on the buffalo the crows that were flying overhead would see our hunters. They then would land on the buffalo's heads and tell them that man was sneaking up on them, allowing the buffalo to escape. As they neared starvation the hunters had a meeting. A plot was hatched and one hunter was chosen to disguise himself as a buffalo, wearing a buffalo skin, and sneak into the herd. When the time was right, the disguised hunter would capture the big white crow, the leader.

"So the next day one of the hunters, disguised in a buffalo skin, went grazing with the herd. As in previous days the Indians tried one more time to sneak up on the buffalo but the crows again warned the herd as the hunters approached. All the buffalo ran away except for the disguised hunter. He continued grazing, waiting.

"The leader of the crows, the biggest white crow, landed on the hunter's head, not knowing that he was falling into a trap.

"'Brother are you deaf? Did you not hear that the hunters are coming? You must flee.'

"Before the crow knew what was happening the hunter grabbed him by the legs and tied a leather lanyard to his feet. The lanyard was attached to a stone so the crow could not fly away. He brought the crow back to the tribe and into a tipi where the council was already gathered. Sitting in a circle was the tribe's council, with the chief and the medicine man.

"'What shall we do with this one father?' a warrior said.

"'We must teach this one a lesson so he and his kind don't spoil our hunts,' the old man said. This was the tribe's wise man. The shaman or medicine man as he is known to most.

"Crow, do you know you are starving our people? We have not had meat on our tables for months and the winter is setting upon us,' the old man said to the crow, trying to reason with him."

"The crow looked at the old man but before he could say anything in his defense another hunter from the back of the circle jumped up and grabbed the crow. Some of the men tried to stop him but he was too quick and he grabbed the crow and threw him into the fire. The crow screamed out as the piece of leather burned. The stone fell off and the crow flew out of the fire and out of the tepee but not before its feathers were singed black. As the crow flew from the tepee the men heard him scream, 'Caw, caw, we will never warn the buffalo again. I will tell the whole Crow nation.' From that day on all crows were born black."

"Did that really happen?" Edda asked.

"After seeing all that's happened today, I think it just may be true," Fala said as water streamed from her fingertips.

Jimmy turned to look behind him and the other children did the same. They all looked at Emily. She wasn't sitting in the circle around Fala, listening to her story, but rather standing, looking like a great warrior guarding a kingdom. Light started to form under Emily's feet and she began to rise off the ground. She hovered over the children. The light pads seemed to be changing in color and shape. She was finally feeling confident, realizing her purpose. She looked out over the children, her Band of Innocence. She raised her sword above her head.

"We are the truth and the light and the future of this world. Our voices shall be heard. The sword of truth shall not be silent.

"The Band of Innocence is complete like a wheel that has no beginning and no end. We are whole. We are one. We have been empowered and we shall empower." All the children's hands touched.

"The truth, the light, the hope, and the innocence." Her voice echoed through the great hall.

A flash of light came from the sword and there was silence. The children looked down and on their right wrists glowed a band of white light. This was the same band of light that Emily had seen on her Aunt's wrist.

The children continued to look down at their arms. Paka tried to wipe it away but it only glowed brighter. The children started talking to one another about themselves as children will do.

"I always had these dreams but I never knew what they meant," Santiago said. "Dreams of swords and a girl flying on pads of light — just like you Emily."

"Your aunt was in most of them. I knew I had seen her before," Edda said.

"Jeez, Edda, you are so right. It was her. I knew it," Paka called out.

The children started to talk about the dreams they'd had. Bands of children through the ages fighting for good; fighting for a cause.

But in a split second they were interrupted. The sword of truth glowed bright and a burst of light shot out against a dark wall. Out of the light a figure appeared.

Aunt Lily walked out of the blast of light that the sword of truth had produced. She walked toward the children and stood with them as they began to circle her.

"My children. I see you have become quick friends. This is good because your bond will be quickly tested. I was hoping we would have had more time to get acquainted before being put to our first test. By now all of you realize that I'm the one who has appeared to you in your dreams. I am also the one who will be your guide through treacherous times. And now an adventure is about to begin. I must warn you: your first test could be your last. You must remember that hate and anger are your greatest enemies."

"Emily, please hold out your sword. My children, this is Haran Kazan."

As Lily speaks the children gather around the sword. Haran Kazan's image appears in the light of the blazing sword of truth.

He is a large, massive man with dark shadows dancing around his face. Lily speaks of the battles she has had with Kazan and the images that project out of the sword's light are in perfect synchronization with what she is saying.

"For years my Band of Innocence battled Kazan and his ruthless corporation. We won many battles against him, helping sustain some purity on this wonderful globe, protecting it from sure disaster.

"Kazan, however, was responsible for shattering our Band of Innocence. He played upon my raw emotion, draining me of my innocence in one moment and thus relieving us of the powers that my band and I had. Who knows what the future would have held had we not been defeated?"

Emily looked in horror at how her aunt was deceived. Suddenly a younger, handsomer version of Kazan appeared in the sword.

"Now he has turned Talonthorn Corporation over to his son, Jason. Jason has taken his father's business and expanded it thirty times over, making him the fifth wealthiest person in the world."

The sword shows the children images of major factories billowing filth into the sky from every kind of industry.

"He has destroyed far more than his father and is twice as ruthless. He currently has children working in sweatshops in seven different Third World countries and he has no qualms about hurting children. Here is the dilemma: he is currently on vacation."

Emily looks confused, "If he is on vacation then why are we being rushed into action?"

"Jason Kazan fancies himself as one of the last great hunters. He has collected the skins and heads of many animals, endangered or not. The more rare, the bigger the prize. His idea of a vacation is getting another trophy to put on his wall. Emily, do you recall our talk on extinction?"

Emily nods her head yes as a large jungle starts to appear in the glow of the sword. As the children watch the image zooms in to a dusty, boulder-strewn ravine. There, at the back wall of the ravine, is a large group of gorillas. They seem to be in a highly excited state. As the image zooms in further, a little white gorilla can be seen clutching what is probably its mother. Its head is buried in a large gorilla's arm. Whether in fear or comfort, the face of this little baby is hidden.

Lily continues as the children all look into the sword's glow.

"Jason has embarked on a journey to a small country in Africa to capture or, if he has to, kill the only white gorilla on the continent. He has hired a team of professional mercenaries who are being paid handsomely to accomplish this mission. You must not only save this magnificent animal but must stop Mr. Kazan's thirst for power and glory at the expense of these animals. It will be difficult but I have the utmost faith in all of you. Be careful, my children, and listen to your hearts. May the truth provide and the innocence guide."

Santiago looks at Fala. "Hey that's a pretty catchy phrase, huh."

"Shhhh," Fala says with a small grin.

Everyone stands with their mouths open and stares at Santiago. Lily disappears into the darkness and the children then turn to Emily.

"Uh oh, I hope my Spirit is strong because I'm feeling a little nauseous," Victor says, looking a little green.

Emily feels a little overwhelmed because all these children are looking to her for some leadership. She slips the sword into a sheath on her back and turns to the children.

Paka looks to where Lily disappeared. "With your aunt gone how will we know where to go?"

"The sword and armor will guide us." Emily feels the armor hugging her body. She feels comfortable and strong.

Victor takes his guitar out and starts strumming it.

"Whenever I feel sad or scared I play my guitar and everything seems okay." He starts to sing his song.

"Did you ever wonder... have you truly seen...?"

Edda turns and faces Victor showing off a huge smile.

"Hey Victor, I really like that song. So do you guys think it could be our theme? We're gonna need a theme."

"It's so beautiful Victor," Fala stares at Victor all starry-eyed.

As the girls talk to Victor light starts to radiate out of the armor, casting a beam about five feet in front of Emily. A ripple starts to appear in the air, where the beam of light ends, the way heat rises from the ground in the summer. Soon an oblong hole forms.

"All right my friends I think a door has opened for us," Emily says.

Victor starts singing louder.

Fala walks over to Victor. "I like it. You have to teach us the words."

Paka puts her arm around Jimmy and yells to Victor, "Sing it louder Victor, it actually is settling the rumblings in my stomach."

"Together, arm in arm we can right all that is wrong. Together the weak is suddenly strong," Victor sings.

"Okay gang, this is our exit. Follow me and above all else remember we are a team," Emily looks back at her band one last time as they get ready to enter the portal. The kids are now all singing the song.

Emily is hovering on her light pads and looks over at Jimmy.

"Jimmy jump up. I have room for one," she says smiling at him. He looks up at her and she feels the love from his soul. Unconditional and overwhelming.

"Wow," she thinks.

Her light pads immediately turn into a long board and she offers Jimmy a hand. He jumps up behind her.

"Thank you," Jimmy mouths.

Emily lets a smile cover her face. "Well, here we go." She needs to be strong for her band and something inside her makes her feel an easy calm.

All the dreams these children have had were about this exact moment in time. These dreams have prepared them for this first adventure.

CHAPTER TWENTY-SEVEN

The Adventure Begins

Emily leads the group of children through the portal. The kids all follow her through without question, for after all, they're the good guys. As the children step through the portal each one is followed by a faint image of each of their respective spirits: the elders that accompany them. Then they are all gone.

As if going through a doorway the children step from the safety of the cool cave into a dusty, hot and sunny landscape. They all squint and wait for their eyes to adjust to the intense sunlight. Emily feels a tap on her shoulder and turns to Jimmy.

Jimmy's thoughts can be heard by all the children.

"I feel a huge wave of fear coming towards us from the east. We must prepare."

"I don't see anything but sun and dust," Fala says, wiping her eyes.

Santiago looks all around. "Okay, I'm geographically challenged and I don't know my right from my left so, uh, where is the east?"

Jimmy points towards the east and the children can see a small cloud of dust coming towards them and black smoke rising up to the sky. A deep rumble can be heard like a freight train, getting louder and louder.

Emily doesn't hesitate and calls to Santiago, "This doesn't look good. Santiago, quickly get us some protection from whatever is coming."

Santiago's arms go up and as if by magic, large, thick bushes pop out of the ground and surround the children just in time to divert a stampede of water buffalo and other animals from running them over. The sound is deafening.

Paka covers her ears and shouts, "I feel so much fear coming from these animals. Let me through, Santiago. I must find out what the animals are running from."

With just a brief thought Paka's body changes into the shape of a wildebeest. She has become this animal totally, with all the snorting and hoof clacking.

"Give me a small opening, Santi," Paka says.

Santiago is a little confused but does as he's asked. He commands the bushes to part for a brief instant and Paka charges through the hole. As Santiago opens the bushes the image of Wiraquocha can be seen surrounding him.

"Is anybody else weirded out by that or is it just me? An animal bossed me around, plus I think she got animal snot on my arm."

Santiago wipes green mucus from his sleeve. He looks around and there's nothing to wipe it from his hand. A vine grows out of the ground, Santiago wipes his hand on the leaf and the vine goes away.

"Muchas gracias, mi amigo. They are so nice to me," Santiago says.

When Paka runs through the bushes they immediately close up. The sound of the animals rushing by is so loud the kids have to rely on their telepathic powers to communicate. Moments later the noise and dust start to settle down and a small bird flies into the circle of thorns and lands on the ground.

Fala runs over to the bird. "Oh, what a cute little bird. Come here, birdie." Edda comes over making bird whistles.

As it hops across the ground it transforms back into Paka. Edda and Fala jump back.

Victor stands to the side. "Wow, how cool."

"Okay my friends, here is what I found out from these poor, scared animals. Some men have set fire to the brush in order to trap that family of gorillas that we saw back in the cave. They are in the ravine we saw and it's just up ahead. We are definitely in Zaire and these men are going to do whatever it takes so they can grab the little white one."

Paka's body starts to transform into the figure of Minona, with sword and shield. "This must be stopped. My creations are not to be hurt or killed and he that harms my babies will suffer the consequences."

Santiago jumps back for a moment and becomes Wiraquocha.

"Sister, you know we cannot harm these humans. They are also your creatures." With that said he returns to the form of Santiago.

Paka ignores Santiago. "I think we all know who laid down the first torch."

"Jason Kazan," Emily says.

Paka is visibly shaken. "Why must they hurt such peaceful creatures?" Paka has tears in her eyes. Emily places her arm around Paka.

"We will stop them, Paka, but we must act quickly to save your friends and remember we go not in anger but in understanding and compassion. Let's not let these men defeat us by using anger as a weapon."

Santiago raises his hands and the bushes disappear back into the Earth. "Thank you, my friends, for the protection."

"When we get closer, Edda, you will call upon the rains to put this fire out. Once this fire is out we all need to make a team effort to restrain and not hurt these men, no matter their faults. Let's get moving."

The children start out towards the fire with Emily ahead of them holding the Sword of Truth out in front. Jimmy is standing behind her on the surfboard made of light. Victor is on Paka, who has changed into a large tiger; Edda is riding on a gust of wind, and Santiago is being carried along the ground by a huge vine.

Fala's legs have turned into water and she is riding a wave behind the rest of the children. Her white crow is by her side. As they get closer the shape of Edda starts to change. No longer that of a child but of the Goddess, Sif.

Sif rises high in the sky, flying above the trees. The children all look up at her as she calls upon the storm spirits.

"Gods of my fathers please grant me the power and the patience to overcome my obstacles. I call upon the rain and the storms to protect and provide for me and my friends. LET THIS BE."

Her voice echoes across the land and lightning shoots from her battle staff high into the sky. The lightning forms into the letters B-O-I for a split second.

Dark rain clouds race across a once beautiful, cloudless sky. The rumble of thunder can be heard and the sky lights up all around Edda.

As the children race towards the gorilla group, the men responsible for the fire are unaware of what is about to happen.

These men who have been hired are some of the most notorious criminals in the world. Guns for hire. They are all carrying automatic weapons and a few of them are still setting fire to those parts of the bush that caused the animals to run for their lives. The only man not carrying a gun is Graham Wellington. He is fanning himself in the intense heat. Graham is dressed impeccably in this desolate wasteland. Jason Kazan emerges from behind Graham with two guards who are laughing. Kazan smiles as a dark shadow crosses his face. Kazan stands tall and walks with an air about him. He walks like a confident man who cares not for anything or anyone. Strolling around as if he's in his own backyard.

Graham looks at Jason and wonders how he came to be the babysitter of such a sadistic animal. Then he remembers. The money. Ah yes, that's it. Good.

"Master Kazan." Even now he calls him master. "The fire seems a tad bit over the top. It is bloody hot already and all that fire caused was a stampede and lots of dust."

Graham dusts off his suit jacket and dabs his head with a handkerchief.

"Ah...Graham. You don't realize what I put into this excursion. I am going to need more than a banana to catch this monkey freakazoid. And I always get my monkey. All those years with my father; I would have thought it would have toughened you up a bit. You'll be back in the air conditioning before you know it. As long as I get this white gorilla. I told you to dress for the occasion." Jason laughs a huge belly laugh.

"God, he sounds just like his father. Yuck," Graham thinks.

Wellington rolls his eyes as Jason checks his watch.

Jason looks up at the sky and around at his men. He is a man on a schedule.

"Okay now listen up. When we approach these apes I don't care what you do to any of the others, but whatever you do don't hurt the white one unless you have to." He looks at his watch again. "Right on schedule."

"Hey, what's that over in the jungle? I think it's one of them," one of the men says. A couple of the men fire at a large dark object that's running just missing it as it ducks behind a tree. Suddenly, from out of nowhere, dark clouds race across the skies. Lightning can be seen crackling and thunder rattles the ground. Graham Wellington looks up as he is suddenly under some of the darkest clouds he has ever seen.

"These clouds came from nowhere. This seems a little odd." Jason says under his breath. All of a sudden the winds pick up and it starts to rain. A fierce rain picks up with lightning and thunder, the kind of rain that bites at the skin and makes it difficult to see. The fire that the men had started is sputtering and going out. Smoke starts to drift into the air as the flames are quickly extinguished.

Graham is always prepared and is the only man in the group standing under an umbrella. Very English and very proper. The umbrella was up before the first drop hit.

One of the local hunters races up a path towards the group of men. He runs over to Jason and in a frenetic voice tells him what he saw.

"I...I don't know how to tell you this, Mr. Kazan. I think I saw a woman flying with lightning coming out of her arms. I swear she had horns on the top of her," but before he can finish Jason turns and quickly knocks this man to the ground.

After hearing this some of the other local men Graham had hired as guides start talking among themselves and looking all around.

Jason had seen this before and wants to stop this kind of talk immediately. These locals can get spooked so easily and then run off into the brush leaving Jason and his men to find their way by themselves.

Graham can hear one of the men say, "I told you this place was haunted. Spirits of the dead, I'm told. I think we should just get out of here. We are going to be cursed."

Jason stands over the man he knocked to the floor. His hands are clenched and the veins in his head can be seen throbbing. Graham looks over and has seen this look before. Someone is going to get hurt, really hurt. Graham stands back because blood always stains — no matter what they say on TV — and if it gets on his clothes here there won't be any way to get it out.

"No, no easy way to get it out of my clothes out here." Graham moves a little further back.

Jason's arm goes back and another thunderous blow connects with the man's jaw, sending blood and teeth into the dusty floor. The man lies still, trying to avoid being hit again. But that doesn't help. He is hit repeatedly. Jason seems to enjoy it.

"See what you've done. Talk like this is infectious and is sure to spook everyone."

Jason eventually stops hitting the man who is now unconscious and bleeding. His face is barely recognizable as the rain and blood mix in the dirt.

"Take him out of here and dump him in the jungle. Maybe he'll get lucky and not be eaten or bitten by something." He turns to the other guides, "I'm going to split up his pay and give you men more at the end of this.

"Now listen up, this is just a storm. One of those freak African storms that roll in and roll out. Let's get the job done. I'm paying you men primo dollars. I want no more talk of flying people or little green men."

Jason walks slowly over to Graham.

"Oh boy here we go," Graham says to himself.

"Wellington, Wellington, you told me you went to great lengths to cover our tracks. If we were followed I won't be happy. And neither will my father."

"Master Jason, this is not my first rodeo, you know. No one — and I mean no one — knows we're here, sir, and no one will ever know we were here. I have covered our tracks coming in and will cover our tracks going out. No matter how messy this becomes."

Graham knows that sometimes Jason can get a little out of hand. The remote village in Guatemala comes to mind. Where

Jason and his men slaughtered a whole village to get a bloody gem that turned out not to be what they had been looking for. Five hundred people dead. Graham had to make it seem as if it the anti-government rebels were responsible. He worked on that for weeks and even then they almost were found out. This kid was dangerous and Graham knew it.

He wasn't like his father, who was disciplined and calculating. This boy was nasty and vicious and cruel. All those little animals that found their lives tormented and ended at the hands of this monster. Even Graham couldn't understand that.

This is yet another reason to make as much money as possible and get out.

"Somewhere, where no one will ever bother me."

Graham knew that soon Jason would grow tired of him. Jason is in his thirties and Graham has been with him since he was a baby but Jason is getting more and more unpredictable.

"I feel like a babysitter and butler all in one. This is embarrassing," Graham thinks, wondering what the men he served with would think if they only knew.

"Just focus on one thing, old boy — the money, the money."

Graham is interrupted in his thoughts of cash.

"Wellington, you listening? You better hope we don't get found out. Last thing I need is to be hounded by the wildlife feds or PETA. I don't need that press. And you wouldn't want to end up like him," he points to the beaten man lying in the bushes, "after all we've been through Graham."

"Get this guy out of here."

Two other men run over and grab the man on the ground. For all concerned he might even be dead but in the jungle, being unconscious, he shortly would be.

"If this job is jeopardized in any way I'll have all your heads on poles. I swear." Jason is pointing at all the men. "No more talk about anything except my prize. You boys have been in the sun too long," Jason starts to chuckle.

"He is so close to losing it completely. I pray I'm not around when that happens. I pray no one is," Graham thinks, smiling at Jason.

"Hey you, Carl! Go out ahead and see if there is anything else up there like maybe Mary Poppins or Sponge Bob." Some of the men start to laugh. A very nervous, let's get past this whole thing kind of laugh.

CHAPTER TWENTY-EIGHT

Encounter

Carl goes out ahead into the brush with his gun poised and ready to be used. He cocks his weapon just so he's ready for anything. There is no reason not to be prepared. Carl looks from side to side pushing the tall grass away. He is a professional and whatever or whoever it is won't surprise him. He brings the gun up pushing the grass away with the barrel. He steps into a small clearing and out of the corner of his eye he sees a small figure. He turns back to see if any of the other men are following him but no one is.

"I need to be sure about this before I report anything to Kazan seeing what happened to that other poor bastard," he says to himself.

Carl turns back and yells to the group, "I'll be right back. I thought I saw something."

If this was someone spying on them they would spy no longer. He walks a little farther into the clearing and on the other side of a tree he sees a small boy dressed in black. He also can smell something burning. Almost like sulfur.

"Must be the fire we started," he thinks. "Thank god this rain is putting a damper on our fire because now I can see a little better."

The boy is sitting in a lotus position. Carl looks around not trusting this at all. What is this kid doing sitting on the ground? As he looks at this child he notices that the skin on his arms and face are all cracked and splitting. There is a red hot liquid flowing out of these cracks.

"Oh jeez this kid has the plague," he thinks.

Carl starts to back up a little never taking his gun sight off of this kid. "Hey you. Kid. What are you doing here?"

The boy doesn't answer. He seems to be in a trance. Carl starts walking around the boy all the while looking around not trusting the situation at all. He is puzzled as to how the boy got here. "Answer me, kid, or I'll put a hole in you the size of a small elephant."

There's no reaction so Carl walks closer and pushes the muzzle of the gun against the kid's back. As the muzzle of the huge elephant gun touches the boy's back it starts to melt and the heat travels quickly up the barrel to the handle.

"Jeez, this thing is getting hot," Carl mumbles as he tries to step back.

He looks at his rifle and sees that the metal is all disfigured. There is no way a bullet is coming out of that gun ever again. This was the last thought Carl remembered.

Victor felt this man getting closer. Victor felt the gun against his back and also the heat of his body melting the metal. As soon as the man was preoccupied with what happened to his rifle Victor brought his body, which was hard as stone now, straight up quickly.

The strength of Victor's upward motion knocks Carl up off his feet and onto his back. The thud to the ground knocks the wind out of him and he is barely able to move. Carl's head hits the ground and his vision is blurry.

Victor stands over the semiconscious man as his body starts to turn into the earth God, Tu Di Gong.

Carl has trouble focusing so of course he thinks it's all a dream. Yes it has to be a dream, a dream of a stone man standing eight feet tall above him with smoke billowing from his body as each raindrop sizzles against the molten skin.

Tu Di Gong brings his arms up as if summoning an unseen force and a mound of dirt shoots up from the ground and covers Carl up to his neck.

Carl is trapped in a dirt-and-rock prison with only his head sticking out. The pressure from the earth containment is just enough to let him breathe, but only very shallow breaths. He can't call out or scream. His body falls into a soft slumber.

"My enemy, you are my friend. You will enjoy a peaceful sleep and when you awaken maybe you will change the way you view the ones that are weaker than you. One down. I wonder how my friends are doing."

Tu Di Gong starts to walk away with smoke wisps rising up from his skin. As he walks — well, lumbers — he is humming the theme song Victor wrote as he slowly turns back into Victor.

All the children know what happened with Victor. The mind connection works wonderfully.

The rains that Sif, the Goddess of the Elements, has created puts out the last of the fires set by Kazan's goons. Sif hovers for a moment, making sure all the flames have been extinguished and then stops the beating rain.

"I am always in your debt, my loves," she says, looking at the bright rainbow that forms across the horizon.

"Mother, that is for you," she says with a huge grin. "If only you man creatures could see this beauty then maybe you wouldn't resort to destroying it."

As she flies back down to the ground, her body transforms back into the young girl, Edda. As Edda starts to look around she hears voices around her.

"Uh oh. I've landed in a hornet's nest."

"Do you need help, Edda?" a voice in her head says. It's Emily.

"Oh no, Em, the fun is just beginning. You have lots to do I'm sure. Meet ya later, alligator, or is that Paka." Edda giggles out loud.

At that moment two men step from some of the charred brush.

"Hey, who the heck are you?" The man turns to his friend. "Hey look at this cute little girl. She looks like one of them albinos."

"Maybe she's the little white monkey." They start to laugh.

Edda continues to smile at the men.

There were two of them. Edda was standing there and these men didn't feel threatened in the least. They also weren't that smart.

"If I were them I'd be asking what the heck would a twelve-year-old girl be doing in this country alone? What morons," Edda thinks.

One of the men does finally realize something is wrong. He raises his gun and points it at Edda.

"Okay enough games kid. Where did you come from? Are your parents around here somewhere?"

As this man is talking to her a third man comes up behind Edda and grabs her, picking her up off the ground. Edda is surprised at first and starts to struggle, kicking her legs.

"Well we've got a little something to bring to Mr. Kazan now, don't we, Lou."

The man holds Edda off the ground when she decides to change into her spirit form. Her body grows back into the Norse warrior, Sif. As Edda grows the man holding her is lifted off the ground.

"I ain't letting go, Lou, I promise. I'm holding on tight," he says.

The man is holding Sif so tight that his legs are now kicking.

"Really my friends, is this any way to treat a lady? This has gone far enough. I cannot play with you all day. So I must put you on ice."

The man holding Sif finally lets go and falls to the ground reaching for his rifle. Edda raises her battle staff as the men start to bring up the barrel of their guns.

With her staff raised, the temperature in the immediate area quickly drops by about 120 degrees. Lou and his friends try to get their rifles aimed at Edda but they start shivering so much that they can't point them.

"Ah I feel a chill in the air my friends. It's quite refreshing isn't it?"

The men have no idea that this is a goddess they are dealing with, not a little girl. She has been here since the beginning of time and with a flick of her small finger could end their existence without them even knowing.

Sif takes a deep breath and she blows out a cold fine mist. As she blows out, her breath forms snowflakes and it starts snowing around the men who are shivering so much they have given up even aiming their guns.

They start to realize that they are freezing to death and their guns won't help them but the drastic drop in temperature has caused the rifles to stick to their sweaty hands much like a tongue on a cold metal pole. Their hands, sweating from the heat, are frozen to their guns.

"Lou I'm stuck," one of the men says as he looks at Lou. Lou has beads of sweat frozen to his face.

Sif looks at these men and in her eyes you can see her disgust. She wants to wipe the planet clean again and do away with man.

"What a waste of time," she thinks. "Mother says you are worth saving. I hope she is right."

As she looks at the men a smile comes over her face.

"Okay, gentlemen, you can drop your weapons." Sif knows full well that these men can't. She laughs, "Oh, come now my friends, drop those mean weapons of yours. Hahahaha."

The men are shaking their arms so that their rifles will fall from their hands but they are frozen in place.

Sif starts to laugh in a big bellowing voice. Her laugh thunders across the plains.

"All these years in the amulet makes the little things like this so enjoyable," she thinks.

In an instant she creates a wall of ice around them, collecting moisture from the air and freezing it. To protect these men, so they wouldn't be hurt by anything.

"I wish I could just let Minona's other creatures eat them. They would be like frozen people pops," she giggles.

Sif changes back into Edda and skips back towards her friends.

In the group of children Emily seems to be discussing strategy with the rest of the band. Seen from afar they look like a normal group of children talking, but up closer you can see how the images change. Children and creators interweaving.

Emily looks concerned. "Edda and Victor have done their part. Fala, head to the camp while Jimmy and I intercept Mr. Kazan. Fala, please be careful because these men may become desperate."

Emily looks at the white crow and winks at it. The crow caws.

Emily pauses for a moment as if she is listening to something. Emily can hear Aunt Lily talking in her head.

"Emily you should also be careful and remember; act only out of purity and innocence."

The children all hear Lily; innocence and purity echoes in their heads as they watch Emily nod silently. She draws her sword and white light emanates from her feet.

"Santi, meet Edda and Victor. When you have them with you, meet Jimmy and I at the ravine. We may need some help with this Jason guy."

Paka steps up. "I'll run ahead and see if I can talk to the gorillas. Maybe there's a way out and I can lead them to safety. Or maybe we can hide. As long as you can hear me you'll know where I am."

CHAPTER TWENTY-NINE

The Hunted

Paka runs ahead of the team so she can lead the gorillas, who she knows must be very frightened. As she starts to run her shape changes into that of a white gorilla figuring it may throw this Kazan off a bit if he does make it to the ravine. She also figures the gorillas will trust her more if she looks and talks like they do.

As she arrives she sees the gorillas huddled together. They are trapped with no way out. The fire has pushed them back into a corner. The only way out is straight past Kazan's camp. Kazan's plan would have worked perfectly. The mothers are hiding their young trying to protect them from the danger that is coming.

As she approaches the group of gorillas a large male starts towards her. Out of the corner of her eye, Paka sees the male approaching but not before noticing a small white baby gorilla attached to its mothers back.

"Ah, so that is the prize he's looking for. Hey, little baby. I swear that no one will hurt you."

Paka steps back and roars a fearsome roar and the sound echoes through the ravine.

The large male gorilla takes a threatening pose directed at Paka. He is the leader of this tribe. He starts sniffing her and circling her, his fist hitting the ground with huge thuds. The hair on his back is standing straight up.

"Who are you? You are not of our tribe and you talk human talk. You also smell somewhat like man but you have our shape. That smell is disgusting to me."

The gorilla holds his nose.

"You are not one of us."

"I am Paka. I am a human but have come to help you. I have the creator spirit in me. The one who made us, man and gorilla alike."

"You were not made with us. You are them. The killers, the darkness owns you. We are the light. We are peace and life. You smell of death and black. We do not need your help. Man is not welcome here."

The male is getting progressively more and more agitated. He is now stomping and banging the back of his hands on the ground.

"It is the humans who attack us and our children. You are the ones that chase us and put us in cages. We never see our families again."

He raises his arms in one last motion.

"Why should I not strike you down right now? What is the reason?"

The group of gorillas start chanting, whooping and jumping, agreeing with their leader. Paka assumes a submissive position. She puts her hands down and her eyes look away.

"I am not like those men. I am a shape changer and my friends and I have come here from across the world to help to save your families from these men. When were you ever able to see this?" Paka changes back into a girl.

As the gorillas call for their leader to strike the little girl her body transforms into the animal goddess Minona. Tall and fearless Minona stands above the gorillas.

When the gorillas see Minona they gasp and one by one they all drop to their knees.

"My queen, we did not know you were here in the shape of this human," the leader says with his head down.

All the gorillas bow and their heads are touching the ground in reverence. From the back of the group the little white baby walks out from behind his mother. The mother tries to grab him but he breaks into a run toward Minona. The baby leaps at the spirit of life and Minona, smiling, opens her arms. The baby jumps right into her arms putting his arms around his Goddess. None of the gorillas get up. Minona puts the little one down and her body changes back into a little girl.

"If you want to strike me down then go ahead but if you really want to save the young ones back away and listen to my plan."

"I am sorry. We did not know,"

"I understand and feel your contempt and mistrust but we must act now for the good of your clan."

The gorillas listen with intent; after all this is the creator.

"We have waited for you, my queen," the male leader says.

For thousands of years the legend of Minona has been handed down from generation to generation. All the animals of the world know of her but most believe she is just a story now. The gorillas of this clan were the true believers and now they will be the ones that will tell all of her coming. In years to come all the animals will hear of the day that the creator came and saved them from certain death.

"I wish I could have been here sooner to protect you," Paka says as she starts to explain her plan to the leader of the gorillas. She has no fear of these animals — and why should she? She is their creator. She is here for them. They now crowd around her.

"We must take cover just in case some of Kazan's men do get through. We will not let these men hurt any of our young; this I swear. We will not give up without a fight."

"Why don't we just strike them down, my lady?" one of the gorillas says.

"We need them. We want to change them so we can add them to our army of light. We need every soul to combat the darkness. Man can be benevolent and good. This is what life should be."

"We must get rock and limbs to form walls to slow them down. You have more friends than you know and they will be coming soon to help us."

Paka has the gorillas form barricades of rock and wood to slow the men down. What was once a clear and open ravine is now full of limbs and rocks. It will be very hard for the men to do a full frontal attack. They will have to pick their way carefully around all the obstacles the gorillas have put in their path.

"Pick up small rocks. We can throw these at the humans to further slow them down."

"But they have boom sticks," one of the gorillas says.

"Yes, I know, and we will stay away from those. We will throw these stones only on my command. Remember, my friends are not far behind. We just have to buy some time for the cavalry."

"The cavalry?" a young female gorilla asks.

"Help, my friends," Paka says.

Inside Paka can hear Minona.

"You are doing a wonderful job, my dear. Keep your head and lead my children."

"I will for they are my children, too," Paka whispers.

CHAPTER THIRTY

The Revelation

Back at the Kazan camp more panic is ensuing as one of the local hunters continues to try and reach other members of the expedition by radio.

Each call the man makes is accompanied by static or silence.

Off to the side of the drama that is unfolding, holding a battery-powered fan, Graham Wellington is noticing the extraordinary events that are taking place around him. It really is beneath his stature to even be here.

"The money, the money. I'm not even sure this is worth it. Wait, what am I saying? Of course it is." He smiles.

"Mr. Kazan. Lou and Matty aren't answering their radios and Carl was found sleeping, buried up to his neck in dirt and rocks. We can't seem to wake him up. I also received a call from Ichow. He has three men with him but he sounded strange and I could hear him shouting something about a cornfield. I'm sure he said cornfield. Here in the middle of nowhere?"

Jason has lost all semblance of patience.

"This is my vacation and I'm supposed to be having fun." Like a spoiled child Jason starts to stamp his feet and clench his fists. "I want that animal. Now, now, do you hear?" Jason the man has reverted to Jason the child: ill-tempered and raging. Jason looks around and sees he is getting no reaction from Graham or anyone so he quickly becomes the man again.

"What the heck is going on? Has everyone lost their minds? Flying people, cornfields..."

A panicked look comes across Graham Wellington. His complexion, which was white to start with, is now completely ashen. He drops his fan to the ground. It finally hits him who may be causing the havoc on this hunt. The look of shock does not go unnoticed.

One of the hunters looks at him and bends to retrieve the dropped fan that is still sputtering on the ground kicking up dust.

Graham mumbles under his breath, "This is impossible. It just can't be. I put an end to them years ago."

Jason's vein is starting to throb the more annoyed he becomes as he turns towards a visibly shaken Graham Wellington.

"What? What are you so upset about? This is my vacation.

Graham, this is going to come back on you. You had better be prepared with an explanation on what went wrong with a simple little snatch and run holiday."

Graham stares at Jason and in a sort of whisper says, "They're here." This reminds Graham of Poltergeist, the movie, but it's completely lost on everyone else. That one thought brings a small smile to Graham's face, be it ever so briefly.

The man who picked up the fan goes to hand it to Graham but Graham just walks by him. He heads for one of the tents and goes inside coming out with a canteen and a pistol. The man with the fan is now using it on himself as Graham turns and silently walks into the jungle.

Jason turns to see the back of Graham as he walks into the jungle.

"Wellington, get back here, now. I am ordering you! Wellington!"

Graham never looks back.

"All right then, someone get me my rifle I guess I'll have to do this myself. You guys start back to camp. As soon as I finish this we're getting out of here."

Kazan grabs a gun from one of the men and screams as he storms out of camp and heads for the ravine.

Ichow Cutter is Jason Kazan's right-hand man and he has carried out everything Jason has ever wanted of him, with precision and discipline, never leaving any stone unturned. But today is another day. A different and new day with lots more stones than ever before. As Graham Wellington is contemplating what's going on and Jason is having a hissy fit, Ichow is about to encounter other problems.

Ichow is a tall man with a long beard. He has had this beard for years and years, tying it together with rubber bands. The longer it gets the more rubber bands, but today he wishes he didn't have this beard. He has never felt such heat before and he isn't sure if it's the weather or the situation. Sweat pours off of him.

Ichow stands with three of Kazan's men. The reason they have stopped is because the path to the ravine has been blocked and they find themselves standing in front of a huge cornfield. They are in shock as they stand and look at this cornfield in the middle of this huge wasteland.

One of the men takes his hat off and wipes his forehead,

"I don't like this, Ichow. I've lived out here in the brush going on twenty-five years and I've never seen corn growing here like this. It looks like one of them farms they had when I was growing up in Idaho, back in the U.S. of A."

The cornstalks stand about seven feet tall. In the distance the men can hear the pounding of something.

They all look at Ichow for direction. "Hey, does that sound like what I think it sounds like?"

Ichow signals his men to draw their guns. Ichow was in Special Ops for the government until he got involved in a "guns for drugs" deal. He was dismissed but never did jail time because he fled the country. He also had the names of some top officials who made a pretty penny for the guns and the drugs. These people thought it best to just let him go.

He then called his old friend Jason Kazan who has kept him busy ever since he was "let go" as he likes to say.

"Nah, can't be. Not out here. Okay let's check this out and let's be careful. I don't want to screw this mission up. Kazan is paying me a lot of money for this and my family can really use it."

The four men spread out and slowly creep through the cornfield. As they move towards the pounding sound each man starts thinking of games he played as a kid. Each of these men has not had thoughts like this in years and years. Why now?

In the center of the field there is a clearing and in that clearing is a child who at first glance looks like he's playing basketball because that's what he is doing, bouncing what looks to be a ball, but the ball he's tossing is all green and looks kind of ratty and worn.

"Hey, Ichow, that kid is speaking Spanish and I swear he said something about Michael Jordan."

One of the other men says this is the heat. They are seeing things. In reality he thinks the whole place is haunted and this is the spirit of the dead but then do the dead play basketball?

The men step out into the clearing and they group together not knowing what to make of this whole situation. One of them starts to laugh.

"Okay, if that's a ghost then maybe it could have looked a little scarier. This is just a fat little kid. Let's shoot him, we'll see if ghosts or illusions bleed and then we can feed him to the jackals."

One of the men raises his gun.

Ichow puts his hand on the muzzle and pushes the gun down.

"Put that down. I need to find out how he got here. There may be more people around and Kazan is going to want to know."

He walks closer to the kid.

"Kid, what is this? And who the heck are you?"

Santiago doesn't look at the men and continues to bounce his green ball. In perfect English and without stopping his dribbling this little boy talks to these four men.

"I'm Michael Jordan and I'm shooting the game-winning three-pointer in the playoff game against the New York Knicks." Santiago looks up at Ichow, "Ya wanna be Patrick Ewing?"

Ichow catches Santiago's eyes. "Okay, so you do speak English and I don't know who the heck you're talking about. What the heck is going on here?"

"Oh he's talking American basketball. Michael Jordan played for the Chicago Bulls and Patrick Ewing was on the New York Knicks. They had a....." The man is quickly cut off.

"Shut up. I don't care about some game." He turns back to the little boy.

"I want to know what in the name of everything are you doing here?"

The men have circled Santiago but he just keeps bouncing what seems to be a ball and spinning it on his finger.

"Okay, kid, just stop fooling around and drop the ball or whatever it is and put your hands on your head. You're coming with us and it's either alive or dead."

Plain and direct as usual, Ichow thinks.

Before anyone can make a move Santiago's shape changes into his spirit form, the body of Wiraquocha.

The men step back as they raise and cock their rifles.

"Let's take this thing out!" Ichow screams but Wiraquocha now stands above them and with a twitch of his hands small roots grow from the ground, grabbing the men's ankles as they move back.

"Hey what the....." one of the men says as they all stumble a little, throwing off his aim.

A gun goes off but it is aimed too high to do any damage. Wiraquocha is holding the ball in his hand and it looks so tiny.

He looks directly at Ichow and tosses him the ball.

"Catch."

Ichow, who has just regained his balance, sees the ball coming at him and instinctively drops his gun, to catch the ball. Not the brightest thing to do but he is surprised.

"I should never have grabbed this," he thinks.

The ball, which turns out to be a ball of vines instantly starts to grow and wrap itself around Ichow.

"What the heck," one of the other men says just before the vines reach out to circle him. In a split second all four men are tied up tight.

The voice of Wiraquocha is low and threatening.

"I never will understand humans. I understand my creations, the plants and trees, but even Minona doesn't understand this animal, man. If she doesn't understand you how can anyone else? Greed and pain is all you know. Well, now my little captives, you will know how to be uncomfortable.

"I've instructed my plant friend to release you by tomorrow or if there is any danger to you but there won't be. We, unlike you, do not hurt but help."

Slowly Wiraquocha starts to turn back into Santiago.

The men are all struggling to get loose but the vines hold tight.

"Stop your struggling because it will get you nowhere. Don't you feel how the more you struggle the tighter the grip? Now listen and you should listen good. I'd get some calamine lotion because my plant friend is a genus toxicodendrum, or for you men the name poison ivy might ring a bell. I may be, as you so plainly stated, fat, but I'm able to walk away."

As Santiago walks away he turns and looks at Ichow, "Look, this is me walking away."

Santiago bends down and picks up a real Wilson basketball and strolls away into the cornfield bouncing the ball.

As he walks through the cornfield the corn stalks start to disappear back into the ground. It was hard for him to get the corn to grow here but the plants came through for him. As the cornfield fades away Santiago bows his head in reverence and thanks his friends.

"Build it and they will come," are the last words the men hear from this child. Santiago's head is filled with old American movie quotes because that's all he saw in his native country.

He starts to laugh as he looks back at the men struggling to get out."Now I have to find Edda and Victor. Where are you?" Santiago calls.

CHAPTER THIRTY-ONE

Realization

Back at Kazan's base camp, Eugene, Kazan's best hunter, is the first to get back to collect everything so there is no evidence that could pin this endeavor on Kazan.

Eugene is brandishing his automatic rifle.

"Mr. Kazan has gone to do his own dirty work," Eugene thinks. "I've never been part of anything Kazan has done that has fallen apart, ever. This one has gone south so quickly. I can't understand it, with all these professional men, this isn't really brain surgery. They are darn monkeys, for God's sake."

All the screaming about a cornfield had stopped and the radio was unusually silent. Something was very weird. He knew it right from the moment those clouds raced across the sky.

"I swear I saw a figure flying above the trees too, but no way was I saying anything." As Eugene is thinking he doesn't notice the water bubbling up from the ground.

He goes over to one of the trucks and jumps up into it.

"We have a good bit of gas and we are all ready to go. I'll just start it up and we'll be all set."

Eugene turns the key but nothing happens. He tries it again and he hears the engine try to turn over but it sounds so strange. He looks out the front window and sees the tents falling down and floating away.

"A flash flood!"

As he jumps down he splashes into about three feet of water.

"Where the hell did this come from? That rain couldn't have produced this much water and it's not flowing, it's just sitting here. What is going on?"

The water is up to Eugene's waist but he had no idea that it was a little late for him to ask questions.

"Swoosh."

Eugene spins as he hears a sound behind him and tries to get his gun up.

As he turns he sees a large white bird coming straight at him.

"What the — it looks like a crow," Eugene thinks as he stumbles back, slipping on wet ground that shouldn't have seen water for months.

Eugene had never counted fear as one of his emotions but as

the bird got closer it looked straight into Eugene's left eye and then and there Eugene felt afraid. He saw the darkness of the past and it felt very cold. The bird stared straight into Eugene's soul.

Thoughts race through Eugene's mind. Visions of ghosts and death, of all the things he killed or hurt in his lifetime at the orders of others. Eugene becomes aware of a blood-curdling scream coming from somewhere. It's too late to react, but he does finally realize that the screams are coming from him. His gun drops from his hand with a splash and he covers his ears with his hands while also trying to put his arms up to block his face. Water is all around him swamping what's left of the campsite and trucks.

As Eugene stands frozen in fear — a word not found in his vocabulary — a figure seems to grow out from the water.

The head rises slowly, as if it had been hiding in the depths of this water.

Eugene stares as the figure grows out of the water and stands above him. Unktahee looks down and then around at the debris floating in the water.

"My waters will cleanse this land from the greed and pain you have brought to Mother." His voice is a soft warble.

Eugene brings his arms down and his first instinct is to lash out.

"What the hell are you?" he screams as he punches his arm up towards this thing's face but his hand travels through the water monster. His arm follows his hand and they both pass right through the watery face with great ease.

The face disappears and then comes back only this time with a grin on it.

Another jab from his other arm produces a fist that travels through the watery god's stomach.

As Eugene stands stunned the water rises higher, covering Eugene. He tries to swim to the top but the water keeps rising.

"I'm drowning, I don't want to die. Please no, not like this," he thinks as it gets harder to hold his breath. Eugene passes out.

The water all around starts to disappear as Eugene is lying on the ground. Unktahee is gone, replaced by Fala, and the white crow that is sitting on her shoulder. Fala bends down and reaches into a pouch she wears on her hip and puts a little sleeping salve under Eugene's nose.

"This will keep you here and you will sleep and dream like a child today, my friend. Flying dreams. High above the clouds. Looking down on your life and seeing the pain you have caused in those that you touched. When you awaken you will see things in a different light, a pure innocent light. Only good thoughts will enter your soul today. And tomorrow is up to you. You will wake up changed, my brother. There will be no looking back."

Fala makes a mental call out to all the children that the camp is secured. She knew Emily and Jimmy were on their way to head off Jason Kazan. Santiago had already met up with Edda and Victor while Paka was with the gorillas so Fala decided to head towards the ravine where they are supposed to all meet.

CHAPTER
THIRTY-TWO

Going it Alone

Jason Kazan is a man on a mission. With gun in hand he picks his way through this dusty, useless land.

"These monkeys should be happy. I'm saving one of them from a life out here in this pit of geography. I won't spoil my vacation even if these dolts want to keep me from having fun. I'm Jason Kazan and I won't be stopped by a bunch of morons. Flying people, cornfields, I think it's heatstroke. They were supposed to be the best in the business. I'm not paying them a red cent and wait till I get Wellington. Walking out on me; that was treason."

A dark inky stain appears on the ground, surrounding Jason Kazan but he is completely unaware that it has engulfed his every step. Even on such a sunny day this black shadow follows Kazan's every move.

Kazan is approaching the ravine but has to pick his path carefully to get around the rocks and downed trees. His men have told him that this place is a clear open area.

"Well this is just another reason not to pay them," he laughs.

Emily and Jimmy had arrived moments earlier on a long board of light. As Kazan picks his way into the ravine Jimmy creeps behind him. Kazan hears something and starts to raise his rifle but before he can swing it around Emily comes into view. She hovers on her oval light pads as the sun reflects off her armor and produces a blinding light.

Kazan thinks he sees a figure but throws that thought away.

"No, there is no one here but me and these apes," Jason says to reassure himself. "I'm not buying into this mass hysteria." His hands go over his eyes as the bright light blinds him. "Blast it, I can't see a thing."

Emily's distraction gives Jimmy enough time to reach out and touch Kazan but Kazan hears him and whirls around, grabbing little Jimmy by the shoulders and lifting him into the air.

Kazan stares into Jimmy's face. "What the hell do we have here? Who are you little boy and where did you come from?"

Jimmy looked for Emily but Emily heard everything Jimmy was thinking. All of the children heard him and they all started to head in his direction, as fast as they could travel.

Jimmy grabs hold of Kazan's wrist and holds on.

Jimmy's thoughts rang out, "He has no fear! I can't possess or change his feelings if he has no feelings."

Emily looks to the sword she holds in her hand.

"I'm sorry we will never know who you are, little one, or how you have come to be in this desolate landscape. I do know that your young life will end at the bottom of this ravine. Hmmm and not even a scream. You are a brave little soul but I have a job to do and you are just another bump in my road. Ta ta."

Kazan starts to raise Jimmy above his head and moves toward the side of the cliff. As Kazan's arms go back, ready to throw Jimmy off the side of the ravine Emily raises the sword high above her. A bolt of light flies from the sword and hits Kazan right in the chest. The light goes deep into his heart.

At that moment Kazan's body is pushed back away from the cliff and his memories are thrust into the past. Instead of having the sensibilities and thoughts of Kazan, the man, he now has all the feelings of Kazan, the child. All his childhood memories come rushing back. He sees himself as a young boy cowering in the corner of his room with his father standing over him.

"This will teach you to be a man, Jason." His father removes his belt. "Men aren't scared, Jason. The dark doesn't make them cry like babies. This will help you to become the man I have become."

With that Kazan's father raises his belt, the buckle illuminated in the burst of lightning coming through the window. Haran Kazan raises the buckle high above his head but before the belt can find its mark Jason is back in the present with Jimmy above his head.

Kazan's thoughts are no longer single-minded but a collection of memories that have been hidden and conveniently stowed away deep in his subconscious.

"Now Jimmy, touch him now," Emily screams with a telepathic urgency.

Her hair is swimming in the air. Electricity is making it stand out and the bright glow from her innocence and the sun's reflection off the armor make her look like a sun going supernova.

With that Jimmy reaches out again just in time to touch Kazan's hand. Kazan throws Jimmy high into the air but Emily swoops down and Jimmy lands with a soft thud on the long platform of light that radiates under Emily. The light board absorbs his fall like it was catching him.

As soon as Jimmy touches Kazan a feeling in the pit of Jason's stomach starts to grow. The sword had instilled the spark of fear in Kazan that Jimmy's touch needed. It was a feeling Jason had not thought about in years. A feeling he had stuffed deep within himself until it wasn't a feeling at all. His fears had been replaced by greed, anger and darkness.

Jason looks visibly shaken as he reaches to pick up his rifle but then he drops it to the ground and his knees start shaking. He trembles as he slumps to the ground and for once in his life he has no control over his emotions. Always wanting to control and be in control, Jason is no longer in either situation.

"What is happening? Get up, Jason. You are Jason Kazan. Powerful. Strong," Jason thinks, trying to convince himself.

Jason looks up and there in front of him holding the Sword of Truth by her side is Emily.

She is shining like a star so intense that Jason has to shield his eyes.

"There's a lesson to be learned, Mr. Kazan. Too long have you been the hunter, smelling the fear in your victims. Looked into the windows of their souls, right before you ended those poor lives. Today you have the opportunity to be hunted and to feel the fear of the animals you've chased down."

Emily's voice echoes like thunder.

"Let the truth provide and my innocence guide."

Emily explodes in light.

With that a cone-shaped vortex is created from the glowing sword. Like a small tornado it engulfs Kazan and when it disappears Kazan stands alone. Emily and Jimmy are gone.

CHAPTER THIRTY-THREE

The Chase/ The Change

The chase is on. Kazan turns and runs with the gorillas right behind him. He can't think straight; all he can feel is these waves of fear and the sense that this has happened before. How many times had he been the hunter and how many times had he smelled the fear of his prey before he extinguished their lives forever? Beautiful gazelles, fierce lions and panthers all running from him. Fear was the only thing they felt before he ended their lives. Painfully and without any mercy.

"I have to get away," is all he thinks as sweat rolls down his face, onto his shirt, sticking it to his torso.

Well now he smelled fear all right but this was different, for this was his own.

He runs as fast as he can but he can hear them getting closer. There is a turn up ahead and Kazan feels that this is his chance to lose them.

"If I can make it around this corner I might just stand a chance," he thinks.

Sweat continues to run down his forehead, stinging his eyes. His legs are aching from running and his heart is racing, about to burst.

He feels the fear subside for a brief moment as he makes this turn. As he makes the turn, the turn to freedom, his fear comes on like a bulldozer. He turned into a ravine that had only one way out. Yes, the way he came in. It was over.

Kazan tries to crawl his way up the rock wall. Visions dance around him of all the animals he has captured this way. So scared that they would make their paws bleed trying to get out of their traps.

Jason slumps to his knees. He hears the voices getting closer and as they do he covers his head and in that short amount of time he sees all the faces of the animals who had shared this same feeling.

"Oh no, what have I been doing?" he cries out. "Please, I'm sorry, so sorry."

This fear was enough to drive most men crazy. Every animal that Jason had killed races through his dark and nasty soul, ripping and pulling his very being in so many painful directions.

"There it is. We've got it now, it's trapped in a corner. These things can be dangerous when they have no way out, so be careful."

The biggest gorilla steps up. "Hurry up and shoot it so we can get paid and get out of here. This thing smells."

Time seems to slow down.

Jason hears the click of a gun like he had heard so many times before. All the animals he had cornered had looked deep into his eyes before he had taken their sight forever and now he feels the need to look into the eyes of his hunter.

As he looks up he can see rifles pointed at him but the only shooting that is happening is by a large white gorilla with a camera. Kazan is shocked as he keeps waiting for a rifle shot that never comes. All he keeps hearing is the clicking of a camera.

As the gorillas look on the white one says, "This is the best specimen we have ever shot. I just love the thrill of the chase."

Kazan's head slumps into his arms. I love the thrill of the chase keeps echoing through his head. "I just love the thrill of the chase," he whispers.

"I love the thrill of the chase," keeps echoing in his head.

Kazan is startled when a hand touches his face.

"Oh god, it's them again. They've come to finish me off," he thinks as he looks up only to see that next to him stands a small boy. The boy's eyes seemed to look deep into Kazan's soul and with his touch Kazan's fear is gone.

This was the child he had held up, how many minutes or days or weeks ago was it. He had lost all sense of time. All he knew was that he was crying. He couldn't remember how long it had been since he had cried. One thing no one seemed to notice was that the darkness was gone. The darkness that had settled on Jason from the moment he was born had disappeared. The sun shone brightly and no patch of shadows could be seen.

Kazan looked around to see children standing around him.

One child was on two light discs floating above the others. Looking like an angel she stared at Jason and started to speak.

"Now Mr. Kazan, how do you feel? Different isn't it, Jason? We have shown you a new road to choose. Whether you follow it is up to you. Jimmy has instilled a spark of compassion in you. That compassion will grow if you let it. Will you pass this next test? We shall see and we will be watching."

The voice was that of Aunt Lily but it came from Emily.

Kazan stares at Emily as she hovers above him. This is an angel, he thinks, who has come to rescue my soul.

Always having something to say, Kazan is speechless. When Kazan looks up again the children are gone.

"That feeling of fear. Oh my god what have I done to these poor souls."

He slowly gets up on his wobbly legs and walks out of the ravine towards his camp. Upon his arrival he sees his men regrouping.

"I don't know who they were," one of the men was saying to the group.

Three of the men are covered in red bumps and constantly scratching themselves but each one of these men is talking about their encounter with some strange children. The men quiet as each one sees Kazan. No one wants to be left for dead like the last guy so they stop talking, just waiting for Jason to explode on them.

"We're finished here. Go get David and let's get him some medical attention. He has a wife and kids and I don't want any more bad mojo now or anytime soon. You men will be well paid and I would like to hire you all permanently. There are so many things to shoot." Jason holds his hands to his eyes making believe he is holding a camera.

"Get it? Shoot? Hahahahaha," Kazan starts to laugh hysterically. Jason spins taking make believe pictures of all the men.

"Get it? Shoot. Get it?" he starts laughing harder.

The men all look at each other, thinking Kazan has lost his mind.

CHAPTER
THIRTY-FOUR

Sunny Days

It's a brand new day and the sun comes up bright and shining this morning. White light is streaming through Elizabeth's windows. Elizabeth does have some control as to how to guide the light through her sometimes dusty panes of glass.

"Ah, look at this little night star sleep. Here, my love, is some warm sunshine to start your day." Elizabeth guides the light to Emily's face and creaks a good morning to her.

As Emily's eyes open she remembers her adventure and quickly jumps up in bed. Her head turns to where Aunt Lily usually is but the chair by the bed is empty.

"Was it all a dream?" Emily thinks. She feels the warm sun on her face and a wide grin is drawn across her face.

"Elizabeth, what a wonderful way to wake up. How has the night treated you?"

Creaks can be heard throughout the house as Elizabeth tells Emily about how her night went. As usual, nothing happened.

Down in the kitchen, Sue and Bill are sitting having breakfast. They got home early that morning and as they walked in Lily already had her coat on and was saying goodbye.

"Is everything ok, Sis?"

"Yes, I just have to go, Bill. Emily is still asleep. You look tired and you have something on your face."

Susan smiles because Bill usually wears more food on his face than he gets in his mouth.

"Well, good seeing you again, Lil. Nice chatting," Bill says mockingly.

Lily roars past him and is gone. Her cane can be seen shining as she almost runs out of sight, leaving the front door wide open.

"You have the oddest family, Billy boy," Susan says. She calls him that when she wants to tease him.

As she says this the whole house creaks.

"Ah Elizabeth. I'm sorry I didn't say good morning," Bill says with a smirk.

Susan and Bill look around and wait. The front door opens wider and then closes by itself.

"I'll never get used to this," Bill says.

"A simple creak is sufficient, Elizabeth," Susan says with smile.

A loud creak is heard throughout the house.

"Ah that's better. Maybe we should ask Elizabeth what is eating Lily," Susan says. All gets quiet not a creak or groan to be heard.

"Or maybe not," Bill says.

Bill and Susan start to laugh. Bill is still looking around waiting for the other shoe to drop but it doesn't.

As Susan heads upstairs he looks at her and falls in love with her again.

"I can't believe how lucky I am," he thinks.

Sue has always noticed that when the house is creaking and groaning Emily is awake. She almost felt as if Elizabeth would never wake Emily up, or that's what she thinks but Sue sometimes also feels silly thinking that the house could actually interact with her daughter.

Susan enters Emily's room.

Emily is lying in bed with the covers up to her neck.

"Oh Emily, I told your aunt to keep the windows closed but they're wide open. I have got to talk to Lily about this," Sue whispers.

Emily opens her eyes.

"Hi Mom. You're home? Where is Aunt Lily?"

"She left as soon as we walked in. She ran out of here like a fire had been set in her shoes and she was trying to stamp them out. Sometimes I don't even think your aunt sleeps at all. By the way, your Dad and I have to go away again in a couple of weeks on another one of his business functions and we need her to stay with you that weekend."

A smile comes over Emily's face as her mother bends to kiss her.

"Come down for some breakfast, okay baby?"

"Okay Mom."

Emily has the covers pulled up tight and as her mom leaves she pulls down the covers to reveal silver armor.

"It wasn't a dream." The house groans and the armor fades as if soaking into her body. Emily goes downstairs and gets her breakfast. Her dad gives her a hug and a kiss on the cheek.

"So did you and your aunt have fun Poobah?"

"Yes we went on an adventure and saved an endangered species," Emily giggles. Bill looks at Sue, "Well that is great Em. I'm sure the uh, endangered species are very happy."

CHAPTER THIRTY-FIVE

Epilogue

A month has gone by and Emily again is woken by Elizabeth and starts to get ready for school. She runs down the steps and her dad is at the breakfast table.

"Emily, you need to hurry. Terry's mom is picking you up for your class museum trip."

"Is that today? Oh jeez. I totally forgot."

Emily gets ready and Carla Kingston beeps the horn. Running out Emily turns around and runs back in. She kisses Susan and Bill and then turns again and runs out. She stops short on the front porch.

"Bye Elizabeth," she says.

"Creak, groan," Elizabeth responds.

"Have a blessed day my little night star," is what Elizabeth means and Emily knows that.

The buses from school are all parked in a row at the museum as Emily helps Mrs. Kingston get Terry out of the car and into her wheelchair.

"You girls have fun. I'll be waiting right here for you two."

Emily starts pushing Terry to the entrance of the museum so they can catch up with her class.

"Oh Emily, this is going to be so cool. And thanks for coming with us."

"Are you kidding, Terry," and they both say at the same time. "That's the way we roll."

All the children go single file out of the buses and into the main entrance of the museum. Little heads all bobbing with huge backpacks. As they enter the museum the teacher calls out to the children.

"Okay we all need to be quiet and get a partner. Oh Emily, I see you have one. Good."

Emily is waving as she stands behind Terry's wheelchair.

As the children walk through the huge foyer they enter one of the exhibit halls.

On the outside of one of the halls is a new exhibit.

There's a placard on an easel. It reads, "Endangered Species Exhibit Photos Donated by Jason W. Kazan."

Emily sees the picture of Jason Kazan holding an award for saving an animal from extinction.

"Oh my God how can that be? We just, uh I think we just," Emily whispers.

"You ok, Em? You look like you've seen a ghost."

"Uh I may have, Terry — or something very ghostly," Emily starts to snicker.

"I need to ask Aunt Lily about this," Emily thinks.

It's a rainy day. A lone figure with an umbrella can be seen walking into an old office building. These are the offices of Talonthorn Industries.

The tall figure can be seen passing a security check and getting into an elevator. Haran Kazan sits in his big chair in his office smoking a large cigar. Shadows dance all around the desk and floor. Occasionally they lie on his face.

Kazan looks at the overhead monitor system and sees a familiar figure stepping from the elevator and walking towards his office doors.

The well-dressed man raps on the door and the doors swing inward.

As the doors open they reveal Graham Wellington walking in wearing a grey pin-striped suit.

"Come on in, Wellington."

Graham is brushing rain droplets from his shoulder.

"It's quite nasty outside, boss."

"Here Wellington, sit by the fire and warm yourself up."

Kazan gets up and walks over to a chair by the massive fireplace. Wellington has a bit of a wry smile on his face.

"Tsk, tsk I had such high hopes for that boy of mine but I guess he was weak. Just like his mother. I will now have to cut him out like a cancer. Let him take his pictures. I will find another. Maybe that other is you, Wellington."

Dark ink-like shadows engulf the room. A low sinister laughter can be heard in the distance.

Graham produces a huge smile. It's just what he wanted to hear.

"I know how to end this, Sir — once and for all." Kazan looks up and smiles as a shadow crosses his face.

The End